The Hitman's Woman

The Hitman's Woman

Devon Vaughn Archer

www.urbanbooks.net

Urban Books, LLC
78 East Industry Court
Deer Park, NY 11729

ISBN 13: 978-1-60162-462-8
ISBN 10: 1-60162-462-x

First Printing September 2011
Printed in the United States of America

10 9 8 7 6 5 4 3 2 1

*This is a work of fiction. Any references or similarities
to actual events, real people, living, or dead, or to real
locales are intended to give the novel a sense of reality. Any similarity in other names, characters, places,
and incidents is entirely coincidental.*

Distributed by Kensington Publishing Corp.
Submit Wholesale Orders to:
Kensington Publishing Corp.
C/O Penguin Group (USA) Inc.
Attention: Order Processing
405 Murray Hill Parkway
East Rutherford, NJ 07073-2316
Phone: 1-800-526-0275
Fax: 1-800-227-9604

The Hitman's Woman

Devon Vaughn Archer

This book is dedicated to my father, who, sadly, passed away in February 2010. He instilled in me a great work ethic and encouraged me to follow my dreams wherever they may lead.

You'll be sorely missed, Dad, by your family and the many others you touched during your seventy-eight years plus of life.

Love always,
—Your eldest son

PROLOGUE

Russell Sheldon was not about to let some two-bit punk intimidate him into giving up one cent of the hard-earned money he'd put into this store. As such, he peered at the shorter, bald man on the other side of the counter, ignoring the wide body who stood behind him as if his shadow.

"What did you say?" the shorter man, who identified himself as Leon, asked, clearly taken aback at the response.

"I said go to hell," Russell responded stubbornly, having put even more force into his words. "If you think you can just walk in here and demand that I give you 'protection' money, you can forget it. I don't need your protection."

The man's jaw clenched. "You hear that, Spencer? He doesn't need my help."

The wide body growled and began to move closer. "Why don't you let me see if I can convince him?"

Leon lifted a hand, stopping him in his tracks. "That won't be necessary. I'm sure that Russ will come around. They all do eventually."

"Don't hold your breath," Russell said. "It's not gonna happen." He hadn't served time in the military and grown up on the mean streets to allow himself to become a slave to someone trying to get something for nothing. "Go find someone else to drain money from. Now, get out of my store, unless you want more trouble than you can handle."

With his licensed Glock within reach beneath the counter, Russell was prepared to use it if necessary. He held the man's steely gaze, not wanting to show any sign of backing down.

"Very well, if you say so," Leon snorted. "The thing is, if I let you off the hook, I'll lose all respect from the other business owners. I can't let that happen."

"That's your problem," Russell said, reaching under the counter for his gun, figuring he might need to defend himself at any moment. He held the gun firmly, pointing it toward the two men. "I know how to use this."

Leon's eyes bulged, and Russell detected the first sign of fear in him and his backup.

"I'll bet you do," Leon said, a sardonic grin on his lips. "Okay, you win. We won't mess around with you. Keep your money." He glanced at the other man. "Let's get out of here."

The wide body glared at Russell, but made no attempt to disobey orders. "Yeah, all right."

"See you around," Leon said snidely.

Russell didn't lower the gun or take his eyes off the two until they were out of his store. Only then did he breathe a sigh of relief. He had taken a stand against some bullies and felt all the better for it. He wished other local business owners would do the same and drive these thugs underground. But he could only do what was best for him.

He put the gun away and thought about his half brother, Dante. It would have been great had they gone into business together. Of course, that was only a pipe dream. Dante was too busy doing his own thing. Russell would have to settle for keeping in touch while they stayed out of each other's hair, as this seemed to work best for them. He glanced at the TV screen above the counter to check the score of the Detroit Lions game. It looked like they were going to pull out a victory.

When the chime rang indicating someone had come into the store, Russell looked up, hoping the man named Leon and his crony weren't back for more harassment. Fortunately, it was someone else. Russell studied the tall, forty-something man with graying, closely cropped hair and soot-colored eyes. There was a half-moon-shaped scar on his cheek. He looked lost.

"Can I help you?" Russell asked.

The man, wearing a topcoat and a glove on one hand, walked up to the counter. "Yeah, maybe. You Russell Sheldon?"

Russell nodded guardedly. "That's me."

The man looked around and back at him. "I have something for you. . . ."

Russell got a bad feeling when the man reached inside his coat. Before he could react, a gun equipped with a silencer was pointing at him.

"This is from Leon," the man said. "It's what happens when you don't do as you're told."

At the last moment, Russell tried to reach for his own gun but was too late. He was hit by a bullet that ripped through his chest, driving him backward. The next bullet landed squarely between his eyes, and Russell saw nothing but blackness.

The killer looked down at his target, the face half-blown away. Showing no remorse, he went around the counter and climbed over the body. He quickly opened the cash register and emptied it. Afterward, in search of the security camera video, he soon found what he was looking for, taking the video and with it any evidence that tied him to the location at that time.

He grabbed a couple of Snickers bars and calmly left the store before anyone else ventured in that he would have to take out. The February cold hit him in the face as he walked a few paces, causing him to blink it back. Getting into his vehicle, he removed the glove and drove two blocks until he came upon a black Lincoln Town Car limousine on the opposite side of the street. He stopped his vehicle when it was aligned with the other car, lowering the window. The passenger window of the limousine came down slightly.

He could barely make out who was inside, but knew acutely well with whom he was dealing. "It's done," he told him succinctly.

There was no response, which spoke volumes to him, before the limousine drove off. He did the same, soon blending into traffic with another mission satisfactorily completed. He would wait patiently until called upon again to silence someone who stepped over the line with no turning back.

ONE

Six Months Later

Dante Sheldon walked into the dimly lit bar in West Hollywood, looking for the private eye he'd hired to investigate the murder of his brother, Russell. According to the police, Russell had been the victim of a simple robbery gone wrong. No one had been arrested, and as far as Dante knew, the case was not being actively pursued by the authorities, who had turned their attention elsewhere. This pissed him off. He hadn't been in close contact with his brother in recent years, as they had drifted apart as they got older and were into different things. But that didn't mean his love for Russell had diminished. He was determined to see that someone would pay for his brother's premature death.

Dante made his way through the place, barely cognizant of the blues music filtering through speakers. He wrinkled his nose at the pungent scent of body odor and mildew. Where the hell was he, anyway? Then he spotted the man who was unmistakable with his blond Rastafarian locks and a black goatee with a center streak of gold. He was sitting at a back table, nursing a drink and seemingly in his element.

Dante approached the table, noticing the briefcase on it. He met the bloodshot eyes of the private investigator.

"There you are," Floyd Artest muttered. "I was starting to think you wouldn't show."

"I ran a little late," Dante said by way of explanation. In fact, if the man hadn't told him he had important information, Dante had been prepared to fire his lazy ass. As it was, this had been a more expensive proposition than he'd anticipated. For the better part of five months, he'd financed the private eye's trips to and from Detroit, assured that he could give him the answers the police had chosen to turn their backs on. But the more time went by and the bills continued to come in, the more Dante had come to believe he was being played for a fool. He had nearly given up on his pursuit of justice when Artest phoned him two hours ago. Now he was counting on not being disappointed or asked for any more money.

He sat down. "What have you got for me?"

"Can I buy you a drink?" Artest asked.

Is he stalling? "I'll pass." Dante peered across the table.

Artest was the first to blink. "That's cool." He sipped his drink. "It wasn't easy, but I uncovered who took out your brother and why."

"I'm listening. . . ."

Artest opened the briefcase and pulled out an envelope. He removed an eight-by-ten photograph and slid it across the table. "Your shooter."

Dante looked at the head shot of a walnut-complexioned male in his forties with short salt-and-pepper hair, a broad nose, and slightly uneven black eyes. There was a scar on his left cheek. The mere thought that this asshole had taken his brother's life gave Dante a chill.

"Name's Eric Fox," Artest said. "He's an enforcer/ hitman in Detroit, working for this crime boss named

Leon Quincy." Artest took another photograph from the envelope and passed it to Dante. "Apart from loan-sharking and pimping, Quincy shakes down business owners on the Northwest side of the city, demanding protection money or else."

Dante stared at the picture of a slender, bald man in his mid- to late thirties. His long face was dark, and his eyes darker.

"Looks like your brother stood up to him and paid the ultimate price."

Dante's brow furrowed as he studied the two photographs, zeroing in on the alleged triggerman. He looked at Artest. "Are you sure you've got your facts straight?"

The private detective held his gaze. "Yeah, I'm sure. I was a cop before deciding to work for myself. I wouldn't have come to you with this if I hadn't double-checked the accuracy. This is your man and the dude he works for."

Dante believed him. He grabbed the envelope and put the photographs back. "Where can I find them?"

"Their addresses are on the back of the pictures. Both stay in the city. Fox lives with a woman, and Quincy, well, from what I could tell, has a different companion every night of the week. He also keeps some muscle handy, so watch your back."

"I can take care of myself." Long before Dante had become a journalist, taking him to such hot spots around the world as Afghanistan and Yemen, he'd been battle tested. First, it was from growing up in a rough neighborhood in Oakland, in a single-parent house-hold where he had to protect himself and his brother from gangs, drug addicts, and other low-life scum. Then there was a brief stint in law enforcement as a re-serve deputy sheriff and firearms instructor before his lifelong dream to earn a living as a writer took center stage. Now he couldn't help but wonder if the preoccupation with his life had cost him precious time that could have been spent with his brother.

Dante took an envelope out of his jacket pocket and passed it to Artest. It was the final cash payment for his services.

Artest riffled through the hundred-dollar bills, then put the envelope away. "Nice doing business with you."

"Everything between us stays that way," Dante said tersely.

"Of course."

"We won't be meeting again."

Artest nodded. "Understood."

Dante stood up. "Don't," he said as Artest was about to do the same. "It's best that we cut our ties right here."

Artest looked up. "No problem." He lifted his glass. "Good luck."

Dante's mouth was a straight line. "I don't believe in luck. Not where it concerns my brother, considering he had anything but good luck. I prefer to make my own destiny, for better or worse."

He walked away without looking back at the private investigator. As far as Dante was concerned, it was all on him now to do what needed to be done. Russell's life would not be cut short without someone paying the piper. That began with Eric Fox and ended with Leon Quincy.

TWO

Eric Fox's penis was only half-erect when he entered his ready-and-waiting woman, Beverly. He was on top of her, stroking her breasts, kissing her full lips—basically doing what he could to get worked up. But it just wasn't happening. Not that he wasn't still sexually attracted to her. Who wouldn't be? She was twenty years his junior and had a sexual appetite he couldn't hope to match in his wildest dreams. That didn't mean he was about to sit by and watch some other man put his dick in her vagina. She was his woman for as long as he said, regardless of whether he was able to put out on a given occasion.

Her breathing quickened as if she was about to come. False alarm, as she went quiet on him again. He tried to think about his lover on the side, figuring that would lead to an erection, along with pushing himself deeper inside Beverly. Instead, that only caused him to go limp.

"Don't stop!" Beverly demanded, clutching his buttocks. "I haven't come in two weeks."

Eric thought about putting his mouth between her legs, a surefire way to give her what she wanted. But he didn't want her to get too spoiled, especially if he wasn't being fulfilled. He lifted off her and looked down at his flaccid penis.

"Sorry, baby," he said in what amounted to only a half-truth. "Guess it takes me longer these days to rock and roll. We'll give it another try later."

"Yeah, right," she pouted. "How often have I heard *that* lately?"

Too often, he conceded. But that was just the way it was. Still, he tried to remain nice about it. He kissed one of her nipples. "I'll take you out to dinner at any restaurant you want."

"I'm not really hungry—not for food, anyway."

Eric kissed her other nipple. He would try another means to appease her. "Go buy yourself something pretty. There's a thousand bucks on the dresser. It's yours."

Beverly wrinkled her face. "So all I am to you now is a prostitute?"

Eric knew she was just being a bitch, so he let it go. "I don't pay for sex. On the other hand, I don't have a problem spending money to make my woman happy. If you have a problem with that—"

"I don't." She did an about-face and gave him an effective smile. "I'll see what I can find to wear just for you."

Eric grinned. "That's more like it." He kissed her mouth and climbed off the bed. Then he grabbed his briefs that were tossed across a leather chair and put them on, followed by pleated khakis.

Beverly propped herself up on an elbow, giving him a nice view of her body. "Where are you going?"

"Just to take care of a little business."

"What kind of business?" There was a touch of suspicion in her voice.

"Nothing you need to worry your pretty head about," he responded evasively. As far as she knew, he was in the investment business. Technically, this was true, as he invested much of the money he earned in stocks, bonds, and a little real estate, making for a comfortable life. What she didn't know wouldn't hurt her. Whereas were she to know that he was an enforcer for a local crime boss, he just might have to kill her.

Beverly Holland waited patiently until Eric left before putting her hand between her legs and giving herself the orgasm he couldn't, or wouldn't, these days. It was becoming clear to her that he couldn't keep up with her in bed. At least not anymore. Maybe this was to be expected. After all, at forty-five, he was past his sexual prime, whereas the twenty-five-year-old woman in her was practically bursting with sexual desire.

Beverly wondered if their arrangement was working anymore. Yes, she loved the material comforts Eric gave her, including sharing his massive house, driving an expensive car, and having all the jewelry and clothes any woman could want. But was that enough? Especially if the man couldn't satisfy her carnal instincts.

Would Eric allow her to leave him if she wanted to? Beverly had her serious doubts about that. He had never shown any violence toward her in the year they had been together and seemed like the legitimate businessman he claimed to be. But there was something in his character and furtive style that made her believe there might be aggressive tendencies beneath the surface.

Maybe I shouldn't tempt fate by walking out. That didn't mean she was prepared to be ignored sexually for the rest of her life. Not when there were other, virile men out there who could satisfy that side of her.

At the moment, Beverly was left to handle that herself. She squeezed her eyes shut and increased the speed as she ran her finger back and forth across her clitoris while she fantasized about a faceless lover. As the buildup reached its peak, her body started to quiver and her breathing sped up. Beverly gasped as the overwhelming feeling of fulfillment started to spread throughout her body.

She lay there for another minute, waiting for the sensations to subside, before her mind cleared and she had to decide how to spend the rest of her day now that she knew Eric would not be around.

Dante rented a car at the Detroit Metropolitan Wayne County Airport. He'd spent the long flight thinking about his brother and what a waste it was to have his life taken away at the young age of twenty-nine, two years younger than Dante. Russell, who had finally seemed to be getting his life back on track after going through an ugly divorce, had moved to Detroit for a new beginning. As far as Dante knew, there was no one serious in Russell's life at the time of his death, as he had been focused on turning his store into a success before rebuilding other aspects of his life. Now he would never get that chance. And Dante would never get to truly know his brother as a man. Or as a father.

Conversely, Russell would never get to see Dante's further evolution through life and whatever it had in store for him. That included a significant other. Though Dante had never been married, he'd known his fair share of women. None had really stood out and tugged on his heartstrings. Maybe it wasn't in the cards for him to find love. Or maybe he just hadn't met the woman who truly did it for him.

Either way, it was an experience he would never get to share with Russell. Dante blamed himself for not reaching out more to his brother, allowing them to bond in adulthood. It always seemed like there would be more time. If only he could do things over. But it didn't work that way when one party was dead.

All that was left was to try to make things right. He was sure Russell would have done the same were the situation reversed and he was the one feeling empty while his brother lay in a pine box in a cemetery.

Dante drove the Cadillac Escalade down the freeway and continued his thoughts about the tragedy that brought him to Detroit for only the second time. The first was little more than two years ago, when Russell first opened his store on Seven Mile Road. On a whim, Dante had decided to drop everything and fly from Nigeria, where he was doing a story about government corruption. He only stayed for two days, but Russell seemed genuinely appreciative, even if there had been moments of strain, mostly in relation to differing points of view on how each should run his life. He wished he could take back every negative thing he said to Russell. If only he had the chance.

Dante pulled into the parking lot of the hotel on Fisher Lane. Traveling light, he carried his one bag inside, checked in, and went to his suite. He looked out the large window and took in the city. There were two men out there intimidating and terrorizing businessmen and women, forcing them to pay up or else. And apparently the authorities weren't doing a damned thing about it. He wouldn't be surprised at all if Leon Quincy had the cops in his hip pocket. Well, Quincy and Eric Fox would get their comeuppance. He would see to that.

Right now, though, he could use a stiff drink. Dante had noticed the lounge downstairs when he came in. He freshened up and headed there.

Beverly was bored. More than that, she was feeling horny. After having spent all of Eric's money and then some, she was looking for a little fun, minus him. Maybe she would have a drink and then some dancing. Eric wasn't much of a dancer with two left feet. She doubted he would be too keen on her dancing with another man. But what he didn't know wouldn't hurt him.

She spotted the hotel. Most hotels had a place to drink and dance, right? Especially the five-star ones like this. It was a good ten miles from where she lived, so there was little chance Eric or one of his friends would see her.

Parking her ruby red Lincoln MKS, Beverly checked her makeup and hair and ran a hand over her black knit dress. Not that she needed to do much to look great. Most men seemed to share that view, and women too. She still wanted to make sure it was all put together nicely, though.

She walked carefully to the hotel in her pointy-toe pumps that had yet to be fully broken in. It would just be her misfortune to fall and break her ankle.

Beverly entered an impressive lobby and wasn't sure which way to head first. Taking a chance, she went to her left and saw the Crescent Lounge. She heard some music—easy listening. Not exactly her taste, but she wouldn't let that stop her from at least having a drink.

Inside the lounge, Beverly immediately laid eyes on the man sitting all by his lonesome at the bar. From where she stood, he was drop-dead gorgeous. Obviously tall and muscular, he was bald-headed, caramel-skinned, and oozed sexuality. She would bet that he was all that and more in the sack. The mere thought turned her on.

Maybe I shouldn't even go there. Otherwise, I just might get myself into trouble.

She ignored the warning bells and felt compelled to talk to him. It never occurred to her that he could be with someone who had gone to the ladies' room. Guess there was only one way to find out.

Beverly moseyed over to the bar and took a seat beside the man, barely able to keep her eyes off him. "Buy a lady a drink?"

He faced her with deep gray eyes flecked with gold. His square-jawed features, as rigid as they were refined, were a cross between Denzel Washington and LL Cool J.

"Sure," he said in a voice heavy with masculinity. "What would you like?"

How about you? "I'll have a Cosmo," she told him, inhaling the powerfully enticing cologne he wore.

"Cosmo, it is." He signaled the bartender and ordered the drink and another one of his own, a cognac cocktail. Then they checked each other out. Beverly sensed he liked what he saw, as did she.

She decided to get the formalities out of the way. "I'm Beverly."

"Dante."

She liked the name. "What's a nice-looking man like you doing here drinking all alone, Dante?"

He considered the question. "Well, since I'm new in town and don't know anyone, I didn't really have much choice. I could ask you the same question."

"So ask," Beverly teased, flipping back her long dark hair.

"All right. What's an attractive woman such as yourself doing in a hotel lounge, asking a stranger to buy her a drink?"

He does like my look. Good start. "Honestly, it was boredom," she said. "I just needed to get out of the house. I ended up here . . . and realized I didn't want to drink alone."

Dante smiled seductively. "You don't have to."

The drinks came on cue. Beverly tasted hers and suddenly felt even more bold in coming on to this man. He struck her as the type who could handle himself if Eric were to walk in at that moment and make trouble. But she would rather forget about Eric for the time being and concentrate on Dante.

"Where are you from?" she thought to ask.

Dante pointed his enchanting eyes at her. "Originally from Oakland, but I've been living in L.A. for a while now."

"Sounds nice," Beverly said, running a finger around the rim of her glass. "I've never been to California, but I like everything I hear about it."

"Seeing is believing. You'll have to check it out for yourself sometime."

"Maybe I will." She would have gone before now if she'd felt she might run into someone like him. "Seems like there's a lot to do there."

Dante chuckled. "California can mean different things to different people."

"What does it mean to you?" she asked directly.

"It means having a place to hang my hat, figuratively speaking, while being able to come and go as I please."

If only life were that simple for me. "What brings you to Detroit, if you don't mind my asking?"

The way he gazed at her, Beverly almost thought he would say she had. Instead, his simple yet firm response was: "Business."

"Just business?"

He tasted his drink. "I'm not opposed to a little pleasure."

She showed her teeth. *Neither am I. Not with you.* "What type of business are you in?" Judging by his casual clothing and easy demeanor, she imagined he might be a college recruiter. Or an insurance salesman.

Maybe even an ex-jock now working as a pitchman for some products.

"I'm a journalist."

That one surprised her, but somehow seemed to fit. "You're here for a story?"

"Something like that." Dante touched her hand, sending sparks flying throughout Beverly's body. "What's your story?"

I knew this was coming. Can't tell him anything he doesn't need to know. "Not much to tell. Just a woman out for a good time," Beverly said casually.

"And also a woman of mystery."

"I thought men were attracted to mysterious women."

His mouth curved upward. "Yeah, that's true. Especially ones as sexy as you."

Beverly's libido rose a few notches. "Do you have a room?" she asked boldly.

"Yes," he said with anticipation.

Her curly lashes batted. "So . . . what are we waiting for?"

"Not a damned thing," he declared.

Dante gazed with appreciation as Beverly stripped naked in his suite. She was like every sexy woman he'd ever dreamed about wrapped into one. With her gorgeous high-cheeked and full-lipped Beyoncé-meets-Alicia-Keys-type looks cloaked in a butterscotch complexion and tall, slender body with ample high breasts and just the right amount of curves, Dante experienced the type of sexual desire he hadn't felt in some time. It was enough to temporarily distract him from his mission.

Dante sensed that Beverly was in a relationship, probably married, and looking for a one-night stand of escapism. Who was he to deny her what she obviously wanted and needed, especially when his wants and needs were every bit as powerful? He had to have this lady who had chosen him to seduce. He'd make sure she wasn't disappointed in the slightest.

Removing his own clothes, Dante wasted little time getting to it. He gripped Beverly's slender waist and lifted her onto the bed. Climbing atop it, he spread her legs and went down on her. He inhaled her scent, turning him on like crazy. She was wet. Very wet. He dragged his tongue across her clitoris and felt Beverly tremble. He licked her several more times while she moaned.

"That feels so good," she uttered. "Don't make me come until you're inside me."

Dante resisted the desire to give her an oral orgasm, enjoying seeing a woman climax from his mouth and tongue. His own libido threatened to overpower him. As such, he was more than ready to accommodate her wishes.

He came up, gazing into her desperate eyes. "I'm going to make love to you now!"

"Please do!"

After hurriedly sliding on a condom, he sandwiched himself between her moist thighs and propelled his erection deep inside her. She immediately clamped hard around his penis, wrapping her legs up high across his back. He used the bed to support his hands and, in rapid-fire motion, thrust himself in and nearly out of her and back again. She met him halfway, slamming herself against his body.

Dante kissed her lips hard and winced as she bit into the side of his mouth. His tongue ran across her teeth and went into her mouth, tasting her. He grabbed hold of one of her breasts, squeezing the hard nipple between two fingers. Beverly's breathing quickened, and she ran long fingernails across his back, causing him to jump.

She cried out as his penis plunged as far as it could go inside her and remained there while he climaxed. Her body went into spasms at the same time, and Dante held Beverly tightly while they rode the wave together. It took a minute or longer before things settled down.

He rolled off her and onto the bed, trying to catch his breath. "Wow!" was all Dante could think to say.

Beverly sighed with a chuckle. "It was pretty wow at that!"

"We can always see if we can top that," he said, finding himself wanting to extend this sexual tryst a bit longer.

"Sounds like fun, but I have to go." On that note, she climbed off the bed. He admired her nice ass and then the rest of her.

"That's cool." He wouldn't try to talk her out of it, not knowing her situation, but assumed it involved another man she was with. "Will I see you again?"

Beverly hurriedly put on her clothes. "That all depends. How long will you be in town?"

Dante considered how long it would take him to kill a man. Then another. But not until he had sized up his adversaries and found out their weaknesses.

"Not sure," he told her candidly. "Depends on how long it takes me to complete the assignment. And maybe if I'll get another chance to see you."

She took her cell phone out of her purse. "What's your cell number?"

He gave it to her, not bothering to ask for hers, figuring he would get it if and when she called him.

"I'll call you if I can see you again," she said.

"All right," Dante replied. "Hope my phone rings and you're on the other end."

He stood up, moved over to her, and planted a deep kiss on her mouth.

She pulled away, touching her lips. "You made your point. Now I really have to go."

I think you'd rather stay. Maybe next time we can make it an all-nighter. "Nice meeting you."

Beverly smiled warmly. "You too."

THREE

As she drove home, Beverly could scarcely believe she had just had sex with a total stranger. Never before had she done such a thing. And she had never been unfaithful to Eric since they had been together. So why now? She had no idea other than that Dante was sexy as hell and it felt right and dangerously appealing to drop her inhibitions and fulfill her sexual desires of the moment.

Dante did not disappoint. In just minutes, which seemed like hours, he had managed to do what Eric hadn't in months: give her an orgasm that she was still reeling from. But it was over now, and she had to remember she was Eric's woman, even if he seemed to see her as just a trophy instead of a woman who needed the type of sexual attention he could not give her. She couldn't ignore the comfortable life he provided for her. She doubted Dante could offer the same or would even want to. For all she knew, he had someone of his own waiting back in California to do what they did tonight. Only more thoroughly, with no need to leave afterward.

Can I really go without ever seeing him again? Or would I only be asking for trouble if I fell prey to temptation and his rock-hard body that turns me on as much as the man's sexual skills?

When Beverly got back to the house, a large Victorian that sat on a hill and was the envy of everyone in the neighborhood, she saw Eric's silver Cadillac CTS-V coupe in the driveway. Usually when he was out on business, he didn't come home until after midnight. Yet here he was. She checked her clothing and smoothed her hair, trying to keep her appearance as unsuspecting as possible. The last thing she needed was for him to think she was cheating on him. As it was, her tryst with Dante was only a one-time thing. Wasn't it?

Stepping inside, her heels clicked on the tile foyer and then on the hardwood floor of the Great Room. There she found Eric sitting on the brown leather sectional, legs sprawled, talking on the phone.

"Yeah, man," he said. "I took care of our little problem." He listened. "There was no resistance or further excuses. Just another day on the job."

Beverly noted that he seemed to be guarded in his words as he looked at her, as if he had something to hide. Or was that only her imagination? Or maybe even guilt about her own little secret?

She gave him a tiny wave and carried her bags up the circular staircase to the master suite. It was huge with an antique king bed and a sitting area with white colonial furnishings. She kicked off her shoes and put the bags on a square glass table. What she needed now after a long day and steamy night was a hot bath.

Beverly was startled when she heard Eric's voice from behind. "Where you been?"

Keep your cool. Otherwise he'll know something happened. She turned around. "Where do you think—shopping. Or have you forgotten that's what you wanted when the sex fizzled?"

He scowled, and then glanced over her shoulder at the bags. "I didn't forget." He peered at her. "Go anywhere else?"

She thought of saying she went for a drink. But even that would likely lead to more questions, and she might end up giving the wrong answers. "I stopped by Marilyn's," she said of her best friend, Marilyn Ramsey. Beverly made a mental note to cover this with her, in case he tried to verify it. "Didn't know I needed to account for my every move."

Eric grinned apologetically. "You don't." He put his arms around her waist. "I just missed you, that's all."

She rolled her eyes. "Since when? Seems to me your work occupies more of your thoughts than I do." Not that she had too much of a problem with this, as it gave her more freedom. But he didn't have to know that.

"Now, don't be like that, baby. Yeah, my work is what keeps us in this house and you spending my money. You're my number-one priority, though. I just want you to be happy."

"I am happy," Beverly told him, and meant it for the most part. She might be happier if the person she came home to every day and made love to was Dante. "Are you?"

Eric smiled. "Yeah, especially when I've got the finest woman in the city to keep me feeling young and energetic."

Beverly wanted to laugh at the energetic part. If he displayed even half the energy in bed that Dante did, then she would never have needed to turn to another man to fulfill her sexual desires. But she had and would have to live with it.

Eric gave her a sloppy wet kiss. She could taste the alcohol on his breath. "So what did you buy?"

"Clothes," she answered, "and a pair of shoes."

"I'm sure they'll look great on you."

"So am I."

He placed a hand on her breast. She pushed it away. "I'm not really in the mood," she told him, doubting he was capable of changing that.

"I thought you were always ready to go?" He slid his hand between her legs.

Beverly yanked it away. "You thought wrong. Right now, I want to take a bath, if you don't mind."

Eric gave a wry chuckle. "Go ahead. Maybe when you're through pampering yourself, you'll be in the mood—"

Don't hold your breath. "Right, maybe." Beverly escaped into the bathroom, sure that he would be asleep by the time she got out. And that was fine by her. She didn't need him to light her fire. Not tonight anyway. A man named Dante had managed to do that exceedingly well and would be a hard act to follow.

After Beverly had disappeared into the bathroom, Eric went through her bags. He admired the clothes and shoes—clogs—imagining them on her. Then he took a look in her purse for anything out of the ordinary. Nothing. It wasn't that he didn't trust her, as she had given him no reason not to—yet.

But he couldn't say the same for other men. Like him, most were dogs who saw women as their sexy playthings. Even another man's lady. Beverly was a beautiful woman, and his alone. He wasn't about to allow anyone else to come between them. Not and live to tell of it.

Eric went back downstairs and grabbed a beer from the refrigerator. He opened it and gulped down a generous amount. He thought about his latest assignment. A salon owner named Kurt Braddock had not only balked at continuing to pay protection money, but had threatened to go to the police. If it had been up to Eric, he would have roughed up the dude a bit, threatened his family, or whatever. But his employer, Leon, wanted the man dead to send a clear message that anyone who even thought about not paying up, and on time, much less going to the cops, would pay a heavy price. It was the ultimate way to keep business owners in line and Leon in business.

So Eric killed Braddock. He'd waited for the man to come outside to empty his trash behind the salon. When staring down the barrel of a gun, the tough-talking Kurt Braddock had turned into a wimp, begging for his life so he could be there for his wife and kid. While a small part of Eric was moved, the better part of him saw it as merely a job that he was paid well to accomplish, leaving no room for sympathy.

It reminded him of the dude he took out six months ago. He, too, let his damned pride get in the way of common sense and what was in his best interests when all was said and done. Unlike Braddock, Russell Sheldon didn't turn timid when faced with death. Instead, he actually tried to go for his own gun as a last-ditch effort to save his business and life. He'd lost on both counts. As had others before him. And more would in the future should they act foolish and decide not to cooperate with Leon.

Eric finished off the beer and grabbed another.

Dante dreamed about Beverly that night. It had been the first time in a while that he had dreamt about anything other than the murder of his brother. Making love to Beverly had reminded Dante of what had been missing in his life—having a woman. While one night with a beautiful woman hardly constituted a relationship, it had reawakened the sexual man in him. And he had no doubt he'd awakened the sexual woman in Beverly, even if she was involved with another man, who was obviously not satisfying her in bed.

Would he ever see her again, giving them both the opportunity to explore more sexual fantasies? Or would she choose to ignore the sexual chemistry between them that had nearly engulfed their very souls and bodies?

By morning, Dante had put his eye back on the ball. Namely, that he was in Detroit for one purpose only: to avenge Russell's death. Anything else would only complicate matters. Especially a highly sex-charged woman who had managed to get under his skin.

After having breakfast in one of the hotel's restaurants, Dante stepped out into the summer sunlight. He allowed it to soak into his skin for a moment before getting in his car and driving to the address he had for Eric Fox. Fox lived in an impressive white Victorian that the man financed with the blood of people he killed for a living. Dante eyed the Cadillac CTS-V coupe and Lincoln in the driveway. Which one belonged to that bastard?

Dante drove around the block and pulled up along the curb a couple of houses down. He had a mind to ring the doorbell and beat the hell out of the man for what he did. But that wasn't his style. Besides, Eric obviously carried a piece, probably at all times, and wouldn't hesitate to use it if his life depended on it.

So Dante waited patiently. He had nearly dosed off when Eric Fox stepped out of the house. Dante glanced at the photograph of the man to be sure. Yes, it was definitely him. He watched Eric, decked out in a navy double-breasted suit and carrying a briefcase, get into the Cadillac.

Dante keep himself inconspicuous as the car backed out of the driveway and drove in the opposite direction from where he was parked. He followed Eric, wanting to see where he went and who he spent time with. As far as Dante was aware, the man didn't have a day job. Not unless you called harassing and killing people during the sunlight hours one.

He followed Eric to a huge house on Cedar Lane. Dante looked at the back of the photograph of Leon Quincy and realized this was where he lived. The idea of taking out two birds with one stone appealed to Dante, except for the fact that now wasn't the time to act recklessly. Especially since he didn't have a piece at the moment to put them out of their misery. Or exact his revenge in an apropos way.

Dante had what he needed for now. He'd be paying Leon a visit real soon, and the bastard would pay dearly for ordering a hit on Russell.

"What's up, man?" Eric said routinely to Spencer Ramsey, one of Leon's boys, there at his beck and call to do whatever needed to be done, short of killing someone. That was Eric's exclusive domain. He wore the badge proudly, never losing a day's sleep over a job that was never personal to him.

"Hey." Spencer spoke in a heavy tone, matching his wide body.

Though taller and in much better physical condition, Eric had his doubts he could take the dude in fair hand-to-hand combat. He wasn't about to try. Not so long as he had a gun that could get the job done.

"I'm here to see Leon," he told Spencer.

"He know you were coming?"

"Yeah." Eric scratched his chin.

"He's in the basement."

Eric walked through the luxurious two-story home with bay windows, plum carpeting, and imported furnishings that made his own place somehow seem inadequate. He walked down the narrow steps and entered the completely finished basement. He could see that he'd interrupted Leon's playtime, as he was sitting on a plush couch surrounded by three sexy young women who couldn't take their hands off him. But Eric wanted to collect what was owed him and see if there was anything else on the agenda.

"Eric, my man," Leon greeted him. "You want one of these lovely ladies to have some fun with?"

Eric was more than a little tempted, especially since he and Beverly hadn't been on the same wavelength in bed recently. But he could find his own women and didn't want to be indebted to the man.

"Thanks, but I'll pass."

Leon furrowed his brow. "Your loss." He removed his hand from between one woman's legs while another was rubbing his chest through an open shirt. "Give me a few minutes, ladies. Help yourself to the bar. We'll pick up where we left off when I'm done with him."

He was a couple of inches under Eric's height, his bald head shining, and a diamond stud earring on one ear. "Let's go upstairs."

Eric followed him. "Sorry if I came at a bad time." Not really, but it sounded good to say.

"It's cool." They went into a sunken-oval-shaped den. "Glad you dealt with that asshole Kurt Braddock."

"Yeah."

Leon chuckled. "That's what I like about you, Eric. You're a man of few words."

Eric grinned. "I let my actions speak for me."

"I can see that. They speak for me too. People need to know I'm not messing around. Either pay up or else!"

Eric found some irony in the words, as this was his position, too, where it concerned his pay. Fortunately, he and Leon saw eye to eye on his value and, as such, there was no trouble between them.

Eric watched as Leon removed an oil painting from the wall, revealing a safe. He dialed the combination, opened it, and removed a stack of bills.

"Here you go," Leon said. "That should square things."

Eric riffled through the new hundred-dollar bills, not bothering to count. Leon had never screwed him before. "Thanks."

"You earned it, as always."

"Any new assignments?" Eric asked, hoping to fatten his bank account even more. Especially with his high-maintenance woman, Beverly, to please.

"I may have something for you soon." Leon put a hand on his shoulder. "I'll be in touch."

"Cool."

"Sure I can't set you up with one of my playthings?"

Eric smiled. "I got all I need at home." Along with something extra on the side.

"Good for you. Give Beverly my regards."

"I will." Eric could imagine that Leon would love to have Beverly as part of his stable. He saw how he looked at her when they got together under the guise of business entertaining. Well, think again. Beverly was strictly hands off. He would see to that.

On the way out the door, Eric ran into Spencer, who was hanging around as if he had nothing better to do. Eric glanced at his face without meeting his eyes. "Catch you later, man."

"Yeah, later," muttered Spencer.

Outside, Eric took in the other nice houses on the block and thought that one day he'd like to set up shop here. If he played his cards right and the investments continued to grow, it just might happen.

Leon Quincy had been involved in crime in one form or another since he was ten years old. His mother sold her body on the streets and in brothels, while his father dealt drugs. Both were in and out of prison while Leon was shuffled around between relatives and family friends who rarely had his best interests at heart. His first criminal activity was shoplifting, progressing into armed robbery and drug dealing. After a stint in prison, he came out wiser, deciding to use his street smarts and ability to get more for less to his advantage.

He wormed his way into the world of Detroit crime boss Vincent Miller, whose successful operation included drug dealing, prostitution, and shakedowns of local business owners. When Vincent died in a car accident, the victim of his own speeding and inebriation, Leon used his wiles and some muscle to take over his business interests while adding profitable loan-sharking. He also got a couple of cops on the payroll to run interference and look the other way when necessary.

Leon was in a comfort zone these days with his business, funneling profits into legitimate investments, encouraging his employees to do the same. Though he had protection in a bodyguard and always carried a piece himself, he was under no illusion that others wouldn't love to take him out if the opportunity presented itself. He had no intention of letting that happen, vowing to go down fighting if it came to that.

He walked with Eric Fox halfway across the hall before leaving it to Spencer to see him out. Leon was generally pleased with Eric's ability to take out those who wouldn't cooperate or otherwise became expendable in a clean hit that didn't lead directly back to him. He wasn't as pleased with the fact that sometimes his hitman seemed to be a bit too independent for his comfort. He supposed he could live with that so long as Eric produced and didn't get greedy.

Leon was attracted to Eric's woman, Beverly. He'd love to make her part of his stable of hoes. If not for the fact that he needed Eric and didn't want him distracted from his duties, Leon would simply take Beverly from him and dare Eric to do anything about it. As it was, Leon had a full load of beautiful women to bed and turn out as he saw fit.

He was approached by Spencer, whom Leon saw as an up-and-coming soldier he could count on so long as he was useful. "Is Fox gone?"

"Yeah," Spencer said. "Did you need something else from him?"

"I'll let him know when I do."

Leon preferred not to have to kill those who could make him money. After all, they were no good to him dead. But he also had to send a message to anyone thinking of resisting paying protection money or double-crossing him that it would come at a steep price. So far, Eric Fox had made that stand up and was clearly ready to do so again when called upon.

"That's cool," Spencer stated. "Do you want me to do a few runs for you?"

"Yeah, later." Leon looked up at his puffy face. "Right now, why don't you come downstairs and have your way with one of my girls?"

"You don't mind?"

"Of course not. That's pretty much all they're good for—giving it up." Leon met his eyes. "I know you've got your own lady, but what happens here stays here."

Spencer grinned, and Leon knew he'd corrupted him. Another way to control his minions.

FOUR

Beverly wore one of her new outfits, a black and ivory floral stretch satin sheath, for lunch with her best friend, Marilyn Ramsey. She was the one person Beverly felt she could trust with her deepest secrets. Unlike other more attractive and thinner women she knew, Beverly didn't see Marilyn as a threat, but rather as someone who had her back and was comfortable in her own skin.

"Wow, look at you," Marilyn said, her black eyes widening as she hand-brushed her dark brown bob.

Beverly gleamed and struck a pose. "Yes, look at me," she uttered. "Fabulous, aren't I?"

"Aren't you always?"

Beverly realized she may have been overdoing it as she studied Marilyn's overweight frame, ill fitted in a paisley print matte jersey. She certainly didn't want to make her feel uncomfortable, particularly when she was itching to confide in Marilyn about her recent sexual rendezvous.

"Why don't we sit down?" Beverly had chosen this outdoor cafe as it was one of her favorites in the city, specializing in Cajun cuisine.

Both ordered crawfish and gumbo, along with red wine.

The waiter had barely left after serving them when Beverly felt the urge to come out with what she couldn't seem to get out of her mind. "I had a one-night stand."

Marilyn's eyes grew. "What?"

Guess it's too late to take it back now. "I had sex with a stranger last night," she reiterated over her wineglass.

"Where? How did you meet him?"

"In his hotel room," Beverly said in a conspiratorial undertone. "We met in the hotel lounge."

Marilyn frowned. "And what were you doing there?"

"I was bored after another sexless experience with Eric and some shopping and just stopped at the first place I saw for a drink," Beverly explained as she envisioned it. "He was sitting at the bar, having a drink. I swear he was the sexiest-looking man I've ever laid eyes on. The sexual chemistry between us was incredible."

"So you jumped his bones?"

Beverly smiled. "I think we jumped each other's bones."

Marilyn tasted her gumbo. "Well, you *are* full of surprises."

"I surprised myself," Beverly admitted.

"Does Eric know?"

Beverly's lips pursed. "What do you think? Of course not. He'd probably kill the guy if he did, assuming he could find him."

"I'm more worried about what he might do to *you*," Marilyn said. "You're my best friend, and I don't want to see you hurt."

"He won't find out," Beverly insisted. At least not from her. And she was sure Marilyn wouldn't breathe a word of it. Aside from their friendship, Marilyn and Eric didn't exactly get along. He felt Marilyn took away some of their time together. She saw him as a control freak. Both had some merit in Beverly's mind. "Besides, I'm a big girl. Eric doesn't own me. We're not even married."

"So does that mean you're breaking up with him?" Marilyn asked while breaking up her crawfish.

"No," Beverly was quick to say. Even if there was definite strain between them in the bedroom, Eric had been good to her and very generous. She'd be a fool to give that up for a stranger who was probably married or had a girlfriend and would be leaving town at any time. "I'm still with Eric. This was just a onetime thing. No one gets hurt by it."

"I suppose." Marilyn licked her fingers. "Tell me about your lover man."

"He's gorgeous," Beverly said dreamily. "Bald, muscular, and did I mention *very* sexy?"

"Yes, I think you did," Marilyn laughed. "Obviously he was just as taken with you."

"Definitely." Beverly thought about how alive and special he made her feel. "We just clicked."

"So why not see him again? Like you said, Eric doesn't own you. Nothing says you can't enjoy some on the side more than once."

"He's from Los Angeles and just in town for business. I'm not sure how long he'll be here. Besides, once is enough for this girl. Any more would be playing with fire."

"Burn, baby, burn," Marilyn joked. "Looks like the fire of desire already scorched the sheets."

"You're crazy, you know that," Beverly laughed.

"Don't hear you denying it."

"That's because it's true. It's also past history. I just want to move on now."

"And what if things never get better between you and Eric in the bedroom?" asked Marilyn. "Are you prepared to deal with his sexual inadequacies forever now that you've gotten a taste of what good sex can really be like?"

That was a question Beverly was not prepared to answer. Already she missed the touch and smell of Dante. And the way he felt filling her insides. Could she really do without that feeling if the opportunity presented itself again?

"I don't know," she told Marilyn honestly. "Oh, by the way, if Eric asks, I was with you last night between eight and ten."

"You were?" Marilyn raised a brow.

"Yes!" Beverly narrowed her eyes.

"I'm just messing with you. Not a problem. You can count on me as cover anytime you need it. That's what best friends are for."

"I know." Beverly smiled, grateful for her friendship and being able to bounce ideas off her. Beverly's thoughts again turned to Dante and how she would love to see him again, even if against her better judgment.

Marilyn Ramsey was admittedly caught off guard when she'd heard that Beverly had slept with another man. She had assumed Beverly knew a good catch when she had one in Eric Fox. Obviously Beverly was more interested in satisfying her sexual needs wherever and with whomever she could.

This was actually a good thing, Marilyn thought, all things considered, as she drove her Subaru Legacy away from the cafe. She was glad to see that Beverly didn't walk on water as had seemed to be the case. She'd been jealous of Beverly since they were in high school. Beverly was prettier, thinner, lighter, and all the guys seemed to fall under her spell with just the batting of her eyes or swaying of her hips.

It had been just the opposite for Marilyn. Few guys paid her much attention in high school and not many more afterward. Seemed as though a big girl couldn't catch a break when competing with the likes of Beverly and other women like her. Certainly not the type of good fortune that Marilyn sought in a man.

Beverly had gotten herself a sugar daddy in Eric. The man gave her everything a woman could ask for, by and large. If he couldn't keep up with her in the bedroom, maybe he had a very good excuse. That was no excuse for her going elsewhere to get some, even if it was playing right into Marilyn's hands.

She knew Eric far better than Beverly did. While Beverly believed he was this upstanding businessman, his business was anything but legitimate. Marilyn understood that he worked for Leon, just as her husband, Spencer, did. But while Spencer got his hands dirty from running drugs, collecting gambling debts, and intimidating people because of his size, he didn't kill people like Eric. She could only imagine how Beverly would react if she knew the truth about her man.

Or that her best friend was sleeping with him behind her back. Marilyn figured it was only fair that she went after Eric. After all, she'd always wanted what Beverly had and it was no different when she moved in with the man. Beverly would never expect her to be capable of seducing Eric. Well, think and think again.

Moreover, Marilyn now had a new weapon to potentially use against her so-called best friend, Beverly. But it was a line she had to tread carefully. She knew damned well Eric had a jealous streak in him a mile long and was fully capable of snapping Beverly's neck if she gave him reason to. It wasn't necessarily the way she wanted to claim Eric as her own. Especially as he might treat the messenger with the same venom as his whoring girlfriend. Marilyn wasn't willing to go there right now, preferring to keep tabs on Beverly and let her dig a deeper hole for herself. She'd cheated on Eric once, and there were no guarantees that she wouldn't cheat again if her new lover hung around. For her part, Marilyn hoped Beverly did keep her affair going. That would just leave her with more opportunities to be with Eric while Beverly was sexually distracted.

Marilyn pulled into the parking lot of the cheap motel. She recognized Eric's Cadillac and parked next to it. The thought of him being inside her made Marilyn's nipples harden. She put lip gloss on, though she expected Eric's lips would take it right off, and made herself smell nice with a bit of Queen perfume along her neckline and dress.

The door opened just as she reached it. Eric stood there. "Hey, baby," she cooed.

His brow creased. "What took you so long?"

"I was having lunch with Beverly." Marilyn knew he would be bothered by that even more than had she said she was with her husband, as if Eric and Beverly were competing for her attention

"Was she with you yesterday too?" he asked, eyeing her keenly.

Marilyn thought about what Beverly must have told him to cover her ass while she was getting hot and sweaty with another man. "Yeah, we hung out," she lied with a straight face. "Why?"

Eric gave her a look of satisfaction. "No reason other than I like to know where she is when she's out and about."

Right. You want to make sure some other dude isn't in her pants. Too late for that. "Let's not talk about her right now," Marilyn said, wanting the occasion to be all about them. Or her.

She got on her knees and unzipped his fly. Pulling out his penis, she ran her fingers across the shaft until he got hard. Then she put him in her mouth, coating his erection in warm saliva. Her tongue teased the tip a bit before going all out to please him.

She looked up at his ecstasy-filled face, knowing his orgasm was forthcoming. It exploded in her mouth while his body shook violently.

"You do that so well," he groaned.

"Only for you," she said dishonestly, knowing that her husband loved her to go down on him too.

"I like that."

Marilyn got to her feet. She pushed him down on the bed and pulled down his pants and underwear. Unlike Beverly, she knew what he wanted and how to give it to him.

She straddled him with her thighs and bent down, putting her big breasts in his face. "Play with them," she ordered.

He obeyed her command, nibbling on them and around the side of her nipples. This got her excited. She returned the favor by guiding her hand up and down the length of his penis and squeezing his testicles until she got a rise out of him.

Marilyn guided herself onto Eric's erection and impaled him deep inside her wet body. She made love to him and came quickly, wishing she had been able to hold out longer. She continued on until he climaxed, imagining all along that she was Beverly, suspecting he was wishing the same.

Beverly called Eric and got his voice mail. She didn't bother leaving a message, assuming he was too busy working to talk to her. She was really only phoning to see if he was preoccupied so he wouldn't be looking for her. Not that he was ever around much in the late afternoon.

What she most wanted was to see Dante again. He had left an impression on her that was impossible to simply sweep aside. Did he feel the same way about her? Or had he already moved on to another woman while he was in the city?

The notion irked Beverly in spite of the fact that she was still tied to Eric. Nevertheless, she felt jealous at the thought of someone else being as sexually complete with Dante as she was last night. *I want him inside me again.* And everything else that came with the hot sex between them.

Beverly started to dial his number, but feared Dante might brush her off. She thought it would be best if she simply went to his hotel room. Risky, yes, as he might not be in, or he might be busy or otherwise preoccupied. *I'll have to take that chance. I need him.*

She drove to the hotel, surprised that he had gotten her to act so daringly based on one time together. *It is what it is.* Even with the threat of Eric somehow finding out, the urge to see Dante again was simply too strong to ignore.

Inside the hotel, Beverly checked the lounge on the chance that Dante might be having a drink again. If so, she hoped he was alone. She saw no sign of him. For a moment, she wondered if it was a foolish idea to go to his room. The man might think she was some crazed woman stalking him.

Maybe he was right. At least about being crazy for the sexual man in him. She would go ahead and show up at his door and whatever happened, happened.

***

Dante sat in his room, strategizing now that he had the jump on where Eric Fox and Leon Quincy stayed. It would obviously not be a smart idea to go after either one in their residences. He definitely wanted revenge in the worst way. But he wasn't keen on spending the rest of his life in prison. Or on death row. That was the last thing he needed in trying to do right by Russell. He doubted, too, that his brother would want revenge to come at the cost of his freedom.

No, he had to be smart about this. He had to find the Achilles' heel of the two men and use it to his advantage in taking them out without the law coming after him. Dante suspected that the authorities would probably think he'd done them a favor by ridding the world of Fox and Quincy. But why take the chance and have the finger point squarely at him in the process?

He drank the beer in his hand and remembered the good old days when he and Russell were tight and took care of each other. Seemed a lifetime ago now. Dante wished he could turn back the hands of time. Unfortunately he couldn't. There was only doing what needed to be done and getting back to his life.

He thought about Beverly. Or, more specifically, their intense sexual encounter. He'd love to go another round or two with her. But she had likely squelched the possibility by returning to whatever life she escaped from briefly to find him. He would have to live with the fact that he had probably seen her for the last time and there wasn't a damned thing he could do about it other than relive the memories of their night of passion. Memories that would stay with him for a very long time.

The knock at the door broke Dante away from his reverie. As his room had already been cleaned, it wasn't housekeeping. And he hadn't ordered room service.

For a moment he tensed, thinking that maybe somehow the men he had come to kill were onto him and were prepared to strike first. But then he realized how unlikely that was. His brother had been killed and cremated six months ago. There was no reason to believe anyone would show up after all this time for justice.

Still, Dante was on guard as he walked to the door. He opened it and smiled when he saw Beverly standing there, looking sexy and very enticing.

FIVE

Beverly had butterflies in her stomach as she took in Dante at the door, feeling a fresh surge of sexual desire encompass her. He was shirtless, as if to show off his six-pack. Tight jeans looked sexier on him than they ever would on her. Not to say that she hadn't provided him with eye candy in wearing a blue sleeveless V-neck silk dress and high-heeled leather sandals.

"Thought I'd take a chance that you might be here," she said, sweeping her long hair to one side.

"Your chance paid off," Dante said, grinning. "Here I am."

"Busy?" She didn't want to presume anything.

"Not too busy for you."

Beverly beamed. "I was hoping you'd say that."

He showed her into the room. "Can I get you something to drink? The wet bar has a little bit of everything."

She thought about it, then decided she'd rather be clearheaded for what was about to happen. "No thanks."

Dante gazed at her. "I wasn't sure if I'd ever see you again."

"Neither was I," she told him truthfully.

"So what made it happen?"

She met his eyes lustfully. "I couldn't get you out of my mind."

"I feel the same way about you," he said, wrapping his arms around her waist. "Yesterday was truly incredible and totally unforgettable."

Beverly couldn't agree more. "Kiss me!" she demanded.

"With pleasure." He tilted his head expertly and brought their mouths together in a hard, tongue-exploring kiss that left Beverly light-headed. Dante unlocked their lips. "How's that for starters?"

She touched her tingling lips. "You're a great kisser."

"I'm an even better lover," he declared in a tone that spoke more of confidence than arrogance.

As he had already shown her that, Beverly could not argue the point. On the contrary, it was the very reason why she had once again thrown caution to the wind and shown up at his door.

"I don't have much time," she warned.

"Then let's not waste even one moment of it," Dante said tersely.

Beverly didn't intend to. She lifted the dress over her head, exposing herself to him in the flesh. Never before had she been so brazen with someone she barely knew. But then a man had never appealed so much to her sexual side.

She watched Dante strip naked as well, put on a condom, and then lift her in one easy motion, carrying her to the bed as their mouths attacked each other salaciously. Beverly gasped as Dante moved his mouth to her breasts, kissing them madly and licking her nipples like lollipops. His lips trailed down her stomach and brushed across the thin triangle of hair before settling between her legs.

Beverly moaned loudly as Dante went to work on her clitoris. She was already wet from the moment she saw him again. Now there was no telling how much nectar she would release from his torturous oral stimulation. She grabbed his shaved head, running her hands across it while keeping his face pressed against her groin so he wouldn't stop what he'd started until he had completed the seduction.

Beverly's body lurched when her orgasm surged. The trembling continued as Dante rose up and moved on top of her. His stiff penis drove into her, and Beverly received it with pleasure, allowing him to penetrate deeper as she wrapped her legs around his buttocks. He began to kiss her feverishly. Beverly tasted herself on his lips, increasing her desire for him that much more.

Dante flipped them around and was on his back, but continued to spear her with his erection, driving Beverly mad as she rode up and down on him, feeling it to her very core. Both their bodies were slick from the frenetic pace and steamy passion. The scent of sex crossed Beverly's nostrils, combining with the onset of another climax that had her drooling with excitement for this man.

When the moment of impact came, Beverly broke her mouth from Dante's and buried her head in his shoulders. He held her buttocks firmly and continually made love to her even as his orgasm practically paralyzed him while wedged deep inside of her.

The bed rocked back and forth from their mutual satisfaction, and sounds of passion escaped their mouths until the fever subsided.

"And I thought it couldn't get any better than last night," Beverly said with a giggle.

Dante lifted his head, kissing her shoulder. "You thought wrong. Looks like we're a sexual match made in heaven."

"I think so." She sucked in a deep breath. "Problem is, you won't be around forever."

"If I were, would it really matter?"

She looked at him. "What does that mean?"

He paused. "Where do you go when we're not together?"

"Oh, that." She tried not to think about it, especially while naked with her limbs still entangled with his.

"Yeah, that," he said, challenging her. "It's cool. I just want to know who and what I'm dealing with here."

Beverly paused but didn't want to shy away from her reality, curious as well about his. "I'm living with a man."

"I see."

"And what do you see?" she asked.

"A beautiful woman in my bed instead of with the man she's seeing."

"We're having some problems in the bedroom," Beverly conceded, and that was an understatement.

Dante kissed her shoulder. "Well, that must be all about him, because you are dynamite in the sack."

She blushed, loving the compliment. "You're pretty hot yourself under or on top of the sheets."

"So why do you stay with him?" Dante flashed a curious look.

Beverly expected the question. The answer wasn't as simple as black and white. "He's taken good care of me," she explained. "He's an older man."

"Obviously it isn't enough just being taken care of, if it's not the right way."

Her lips pursed. "It wasn't always this way."

"But it is now." Dante touched her, sending sensations through Beverly. "Maybe it's time to move on?"

She arched an eyebrow. "You mean with you?"

"Not necessarily." He rubbed his nose. "I'm only saying that if it's not happening in the sex department, forcing you to look elsewhere, maybe you need to re-think your priorities."

"And what are *your* priorities?" Beverly asked point-edly, deciding it was time to turn the tables.

Dante hesitated. "Right now, you." He kissed one of her breasts.

As good as it felt, she was not about to let him off the hook. "Are you married?"

"Nope." He kissed the other breast.

"Girlfriend?"

"Not the last time I looked."

"Why not?" It was an honest question, even if Beverly was relieved that she had him all to herself. At least for now.

Dante mulled over the question. "Guess I've been too focused on work."

"Sounds like you need to work on your own priori-ties." She ran a hand across his smooth face. "Or are you satisfied having hot sex with a stranger, and then being on your way?"

He put his finger between her legs and then sucked it. "I'm never totally satisfied, but you're a very good step in the right direction." He kissed her passionately. "You're fast becoming less like a stranger and more like someone I'm getting to know very well in all the ways that count most."

Beverly felt her temperature once again beginning to rise. His assessment of their familiarity with each other was right on the money. The thought that it would likely be ending soon was almost unbearable. But until then, she intended to milk the sexual magnetism be-tween them for all it was worth.

***

Admittedly, Dante had been unprepared for Beverly to walk into his life, bringing with her the sexual courage and openness that had been lacking in his world. He didn't make a habit of sleeping with another man's woman. On the other hand, he couldn't be blamed if the dude couldn't keep his woman satisfied. That fell on Dante's broad shoulders for the short term, and he was more than up to the task.

After going another round with Beverly in which they explored every part of each other and came back for more before climaxing together in a powerful burst of energy, Dante watched her walk away. This time the question was no longer, would they see each other again, but when? He loved making love to this vivacious woman and could do so every day of the week.

Except for the fact that he was in town on a mission. It was a mission he would not pass up, not even for the opportunity to be with Beverly. Besides, she seemed comfortable giving herself to two men, though apparently only one was getting some. Dante accepted the limitations of their tryst, given that he, too, had other obligations, after which he would be leaving Detroit and getting back to his real life. Right now, there was no room for anyone on a steady basis. But if there were, he couldn't think of a better-looking, sexier woman he would want to try to build something with than Beverly. Too bad neither of them was at that place in their lives to go there.

He got dressed and drove across town to Primrose Avenue, where a friend of Russell's named Wesley Carson lived. Dante had spoken to him briefly over the phone the day before. Russell had introduced them when Dante visited two years ago. As someone his brother trusted, Dante hoped that talking to him might add greater closure in his loss.

When Dante got to the door of the modest ranch style home, it was opened by a little girl.

"Hi," she said with a bright smile and a front tooth missing.

"Hey, there," he said and looked up to find a dark-haired, tall, slender man above her whom Dante recognized as Wesley Carson.

"Nice to see you again, Dante."

"You too."

Wesley shook his hand. "Sorry it wasn't under better circumstances."

"Same here." Dante gazed again at the girl, who put her thumb in her mouth.

"This is my daughter, April," Wesley said.

Dante grinned at her. "Pretty name."

Wesley patted him on the shoulder. "Come on in."

Dante stepped into the living room, where a big-screen television was tuned to a Tigers baseball game against the New York Yankees.

"The grown-ups are going to talk right now," Wesley told his daughter. "Go play."

She tilted her head sideways at Dante. "Bye."

"Bye." He wondered what it would be like to have a daughter or son. Russell had talked about having kids before his divorce and afterward, should he meet someone else and remarry. Dante was still open to the possibility, if he were to settle down with a woman who was of the same mind.

"Can I get you a beer, wine, or a soft drink?" asked Wesley.

"Beer."

A moment later, Dante had a can in hand and was sitting across from Wesley. "My wife, Doris, is working the afternoon shift at the hospital where she's a nurse," he said. "Wish she'd been here to meet you."

"I'll probably be in town for a little while," Dante indicated. "Hopefully, we can get together again before I leave."

"I'd like that."

Dante put the can to his mouth thoughtfully. He hated being in Detroit when Russell was dead and buried, no longer around to hang out. His brother should never have been denied the chance to play out his dreams for tomorrow.

"I'm really sad about Russell's death," Wesley said, as though he could read his mind. "He was a good man."

"I appreciate that." Dante looked at him. "He thought a lot of you too."

"I could say the same about you. Russell used to tell me all the time how you two used to raise hell as kids."

Dante smiled. "Yeah, we got into a bit of trouble—and out of it."

"He really admired your work as a journalist," Wesley remarked. "Russell showed me a couple of articles you wrote. They were great."

"Thanks." Dante drank more beer. "I like what I do. I also respected how Russell came to Detroit and tried to start over with his business." He paused. "Until they took his life and destroyed what he had going for him."

Wesley drank his beer dejectedly. "Yeah, it was a damned shame. And for what? To steal what little money he had?"

"I think it had more to do with making him a slave to some punk who thought he owned the neighborhood," Dante said, his jaw set.

Wesley raised a brow. "Not sure I follow you."

Dante pondered whether to keep what he knew in check or share it with someone who was in Russell's corner. He decided to go somewhere in between. "Let's just say I have it on good authority that Russell was the victim of a shakedown. Seems like all the local businesses were essentially being held hostage by someone who demanded protection money or else."

"Wow. I never read anything about—"

"That's because most people were too afraid to come out with it. Or risk having the same thing happen," Dante said angrily.

"Well, are the police doing anything about it?"

"The case has gone nowhere with them, aside from in some cold case file." Dante kept to himself his suspicions that some members of the police department were on the take.

"So there's nothing that can be done to bring those responsible to justice?"

Dante paused. "Hope for a lucky break."

Wesley's brow creased. "Not many of those to be found in Detroit these days."

"I get that." He could only make his own luck, and certainly there would be hell to pay for both Eric Fox and Leon Quincy. "Anyway, I'd better get out of here." He finished off the beer and stood.

"Thanks for dropping by," Wesley said. "If there's anything I can do for you while you're in town, don't hesitate to ask."

Dante shook his hand thoughtfully. "I'll keep that in mind."

In his car, Dante's eyes watered. He hadn't wanted to get emotional, but he did while thinking about Russell and his tragic, untimely death. It was nice to know that there was someone other than himself who hadn't forgotten his little brother. He would see to it that two other people would remember what Russell had stood for before they took him away.

SIX

That evening, Beverly went out to a restaurant with Eric for dinner. Though her mother had taught her how to cook, she almost never used the kitchen, preferring the luxury of being served whatever suited her appetite. That included sex. Men had always been there to give her nice things, and she saw no reason not to take them. Living with Eric had provided her with the greatest comforts yet, allowing her the opportunity to be pampered, wined, and dined to her heart's content.

But it didn't include having children. She had always hoped to have a child someday. That wasn't in the cards for Eric. He had made that clear from the start, claiming that was the reason behind his divorce. Beverly hadn't argued the point, as she felt their relationship could only last so long. Maybe the next man in her life would feel differently.

Maybe Dante could be that man. She envisioned herself living with him in Los Angeles, making love every day and later deciding to make it official in hooking up and having their love child. She realized it was only a fantasy. But that didn't stop her from longing to be with someone who seemed to get her. At least where it concerned her sexual appetite. The thought of making love to Dante a few hours ago sent heat up and down Beverly's spine. The man had definitely gotten under her skin. She could not shake her deep desire to have him inside her, stimulating nonstop. Not even when sitting across from the man she lived with.

"What are you thinking about?" Eric asked, slicing a knife into a thick pork chop.

Beverly spooned some peas. "Nothing," she lied. *Can't exactly tell you about Dante and what we've done together the past two days.*

"Now you're lying to me. I've got eyes, and you were definitely somewhere else. Where was that?"

Beverly felt the coldness of his gaze. *Think fast.* "All right, if you must know, I was trying to decide where to get my hair done tomorrow. My regular hairdresser went to Alabama to attend her cousin's wedding."

"So why not wait until she gets back?"

"Why should I?" Beverly responded. "I need to repair some split ends and maybe color my hair a little."

His eyes swept over her hair, which was clipped while hanging across her shoulders. "I like the way it looks now."

"You'll like it even better afterward," she promised. "I want everything to be as good as it can be for you, honey." And maybe for Dante as well.

Eric dabbed the corners of his mouth. "What else do you need to beautify yourself?"

"Hmm . . ." Since he was asking, Beverly felt she might as well take full advantage. "A manicure and pedicure would be nice."

"So have them done."

She smiled, while wondering what else she could squeeze out of him. "As part of my staying in shape, I'd love to join a spa fitness club that just opened and hone my body with some Pilates, yoga, and whatever."

Eric grinned appraisingly. "Go ahead and join. I want you to keep looking great and be happy."

"Thank you." Beverly wouldn't press her luck by asking for more right now, especially when she had eyes for another man. "You might even want to join."

"I don't think so," he said as expected. "Too busy for that."

Excuses, excuses. She wanted to suggest it might help him get into better shape for sex but no longer wished to encourage him in that department.

"Well, I'll work out there for both of us."

"You do that." Eric started eating again. "I was thinking that maybe in a couple of months we could go to the Bahamas for a vacation."

Bahamas? It wasn't so long ago that Beverly would have jumped at the opportunity. But now she wasn't so sure. Going on romantic escapades was supposed to result in passion and lots of it. Would that be the case this time? Or would he still be nothing more than a big dud in bed? Did she dare find out? Would her affair with Dante be over by then or have only just begun?

"So what do you think . . . ?" A note of impatience spread across his face.

"That sounds nice," she told him, figuring the idea would probably disappear as time went by.

"Good. I'll look into it."

Don't do me any favors. Beverly smiled and sipped her drink, while turning her thoughts once more to Dante.

Eric sensed that Beverly was not her usual self, which concerned him. Though the magic had worn off for them sexually, he still liked having her as his lady and wouldn't let her walk away into another man's arms. If it took pampering to please her, in case he couldn't keep up in other areas, then so be it. The trip to the Bahamas could be just what they needed to get more fire into their relationship. It was worth a try. Too bad he couldn't bring Marilyn along for the ride. A threesome between them could be fun.

When they got home, Eric felt in the mood for sex. He wouldn't take no for an answer. In the great room, he began kissing Beverly.

"Let's go upstairs," she said hurriedly.

"Let's not," he responded, grabbing her breasts. "I want you right here."

She put up only mild resistance before looking him in the face. "If that's what you want."

It was. The bedroom never seemed to do it for him anymore where it concerned her. They got naked, and Eric scanned Beverly's sweet body up and down, feeling himself become aroused. He had her lean over the arm of the sectional and put his penis into Beverly's vagina from behind. She was tight and not as wet as he preferred. He brushed back his own slight discomfort and pushed himself in deeper, gripping her shoulders while he moved in and out.

Beverly cried out, which Eric interpreted as her having an orgasm. His orgasm wasn't coming as easily, even when envisioning himself inside of Marilyn or some other woman he'd bedded. He tried harder, plunging forward, breathing irregularly as Beverly began to loosen up inside. Eric felt his erection begin to weaken, causing him to go quicker in slamming himself against her buttocks. Finally he had a halfhearted climax, slumping onto her moist body afterward.

"Was it good for you?" Eric asked, lifting back to his feet.

"Do you even have to ask?" Beverly responded sarcastically, crawling across the sectional and away from him. "You got what you wanted. Let's just leave it at that."

"Did I hurt you?" He regarded her with only mild interest.

"No." She stood and gathered her clothes. "I'm used to your rough style of doing things."

"It'll get better again," Eric promised, though far from certain if he could deliver. He was more intent on making sure no one else tried to take his place in between her legs. What he wasn't giving her in the sex department, he was more than making up for in treating Beverly like a queen. He doubted she would get the same from some punk her own age. Not if he had a say in the matter.

The following morning, Beverly went to a nearby salon to have her hair and nails done. Marilyn had recommended the place. Beverly was still sore from last night. As usual, Eric thought only of himself when having sex with her. No foreplay. No oral stimulation. No nothing but wham, bam, thank you, ma'am. She wondered if it was worth it to put up with his sexual inadequacies in order to have everything else that came with being Eric Fox's woman.

Especially when she knew there were other men out there who were so much more compatible with her sexually—like Dante. Not to mention, he was so damned attractive and closer to her age. Was that enough to walk away from Eric? Or were she and Dante only good for hot sex?

"Someone's getting the royal treatment for that special man," hummed Felecia, who was polishing Beverly's toenails.

"Actually, I'm doing this for myself," Beverly said, though admittedly, she was hoping to turn heads with her new haircut and coloring. She also loved having her feet massaged and kissed by a man and wanted them to look good in the process.

"Absolutely nothing wrong with that, girlfriend. You're a beautiful woman and should be able to appreciate having that brought out even more with some coddling."

"Not to say that my man won't appreciate this." Beverly was thinking of Dante instead of Eric.

"Of course he will. What normal man wouldn't?"

Beverly smiled. "True."

"So you and Marilyn are pretty tight, huh?"

"Best of friends."

"Cool. She's a trip. But definitely driven," Felecia said. "That girl knows what she wants and won't stop until she gets it."

Beverly laughed. "Are you sure we're talking about the *same* Marilyn?" The one she knew was a nice, loyal person, but the last word Beverly would have attached to her was *driven*. Marilyn seemed perfectly content in her little world, with little interest in changing the status quo. Or was she missing something?

Felecia described Marilyn, convincing Beverly that they were speaking about the same person. "Marilyn's one of my best customers," Felecia stated. "Hopefully, I've got you now as a new customer."

"I think you do." Beverly smiled and wondered how she could move back and forth between two good hairdressers without anyone being bent out of shape. "I'll have to speak with Marilyn and see what's up. If she's motivated about something, maybe she'll share it with me."

"I'm sure she will." Felecia moved to Beverly's other foot. "Now sit back and enjoy."

Beverly intended to and would use the time to think about Dante and what she wished badly they were doing right now.

SEVEN

"Your hair," gushed Marilyn, her eyes glued to Beverly.

"You like it?" Beverly had decided to drop by her girlfriend's house so she could get a first look at her trimmed hair with blond highlights.

"I love it. Felecia did a great job." Marilyn was eating a donut. "Has Eric seen it yet?"

"I came here straight from the salon." Beverly wondered if her new hairdo would appeal to Dante.

"I'm sure he'll think it's great," Marilyn said. "You want a donut?"

"I'll pass. Those things do wonders to clog the arteries."

Marilyn frowned. "I think they'll clog no matter what we eat."

"You're probably right," Beverly said if only to appease her.

They went into the small breakfast room and Beverly sat at the table. It was cluttered and Beverly wasn't sure how Marilyn could find anything she needed.

"Can I at least pour you a glass of freshly squeezed lemonade?" Marilyn asked.

"Yes, please." Beverly ran fingers through her hair while eyeing Marilyn pouring the lemonade into a tall glass. "Felecia and I were talking about you."

Marilyn handed her the glass. "Yeah? What about?"

"She said you were driven."

"I am." Marilyn met her eyes. "Just like you, I want whatever I can get out of this life."

"Such as?" Beverly was curious.

Marilyn paused, sitting down. "Well, I'm thinking about going back to school to get my degree."

Beverly raised a brow. "That's news to me."

"Guess I hadn't gotten around to telling you."

Beverly had a degree in liberal arts but never did anything with it. She'd never felt the need to. Maybe she still could make her education count for something. "I'm happy you're going back to school."

"So am I." Marilyn leaned back in the chair. "Now I just need to get the courage to tell Spencer. He's so cheap that he'd probably think it was just throwing away money."

Beverly was inclined to agree, though she didn't know Spencer very well. "Maybe he'll surprise you," she said, giving her hope.

"Enough about me." Marilyn sipped lemonade. "Any news about your onetime lover?"

Beverly felt a tingle between her legs thinking about him, the soreness she felt earlier all but gone. "It's two times lover now," she announced boldly.

Marilyn's eyes bulged. "You're really bad, girl—very bad."

"Maybe just a little." Beverly giggled.

"I figured the great sex might be too much to pass up again, especially if he's only going to be around for a little while."

"I'm not sure when he's leaving," Beverly said pensively. "We just really have a great sexual chemistry thing going."

Marilyn chuckled. "In other words, you're hooked."

"You could probably say that. At least for now I am." She didn't even want to think about the void left once he went back to California.

"You'd better be careful," warned Marilyn while giving her a look. "If Eric ever found out—"

"He won't," Beverly said confidently. *Am I fooling myself? Or can I really keep being his woman while longing to be with another man?*

"I hope not."

"You're the only one who knows," Beverly pointed out.

"My lips are sealed," Marilyn promised, putting a finger to her lips.

"I know that." Beverly took comfort in knowing she could, and would, keep a secret as her best friend.

"All I'm saying is to be careful if you plan to keep getting some on the side."

"I will be." Beverly twisted her lips. "Eric and I had sex last night. Or should I say, *he* had sex while I was bent over like his damned dog."

"Doesn't sound like it was much fun," Marilyn voiced, crinkling her nose.

"Not unless you call not being lubricated while he shoved his penis inside me from behind fun. At least he had trouble maintaining an erection, as usual, so it was over soon enough."

Marilyn gazed at her. "If he can't satisfy you, why not get out of the relationship and give this other man your full attention—and vice versa?"

"Don't think it's not something I haven't thought about," Beverly responded honestly. "Unfortunately, it's not that simple. I can't just walk out on Eric for someone I've had sex with but still don't know very well. I'm certainly not ready to just up and move to Los Angeles, not that he has invited me or anything. Right now, I want to keep things as they are with Eric *and* maybe the other guy—and just see what happens. . . ."

Marilyn remained mute for a moment. "Whatever you say. I just hope you know what you're doing."

"I hope so too." Beverly drank more lemonade and thought about Eric's plans for a trip to the Bahamas. If things had not gotten any better for them in the bedroom by then, could she truly accompany him to such a romantic spot? Especially if another man occupied her mind in ways Eric no longer could.

She heard the front door open, and they both looked down the hallway as Spencer Ramsey entered, carrying a bag of groceries.

"What's up?" he said, eyeing Beverly.

"I'm good," she told him.

In his early thirties, Spencer had a large frame and closely cropped dark hair. Marilyn had married him three years ago. Beverly had been her maid of honor, though she was skeptical the relationship would last. Marilyn had started seeing Spencer on the rebound after breaking up with her married lover. Though Beverly saw the two as a physical match, she wondered if Marilyn was too high maintenance for Spencer. Or if she would leave him in a snap if someone better and wealthier were to come along.

Beverly recalled that she had been introduced to Eric while attending a barbecue picnic at a park. Eric was a colleague of Spencer's—both of whom worked for Leon Quincy. Though Beverly hadn't exactly been looking for anyone, men always seemed to gravitate toward her, not counting the fact that she was the one who had approached Dante. In spite of being older, Eric, with his handsome features, charming personality, and generosity, won Beverly over. Marilyn seemed to approve, and Spencer vouched for him, giving her an added measure of acceptance in dating Eric.

But that was then and this was now. Beverly could only wait and see how things played out with Eric now that Dante had come along and stolen some of his thunder.

"How's Leon these days?" Beverly asked Spencer as he began putting away groceries. She had met Eric's sharply dressed, suave boss, and he seemed like a nice enough guy, though Eric rarely talked about him.

"Leon's cool," he replied, glancing at Marilyn. "Eric can probably tell you more about him."

Beverly wasn't really sure what he meant by that and didn't follow up, assuming it was merely a figure of speech in case she wanted more details about the man who paid Eric's salary.

She glanced at her watch. "I'd better get out of here," she told Marilyn.

"Thanks for dropping by," Marilyn told her at the door, then lowered her voice. "If you run into any problems trying to juggle two men, let me know."

"I will." Beverly smiled and gave her a little hug. She was happy to have Marilyn's friendship, especially with her mother no longer in the city to drop by and visit whenever she liked. "See you later."

Marilyn waved at Beverly as she drove off before the smile on her face turned to a scowl. *That bitch. She wants to have her cake and eat it too.* When she had a smooth-talking, charismatic man like Eric, why was Beverly instead pining for some sex stud who didn't even stay in Detroit? Eric deserved better from his woman, even if he had his own dirty little secrets. But how could she spill the beans without jeopardizing her position with both of them? Could she do more harm than good in coming out with it? Especially when she had her own marriage to consider. Or was it even worth considering when she looked at it squarely? *Guess I'll just keep my mouth zipped till I'm certain it's in my best interests to expose Beverly's sordid affair.*

Fifteen minutes later, Spencer was on top of Marilyn. She squeezed his penis inside her vagina, causing him to groan with pleasure. She used a finger to rub her own clitoris as she fantasized that it was Eric impaling and pleasuring her. Once she'd come, Marilyn wanted to hurry up and get it over with.

Spencer seemed to hear her pleas, grunting loudly, his big body shaking as he reached his orgasm. Afterward, Marilyn rolled him off her.

"Was it as good for you as me, babe?" he asked, sucking in a deep breath.

"Yeah, sure," she said, trying only halfheartedly to sound as if she meant it.

He flashed his teeth. "I could tell."

It wasn't because of you. "No reason to hide it."

"You're the best." Spencer kissed the damp spot between her breasts.

Marilyn liked it better when Eric's mouth was all over her. "Don't you have to get back to work?"

"Trying to get rid of me?"

Isn't it obvious? "I just don't want you to get on Leon's bad side." Not to mention she had her favorite soap operas to watch.

"Me and Leon are tight," Spencer bragged.

"As tight as he is with Eric?"

Spencer's mouth contracted. "Yeah. Eric ain't nobody special. He does his job, just like I do."

But he's paid better and treated with more respect. Which was partly why she wished he was her man fulltime instead of part-time. More than that, the fact that Beverly had him and all the perks infuriated Marilyn.

She would change that soon. And then she wouldn't have to put up with Spencer's fat ass anymore.

"You're right," she told him sweetly. "You're every bit as special as Beverly's man."

"Glad you think so."

"That's why I married you. I got someone who takes good care of me."

Spencer grinned. "You got that right. If anyone ever tries anything with you, let me know and I'll make them pay."

The only one who would be paying for anything in this relationship was him when she filed for divorce, demanding everything that she was owed for being his wife. Until then, she would have to bide her time and watch as Beverly self-destructed and she was there to pick up the pieces for Eric.

Spencer felt good after getting off inside Marilyn. The fact that he was giving her what she needed, too, made him happy. From the first time he'd laid eyes on Marilyn, he knew she was his type of lady. He'd always been attracted to curvaceous women. The fact that she had a bit of attitude was cool too. He knew she loved him, and he could put up with any sassiness she brought to the table.

He would take Marilyn any day of the week over her friend Beverly. Not to say that Spencer didn't find Eric's woman nice on the eyes. It was just that she was too much into herself for his liking. She was also clueless in somehow believing Eric to be someone he wasn't. But that was her problem—and Eric's.

Spencer had to focus on his life and taking care of business and Marilyn, not necessarily in that order. He gave Marilyn's juicy lips a kiss and left her naked on the bed, no doubt wishing he could stick around and make love again and again. If only there was time for that, he'd be all over her every day. But he had to make a living and keep his boss satisfied that he could be counted on to hold his own weight as a member of his posse.

Driving down Seven Mile Road, Spencer wondered if Marilyn might be ready to have a kid. He'd brought it up a few times, but she had told him they could go there a few years down the line, after enjoying each other's company. He'd grown up with a houseful of siblings. Although he wasn't close to any of them, he expected he would be a much better dad than his old man ever was. And he was sure Marilyn had a good mother somewhere in her.

Spencer noticed that the convenience store on the corner ahead was open again. It had been shut down for about six months. Or ever since the dude who owned it had been offed after deciding he valued his money more than his life. Spencer parked his car so he could take a look inside.

He entered the store and saw that it was definitely up and running. Behind the counter, he noted a dark-skinned, medium-sized man wearing glasses, with short black hair and a goatee. He guessed the man was around forty.

"Can I help you?" he asked evenly.

Spencer was nonchalant. "I'm cool. Just looking around."

"No problem."

Spencer walked casually through the store. Not much had changed from before. Except the owner. He didn't seem like he would be much of a problem. Not if he knew what was good for him.

Grabbing a big bag of potato chips and a large Coke, Spencer put them on the counter and watched the man ring it up and tell him the cost. He gave the man cash.

"Thanks," he said in a friendly tone. "Hope you come back again."

Spencer nodded. *Oh yeah, you'll see me again and again. Might as well get used to it.*

Back in his car, Spencer hit the road, eager to see Leon. He would want to know about this.

Dante walked into the police precinct, passing by an officer who was roughly handling a foul mouthed, tattooed man in handcuffs. He saw a woman wearing little clothing and stilettos being led in a different direction by another officer. Other people were milling about or pleading their case to anyone who would listen.

Dante tried to ignore all this, distracting as it was, and concentrate on his purpose for being there. He wanted to see if there were any new developments in the murder of his brother. Based on what had happened thus far, or hadn't happened, he wasn't expecting any earth-shattering revelations. It also occurred to Dante that if there had been any police officers on the take who worked for Leon Quincy, he could be putting an *X* on his own back by exposing himself.

It was a risk Dante was willing to take to try to get justice for Russell the right way. *I'd rather not have to kill the assholes responsible for his death if the cops would only do their job.* He also wanted to reassure himself that the private investigator had led him down the right path before taking measures into his own hands with no turning back.

Dante went up to the desk where an officer was chewing gum and appeared to be bored. He looked up at Dante. "How can I help you?"

"My brother was murdered six months ago," he responded equably. "I'd like to talk to the detective who investigated the case."

"What was your brother's name?"

"Russell Sheldon."

The officer typed it up on a computer and watched the screen. "Sheldon . . . store robbery . . . That him?"

"Yes," Dante responded.

"Looks like Detective Scott McCoy was in charge of the investigation. Let me see if he's here. . . ."

Dante watched as he made a call and reached the detective, exchanging words with him.

"What's your name?" the officer asked.

"Dante Sheldon."

He relayed the information to the detective and hung up. "Detective McCoy's office is on the fourth floor. He'll be expecting you."

"Thanks." Dante walked through the busy station and took the elevator up. He easily found the detective's office, which was stuck in the middle of two others. A forty-something, gray-haired man was sitting at a desk cluttered with files.

"Detective McCoy?"

"Yeah, I'm McCoy. You must be Dante Sheldon?"

Dante nodded, leaning over and shaking his large hand.

"I think we talked over the phone a few months back about your brother, Russell," McCoy recalled.

"That's right," confirmed Dante, remembering feeling totally unsatisfied about the terse conversation.

"I pulled up the file. Have a seat."

Dante sat in the metal chair across from his desk, wondering if he should just dive into what he knew or wait and see what the detective had to say, if anything.

"I take it you want to know if we've come up with any new leads on your brother's death?" McCoy asked.

"I traveled across the country from California, so, yes, I would like to know if you are any closer to solving my brother's murder." Dante realized his response was sarcastic, but he wasn't in the mood to be nice.

"Maybe you should have called before coming all this way—if that was your sole purpose for being in Detroit." McCoy sighed. "Afraid I don't have much more to tell you. Your brother was the victim of a robbery. Unfortunately, with the way the economy is these days—especially in Detroit—robbery has become all too common with people looking to feed themselves, their drug habits, you name it."

"Has anyone been arrested?" Dante peered at him. "Or even brought in for questioning?"

"We've questioned some people, but there have been no arrests."

"So what you're telling me is that the case has been swept under the rug?"

McCoy frowned. "We never sweep cases under the rug. This is still an ongoing investigation. But I'll be honest with you, we have a lot of current investigations and not nearly enough manpower to devote as much time to all of them as we'd like. Your brother was in the wrong place at the wrong time, though in his own store. Unless someone comes forward with new and compelling information, it's probably a long shot that we'll get the person responsible for shooting him."

Dante was afraid he would say that. It sounded very much like Russell's death had gotten lost in the shuffle, either through incompetence or by design. Either way, it left Dante more than a bit unsettled. "What if it wasn't a simple case of robbery?"

McCoy met his gaze sharply. "What are you saying?"

"What if Russell was the victim of an attempted shakedown?"

"By who?"

Dante looked away thoughtfully. He hesitated to open up a can of worms he couldn't close and the detective probably wouldn't. "You tell me." He put the onus back on him. "There is a string of businesses on the block where my brother had his store. Have you talked to any of the owners about being pressured to pay up or else?"

McCoy laughed deprecatingly. "I think you've been watching too many gangster movies, Mr. Sheldon. This is Detroit, not New York or Chicago."

"You just said that you have more crime going on than you can handle," Dante tossed back at him. "My brother's death may *not* have been the result of an armed robbery, no matter how it may have seemed!"

McCoy's nostrils flared. "Listen, I don't think I need you telling me how to do my job. We investigate all angles whenever there's a homicide in the city. Standard policy. It was concluded that robbery was the motive after the investigation, not before. And, for the record, we did talk to local business owners and none of them said they were victims of a shakedown. Now, if you have solid proof to back up your suspicions, give it to me and I'll check it out. Otherwise, I suggest you leave police work to the professionals and go back to your life." He paused. "Well?"

Dante thought twice about mentioning Leon Quincy and Eric Fox by name. He had a feeling it would do no good, particularly if cops were on Quincy's payroll. And it could be very bad for Dante if he tipped his hand and either had Quincy and the man he paid to kill Russell on his case or had the law after him when all was said and done. No, he would have to stick with his plan and take matters into his own hands. It was the only way Russell would ever see justice.

"I don't have any proof," he told the detective with a slow breath. "I'm sorry if I came down too hard on you. Guess I'm just frustrated that my brother has been dead for over six months and no one's in police custody for it."

"Believe me, I feel your pain," McCoy claimed, sitting back. "So do many others in this city and other big cities across the country. All I can tell you is that we won't stop trying to find your brother's killer. Unfortunately, that has to be balanced with new cases that come across my desk and are given priority over old ones. Sorry I can't give you any more at the moment."

"So am I, but I wanted to try, anyway." Dante stood up. "Thanks for seeing me."

"No problem. If you leave your number, I'll be sure to give you a ring if anything comes up."

Dante gave the number, figuring that would help serve as cover as he went about his mission to make Russell's killers pay the ultimate price.

Beverly was driving and thinking about how much she wanted Dante to make love to her. In spite of this and being only five minutes away from his hotel, she couldn't just show up at his door again, not knowing if he would be there or welcome her naked with powerful open arms.

Why am I lusting so much for this man? Is he really that good in bed? Or has Eric become that bad?

Beverly dismissed the questions, preferring to focus on Dante taking her to bed, to hell with everything else. She got out her cell phone and dialed his number.

"Hey," he answered in a voice deep with sexuality.

"Are you at the hotel?" she asked with a sense of desperation.

"Yeah, for a bit."

"I have about an hour that we can use if you're available."

"I'm available," he said eagerly. "Where are you now?"

"A block away," she told him.

"See you soon."

Beverly smiled as he disconnected. Clearly the man wanted her body as much as she wanted his. And she couldn't wait for his tongue to tease her in all the right places and for hers to do the same to him.

When her cell phone rang, Beverly thought it might be Dante. Instead her caller ID showed it was Eric. She debated whether to answer. Given his suspicious nature of late, she decided to.

"What are you up to?" he asked.

"Nothing, really."

"Thought I'd pick up some Chinese takeout for dinner tonight."

"Sounds good." It wasn't her favorite cuisine, but she didn't plan to eat much, anyway, as Dante was about to satisfy her appetite.

"Do you want red or white wine with it?" Eric asked.

Whatever. "You pick."

"White."

"Then we'll go with white." She pulled into the hotel parking lot. "I have to go."

"Trying to get rid of me?" He paused long enough to make her believe he was serious before Beverly heard a chuckle. "Just kidding. I've got some things to do myself before coming home."

"I'll be waiting for you," she said nicely, hoping it sounded convincing even as she had her mind on someone else.

***

The moment Beverly stepped inside the room, Dante didn't waste any time kissing her as she kissed him back aggressively, while they started ripping each other's clothes off. He needed the distraction after being disappointed that he would not get any justice from the Detroit Police Department, leaving the burden entirely on his shoulders. He would think about that later.

Right now, it was all about Beverly, a sexy lady that appealed to every desirous bone in his body. He lifted her up naked against the wall, wanting to make love right then and there. Sandwiching himself between her thighs, Dante stuck his hard penis covered by a lubricated condom inside Beverly. He waited as she wrapped her long legs around his waist before thrusting deep into her vagina. She was wet and clearly wanted him in the worst way. He was more than accommodating. He began kissing her again, his mouth open, as was hers. She sucked his top and lower lips, and he returned the favor, loving her taste that included mint.

Dante turned them around, putting himself against the wall. He held her tightly while bringing Beverly up and down on his erection. She moaned and clutched his shoulders as she absorbed his mighty thrusts. He got turned on even more as her long hair fell onto his face. He liked what she had done to it, giving her an even sexier look, if that was possible.

"I'm coming. I'm coming," gasped Beverly, breaking away from his mouth and running her tongue across the side of his head.

"I'm coming, now too," Dante said in a throaty voice, feeling the surge take hold of him.

Dripping with perspiration, he carried her to the bed while they were still locked, and both fell onto it, where Dante was able to propel himself even deeper inside her as Beverly splayed her legs as far apart as possible, grunting each time she absorbed his slamming thrusts into her. She cried out as her orgasm shook her body wildly. Driven by her response to his lovemaking, Dante yielded to his own powerful need to release his seed inside her.

They smothered each other in kisses, and Beverly brought her legs up and tight against his body as they rode the sexual heights together, holding nothing back in their craving for satisfaction. Dante moved rapidly in and out of Beverly's tight vagina during his climax, eliciting screams of pleasure and passion from her and the same from him.

Afterward, Dante breathed in the intoxicating scent of their sex, holding Beverly as she lay with her head on his chest.

"What is it about you that keeps me coming back for more?" she asked, looking up at him.

He grinned seductively. "It's not about me. It's about us," he told her. "We have this incredible sexual chemistry that simply won't fade away." He didn't even want to think about the void that would be left once he was back in Los Angeles and no longer around to have sex with her.

"I agree." Beverly kissed his lips, licking her own. "Hmm . . . so what do you propose we do about this sexual addiction?"

"I thought we just did it," Dante answered.

"Did we ever." She gave him a serious look. "But what about down the line? Are we really going to say our good-byes forever when you leave town?"

He considered the questions, not wanting to make any promises, even if her sexual hold on him was more powerful than that of anyone who had come along in his life up to this point.

Still, Dante didn't relish the thought of never being inside Beverly again once he had completed his mission in Detroit. Yet there was no way he could stay there, either, as the memories of Russell's death were far too painful. Not to mention his real life was elsewhere.

"Forever is a long damned time," Dante said, cuddling her. "Maybe you should think about visiting L.A. sometime."

"Really?" Her eyes widened.

"Why not, if you can get away? No reason why we can't enjoy this as much in my neck of the woods as yours."

Beverly beamed. "I'd like that. I'm not too sure the man I'm staying with would, but that's his problem."

Dante laughed, choosing to ignore that she wasn't giving herself only to him. "Yeah. Ours is keeping our hands and bodies off each other."

"Some problem to have, huh?" She slid her leg between his crotch seductively.

"Definitely a major issue that we'll have to deal with in our own way."

With that in mind, Dante planted a big kiss on Beverly's lips and she reciprocated in kind.

"Suck my toes," Beverly demanded, sticking her foot in Dante's face. They had just had another no-holds-barred sex session, and now she was feeling playful.

"Whatever suits your fancy," Dante said and put her daddy toe in his mouth, sucking it slowly and sensually. He gave the same treatment to her other toes. "How's that feel?"

"Hmm . . ." Beverly closed her eyes to the toe caresses with his lips and tongue. "Feels incredible. Don't stop."

Dante continued, moving to the other foot while massaging her heel at the same time with steady hands. "You're really enjoying this, aren't you?"

"Yes, but not quite as much as when I'm riding your penis deep inside me," she admitted boldly. "There's still time for another go at it." She was hoping that he didn't take forever to get off. She certainly wouldn't. Not as hot as he made her every time he was near.

"In that case, I'll come back to your feet another time." Dante got between her legs and Beverly watched his penis become erect instantly. "Your vagina deserves my attention right now."

She gasped when he drove himself into her. "Give me all the attention you have," she cooed.

Beverly shamelessly raked her newly manicured nails across Dante's back as he impaled her deeply and fluidly. She wanted him like no one before and threw herself into the joy of sex that sizzled between them. With her legs cradling his buttocks, she levitated with each potent thrust, bringing him deeper inside her and setting her soul on fire. She covered his mouth with hers, kissing him for all he was worth.

When another powerful climax affected every part of her body, Beverly shook violently. A few moments later, Dante had his orgasm, quivering wildly throughout. She held him tightly, relishing in his triumph and theirs together.

Though it pained her to do so, Beverly said her goodbyes to Dante with a stirring kiss. She wished they could stay in bed 24/7 and enjoy each other's body up and down. But they weren't there yet. Maybe never would be. Right now, her life was still in Detroit. With Eric. She couldn't recklessly throw that away by moving across the country. Especially when Dante had not invited her to do so, instead suggesting that she visit him in California.

Was that enough for the long run—limiting their sexual trysts to visits back and forth? She didn't want to look that far ahead. Only at the here and now. Along with the man who made her his slave in bed. Or was it the other way around?

Beverly was happy to see that Eric had not beaten her home, given that she had found herself having red-hot sex with Dante longer than planned. She went inside and put lip gloss back on her mouth to replace what he had taken off. Then she got her hair back together and changed clothes, hoping it would take away the scent of sex that still infiltrated her nostrils.

Afterward, she peeked out the window and saw Eric's car pull into the driveway. He got out and stretched his limbs before moving up the walkway. Sucking in a deep breath, Beverly readied herself for some Chinese food, wine, and keeping up appearances in pretending to be happy with someone who was not really doing it for her anymore.

EIGHT

Leon was sipping a cocktail and chilling out by his pool with two of his sexy playthings when he saw Spencer entering his backyard. Since he hadn't summoned Spencer and did not particularly like his downtime being interrupted unless there was a damned good reason, Leon assumed something was on his mind.

"I need to talk to you," Spencer said.

Leon frowned. "Take a dip," he ordered the bikini-clad women. "I'll join you shortly at the deep end."

"Don't take too long," the red-haired one with big breasts said, "otherwise we might have to start the party without you."

He chuckled, feeling horny looking at her ass. "Don't do that. We'll party together."

They dove into the pool and water splashed onto Spencer. He muttered an expletive.

"Maybe you need to get wet more often," Leon said with amusement.

"Yeah, soon as I learn to swim."

"My girls will teach you."

"Might take you up on that sometime," Spencer said.

Leon doubted that. He could always tell when someone was afraid of something. Usually it was him. In this case, Spencer, big as he was, didn't have the nerve to challenge him. But that was his business. So long as he did what was asked of him, Leon was cool with that.

He tasted his drink. "So what do you want to talk to me about?"

"You know that store on Seven Mile where that dude, Russell, did his thing?"

Leon recalled it well enough. He made a habit of remembering who died while on his watch. Especially when the bastard didn't have to, but chose death over common sense.

"What about it?" he asked.

"It's reopened."

"Did he come back from the dead?" joked Leon.

"No, someone new is running it now. A man in his forties. Far as I could tell, he was operating it alone."

"I see." That was very good news for Leon, as the store sat on a prime corner lot with lots of traffic coming and going. This meant another moneymaking opportunity if the owner wanted to remain in business safely. *Hopefully he won't be a dumb ass like his predecessor.* If so, then he might as well buy his burial plot, for he would need it. "We'll give him a little longer to settle in, then pay a visit."

"Okay."

"Maybe we'll become good friends." Leon laughed sardonically, prompting Spencer to do the same. "While you're here, I need you to go pick up a package for me."

"Sure. Where to?"

Leon gave him the address. The prepaid package contained crack cocaine, which would make him a nice profit. "I'll let them know you're coming."

He watched Spencer lumber away, then turned his attention back to his girls, feeling aroused. Leon finished off his drink, dropped the towel from his shoulder, and dove into the pool.

***

At 4:00 P.M. the following day, Eric found time to slip away to the motel for his usual rendezvous with Marilyn. He stood tall while she sucked on his penis, engorged with blood, and making him feel hot and bothered. Why couldn't Beverly do that? If she primped less and spent more time trying to please him any way he wished, then he might not need to get his from another woman.

Who was he kidding? There would *always* be someone on the side. If not the sex-starved Marilyn, it would be someone else. He would be the first to admit that most men had to have more than one woman to satisfy them. That was just the way it was, and he saw no reason to buck the system. The fact that he was fooling around with Spencer's woman made no difference to him. So long as the man didn't try to return the favor by bedding Beverly, they were cool.

When Eric felt himself getting close to climaxing, he pulled Marilyn up from her knees. He pushed her onto a chair and got quickly between her thighs, sticking his erection inside her vagina.

"Do me, baby," she urged. "Let me have all of you!"

He assumed she was referring to his penis. As such, Eric was happy to oblige. He leaned over her, using the chair's arms to brace himself, and slammed into her. She grabbed hold of his waist and moved her body hard up against his time and time again.

"I'm coming," she yelled. "Don't stop. Don't stop!"

As if he had any intention of stopping before getting what he came there for. Eric continued his quest in that regard, giving Marilyn a solid, wet kiss on the lips and nibbling at her breasts. She practically jumped off the chair when she came, coating his erection.

He returned the favor shortly thereafter, moaning as the moment hit him and he got his release while wedged deep inside her. When he was done, he pulled his pants up, zipping the fly.

"That was so good," Marilyn murmured. "I always feel so feminine and sexy when we're together."

Eric didn't see her as especially feminine and certainly not sexy. But she was a good lay and knew what it took to please him.

"That's because you are," he told her, lying through his teeth.

"More feminine and sexier than Beverly?" she asked, challenging him.

Eric resisted laughing out loud, managing to keep a straight face. "Yeah, I'd have to say that." *Not in this lifetime.* Didn't mean Beverly was as satisfying, though, in bed these days.

Marilyn giggled. "Just wanted to hear the words. I'll always be here for you, Eric. All you have to do is call me, and I'll come."

He liked hearing that. Especially given the fact she was more than willing to satisfy his needs. Made him wonder if she had anything left to please her husband. Or was he getting his elsewhere too?

Eric grinned with confidence, having her right where he wanted. "I know."

Marilyn was happy to know that Eric felt about her the same way she did about him. She hated that he was going back to Beverly, pretending to want her in bed while fantasizing about his lover. Worse was that Beverly didn't really give a damn about Eric, wanting him only for his money and material comforts, while pining for this mystery man who was giving her multiple orgasms. Though every fiber in Marilyn wanted nothing more than to see Beverly suffer the consequences for cheating on Eric, common sense dictated that betraying Beverly's trust could come with unintended consequences. Like losing Eric before Marilyn ever had him firmly in her grasp. She definitely intended to have the man all to herself, but she had to be smart about it.

The way things were going, she suspected it was only a matter of time before Beverly slipped up. Or outright confessed her infidelity and wanted to leave Eric. Then Marilyn planned to be there to comfort him in any way he wanted, regardless of what happened to Beverly as a result. Until such time, she was stuck with Spencer and what little satisfaction he brought to the table.

Marilyn got up from the chair Eric had placed her in while jamming his penis inside her, wishing it were still there and their mouths locked in perpetual harmony. She took delight in knowing that her scent was all over Eric, making sure she touched and kissed him everywhere she could. That way he would carry a bit of her wherever he went. Including when having sex with Beverly, knowing how unsatisfying it was for her *and* him.

"When do you want to get together again?" Marilyn looked up at Eric's eyes greedily.

He shrugged. "Whenever I can get away. Of course, you'll have to be able to do the same."

"Don't worry about that," she promised. "I can get away almost any time."

"Spencer gives you that much leeway, huh?"

"He's usually too busy doing stuff for Leon to pay much attention to my coming and going." She brushed her breasts against his chest. "If Spencer were more of his own man like you, maybe he would be more suspicious."

"He probably thinks you wouldn't want anyone but him," suggested Eric.

"We both know better than that." Marilyn again pressed her breasts into him, feeling his hard-on.

"Yeah, I guess so."

"Must be nice to have two women falling all over you."

"Only one woman really knows how to treat me right," he said, stroking her cheek.

"Wonder why?" Marilyn said with a catch in her voice. "Maybe Beverly's getting it somewhere else."

"She better not be." Eric's brow furrowed. "Do you know something you aren't telling me?"

"Of course not," she said convincingly. "If she were cheating on you, I'd know about it."

"Then why even suggest such a thing?" he demanded.

"Just to get a reaction is all." Marilyn swallowed under the weight of his glare. "I'm only saying she'd better start paying more attention to her man or she'll lose him to someone else." *Hope I didn't blow it.*

He grinned. "Maybe *you* should tell Beverly to get her act together."

"I will, so long as it won't cause me to lose you," she stressed.

"It won't," he promised. "We need each other."

I sure do need you. "You're right."

Eric gave her a steady gaze. "Do me a favor. Keep an eye out on Beverly when I'm not around."

"You mean spy on her?"

"Yeah, something like that," he said unapologetically. "If you see her doing anything that arouses your suspicions or otherwise is out of line, let me know."

"I can do that." *Be careful what you ask for. You just might find out the dirty truth about your precious Beverly and her lover.* Marilyn wasn't sure he could handle that. Or what the fallout might be. It was something she was bracing herself for, hoping it worked in her favor.

"Cool." Eric smiled sideways.

"I'm sure she's being true to you, even if she's not giving her all in bed."

"Yeah, she'd better be." He put his shirt on. "Got to get going. Beverly's expecting me, and I don't want to disappoint."

"Of course not." Marilyn bit back her ire, wishing he showed the same type of dedication to not disappointing her. Wanting to leave him with something to think about, she took the initiative and held Eric's cheeks while she gave him a hard kiss on the lips.

NINE

Dante walked in the store that had once been owned by his brother. It was more difficult than he had anticipated. Memories flooded his head from the first time he had come in there and Russell proudly showed off his business and what he hoped would be a mainstay in the community. Dante had enjoyed the short tour and could see just how dedicated his brother was to making it a success. He had even offered to give Russell money to help with any up-front expenses, but he had refused, preferring to make it or break it in the business on his own. Dante respected that and offered all the moral support he could, confident that Russell could succeed at anything he made up his mind to.

Moving around with a basket, Dante grabbed a package of razors, a bag of chocolate chip cookies, a couple bottles of beer, a box of condoms, and a newspaper. In his mind, he believed he was purchasing these items in memory of Russell and all the others who had died as a result of refusing to back down to intimidation by giving up money that belonged to them.

Dante walked up to the counter and put his items on it. He observed the owner, a casually dressed man in his early forties, who had just finished taking care of another customer.

"Did you find everything you need?" he asked in a friendly voice.

"Sure did. Thanks." Dante watched him ring up the items. "How long have you been open?"

"Two weeks and thirteen hours."

Dante grinned. "Keeping track down to the hour, are you?"

The man chuckled. "Guess when you first open a business, everything stays with you."

Dante knew that all too well, as Russell had expressed the same enthusiasm and attention to detail. He paid his bill in cash. "I knew the previous owner."

The man raised a brow. "That right?"

"Yeah." He didn't want to go any further than that and risk somehow blowing his cover and his purpose for being in town. "He was a good guy."

"Heard he was killed in, what, a robbery?"

"That's what they tell me," Dante said glumly.

"Doesn't sound like you buy it."

Dante met his eyes. Was that normal inquisitiveness for a store owner who had every right to be at least a little concerned? Or was it something more?

"I can only go by what I heard," he said to the man.

"I won't lie. That certainly concerns me. This area is not as safe as it once was. But I have a wife out of work and a mortgage. When this opportunity came up, I felt I had to go for it."

"I understand," Dante told him, feeling no animosity that he'd wound up with the store that belonged to Russell, and always would as far as he was concerned. He grabbed the bag. "I wish you the best of luck."

"Thanks."

"That said, I'd still watch my back if I were you. Last I heard, whoever killed Russell was never caught."

"If someone tries to rob me, I'll have an answer waiting for him beneath this counter," the man said confidently. "I want this store to succeed."

So did Russell, but it was all for naught. Dante forced a smile. "Maybe it will with that attitude. Take care."

"You too."

Dante headed out of the store and was shocked when he saw Leon Quincy approaching. He'd locked the bastard's ugly mug in his mind indelibly. Quincy was accompanied by a larger man. For an instant, Dante locked eyes with the person who'd ordered the hit on his brother. He wanted badly to take a swing at him and wipe that smug look off his face. If lucky, one blow was all it would take to put him out for good.

Quincy peered back at him, as if daring to make a move.

It was Dante who averted his gaze first, backing down from his dark thoughts. The last thing he wanted was to arouse the suspicions of the man he planned to take out when Leon least expected it and without a bodyguard there to save his ass. After he had walked past them, Dante turned back and looked at the men about to enter the store. Neither gave him any further attention, totally oblivious to who he was as the brother of Russell Sheldon. He wondered if they had already put the squeeze on the new store owner for so-called protection money. The man struck Dante as one who would not give in to pressure from thugs. But what did he know? Could be the owner was also smart enough to realize it wasn't worth dying to take a stand.

Am I saying that Russell did a stupid thing for getting himself killed? Dante shook off the implication, not wanting for a moment to blame his brother for his own murder, especially when the real people responsible were still walking the damned streets like they owned them while the police turned a blind eye.

Once in his car, Dante sucked in a deep breath to reduce his anger. He had to keep a cool head if he was going to take care of business successfully and not be held accountable afterward. If all were right with the world, he would have preferred to lose himself in Beverly's sexual heat and see where that took them beyond a few stolen afternoons in bed. But he had an agenda that couldn't be ignored or pushed to the sidelines. Not even for the chance of building something with a lady who seemed to want to move beyond her unsatisfying life. Maybe once the score with Leon Quincy and Eric Fox was settled, Dante and Beverly would have a chance to take things to the next level.

Dante backed out of the parking spot. Through the window, he could see Leon and his henchman talking, as if plotting strategy in dealing with the latest object of their pressure and criminality. He would give anything to be a fly on the wall and see what they were up to. But to go back inside would only draw their attention and put him in harm's way ahead of time.

He drove off, confident that Leon Quincy hadn't seen the last of him and would pay for what he'd done to Russell.

Leon entered the store with Spencer. It was changed slightly from the previous owner's setup. But the operation was still the same. It was a moneymaking machine, and Leon wanted—no, demanded—his piece of the action.

"Look around and see if you see anyone," he ordered Spencer.

"All right."

"I'll see you up front." Leon moseyed about, checking out the setup. He knew they had a security camera that captured everything. No problem. If the dude was stupid enough to go to the cops, the ones he had on his payroll would take care of it. In the meantime, he wouldn't be deterred in establishing his territory and fattening his wallet at the same time.

Spencer joined him near the counter. "No one else here."

"Good," Leon said with satisfaction. "Keep your eye on the front door, but stay close by."

He watched Spencer separate from him, and then Leon eyed the owner, who seemed liked a bookworm behind those glasses. He also had no sense of style, wearing clothing from the last century, which, as far as Leon was concerned, was another reason not to show him respect.

"Can I help you?" he asked.

Leon grinned crookedly. "Actually I'm here to help you."

"Excuse me?"

Leon lost the grin and delivered his prepared speech. "My name is Leon. We have a lot of crime in this area with burglaries, gangs, drug addicts, and other trouble-makers. Stores like yours are prime targets for those looking to get something for nothing. I can offer you protection from anyone who might decide to come after you or your business."

The man's brow creased. "Thanks, but no thanks. I got all the protection I need." He pulled out a gun and set it on the counter menacingly.

Leon bit his lower lip and suppressed a laugh. Looked like a forty-five caliber. They all start off playing tough guys. The smart ones eventually saw the light. The others wished they had seen it before it was too late.

Out of the corner of his eye, Leon saw Spencer come forward, as if ready to take away that gun and make the man eat it. Leon put up a hand, stopping him in his tracks. "I'll handle it."

Spencer glared at the man and took a couple of steps toward the front door.

Leon directed his attention back to the store owner. "I know you think having that gun will solve all your problems. Trust me, it won't. The last man to own this store had the same don't-mess-with-me attitude. He ended up dead."

The owner flinched. "You're saying you killed him?"

Leon was too wise to fall into that trap, even if he didn't believe for one moment he was dealing with an undercover cop looking to get the goods on him. Not that he would put it past them, all things considered. Better safe than sorry. "Me? I'm not a killer," he said with a straight face. "I heard the dude was shot to death during a robbery. But it would never have happened had he played ball with me. I could have protected him, and he would still be in business instead of six feet under."

"Why should I believe you can protect me?"

Good question. "What's your name?"

The man hesitated. "Paul Kline."

"Well, Paul Kline, as I said, my name's Leon. You might say this is my turf. Everyone knows that I take care of those who take care of me. Ask some of your business neighbors and they'll tell you no one's messing with them."

Paul touched his glasses. "Exactly how much protection money are we talking about here?"

Leon sized him up, trying to figure how much he could squeeze out of him. Every store owner had a breaking point, and he tried not to go over it, realizing as a businessman he had to operate within reason to keep profits coming in. Of course, this store was in a great location and would generate a decent amount of revenue.

"Twenty-five hundred a month," he said. For now. Later, once he had hooked the man, he would raise the amount to bring it more in line with other business owners operating on his turf.

"That's a lot," complained Paul. "I'm not a rich man."

"It's actually a discount because you're new around here," Leon pointed out. "I also know that you'll make good money in this location. Wouldn't want to see you lose more than you bring in by having bad guys constantly target your store for this and that. Even having a security system and gun won't deter most who don't have much to lose if they're shot or put in jail. You, on the other hand, stand to lose a lot by taking unnecessary chances. I'll keep the threats to your livelihood at bay, and you'll have some peace of mind."

Paul stared at him thoughtfully, his hand on the counter near the gun. "I'll need to think about it . . . talk it over with my wife."

"Not a problem." Leon rubbed his nose. He saw no reason to be too demanding, too soon, sensing the man would come around. "Just don't take too long. I wouldn't want anything to happen to your business before the protection kicks into gear."

"I'll let you know," Paul said tersely.

Leon nodded at Spencer to come over. "I think we're done here for today." He looked at Paul Kline, then his weapon. "You might want to put that away now. You don't want any of your customers to get the wrong idea. See you soon."

He walked away from the store owner, with Spencer following, and felt triumphant, as if he'd already snagged the dude man. More money in his pocket and a further grip on other business owners in the neighborhood who might be thinking about resisting his demands to remain in business.

In spite of brimming with confidence over his latest catch, Leon hadn't gotten where he was by taking too much for granted. He got out his cell phone and dialed Detective Stanley Dillard, his contact at the police department.

"Dillard," he answered sluggishly.

"It's Q," Leon said, using the nickname that he went by when doing business. "I got a little assignment for you."

"I'm listening."

"The store that Russell Sheldon owned has a new owner. Name's Paul Kline. I need you to check him out, make sure he's legit and not one of your undercovers."

"I doubt we have the manpower for that these days," Dillard said. "No reason to get paranoid."

"Just do it!" Leon demanded, not wanting to assume anything when it was his neck on the line. "Remember, you have as much to lose as I do if my operation goes up in smoke."

"Are you threatening me?" Dillard challenged. "'Cause if you are—"

"Not a threat." Leon softened his tone, glancing at Spencer. He couldn't afford to alienate Dillard or his other contact with the Detroit PD, Officer Roger Menendez. "I just want to make sure I have all the bases covered before doing business with this Paul Kline. You'll get your piece of the action, as usual."

"All right, all right. I'll check him out."

"Good." Leon disconnected with a sly grin on his face. What he wanted, he usually got. In this case, it was peace of mind and what he expected would be another store to get his cut of the profits from.

***

FBI Special Agent Ben Taylor calmly watched as Leon, which he knew was short for Leon Quincy, exited the store with one of his minions named Spencer Ramsey. Ben had gone undercover as part of an investigation into racketeering against Quincy that included shakedowns, prostitution, loan-sharking, police corruption, and possibly murder. Ben had used the name Paul Kline as his store owner front, hoping Leon Quincy would swallow the bait and come after him. And the asshole had done just that.

Ben bristled at the intimidation tactics Quincy used in forcing business owners to capitulate to his demands or else. They had long suspected that the crime boss had been behind some recent murders of local businessmen, including Russell Sheldon, the previous owner of the store, but lacked hard evidence or witnesses who would come forward. There was also strong reason to believe that Quincy had at least two police officers in his hip pocket.

Ben put the gun away. It wasn't his department-issued revolver, but rather a cheaper gun they had borrowed from the evidence locker that wouldn't likely tip Quincy's hand that he was dealing with an FBI agent, rather than a store owner he could walk all over. They had reopened the store, complete with stocking shelves and serving the community. All the while, the plan was to lure Leon Quincy and his cronies into thinking they had an easy mark to continue their reign of terror over local businesses. Now they just needed to build their case and then nail Quincy's ass to the ground before hauling him off for a long stint in federal prison.

Ben heard the bell, indicating someone had entered the store. He looked up and saw a leggy, shapely blonde walking toward him. Almost for effect, she grabbed a box of donuts off the shelf and set it on the counter.

"Will that be all?" he asked her with a serious face.

She smiled. "I may want more later, if you're nice about it."

He rang up the donuts. "I'm always nice, other than to bastards who shake down gullible people and expect to get away with it."

"Maybe we can put a stop to that—at least in this instance," she said.

"Yeah, I think you're right, Special Agent Fry." Ben grinned at his partner, Lynn Fry, whom he'd gotten to know well in more ways than one since they'd been paired two years ago. Together, they had taken down their fair share of lowlifes, and he saw no reason why they couldn't in this case. "Leon Quincy is going down!"

Lynn's green-blue eyes met his. "Let's hope so." She paid for her purchase like any customer would.

"I take it you saw and recorded my little chat with the man?"

She nodded. "Every word. He's a deceptively scary one."

"Yeah, especially to those who can't fend for themselves."

"I doubt that will be a problem for you—not with what you're packing below."

Ben grinned, wondering if her words were deliberately meant to have a dual meaning. He guessed yes by the look on her attractive face. It got his libido going. He ignored that for the moment, focusing on the investigation. "I think I can handle myself well enough as an FBI agent. But as Paul Kline, I have to tread water carefully until we reel our fish in all the way."

Lynn smiled. "Quincy will never know what hit him until it's too late."

"I agree," Ben said, resisting the urge to reach across the counter and touch her. "Until such time, I'll continue to do my part as a store owner who will gladly pay for protection and to see Leon Quincy further incriminate himself."

The door opened and a middle-aged couple walked in.

"Guess I'd better get back to work," Ben said.

"Me too." Lynn spoke lowly. "See you later."

"That's a promise." He raised his voice louder for the others to hear. "Enjoy your donuts and have a nice evening."

"You too."

TEN

On Friday afternoon, Beverly took full advantage of her new spa membership with a Pilates workout. She enjoyed the physical fitness program in working all parts of her body. It wasn't quite the turn-on of a sexual workout with Dante, but it helped keep her in shape for what were becoming all-consuming and energetic sexual get-togethers with him. Beverly found herself fantasizing more and more about Dante when they were apart, wondering what positions they should try next and how many orgasms she would have before exhaustion overtook her or him.

The thought that Dante wouldn't stick around the city forever bothered Beverly deeply. He hadn't talked about the story he was working on or how long it would take to complete it. Was it any of her business? Should she be satisfied with the time they had together and not seek more from him than he wanted to give?

Problem was, she didn't want to see their affair, if you could call it that, come to a halt. And along with it her suddenly reinvigorated sex life. The idea of having to return to satisfying herself to make up for Eric's inadequacies troubled Beverly. She deserved better. But she also deserved to be treated like a queen and provided with whatever it took to keep her happy. She wasn't sure Dante was up to the task outside the bedroom. Not to mention he hadn't exactly gone out of his way to say he wanted her over and beyond the times she came to him. Was he trying to tell her not to get too wrapped up in him? Or did he think she was too tied into her life to want to make any drastic changes?

After the Pilates class, Beverly stepped into the whirlpool tub. She closed her eyes and let the warm, pulsating water soothe her body while fantasizing that Dante was there making love to her.

"Well, look who's here." The voice caught Beverly's attention, snapping her out of her reverie.

She opened her eyes and saw Eric's thirty something ex, Gloria Fox, standing there in a skimpy bikini, leering at her. "Gloria . . ."

"Good to see you still remember me as the woman whose man you stole."

"I didn't steal Eric from you," Beverly defended herself. Yes, he was still married when they first got together, but Eric and Gloria were already living apart and officially separated. Even more odd to Beverly was that, at the time, Gloria suggested she was doing her a favor by getting Eric out of her life for good so she could move on. Now she seemed to be reversing her position. But Beverly was not going to be her punching bag by taking blame for a relationship that by all accounts had been pretty volatile and destined to fail. "Your marriage was, over."

Gloria got into the whirlpool opposite Beverly and brushed her auburn Senegalese twists to the side. "Say what you want, but we *both* know the truth."

"And what truth is that?" Beverly hesitated to ask.

"That you're nothing but a damned gold digger."

Beverly frowned. Admittedly, she was attracted to Eric because he was well off and treated her accordingly. It was never only about the money, though, but she doubted she could convince Gloria of that. Maybe she shouldn't even try.

"Eric pursued me, not the other way around," Beverly snapped. "I'm sorry if you're still pining after him. I can't help that."

Gloria's face contorted into a sneer. "All Eric saw in you was a young piece of ass that he could entertain himself with while pretending he was twenty years younger. Just as soon as someone else comes along, he'll kick you to the curb without giving it a second thought."

"That may be," allowed Beverly, "but he sure as hell won't go back to you. Get over it and move on with your life."

"You bitch!" Gloria spat. "I don't need your damned advice on how to live."

"And I don't need yours, thank you. If you have a beef with me being with Eric, I suggest you talk to him. I don't have to take this crap."

"Not if you leave him be and go hang out with someone your *own* age."

"Are you threatening me now?" Beverly asked tentatively, her mind wandering to the man she was hanging out with on the side, who was closer to her age and everything Eric wasn't.

Gloria's eyes narrowed. "If I were threatening you, you'd know it. I'm just giving you some friendly advice. I suggest you take it."

"Go to hell!" Beverly climbed out of the spa. "If you think you can win Eric back, be my guest."

She walked away on that note, sure that Gloria would follow her to the locker room and that they might actually come to blows. Thankfully, that didn't happen. Beverly sucked in a deep breath. She had to calm down, lower her blood pressure. She wasn't used to being verbally attacked by another woman. Especially a woman scorned—the most dangerous kind.

I'll have to have a talk with Eric and let him know just how unstable his ex-wife is. Will he rein her in? Or will I have to constantly look over my shoulder for fear that she might try to stab me in the back? Or worse?

Beverly left the spa, fearful that Gloria would be waiting outside to accost her. Fortunately, she wasn't. Didn't mean the crazy woman wouldn't still come after her if she didn't break up with Eric.

Maybe she should just quit while she was ahead and start over with Dante. But would Eric step aside graciously? Or be as threatening in losing her as Gloria was?

Furthermore, Beverly wasn't sure she could count on Dante to take her for who she was outside the bedroom. She couldn't walk away from what Eric offered on a wing and prayer.

Unless, of course, she was pushed out.

Dante walked into the bar called Earl's Drinks on the east side of the city wearing a Detroit Tigers cap. A friend of his in L.A. had suggested it was a place where anyone could get anything, no questions asked, for the right price. He took a leap of faith that was true, as he needed to secure a piece that didn't require him going through the typical registration process.

The bar was not particularly busy at five o'clock, which suited Dante just fine. The fewer people who saw him, the better. He stepped up to the bar. Behind it, a slender female bartender with pixie braids was putting bottles on the shelf behind her.

"What would you like?" she asked over her shoulder.

"Whiskey."

"Whiskey, it is." She grabbed a glass and poured.

Dante set down some bills. "I'm also looking for something else."

She raised a brow. "Yeah? What's that?"

Dante paused. "I need a gun for protection," he stressed. "I was told I could get one here."

She moved closer to the counter. "Why not get one from a gun store?"

"I wouldn't pass the background check," Dante lied, tasting the drink. "Don't ask me why."

"Okay, I won't. What type of gun you looking for?"

"A handgun with a silencer," he said straightforwardly.

She scratched her head. "How much you willing to spend?"

Dante wasn't particularly comfortable arbitrarily giving an amount. He didn't want to give a false impression that no amount was too much. Or possibly set himself up for a double cross.

"Let's just say I can pay anything that's not too unreasonable."

"By whose definition?" she asked, batting her eyes skeptically.

"Yours," he responded. "Assuming you're the person I'd be dealing with."

"I'm not." She put her hands on the counter. "His name is Lamb."

"Lamb?" Dante wanted to make sure he had it correct.

"Yeah, Lamb," she said. "And your name?"

"Dirk," he responded evenly.

She studied him. "You're not a cop or something, are you?"

"Not even close." He looked her in the eye. "Just a dude who needs an untraceable gun without a lot of questions."

She paused. "All right. Come back here tomorrow at eight and bring three hundred in cash. Lamb will be waiting for you."

Dante thought about protesting what was highway robbery for a gun that was likely stolen. Maybe more than once. But he wasn't in a position to argue about dollars and cents, since he needed the weapon to finish the job with a couple of clean hits that he came to Detroit to do.

"I'll be here," he said, finishing off the drink.

"Another round?"

"I'll pass." She'd taken enough of his money for one day.

On the way back to the hotel, Dante stopped at an ATM and withdrew three hundred dollars. He wondered if this was truly the right way to go in settling the score. Did he really need to take out two punks to avenge a cold-blooded hit? It took only a moment or two to convince him that it had to be done for Russell. He doubted his brother could ever rest in peace while the persons responsible for his death were still walking around free.

And, frankly, neither could he.

Dante turned his attention to Beverly. It was frustrating that he couldn't call, text, or e-mail her to get together. It all had to come from her end. She was playing it safe. Not that he could blame her. Maybe the man she was staying with had violent tendencies, though Dante couldn't recall seeing a mark on her. Or perhaps she was simply protecting her means for support, not wanting to lose it over a fling.

Was that all they were—a fling? Dante supposed that's what it was. They had blazing hot sex and nothing else. Even if he wished there could be more, she seemed comfortable enough getting together at her leisure and not his. Then there was the reality that his days in Detroit were numbered. He wasn't sure if either of them was prepared to keep their relationship alive beyond that.

It didn't stop him from wishing Beverly would call as Dante stood in his room and checked his cell phone for messages. Better yet, he'd like to see her walk in that door right now, get naked, and have some fun that would leave them both happily and lustfully exhausted.

"Your ex practically attacked me at the spa today," Beverly complained.

Eric was standing by his pool table, cue stick in hand, while she stood on the other side. "Gloria?" he asked, like it could be anyone else, since he had only been married one regrettable time. Having a good-looking live-in girlfriend who wasn't on his ass twenty-four—seven about one thing or another was much more preferable.

"Yes, Gloria," she reaffirmed, a hand on her hip. "She came in there accusing me of stealing you away from her."

He sighed. "You didn't steal me from her."

"I know that. Maybe *you* should tell her."

Eric lined up the shot. "Gloria's harmless," he said and hit the four ball. Didn't mean he wanted her showing up and getting in Beverly's face. Not after all this time.

"Are you trying to convince yourself of that or me?" Beverly asked, her tone telling him what she thought. "The woman's crazy. I could see it in her eyes."

He gave a mirthless chuckle. "Let's not get too carried away. She probably had too much to drink and went off."

"So you're defending her now?" Beverly pointed an accusing finger at him. "What's that about?"

"I'm not defending her," Eric said. He only wanted to enjoy a game of pool all by his lonesome, but apparently that wasn't going to happen. "Look, I'll talk to her, okay?"

"I wish you would, so she can get off my case."

"Fine." He lined up another shot and looked at her. "Anything else?"

Beverly moistened her lips. "She wants you back."

Eric cocked a brow in disbelief. "That what she told you?"

"Yes, in so many words."

Damn. He had hoped Gloria would have gotten him out of her system by now. He sure as hell had gotten her out of his.

"Well, I don't want her," Eric made clear. "Been there, done that. I'm happy where I am right now—with you."

Beverly rolled her eyes. "You sure about that?"

He put the stick down on the pool table and walked around it to Beverly, putting his arms around her. "Yeah, I'm sure." To prove it, he tilted his head and kissed her on the mouth, tasting the wine she'd been drinking. The show of affection didn't give him an erection, as had once been the case whenever Eric was even close to Beverly. That notwithstanding, she was still drop-dead gorgeous, and he liked having her in his life. Right now, he had no plans to change that. Certainly not for the likes of his ex-wife and all her over-the-top drama.

Or, for that matter, his sexual diversion in Marilyn.

***

"Play with my nipples," Beverly directed Dante as she straddled his firm body with her legs, feeling his erection deep inside her. She had boldly used the time while Eric was out trying to get his ex to back off to have her own little outside activity. And she could think of no other person she wanted to be with.

Dante's sure fingers caressed her nipples, making them rock hard and sending delightful sensations throughout Beverly's body. "That feel good?"

"Feels wonderful," she gushed. "Just like having you in me."

"It feels good to me too." He began massaging her breasts. "And you feel good."

His words and actions caused things to heat up. Beverly began to move more swiftly up and down the length of his penis, making sure it hit the mark each time she impaled herself fully. She fell onto Dante and began sucking his lips. She stuck her tongue in his mouth and tasted herself from when he'd gone down on her a little earlier.

Dante cupped Beverly's buttocks and easily turned them around. She gasped when, on his knees, he lifted her and brought her down hard on his erection. It turned her on, as if she weren't already wildly excited about making love to him. She followed his lead and pushed herself onto him time and time again while they kissed passionately. Beverly fought to catch her breath as the orgasm overtook her, causing her body to vibrate almost out of control.

Even as she luxuriated in the incredible feeling of satisfaction, her body braced itself as Dante's own powerful climax caused him to shudder violently. Beverly clung to him tightly, their mouths still locked in succulent harmony, bodies slick from the onslaught of desires fulfilled, and embraced the frenetic culmination of their sex. Their sighs and moans were like music in Beverly's ears, and she wished they could sustain what had just occurred. She took solace in the notion that neither seemed to want to back away from the mind-blowing, earth-shattering sex that brought them together in ways Beverly could hardly have conceived.

"So what does he think you're doing when you come to me?" Dante asked as Beverly lay on him.

"Shopping or visiting a friend," she said. "Sometimes he thinks I'm seeing a movie."

"He never gets suspicious?"

She ran her fingers across his chest. "Yes, he does," she admitted. "But I cover my tracks well."

He chuckled. "So you're not only sexy as hell, but a pretty clever lady too."

"True. Guess I'm willing to do what it takes to go after what I want. In this case, it's you."

Dante ran his fingers through her hair. "What do you think he'd do if he ever found out you were sleeping with another man?"

"I honestly don't know." *I don't think I want to know.* Beverly thought about it. She strongly suspected that Eric would not take it like a man, but instead, as though he owned her. She wasn't eager to go down that road, even though she might have to sooner or later.

"Would you ever want to leave him?" Dante asked.

"I've thought about it," Beverly confessed. "It would depend on whether I had a better offer." *Such as staying with you.*

"What about simply leaving because it's no longer happening for you?"

"I never said it wasn't happening. At least not in every capacity. He's treated me right in some ways that are important to me."

Dante looked at her face. "You mean he's provided for you?"

Beverly thought about the gold digger tag Gloria had placed on her. Would Dante assume this as well? "Yes, he takes care of me financially. But it's more than that. Since he's older, I respect his wisdom and like the way he makes me feel more mature."

I can't believe I am singing the praises for Eric to the man I'm having sex with. Maybe it was a way to protect herself from hurt by falling too strongly for Dante, who didn't figure to be around much longer. Or might his plans have changed?

"How do I make you feel?" Dante asked.

Beverly kissed his chest. "Very sexy and desired."

"Maybe that's because you *are* very sexy *and* highly desirable."

She smiled. "I'm glad you feel that way."

"Did you think for one instant that I didn't?"

"Not really. Guess that's why I'm here with you and wish I didn't have to leave."

"So do I." Dante stroked her thigh. "You might have to ask yourself at some point if staying with this man is worth what you're not getting from him."

"Maybe you're right," she said, feeling the heat from his hand sliding up her leg. "I will have to weigh that in my mind." *You're not making it any easier, wanting you the way I do.* "Tell me about your assignment."

His hand stopped suddenly. "Assignment?"

"Yes, the story you're working on."

He paused. "I'm doing an exposé on sex trafficking in the city."

Her eyes widened. "Prostitution?"

"Yes, only involving mostly females who are forced or tricked into selling their bodies on the streets as a form of sexual slavery," Dante explained knowledgeably. "The victims are usually brought to the United States from Eastern Europe and Asia. But they also come from such places as Haiti, or even within this country."

"Wow," Beverly said thoughtfully. "Didn't realize that went on here."

"Most people don't."

"Who do you write for?"

"Several organizations," he said. "AP, *LA Times, Newsweek* . . ."

She was impressed and curious as well. "How long will it take you to complete your assignment?"

Dante lowered his face, brushing his lips across hers. "That all depends."

"Hmm." She licked his lips. "On what?"

"On how long I find myself distracted from my mission."

Beverly was aroused. "What if that lasted for quite a while?" she asked teasingly.

He dribbled a finger across her clitoris, causing Beverly to shudder, and then slid it inside her wet vagina, brought it out, and sucked it. "Then I guess I'll just have to deal with it. Or should I say, we will?"

She grabbed hold of his hard penis and began to caress him. "I think we're already doing just that."

For some reason, Dante hadn't expected Beverly to ask him about his writing assignment. She'd seemed to be interested only in the blazing sexual chemistry between them, which had also dominated his thoughts. Having to think quickly on his feet, the sex trafficking tale was perfect, considering he'd just done such a story about young women being brought to the Pacific Northwest from Russia and turned into sex slaves. It wasn't too far off the mark to believe the same thing was happening in Detroit, with a large population of people living there from Eastern Europe, where sex trafficking and forced prostitution were rampant.

That sure beat telling Beverly that he was in town to avenge the murder of his younger brother. Or that he wouldn't rest until the men responsible had breathed their last breath. Dante doubted she would understand. How could she, unless she had walked in his shoes?

In truth, he knew almost nothing about her life, other than that she was living with an older man who provided her with the financial means to lead a good life. That included seducing Dante, while her sugar daddy was none the wiser. But that hardly stacked up to Dante's situation, where he was still dealing with the loss of a brother and his plans to kill two people as a consequence.

Would Beverly still want to cheat on her man with him if she knew what was really going on in Dante's head? Or would she be glad to have a ho-hum man to go home to and protect her from the dirty, dangerous world they lived in?

They had sex again and Dante worked up a good sweat as Beverly seemed to be able to go on forever. He'd never been with such a woman before whose body seemed made for his touch and taste. It was clear to Dante that she was just as much into him. He could well imagine that if Beverly were living in Los Angeles, they might have a future together. But she was living with a man in Detroit, and it seemed like she wanted to stay put as a security blanket.

"It would depend on whether I had a better offer," she'd said.

What type of offer was she looking for? Dante pondered the question after seeing Beverly out the door and receiving a stirring kiss to remind him of what he was missing whenever she wasn't there. And, just as important, what he had to look forward to the next time they got together.

Does she want a full-time lover? Or something much more?

Was he capable of giving a commitment to a woman? Or would he always stick to playing it safe without having to deal with love and romance?

Dante left those questions for another time as he went down to the bar and thought about his meeting tomorrow night with the man named Lamb.

Eric stood at the door of the ranch home he once lived in before he lost it as part of the divorce settlement with his ex-wife. He didn't relish the idea of returning. She'd given him nothing but grief in the last years of their marriage. Apart from trying to make him someone he wasn't, she got into his business too much—a dangerous thing that she should have wanted no part of had she known what was best for her. He'd finally had enough when she'd demanded he give her a child or she would find someone who would.

Under other circumstances, Eric might have killed her for threatening to sleep with another man. But in this instance, as he wanted no children, especially with her, he welcomed the chance to bolt and let her do her thing with whomever she wished, as long as it wasn't him. Since he'd been unfaithful throughout their marriage, Eric also liked the freedom the breakup gave him. It afforded him the opportunity to meet Beverly and put Gloria out of his mind once and for all.

Only now she had resurfaced and was trying to come between him and Beverly. He wasn't about to let that happen. He glanced at her Ford Focus in the driveway and rang the doorbell.

The door opened. Gloria stood there, wearing a robe and slippers. "Guess your girlfriend told you we ran into each other, huh?"

"She told me," Eric said stiffly. "Can I come in?"

She seemed to think about it for a moment before stepping aside. He walked through the entryway, picking up the scent of fried chicken. From what he could see in the living room, the place was still in immaculate condition, as she'd always liked it. Personally, he would have preferred it less pristine so it seemed more like a home.

"Do you want some chicken?" Gloria asked. "I made turnip greens and corn bread too. Your favorites."

"I'll pass." Though it was tempting, Eric didn't want to get caught up in what was obviously her attempt to seduce him with food and the generous amount of skin showing beneath the robe, as if to remind him what he was missing.

Gloria ran a finger down her chest and stopped at her cleavage. "Bet she can't make you the type of meals a man needs."

Eric couldn't argue the point, since cooking certainly wasn't a strong suit for Beverly. Fortunately, she worked for him in ways that Gloria never could. "What do you think you're doing?"

"Trying to show you what you're missing and can still have," she responded bluntly. She stepped close to him, and he smelled her perfume, along with the alcohol on her breath.

"I don't want you anymore," he said coldly. "I thought I made that clear."

She draped her arms around his neck. "Men say a lot of things they don't mean. So do women. We both said some things we shouldn't have. You've had enough fun with that oversexed bimbo. Come back to me and let a *real* woman take care of you."

She laid into his lips with a mushy kiss before Eric broke away, wiping his mouth. "Enough, Gloria! There's no going back for us. Not for me, anyway."

"Why not?" she asked. "I understand you better than she ever could."

"Maybe that's part of the problem," he allowed. "You know me too damn well, some of my deep, dark secrets. It's best that we don't go there anymore."

Gloria opened her robe, revealing her large breasts and nude body. "This is all still here for you. Tell me I'm not turning you on."

Eric had to admit that he was aroused. But he wasn't willing to give her an inch that she would use to try to drive a further wedge between him and Beverly. Besides, he already had Marilyn on the side and prostitutes when Beverly and Marilyn weren't what he needed at a given time.

He closed her robe and tied the belt. "Give it up. I don't want you anymore."

"Bastard." Her face contorted into a scowl. "You really think she's going to stick around once someone better, younger, and more attentive shows up? Come back to someone who appreciates you, warts and all."

"You should have thought of that earlier, before things got out of hand," Eric told her unsympathetically. "As far as Beverly, she's none of your damned business."

"You made her my business when you went after her instead of making an effort to try to save our marriage."

He'd had about enough of this. Grabbing her shoulders, Eric got in Gloria's face. "Now, you listen to me. I want you to leave Beverly alone."

"Or *what?*" Her voice shook. "You're going to kill me?"

His face darkened. "I think you know the answer to that. We made a clean break, and I want it to stay that way. I strongly suggest you forget all about me and Beverly—and keep your mouth shut about things that don't concern you. Otherwise, I might forget what we once had before you threw it all away!"

Eric saw the fear in her eyes, even as she tried to be the stubborn bitch she'd always been. He was sure his words had sunk in and she wouldn't cause further trouble for him.

ELEVEN

The following day, Beverly had lunch with Marilyn at a restaurant in nearby Southfield. After listening to Marilyn drone on about the happenings of her favorite soap opera and a fight she'd had with Spencer, it was Beverly's turn to talk about her run-in with Gloria and hot sex with Dante.

"And I thought there was drama in my life," Marilyn said, putting down a rib and licking the barbecue sauce from her fingers. "I can't believe Gloria. The nerve of that woman."

"My sentiments exactly." Beverly forked a couple of ranch fries. "If you'd seen the way she looked at me . . . very creepy."

Marilyn's mouth hung open. "She really thinks Eric would dump you for *her?*"

"Apparently."

"As if." Marilyn rolled her eyes. "Look at her and look at *you.*"

Beverly smiled, flattered. She knew it wasn't just about looks. Gloria had her hooks into Eric longer than she had and might be able to sway him if she tried hard enough. Maybe that wouldn't be such a bad thing. If it was Eric who decided to end their relationship, she would accept it and move on, rather than leaving him and possibly being left with no one should Dante not be up to the challenge of being more than a great lover.

"You never know," Beverly told her friend. "Gloria seemed pretty confident that she brought more to the table than I ever could."

"And what did Eric have to say about this?" Marilyn regarded her with interest.

"He tried to dismiss it as nothing to worry about," Beverly said. "He said she was harmless. But then he went to talk to her."

"And . . . ?" Marilyn pressed.

Beverly grabbed a biscuit. "Eric said he took care of it."

"What does that mean?"

"According to him, she was hoping they could get back together. He told her that wasn't going to happen and to stay away from me."

Marilyn picked up a rib. "Think she'll listen to him?"

"Eric seems to think so," she responded. "That's good enough for me until proven otherwise."

"Me too. I wouldn't want Gloria messing things up between you and Eric," Marilyn said. "Or should I say, you and lover boy?"

If Beverly hadn't known better, she'd think her friend had a sore spot because she was getting some outside her relationship while Marilyn wasn't. *I can't help it if I found a man who fulfils my every sexual need and seems tireless in the process. Unlike Eric.*

"Dante has nothing to do with any of this," Beverly made clear.

"Oh, so his name is Dante," Marilyn uttered. "I like it."

"Seems to fit him," Beverly admitted.

"So did he cheer you up last night?"

Beverly smiled thoughtfully. "You could say that. The man is insatiable."

"So are you."

"I suppose so," Beverly said unabashedly.

Marilyn gazed across the table at Beverly. "And where does Eric fit into this equation? Or does he?"

Beverly wasn't quite sure how to answer that or what she expected her to say. It was complicated for sure, as Beverly found herself meandering between the safety with Eric and the sexual freedom and energy she had with Dante. Why couldn't she have it all in one man?

"Eric is still my man," she told her.

"Doesn't sound like it," Marilyn said. "Sounds like Dante pretty much has your undivided attention these days."

"He doesn't," Beverly said, picking up her glass of water and sipping. "Yes, we're having sex, but I know he won't be around forever and Eric will be." *Or am I giving him too much credit that he'll be there no matter what?*

"So you want him, but you don't want him?" Marilyn frowned. "Maybe you should give up Eric and take your chances with Dante. You're obviously hooked on the man."

"Don't think the thought hasn't crossed my mind." In fact, Beverly was thinking about it more and more with each sexual adventure she had with Dante and the pain she felt when apart from him. But she was also a realist and wasn't about to put the cart before the horse. "I'm not going to make any hasty decisions I may live to regret. I like things as they are right now. I'll have to see how it plays out. Once Dante goes back to California, it may end things between us. Or it could be an avenue I can explore for the future."

"I'm not trying to give you a hard time," Marilyn stressed, wiping her mouth with a napkin. "I just don't want to see you get hurt trying to play two men at once."

"Like they don't do the same to us every chance they get," Beverly said, though feeling a little guilty. "I'm not trying to justify anything. This just happened with Dante when my sex life with Eric was lousy."

Marilyn narrowed her eyes. "You're saying you think Eric's unfaithful?"

Was he? She had no way of knowing for sure. "No," Beverly responded, giving Eric the benefit of the doubt that if he was having trouble getting it up with her, he probably wasn't trying to get it up with another woman. Least of all Gloria. Beverly recalled that she had once accused Eric of cheating on her with a girlfriend, Tenesia White. Both had denied it, and she couldn't prove otherwise. Beverly was still suspicious, but let it go once Tenesia left town. "I'm only saying that women should be allowed to get what makes them happy from more than one place, the same as men."

"You're right," Marilyn said and smiled. "Why not enjoy what's on the table, so to speak, if it presents itself?"

"You think?"

"Yeah. It's not like you and Eric are married or anything. Same is true with Dante. Sounds like he accepts the limitations of your arrangement for what they are. Maybe in his own way, the same is true for Eric."

"I'm glad you feel that way," Beverly expressed.

"Of course I do. As your best friend, I want you to be able to indulge your fantasies with Dante, Eric, or anyone else."

"I want you to do the same," Beverly said. "Is Spencer getting the job done to your satisfaction these days?" They seemed happily married, even if the occasional argument put them at odds. Or was it all just a front with trouble lurking in the shadows?

"Yeah, we're pretty cool," Marilyn told her levelly. "He takes care of my needs as well as can be expected."

Beverly chuckled. "Unless, of course, you expect more than you get."

"Good point." Marilyn laughed. "I take care of my own needs, first and foremost. That way, anything I get from Spencer is like icing on the cake."

"Sounds like you've got a sweet tooth," joked Beverly, seeing nothing wrong with self-satisfaction if your man was lacking in that department.

"Ditto," she countered. "Guess that's what makes us who we are and who we choose to be with to feed our sugar addiction."

Beverly smiled, agreeing wholeheartedly as she thought about Dante's penchant for giving her the fix she needed every time.

That bitch, Marilyn mused after leaving the restaurant in her car and heading to the motel where she had prearranged and timed it perfectly to meet with Eric. How dare she whine about Gloria trying to win back Eric when Beverly was two-timing him herself! Not that she was complaining too much, as Beverly's infidelity was playing right into her hands. Soon she would wrest Eric from her, and Beverly could shack up with her lover, assuming he cared enough for her aside from sex.

But Gloria was another story altogether. Marilyn was happy to hear that Eric had put her in her place. It was enough having to play second fiddle to Beverly for the time being. The last thing she needed was to also have to compete with his ex, who must have gotten desperate after the man she was bedding dumped her. Marilyn knew all about it, as Hal Ketchum was her cousin and practically bragged about it.

You can't have Eric. He's mine. Or at least he would be after finding out that Beverly wasn't worth spending a fortune on. Not when he could have someone low maintenance by comparison who would be true to him once Beverly was out of the picture.

Marilyn grinned at the thought of finally being with someone who could appreciate her, rather than take her for granted, which was all that Spencer seemed to do. They had sparred verbally when he complained about the house not being clean enough for his liking, while having the audacity to deny her the new big-screen television she wanted, as though it cost too much. Had she been married to Eric, he would've bought it without giving it a second thought. In fact, he'd done that very thing last month, when Beverly sweet-talked him into it. She couldn't stand how Beverly had him wrapped around her little finger, all the while playing him for a fool.

Better enjoy it while you can, girlfriend. You're playing a dangerous game you're bound to lose. Messing around with two men is stupid—unless you know what you're doing.

Marilyn was confident she was in control as a mistress and a wife, even if, at times, it could be challenging, to say the least, juggling the two. One day in the foreseeable future she wouldn't have to do that anymore—discarding Spencer for a real man in Eric.

At the motel, Marilyn wasted no time getting down to business. She performed oral sex on Eric, got him hard, and then spread her legs wide on the bed and watched as he went to work, thrusting his penis into her over and over, kissing her breasts, and breathing unevenly into her ear until he got off.

Her orgasm came and left the moment he entered her. But she pretended to be ecstatic with desire for him while waiting for him to climax. Unlike Beverly, she had no issue with Eric not being the sexual beast he probably was when with Gloria. Marilyn was perfectly content to take what he had to give, which was more than what Beverly got, in exchange for becoming his number-one lady and all the perks that went with it.

Eric squeezed his eyes shut and imagined it was Beverly he was penetrating instead of Marilyn. If only he could get it up consistently when he was with his woman. But what difference did it make? As long as he was getting off inside someone while he still had the beautiful Beverly to come home to, he was good.

He planted his hands on the bed and pushed himself back and forth against Marilyn's body, thrusting deep inside her as she moaned loudly, turning him on even more. He kissed her, and she wrapped her arms firmly around his head, sucking his lips like candy. When Eric felt his surge coming, he unlocked their mouths so he could breathe while picking up the pace in his powerful thrusts and active imagination.

With one long grunt, he released his seed well within her, his buttocks clutched in orgasmic agony until the deed was done. Afterward, Eric rolled off Marilyn, lying on his back to regain his equilibrium.

"That was nice," she cooed, looking at him. "*Very* nice."

"Yeah, it was great." He told her what she wanted to hear, and meant it insofar as being able to get a hard-on and delivering the goods when all was said and done. He wasn't sure how much longer this would last between them. Maybe things with Beverly would get back to the way they used to be when they went at it practically night and day. Or someone else might emerge as his sex kitten to keep the juices flowing when things were stale at home.

"Beverly told me about her little episode with Gloria," Marilyn said casually.

Eric wasn't surprised. After all, Beverly told her everything, it seemed. If only she had a clue that her best friend was stabbing her in the back. Then maybe Beverly would learn to keep their issues at home, where they should be. He had a mind to burst her bubble and watch Beverly come crawling back to him in humiliation. But that wouldn't benefit him nearly as much as the present arrangement. He was quite content bedding Beverly's friend and Spencer's wife. It gave Eric the best of all worlds while answering only to himself and his needs. Aside from that, he needed Marilyn to keep an eye on Beverly to make sure she wasn't two-timing him or otherwise up to no good.

"Gloria was drunk and said some stupid things she didn't really mean," he said dismissively.

"You sure about that?"

She meant every word that came out of her mouth, but he'd dealt with it. "Yeah. She won't be bothering Beverly anymore."

"I'm glad," Marilyn said. "I know you have a history with Gloria, but you have me now to be yourself with."

Eric suppressed a laugh. "Yeah, I do." He also had Beverly, whom he had no intention of tossing aside for Marilyn, Gloria, or anyone else.

"We make a good team."

"Yeah." At least where it concerned having sex the way he liked it.

"Do you want to do it again?" Marilyn asked. "Spencer thinks I'm still with Beverly."

Eric considered the offer, seeing it as a great way to reenergize his libido for when he and Beverly could turn up the heat again. But he had other things to do than spend all day in bed with someone who had nothing else to do other than pick her nose and daydream. He wondered how much action Spencer was getting from his wife. Or was he too busy hanging out with Leon Quincy's hoes to worry about her?

"Can't," Eric said, feigning a tone of regret. "Got some business to take care of."

"For Leon?" she asked curiously.

He eyed her, well aware that, unlike Beverly, she knew the type of business he was in, like her husband. Marilyn seemed to get a thrill out of being with men involved in criminal activity, as though it were a damned movie. Eric had no problem with it, as he was sure she wouldn't say or do anything stupid, similar to Gloria, at the end of the day. Beverly could be a different story. He wanted her to see him as a legitimate businessman who could do no wrong to speak of. If she should get wind of what he did on the side, he would deal with it then.

"Yeah, he wants me to ruffle a few feathers." Eric downplayed it. "No big deal." In fact, it could be a really big deal if the man he was going to see didn't play ball.

Marilyn lifted onto an elbow. "Do you want to get together next Tuesday?"

"Maybe." He looked at her large breasts. "I'll let you know."

She kissed him while grabbing his penis. "That's good enough for me."

Eric was aroused from her touch but ignored it, slipping away from her and off the bed. He turned his thoughts to Beverly and that trip to the Bahamas they talked about.

TWELVE

At 7:00 P.M., Ben Taylor unlocked the door to the house he rented on Appleton Street. It was part of the elaborate cover he had undertaken as an FBI agent posing as shopkeeper Paul Kline. Not wanting to take any chances that Leon Quincy might check him out and discover that they were laying a trap for his ass, they went the extra mile to make Paul Kline very believable. Including having a wife, though Ben had never been married.

He stepped inside the foyer. The scent of perfume hit his nostrils. In the living room he saw his partner and fake wife, Lynn Fry, sitting sexily on the couch.

She smiled at him. "Thought my hubby would never make it home."

Ben grinned, sitting beside her. "Had to wait until my replacement filled in at the store," he said of Special Agent Geoffrey Turner. "I'm expecting Quincy and his crony to show up anytime to collect on his protection money."

"Pretty soon there won't be anyone to protect him from doing hard time," she said.

"Let's hope it works out that way. The man's definitely slick and hard to pin down and make it stick."

Lynn brushed against him. "We'll make it stick this time," she said confidently. "We've got a tail on Officer Roger Menendez and Detective Stanley Dillard of the Detroit PD." Both men were strongly suspected of being on Quincy's payroll, though careful to keep from incriminating themselves. "As soon as they slip up, we'll nail their asses to the ground."

"Yeah, I think it's only a matter of time before Quincy's entire operation goes up in smoke," Ben told her in agreement.

"Then our charade as man and wife will be over." She made a pretty face.

Ben found it sexy, as he suspected she wanted. "That may be. But the rest has only just begun."

"Oh, and what might that be?" she teased. "If you're talking about the sandwiches I brought home for dinner, they're in the kitchen, ready to heat up in the microwave."

He ran a hand along the side of her face as a wave of desire coursed through him. "I'm talking about me and you."

"You and me, huh?" Her aquamarine eyes flashed. "Do you know something that I don't?"

Ben grinned. "Why don't we find out?" He gave her a quick kiss on the lips. "Actually, there's a familiar ring to that. Very familiar and a big turn-on."

Lynn kissed him and licked her lips. "You've got a good point there. Maybe we should take this to the bedroom?"

"What about those sandwiches?" he asked, half joking.

"What about them? Are you really hungry?"

He regarded her lustfully. "Yeah, only not for food."

"Then let's do something about that other type of hunger," Lynn said with urgency in her voice as she stood, taking his hand.

Ben followed her into the bedroom, where he took her in his arms and laid a passionate kiss on her, receiving back as much as he gave. They stopped long enough to strip off their clothing and hop into bed. Ben played with Lynn's creamy white, small breasts and tautened pink nipples while she moved atop him up and down on his erection. She was a tight fit and getting tighter as her arousal increased.

Lynn brought her face down and went after his lips. He took her tongue in his mouth, tickling his gum. Ben grabbed her thighs and brought his body up heartily to meet hers with each time she came down on him. He lost his breath as his orgasm erupted, sending shock waves throughout him.

Simultaneously Lynn came, quavering atop Ben. She cried out, and he held her waist, assisting in impaling her deeply in making sure it was as powerful a feeling as his. At the end of her journey, she finished things off by kissing him voraciously.

When it was over, Ben turned his thoughts back to the matter at hand. Namely, getting the goods on Leon Quincy to put him away for the rest of his life.

Leon Quincy inhaled the sexual scent of a ho named Angie while kissing her clitoris above his face, even as another ho named Shania sat on his penis, making love to it. He loved these threesomes and sometimes even had four women at once. He believed variety was the spice of life and fully embraced the notion. He grunted as he got off inside Shania's vagina and brought a climax to Angie as she sat on his face at the same time.

Already high as a kite from smoking marijuana, Leon felt twice as nice from the orgasm. When his cell phone rang, he considered letting voice mail pick up. But since he was expecting some important calls and didn't like to be kept waiting where it concerned business, he extricated himself from the hoes.

"Why don't you go at it with each other for a while?" he told them salaciously. "I won't be long before joining you."

Climbing off the bed, he grabbed the phone off a table. The caller ID showed it was Detective Stanley Dillard.

"Hey, what's up?" Leon asked the detective casually.

"I checked out Paul Kline," he said. "The man appears to be what he says. He has the proper permits for the store in order. He and his wife, Lynn, are staying at a place on Appleton Street."

Leon sighed. "Good. I'm happy to hear it. I'll be paying Kline another visit shortly."

"When do I get my piece of the action?"

"Same time and place as usual."

"Fine." Dillard paused. "Everything else in order?"

"Yeah, no problems to speak of." Then a thought occurred to Leon. "One of my girls, Kelly, was busted last night for soliciting an undercover cop. What can you do about it?" He was used to bailing them out and sending them back out on the streets, but didn't mind getting another hook into the detective as insurance that he wouldn't lose his nerve down the line. Or rat him out.

"What's in it for me?" Dillard asked.

Leon glanced at the hoes in bed, wrapped up in sixty-nine and turning him on. "My gratitude," he expressed. "You can also have your way with her as a freebie. Just make sure she's still able to work after you're done." He was aware the detective was married with three kids, but it never stopped him before from taking advantage of their arrangement.

"I'll see what I can do," Dillard said.

Leon took that as an indication that he could count on his help to get her released, further linking them for future business. He hung up, smiling with satisfaction, and ready to get back to some sexual fun and frolic.

***

At eight o'clock, Dante walked into the bar. He hoped he hadn't made a big mistake in trusting this Lamb dude to get him what he needed. But he wasn't exactly in a position to buy a gun legally and then turn around and shoot someone with it. Or, in this case, two people. He'd have to take his chances and let the chips fall where they may.

It was a little busier than the previous night. Dante stepped up to the bar and got the attention of the female bartender.

"You bring the money?" she asked.

"Yeah," he told her.

She looked over his shoulder. "Go through that door. Lamb's waiting for you behind the bar."

Dante gave her a direct look. "Can I trust you . . . him?" He didn't want to walk into a trap where he ended up with nothing, including losing the money.

She held his gaze. "You've got nothin' to worry about, so long as you're playin' straight with me."

"I am," he assured her.

She smiled. "Okay, then everything's cool."

Dante walked toward an exit door and stepped out into the alley. He saw a Dumpster and what looked to be a dark-skinned homeless man with disheveled clothing and a scraggly beard. For an instant, Dante thought about heading back inside.

Then he heard the man say in a deep tone, "You lookin' for me?"

Dante took a step toward him. "You Lamb?"

"Yeah, that's me." He peered at Dante. "You Dirk?"

Dante nodded uneasily.

Lamb shuffled toward him. His baggy clothing was torn and filthy. "You got somethin' for me?"

Dante raised a brow. "I think it's supposed to be the other way around."

Lamb's eyes became slits. "The money first."

Since he was at a disadvantage but didn't want to leave empty-handed, Dante took the money out of his pocket—three one-hundred-dollar bills—and handed it to him. He watched the man as he spread the bills like cards and then stuffed them in his pocket.

"Now I'd like what I paid you for," Dante said tersely.

Lamb ran a hand across his mouth. "Chill. I got what you want." He removed a brown bag from inside his jacket. "Here."

Dante took the bag, opened it, and pulled out the weapon with a handkerchief. He recognized it as a semiautomatic pistol equipped with a silencer. He checked out the detachable magazine and saw it was loaded. After placing the weapon back in the bag, Dante gazed at Lamb.

"That what you wanted?" Lamb asked.

Dante nodded. "Yeah."

"Cool. You need somethin' else, you know how to reach me."

"I'll keep that in mind," Dante said, though figuring he had just what he needed and hoped to never have to see Lamb again. "Have a good one."

Dante walked away from the man toward the door of the bar, almost believing that Lamb might attack him once his back was turned, reclaiming the gun for another sucker. Only when Dante looked over his shoulder, he saw that Lamb had vanished like an illegal gun dealer in the night.

Inside the bar, Dante came upon the bartender.

"Did you get it handled?" she asked.

"Yeah," he responded simply.

She looked up at him. "Would you like a drink?"

Dante's first thought was that he wanted to get the hell away from there as fast as he could. But since there was no indication he had been set up, and he had a little time on his hands to assess his next move, he told her, "Why not?"

Eric had his arm around Beverly's shoulder as they sat in the living room, watching a movie on the fifty-inch plasma TV that he'd given her for her birthday. She loved it and had thought nothing could be better. But that was before Dante entered her life and turned things upside down. Now she found herself thinking about him even when she honestly wanted to enjoy the romantic movie she had chosen to watch with Eric.

What are you doing to me, Dante? Beverly allowed her mind to wander even further, thinking about him making love to her in her own bed. She imagined that the orgasms from his mouth and penis would come at her in waves. *Am I really fantasizing about Dante while in Eric's arms?*

"Not falling to sleep on me, are you, baby?" Eric's voice broke into her thoughts.

Beverly glanced over at him. "That's your domain, isn't it?" she asked wryly.

He tossed his head back with a laugh. "That was a low blow."

"Sorry, I couldn't resist." Not to mention it had been true of late.

"I forgive you." Eric nibbled on her ear. "Sorry if my energy level hasn't always been where I want it to be. Maybe I can make it up to you tonight. . . ."

She pushed his face away. "Don't make promises you can't keep." Not that she wanted to have sex with him tonight. She'd rather just go to sleep, unless, of course, she was intimate with Dante tonight. But that would definitely be pushing it. Eric would certainly find out. Then there was no telling what the fallout would be. She could wind up losing both men. Where would that leave her?

"I had that coming." Eric maintained his arm around her. "I'll try harder in the future."

Don't do me any favors. Beverly refocused her attention on the TV screen, then yawned, deciding she'd better cut this short. She looked at him. "Maybe you should go to the pool hall, after all."

Eric raised his brow. "I thought you wanted a nice evening together watching television?"

"I did," Beverly said, wishing now she had never talked him out of going to play pool. She had thought it was a better idea for them to spend more time together, maybe reconnect on a romantic and sexual level. Now she wondered if Dante had made that a lost cause. "I'm not really getting into the movie the way I thought I would. I think I'm just going to call it a night early."

"Want me to join you?" he asked in a seductive voice.

"I'm going to go soak in the Jacuzzi first," she said quickly. "Go ahead and play pool."

Eric lifted his arm off her shoulder. "You sure?"

"Yes." Beverly looked at him sweetly. "We can pick a better movie next time." She cut the TV off, satisfied that he would do his thing tonight and she would do hers.

Eric wasn't overly eager to play pool. Especially given that there was usually no competition at the pool hall. Certainly no competition worthy of being invited to his house for some private pool playing. But since Beverly had flaked out on him and put the brakes on the movie, which he'd thought could help get him in the mood, he decided he may as well hang out for a while. Maybe afterward he would wake her up for sex and not take no for an answer. Or, more likely, he'd conk out himself, finding that he couldn't get it up for her. Not after a few drinks. And the way Marilyn had worn him out.

The Northside Pool Center was on Eight Mile Road and semi-crowded as always, or at least it was on the days Eric came to play. There were a dozen tables, along with a couple of pinball machines and arcade games. After getting a mug of beer, he found an empty table and got his pool stick out of its cover and assembled it. He wondered if anyone hanging around would dare challenge him to a game so he could kick their ass.

He began hitting balls, nailing them in different pockets. When Eric saw an older man watching him, he invited him to play if only to give himself something to do other than perfect his game.

Turned out the man was little competition for him. Eric wondered if maybe he should have stuck it out with Beverly. Maybe after her fun in the hot tub they could have heated up the sheets in the bedroom. Or not. He was still committed to keeping her in his life, even if the sex between them continued to be lukewarm at best.

In the Jacuzzi, Beverly enjoyed a glass of wine and some fresh fantasies now that she was alone. She pictured Dante all over her and deep inside her. Beverly heightened the visual image by masturbating, imagining that it was his nimble finger moving back and forth across her clitoris. She got really wet, and it had nothing to do with the water that surrounded her.

When it became too much, she let up, wanting to savor the experience before coming too soon. Dante made her so horny, it was driving her crazy with lust. She had a mind to take her chances and go to the hotel right now. But it was later than their usual trysts, and once they got going, it was easy to lose track of the time. How would she explain it to Eric if he was back before her after she told him she was going to sleep after the Jacuzzi? She didn't take him for a fool, in spite of having a lover behind his back.

It's probably best not to play with fire tonight and risk getting burned by one man, or both.

That didn't mean she wasn't up for a little naughtiness if Dante was available. She got up and strode across the tile and onto the bedroom hardwood floor, grabbing her cell phone and going back to the tub, where the jet-driven water once more gave her a hydro massage.

She called Dante. *Please pick up.*

He did. "Hey."

"Hi." Beverly smiled. "What are you doing?"

"I'm working," he said.

"Too bad." She frowned. "So are you out cruising the streets, looking for hookers to interview?"

"Not exactly." Dante paused. "I'm in my car, but between stops. I have spoken to some of the women who have been trafficked. Mainly, though, it's about observation, seeing what the cops have to say and others who are affected by this dirty business."

Beverly yawned. This might be more interesting if she wasn't so hot for him right now. *I will be your whore anytime.*

"What are you up to?" he asked.

"Oh, I'm just sitting here in the Jacuzzi all by my lonesome, wondering how spicy it would be to have phone sex with you."

Dante chuckled lasciviously. "Something tells me it would be hotter than hot."

Beverly began to rub herself. "I'd love for you to talk dirty to me."

"You mean like saying how I would lick you incessantly if I were there?"

"Uh-huh," she moaned.

"My face would burrow its way between your legs, and once I wrapped my lips around your clit, I would have you begging me to stick my dick deep inside you."

"Oh . . ." Beverly gasped, picking up the pace with her finger. "Stick it inside me, please."

"Yeah, I'll penetrate your tight vagina and put my tongue down your throat at the same time while rubbing your nipples until they felt like bursting with joy."

Beverly moaned. She was coming in that moment and was practically paralyzed by the sensations. She made sure Dante knew what was happening. When it was over, she smiled with just the slightest embarrassment.

"Thank you," she murmured.

"My pleasure," he said smoothly. "I'm glad you got off and I could help."

If he only knew just how much. "Next time we'll make love in person," she promised.

"I'd like that."

"Well, I'd better let you get back to your research," Beverly said reluctantly, wishing they could spend hours doing over the phone what they did while naked in his hotel room.

"Thanks," Dante said. "Enjoy your Jacuzzi."

"Always do." ˉ

He disconnected, and she immediately felt his absence, while wondering if he felt hers just as much.

THIRTEEN

Dante smiled when he thought about Beverly and how much she turned him on. He hadn't expected her to call for some phone sex. Though the timing was off, he could tell that she desperately needed to hear his voice to put her over the top. He gave her what she wanted and found himself wishing he had been there to deliver it in person. The woman was sexually amazing and had single-handedly heightened his libido at a time when his greater focus was elsewhere.

While Beverly was a great and sexy diversion, Dante put his eye back on the ball. He had been following Eric Fox since he left his house. Dante had vacillated between simply gunning the bastard down at the first opportunity and waiting to catch him in a secluded location. Once he had disposed of the one who shot Russell, he would go after the man who ordered the hit.

Dante followed Eric to a pool hall. *So the man takes a breather from murdering people by playing pool.* It was something Dante had become pretty good at himself. He had started playing pool in college and had his own table back at his place in L.A. Only he hadn't come to Detroit to play some damned pool. Certainly not with the likes of a hitman.

Doesn't mean I can't go inside, check it out, and see what he's up to.

After giving it some thought, Dante decided to leave the gun inside the car. He put it in the glove compartment for safekeeping. It would be just his luck that the cops would bust him for possession of an illegal and loaded firearm. While they hauled his ass off to jail, Eric Fox would still be free as a bird. *I can't let that happen.*

Dante stepped into the pool hall. It wasn't too crowded, but enough so that he didn't spot Eric immediately. Then he saw him at a pool table at the end of the hall. He was laughing with some others who had gathered around to watch him do his thing, seemingly with proficiency above the norm.

Moseying over to the group of spectators, Dante watched up close as Eric dusted off a would-be competitor. He invited any other challengers, putting a hundred dollars on the line to anyone who could match it, winner take all. When no one stepped up, Eric chuckled arrogantly.

Suddenly, he honed in on Dante, who matched his hard gaze. "What about you, bro?" he asked.

Dante kept a straight face. "What about me?"

"You play pool? Or are you just hanging out to watch a master at work?"

"I play a little," Dante said coolly.

"Are you up for a game of eight ball?" Eric asked. "Since I'm in a generous mood, I'll let you put up fifty and I'll spot you a couple of balls."

If this was any other circumstance, Dante would have laughed out loud. Who the hell did this bastard think he was? But why not take the bait? It just might be a means to an end he could exploit in setting the asshole up for the kill.

"You're on." Dante took a fifty-dollar bill out of his wallet and set it on the edge of the pool table. Though he certainly didn't need it, he would even take Eric up on spotting him two balls to give him a false sense of security.

Eric grinned. "You break."

Dante grabbed one of the hall pool sticks that seemed a good fit. He noted that Eric had his own stick to match his ego. Well, he would bring it crashing down. And soon he'd be dead and could rot in hell for eternity.

After lining up the white ball, Dante shot it into the other balls, two of which fell in holes, and he was off and running. He deliberately missed once, giving Eric a turn, hoping that he wouldn't be able to run the table.

"Not bad," hummed Eric. "But not good enough."

"Let's see if you can do better," Dante challenged him, counting on his supreme confidence to be his undoing in more ways than one.

When Eric missed what seemed to be an easy shot, perhaps distracted by a Sanaa Lathan look-alike who peeked in on the action, Dante took over. He made it count, clearing the table and pinpointing the eight ball in a corner pocket.

As onlookers cheered and gave him and each other high fives, Dante downplayed it as just luck. This seemed to further incense Eric, whose shine had dulled after losing one game.

"Let's go another," Eric demanded. "Only this time for the hundred and fifty dollars you won. And no handicap. Or do you not have the balls to take me on fair and square?"

Dante peered at him. They were roughly the same height, give or take an inch, and of similar build. It looked like Eric worked out to some degree, as did he. Nevertheless, Eric was older, and Dante believed he could take him in hand-to-hand combat if push came to shove. Only he had no intention of getting into a street brawl with the man and possibly being the victim of a lucky punch. Using the gun he'd bought was the best way to ensure that his revenge was decisive and final.

"Yeah, I've got the balls," he told him, meeting his eyes sharply while putting down the money.

Eric nodded and smiled. "Then let's do it."

"You break first this time," Dante said, feeling confident that he could beat him under any circumstances, causing Eric to lower his defenses and become more vulnerable for what was headed his way.

"By the way, what's your name?" Eric asked the man who had given him unexpected competition in the pool hall.

"Dante."

Eric gave him the once-over. He was about ten years younger, maybe an inch taller, had a shaved head, and looked to be in better shape than him, though Eric liked to think he was pretty fit for forty-five. He was surprised that the dude actually beat him, even with the handicap. Was he losing his touch before an audience and after lots of practice at home? Or had he been playing him?

He forced himself to smile. "I'm Eric." He stuck out a hand, wanting to give the guise that he wasn't a sore loser. Of course he was. He didn't like losing anything. That included his woman, Beverly. But he would strike up losing the pool game to having a couple of drinks, which threw off his game, and luck, as Dante had suggested.

Dante shook his hand. He had a firm grip. Eric liked that. Maybe he'd finally have some competition at the pool table. He lined the balls up and then broke them with a powerful thrust of the white ball, but knocked only one ball into the hole.

"Haven't seen you around here before," Eric said while taking his sweet time setting up the next shot.

"Good reason for that," Dante said calmly. "I'm just in town for business."

"What type business are you in?" Eric was curious. He didn't see him in law enforcement. Nor could he picture the man in the business of killing people like him.

"I'm a writer."

Eric sized up the shot. "What do you write?"

"I write about current events, war, government corruption, sex trafficking, stuff like that."

"Cool." Eric called and sank another shot, feeling he was on a roll. "Which one of those has you in Detroit? And where are you from?"

Dante grimaced. "You ask a lot of questions. Are we here to play pool or what?"

Eric chuckled. "Didn't mean to get into your business." *Actually, I did. Are you hiding something?*

Dante smiled. "I was just messing with you, man. I'm from L.A. and was sent here to look into the local world of sex trafficking."

"Sex trafficking, huh?" Eric wondered if that was part of Leon's activities. He knew about the stable of women under Leon's control and wouldn't be surprised at all if he was involved with international sex trafficking. But that was his problem. All Eric cared about was handling his business when called upon.

"Yeah," said Dante. "From what I gather, it's a much smaller issue here than L.A."

"Not surprised. Everything here is small compared to there." Eric lost his train of thought for just an instant after identifying a shot and flubbing it. He cursed under his breath. "It's on you."

"Thanks." Dante took the opportunity afforded him and sank shot after shot until there was one ball left. "Eight ball in the corner . . ."

He calmly sank it, and Eric got a bad feeling that he'd underestimated the man. "You win," he conceded, blaming himself for not taking Dante seriously enough.

"Looks that way," Dante said, grinning. He pocketed the cash triumphantly.

"How about one more game?" Eric pleaded. He hated the thought of losing not once, but twice, though he'd gained a certain measure of respect for Dante as a result.

"Wish I could, but I have to go." Dante set the stick down.

"Come on now, at least give me the chance to win my money back."

"Maybe another time."

Eric's brow creased. "Obviously you're a better player than you let on. Now you want to take the money and run?"

Dante laughed. "Never said I couldn't play. Only that I played a little, which is true. I'm sure you can easily win that money back with anyone in here."

"Probably," conceded Eric, balancing his stick against the side of the table. "But none of them would be you."

"True."

"How long are you going to be in town?"

"A few days," Dante said. "Maybe a little longer."

"Maybe you can drop by my place so we can play some serious pool," Eric suggested. He liked the idea of playing someone who would give him a stiff challenge. Beverly had complained often enough that they never seemed to have guests over. On the whole, he preferred it that way. The more people you knew, the more they tended to get in your business, which could be bad for their health. In this case, since Dante was only going to be around for a short while, there was little chance he could be a threat to what Eric had going on. Including Beverly.

"When?" Dante asked.

"How about tomorrow night, say, around seven?"

Dante twisted his lips in thought. "Yeah, that could work."

Eric grinned. "Great." He gave him the address and the quickest route to get there.

"See you then," Dante told him and left.

Eric finished off his beer and decided it was time for him to call it quits too. He wondered if Beverly had gone to bed or if she'd gained her second wind. He wasn't exactly in the mood for sex tonight but wouldn't reject her if she was up for it. Or maybe he would make love to her, anyway, just for the hell of it and to remind her that she was his and his alone. He saw no reason to change that anytime soon.

Dante stepped outside into the humid night. He could barely believe he'd just accepted an invitation to visit the man who shot his brother to death in cold blood. On the other hand, it couldn't have worked out better. He had gained the bastard's trust and would see him in a place where perhaps he was most vulnerable. *Then I'll have him right where I want him.* Maybe he would blow Eric's head off then and there and be done with it, splattering his brains all over his pool table.

After getting inside his car, Dante checked his cell phone for messages. One was from his buddy and colleague, James Barbour. There were two messages from Beverly. He listened. Both were sexually stimulating and unabashedly grateful for their earlier chat, hoping to repeat it when she couldn't come to him. Dante smiled, not at all averse to some hanky-panky through phone sex, though it couldn't compare to hot action body to body. Beverly was more than his match in the bedroom, giving every bit as much as she received, and then some. This made her even more alluring and aroused him in anticipation of the next time they could tear each other's clothes off and get down and dirty in his hotel room until both had climaxes that left their heads spinning and bodies soaked with perspiration from the sexual heat.

Right now, though, his thoughts were on Eric Fox and the chance to exact some justice. Dante drove off, feeling he had taken a step in the right direction in that regard. He looked forward to paying the man a visit tomorrow night.

Dante found himself parked just a couple of doors from Leon Quincy's house. And to his surprise, he actually saw the man standing on the porch all by his lonesome. Maybe this was the opportune time to take him out and get half the job done. Dante took the gun out of the glove compartment. His palm was sweaty and his heart seemed to skip a beat at the thought of killing a man who deserved nothing less than death.

He got out of the car and approached the house, figuring one clean hit to the head should do the trick. But before he could put the plan into action, Leon went inside the house and closed the door. Dante doubted if the man ever even saw him, so self-absorbed was he.

Standing in front of the house briefly, Dante had a mind to just go up to it, ring the bell, and hope the asshole opened the door. Then he could watch him squirm before ending his life. But the risks of such an action were too great for Dante to make such a move. Could be that one of Leon's heavies came out firing without asking any questions and he wound up being the one dead, joining his brother in an early grave.

And so he retreated, having missed the golden opportunity, but sure there would be others to get the job done.

Just as would be the case when setting his sights on Leon's gun for hire, Eric Fox.

At ten o'clock, Spencer made the rounds on the corners where Leon's streetwalkers did their thing. His job was to collect their earnings thus far. Leon would give them whatever money he deemed necessary later. Personally, Spencer felt they received far too little for what they did on their backs and knees. But it wasn't his call. And no one made them work for a pimp like Leon. It wasn't like the South American, Russian, and Filipino women who worked downtown and on the east side for crime cartels and Asian gangs. These were women who chose to break away from home or bad asses in their lives to prostitute themselves when they weren't whoring for Leon in his bed.

Spencer walked up to Gail, a twenty-year-old who had been in Detroit only a few days before she came to Leon's attention. He'd put her out on the streets in less than a week.

"Getting any action?" he asked her.

She flipped her blond extensions to one side. "A little."

"I need what you've made so far."

Her fake lashes fluttered. "It ain't much."

"Leon won't be happy to hear that," he warned, though he knew she couldn't make johns materialize out of thin air.

"Is he ever happy?" she asked courageously.

"Yeah, when his operation's running smoothly."

Gail removed a wad of bills from her bra. "Here. It's all I've got."

Spencer flipped through the cash. "Okay." He met her eyes. "You all right?"

She smiled thinly with full lips. "Yeah, I'm cool. Just wish it wasn't such a slow night."

"Maybe it will pick up," he told her. "See you later."

Gail went back to work and Spencer finished his assignment and headed over to Leon's place to give him the money. Spencer thought about Marilyn. He was currently in the doghouse with her after their little argument. He blamed himself for starting it. Could he honestly expect her to be someone she wasn't? Was it too much to ask for someone who always sat on her ass and rarely went out to tidy things up?

He loved her in spite of it. She got him and gave him enough leeway to do pretty much what he wanted with few questions asked. Most other women would have been overly suspicious and nitpicking his every move. *I need to get back on her good side.*

Spencer arrived at Leon's house and gave him the girls' earnings. He even threw in fifty bucks of his own money to bring the total up a bit.

Leon wrinkled his nose after he counted the cash. "Guess it's better than nothing at all."

"Yeah," Spencer agreed.

Leon handed him a hundred dollars. "Don't spend it all in one place."

"I won't." Spencer didn't argue about the fifty he ended up with for the work, since he chose to give up as much.

He used most of it to buy Marilyn some roses, presenting them to her when he got home.

"Thanks," she told him, grinning.

"Sorry about last night."

"Don't worry about it," she said.

"Seriously?" He looked at her, expecting more resistance.

"Yes," Marilyn said. "We both said things we didn't mean."

"You're right."

She put the roses down and grabbed him. "I want to have sex."

"Now?" Not that he had any problem with it.

"Yes, now. Makeup sex is the best kind, don't you think?"

Spencer grinned broadly, instantly getting a hard-on. "Oh yeah, definitely."

"I thought you'd agree." She took him by the hand to their bedroom, and they made love like he couldn't remember but would never forget.

The following morning, Spencer used his credit card to purchase Marilyn a big-screen television with access to the Internet, surprising her with it.

FOURTEEN

"I've missed you too, Mom," Beverly said over the phone the next afternoon as she sat on the patio, talking to her mother, Etta Holland. She had moved from Detroit to Atlanta four months ago with Beverly's younger brother, Cody, and her stepfather. Beverly had been sad to see them leave, but understood they had to go since her stepfather had a job transfer. Her mother had actually tried to get her to move too, telling Beverly they had plenty of room and she was more than welcome to stay with them until she could find a place of her own. But since she was happily living with Eric then, she saw no reason to upend her world for an unknown future.

"Tell me you've finally come to your senses and have left Eric," Etta said, never shy to give her opinion.

Beverly cracked a smile. Her mother had never liked Eric, believing he was too old for her and too set in his ways. She was also concerned that he had not gotten over his ex-wife and seemed like he was hiding something. Beverly had dismissed her mother's concerns as nothing more than those of an overprotective mother who didn't want to let her make her own choices in life. Including men. Most of the men she'd dated had failed to impress her mother. She always found one reason or another to reject them as unworthy of her daughter.

Eric was no different and, if possible, might have left an even worse impression on Etta, who was a year younger than Eric. As stubborn as her mother could be, Beverly had steadfastly defended him, believing it to be in her best interests and not wanting to end a relationship prematurely simply because her mother had issues with Eric, who had tried hard to get her to accept him for who he was.

"No, Mom, I haven't left Eric," Beverly almost hated to say, though she now had reason to seriously consider the prospect. "Sorry to disappoint you."

"I'm not disappointed," her mother said. "I'm just worried that in being with a man so much older and seemingly with different values than you, you're missing out on being with someone you have much more in common with."

"You don't have to worry about me. I'm fine. Eric wants to make me happy."

"But *are* you happy? Or are you playing the role he wants you to just so you can keep living in that fancy house of his?"

Beverly's temper flared. *Here we go again.* "There's nothing wrong with being taken care of by a man," she voiced. "And that includes living in his house."

"So why not marry him?" Etta questioned. "That would be the proper thing to do if he really cared about you and vice versa."

"We've already talked about this," Beverly said with a sigh. "He's not looking for that right now, and neither am I."

"And what *exactly* are you looking for?"

Beverly contemplated the question. What did she want that she didn't already have? The answer was obvious. Dante was the man she wanted. Beyond the mind-blowing great sex they had, somehow she could picture herself being married to him, though they were not even really dating at this point. And she wasn't sure he was or would ever be the marrying type.

Should I or shouldn't I mention it to her? She decided to spill at least part of the beans, if only to put her mother's mind somewhat at ease.

"I've been kind of seeing another man," she confessed.

"Oh? And how long has this been going on?"

"Not long."

"I take it Eric has no idea?" Etta asked.

"I don't think so." Beverly saw little indication that he suspected anything. Or was she only deluding herself?

"Who is he?"

Beverly took a sip of her soft drink. "His name's Dante."

"Where did you meet?"

Maybe she shouldn't say, or she'd be scolded for picking up a stranger in a bar. "At the store," she lied. "We just hit it off."

"You mean the same way you hit it off with Eric?" her mother asked sardonically.

"It's not the same," Beverly assured her. "Dante's completely different."

"You mean he's younger? Better looking? Richer? What?"

"Yes to the first two," Beverly responded. "Not richer. We are, uh, more sexually compatible." *Should I be telling her about my sex life?*

"You need more than sex to make a relationship work," Etta said.

"I know that. But it's hard to make it work right without good sex."

"So does that mean you and Eric aren't having good sex?"

Beverly colored. "It hasn't really been very good lately," she conceded.

"And that's why you're going behind his back with this other man?" Etta asked.

Beverly sighed. "That's how it began."

"If sex is that important to you, why don't you just leave Eric and take up with Dante?"

Beverly knew that was coming. She wished she could give a short and simple answer. "It's complicated."

"What's complicated about it?" demanded Etta. "Is it Eric's money that's keeping you with him? Or is it that Dante is only interested in having sex with you?"

"Maybe a little of both," Beverly answered. "I'm so confused. I just need more time to see how things play out with Dante before deciding if I want to end things with Eric." She was also concerned about how Eric would react. Would he step aside and give her back her freedom without much resistance? Or would he go after Dante as a jealous and angry man?

Then Beverly still wasn't certain if what she had with Dante had legs beyond their sexual chemistry. Or was he attracted to her mainly because she was tied to someone else, making it a safer bet for him with no commitment?

"You're playing with fire, Beverly," Etta warned. "My advice is to make a decision fast and act on it before someone—including yourself—gets hurt with you trying to hang on to two different men."

Beverly heard a car pull up in the driveway. She assumed it was Eric. The last thing she wanted was to have him hear her talking about this.

"I have to go," she told her mother. "I'll call you again soon."

"You'd better. Please be careful in what you choose to do."

"I will," promised Beverly. "Love you."

She put the phone on the glass table and, after grabbing her drink, drew in a deep breath thoughtfully. In spite of opening up a whole new can of worms by letting her mother in on her little secret, Beverly was glad she had. Her mother had always been the voice of reason, even if she didn't always listen to her. On the other hand, this only played to her mother's belief from the start that Eric wasn't right for her. Beverly wondered if that was beginning to catch up with her.

"What are you up to?" Eric's voice boomed as he stepped out onto the patio.

She looked up at him, dressed professionally in a gray double-breasted suit. He somehow suddenly looked every bit his age. Or was that an illusion because of the chat she'd just had with her mother?

"Just relaxing," she told him.

He smiled and grabbed her soft drink. "You mind?"

She preferred he got his own drink. "Be my guest."

Eric gulped down a nice amount and put the can on the table. "A friend is dropping by later to shoot some pool."

"Who?" Beverly asked. Not that she cared, as long as he didn't hit on her like so many men she couldn't care less about. It just came as a surprise to her since Eric didn't have that many friends besides her and some people he worked with. Most of them never came to the house.

"Just someone I met at the pool hall. He kicked my ass on the table, and now I'm hoping to have a little payback."

"Sounds like fun," she said wryly.

"We'll see about that. Anyway, stick around and be my good luck charm."

Beverly flinched. "I wasn't going anywhere." Had he expected her to go somewhere? She'd love to be with

Dante while he was playing pool. But Eric had decided to keep an eye on her. Or, more likely, show off his trophy girlfriend to his new pool pal.

She would go through the motions while dreaming about making love to Dante. Then, at the next opportunity, she would turn the dream into an erotic reality.

"Good," Eric said. He leaned over and kissed her before heading back into the house.

Beverly sipped her drink and decided this was a perfect time to start on her sex fantasy with Dante.

Marilyn was glad her gamble paid off. She'd bet that after giving Spencer the cold shoulder long enough, he would give her what she wanted. Reversing her strategy, she'd pretended to get turned on by him, allowing him to have his way with her. Worked like a charm. Now she had the big TV that matched Beverly's, meaning bragging rights.

But she wanted much more than that. She wanted Beverly's man and intended to have him. Last night, Spencer had been a poor substitute for Eric. Though he was a big man, his penis did not measure up to Eric's when hard. Or to what Eric could do with it. Once upon a time that was all Beverly could talk about. Now it seemed like ancient history, as Beverly had turned her back on him in favor of a young stud she apparently had eating out of her hands. That left it up to Marilyn to pick up the slack with Eric, and she was more than up to the task.

She needed to secure her position as the woman of Eric's future. That meant dealing with his past prior to Beverly entering the picture. Marilyn had decided to pay Gloria Fox a little visit. She was not about to let that bitch somehow worm her way back into Eric's life.

Not after all she'd done to steal him away from Beverly.
He's mine, and I'll be damned if you or anyone else at-
tempts to change that.

Marilyn sucked in breath as she rang the doorbell.
If she was a trifle nervous, it wasn't because of Gloria, whose ass she could kick any day of the week, but
rather Eric, whom she didn't want this getting back to.
It could spoil all the strides she made. She considered
it worth the risk to put Gloria in her place.

Gloria opened the door and gave her a surprised
look. "Marilyn!"

"Yeah, it's me." They had run into each other a few
times. Once was when Gloria was still married to Eric
and they were at the same picnic as Marilyn and Spencer. Even then, Marilyn was attracted to Eric. But it was
only when he and Beverly hooked up that she wanted
him for herself. On another occasion, Gloria had barged
in when Marilyn was having lunch with Beverly. In spite
of Gloria acting holier than thou, Marilyn viewed her as
strictly yesterday's news. The last time she saw the bitch
was at a wedding in which Gloria was accompanied by
Marilyn's cousin, Hal Ketchum.

"What are you doing here?" Gloria asked.

"We need to talk," Marilyn said toughly, pushing her
way past Gloria and into the house.

Gloria rounded on her. "I don't think we have anything to talk about."

Marilyn stepped inside the living room, waiting for
Gloria to follow, which she did. "Do us both a favor and
leave Beverly and Eric alone."

"What business is it of yours?" Gloria asked, holding
her ground. "Or did Beverly send you here to do her
dirty work?"

Marilyn was mildly amused at the thought of making
Beverly the bad one. That way, if this blew up, it would
be in Beverly's face and not hers.

"Doesn't matter," she said slyly. "What does is that Beverly and Eric are friends of mine. They're happy, and I don't want to see you screwing that up."

Gloria laughed. "First, Eric threatens me, and now you bring your fat ass into my house, trying to tell me what to do. If their relationship was so secure, why do I believe otherwise?"

"Maybe because you're too stupid to know when to leave well enough alone." Marilyn's mouth became a straight line. "Or maybe you're trying to get back something that's gone forever after Hal tossed you to the curb."

"You bitch," cursed Gloria. "How dare you come over here and—"

"How dare you call me a bitch!" Marilyn cut her off and got right up to her face. "If anyone's a bitch, it's *you*. When you mess with my best friend and Eric, you're messing with me. You don't want to do that, because I never fight fair and square. I will kick your ass up and down this block and make you wish you'd stayed out of Eric's life."

"Is this about Eric or Beverly?" Gloria asked curiously, trembling. "You want him for yourself, don't you?"

Marilyn would not let her bait her into a confession, as it would only jeopardize her plans to be with Eric. "Get real," she slung at her. "I'm happily married to Spencer. This is all about you!" She pushed Gloria hard enough that she stumbled off balance before catching herself. "Find yourself another man and leave Eric and Beverly the hell alone. Otherwise, there's no telling what might happen. . . ."

Marilyn glared at her and sensed that Gloria realized she meant business. Just as she knew Eric did. She left the house and got in her car, barely able to hold back the satisfaction she felt in defending her territory. At least it would be once Beverly was out of the picture for good. Until then, Marilyn intended to continue to service Eric at every opportunity while waiting impatiently for the day that she moved into his house and bed for good.

FIFTEEN

Beverly could hardly believe her eyes when she saw her onetime friend Tenesia White standing at the door. It had been nearly a year since Tenesia moved to London with a reggae musician she met on the Internet. Beverly had considered her a close confidant before she discovered she was hitting on Eric and was pretty sure there was much more to the story than just flirting. She had seen the way they seemed to be all over each other on the dance floor, as though making love on their feet. Of course, Tenesia had insisted it was all in Beverly's head and that she was merely being friendly to her man. Eric had dismissed the whole thing as just some innocent flirting and nothing more, making Beverly feel insecure and wonder if it was all in her head.

Then Tenesia set her sights on someone else and fled Detroit. Their relationship had been strained ever since, with only the occasional phone chat or e-mail. In fact, it was about a month ago that Beverly had last heard from Tenesia by e-mail. She hadn't said anything about coming back to Detroit. Was it for a visit or permanent?

"Hey, girl," Tenesia said, giving Beverly a big hug. "Surprise!"

"Yes, it is." Beverly studied her. She was a couple of inches taller, with a model's slender physique, a creamy caramel complexion, and pouty lips. Her black hair was cut short and perfectly coiffed. As always, she was sharply dressed, wearing an eye-catching apple-red V-neck top, black, slimming boot-cut jeans, and wedge high heels.

Beverly had always felt a little envious of Tenesia, whom she considered more beautiful and maybe even sexier than she. Those feelings had come to a head when she suspected Tenesia of going after Eric. She wondered now if she had overreacted in accusing Tenesia of something she might have been totally innocent of.

"You look great," Tenesia said, eyeing her up and down. "But why am I not surprised?"

"Look who's talking!" Beverly felt self-conscious for some reason, even though she was dressed for company in a purple sleeveless halter and sandals. Her hair was curled nicely, and the touch of makeup she wore was just right to brighten her complexion. But was that enough to keep Eric's eyes on her and not on Tenesia? Or would she be gone before he even knew she was there?

"Well, aren't you going to invite me in?" Tenesia flashed bold brown eyes at her.

"Of course." Beverly realized she was being silly and had nothing to worry about, especially since she had her eye on another man. She stepped aside and watched Tenesia strut past her. "So how long have you been in town?"

Tenesia faced her. "Since last night. I thought about calling, but wasn't sure you'd want to hear from me, so—"

So you decided to come by unannounced instead. "Where are you staying?" *Please don't say you want to stay here.*

"At my mother's," Tenesia said, making herself comfortable on a chair.

"Is she all right?" Beverly had heard that she had been ill. She felt a twinge of guilt that she had never gone to see her since Tenesia left.

"She has her good and bad days, but she's dealing with it."

"Did you come back to see her or . . ."

Tenesia frowned. "Actually, I've moved back to Detroit."

Beverly cocked a brow. "What happened to your reggae man?"

"He's still there. Things just stopped working for us, so I left," Tenesia said.

"What things?" Beverly couldn't help but ask as she sat down.

Tenesia jutted her chin. "If you must know, he cheated on me. Not once, but twice, that I know of. Guess I should've thought it through more carefully before hopping on a plane for England."

"You went with what seemed right at the time," Beverly pointed out, feeling sorry for her. "You can't blame yourself that he turned out to be a dog." *What does that make me since I'm doing the same thing to Eric?*

"I know. It still hurts, though. But I'll get over it." Tenesia gazed at her in a moment of awkward silence. "How's Eric?"

"Fine." Beverly knew that she must have seen his car in the driveway. She suspected Tenesia was dying to see him. Or was that her insecurity kicking up again? "He's down in the basement, playing pool, waiting for his friend to come over."

"Look, I want you to know that nothing happened between us."

"I believe you," Beverly told her. "I'm sorry I accused you. I should've known I could trust you as much as I can Marilyn."

"Thanks." Tenesia smiled. "How is she, anyway?"

"Marilyn's great. She and Spencer are happy."

"That's cool." Tenesia gave her a direct look. "Are you?"

Beverly sighed, not wanting to say anything that would stir the pot and possibly get back to Eric. "Of course. Things are great in my life, and with Eric." She only wished it were that cut and dry. Dante had certainly complicated things as far as her conflicting emotions and enhanced sexual desire.

"I thought I heard some chatter up here." Eric's voice broke into Beverly's thoughts as he stepped into the living room. "Well, look who's here. . . ."

"Hey, Eric," Tenesia said cheerfully.

"How the hell are you?" he asked, grinning sideways.

"I'm good," she said. "Or at least I try to be."

Eric laughed as he glanced at Beverly uneasily. He gave Tenesia a hug and kiss on the cheek. "Nice to see you again."

"You too."

Beverly watched this show of affection, which had her wondering all over again if the connection they shared went beyond platonic friendship. To her surprise, it didn't affect her so much one way or the other. In some respects, she did not mind if Tenesia and Eric hooked up, if this was what they chose to do. That way, she could turn her full attention to Dante—a man who aroused Beverly like no one before him. He was even beginning to creep into her psyche beyond pure sexual appeal. Admittedly, giving up what Eric had to offer for someone who had offered her little beyond great sex was a scary proposition for Beverly. But she was starting to realize that the notion of life without Dante's hot body, torrid kisses, caresses, scent, and lovemaking was even scarier.

***

Tenesia White took one look at Eric and could see that he hadn't changed a bit. He was still a snake in the grass disguised as a devoted boyfriend to Beverly. It pained Tenesia to think that her once good friend had it all wrong about her coming on to Eric and jumping his bones. In fact, it was Eric who shamelessly flirted with her and actually suggested they get a hotel room and release all inhibitions. Of course, she'd rejected any such sexual tryst with Beverly's man. That didn't stop Beverly from making false accusations against her, though.

While defending herself, Tenesia had stopped short of coming clean about Eric's sexual advances, certain that Beverly would have only blamed it on her for instigating such. Girls always found it easier to turn on each other than blame the man, even though men were usually the guilty ones. Tenesia suspected that if it hadn't been her, Eric would have likely found someone else to get his rocks off with. Beverly would come to see him for what he was sooner or later.

Tenesia had no intention of telling Beverly what she thought and stirring up old and bitter feelings, especially when her love life had gone to hell and back. It seemed like she'd ended up with one loser after another. Her musician boyfriend, Manute, was a perfect example. She'd thought they really had something special. Turned out he was just another player, wanting twice as much as he gave and as many women to bed as possible.

Now she was back in Detroit, still licking her wounds and hoping to make things right with Beverly again, if that were possible. At least Beverly seemed to be willing to let bygones be bygones and meet her halfway. That was more than Tenesia wanted from Manute or even Eric, for that matter.

"So how long are you sticking around?" he asked as they sat on stools in the kitchen, sipping wine.

"For a while," Tenesia said, feeling Beverly's eyes on her. "London wasn't what I'd hoped it would be, so I guess you could say I'm starting over where I belong."

"Sorry it didn't work out for you." Eric lifted his wineglass thoughtfully. "But I'm sure Beverly's happy that you're back. It gives her someone else to hang out with other than Marilyn all the time."

Tenesia wasn't so sure Beverly was happy to see her back in Detroit. She doubted Marilyn would be. They had always been in silent competition to be Beverly's best friend until Tenesia lost the battle when Beverly thought she was trying to steal her man. She only hoped Beverly believed now that she had absolutely no interest in Eric. Maybe there was someone else out there for her. But she wasn't about to hold her breath in that regard.

Dante stood at the front door of Eric Fox's house. He could hear chatter inside with at least one female voice. He recalled from his private investigator that Eric was living with a woman. It made him seem all too human rather than the murdering monster Dante saw him as. He refused to allow himself to get too caught up in Eric's personal relationships. That wasn't what this was about. He could only hope she didn't get caught in the cross fire.

Dante rang the doorbell while thinking of the very personal nature of his vendetta as Russell's face flashed in his head.

The door opened, and Eric stood there, grinning. "You made it."

Dante pasted a fake smile on his lips. "Had to give you a chance to win your money back."

Eric laughed. "Or take even more away from me."

"Yeah, that too."

"Come on in."

Dante stepped inside, bypassing an attractive mahogany accent table in the foyer. He could hear what now sounded like two women speaking. One of the voices had an air of familiarity.

Eric led him into the kitchen. "Ladies, this is Dante, my buddy from the pool hall." He moved to Beverly, who was seated, and placed a proprietary arm across her shoulders. "This is my lady, Beverly, and her friend Tenesia."

Dante was stunned as he locked eyes with Beverly. She seemed just as shocked to see him. What the hell was she doing there—with *him*, of all people? Was she *actually* Eric's girlfriend? *This is the older man she's living with and comes back to every time she has steamy sex with me?*

A mixture of anger and jealousy ripped through Dante like a hurricane in what seemed like the longest moment of his life. He scarcely knew what to think or how to react. He hadn't counted on this turn of events in his plan to kill Eric Fox. Doing so would be at the expense of a woman whom Dante had gotten to know very intimately and had admittedly begun to develop feelings for as a result of their hot and heavy affair.

"Hi, to both of you." The words managed to come out.

"Hi," Beverly said in a low voice, her eyes wide and unblinking, as though he had stabbed her in the back.

"Nice to meet you," Tenesia said in a decidedly more upbeat tone.

Dante finally broke his gaze on Beverly to look at her friend. Though Beverly was better looking, Tenesia was not far behind in the looks department. He liked her hairstyle and the way her legs were crossed teasingly. He wondered if she was privy to what was going on between him and Beverly.

"Do you want something to drink?" Eric asked him.

Dante noted that there was a bottle of red wine on the table that everyone was drinking. "I'll have some wine."

Eric took out a goblet, half filled it, and handed it to Dante. "Let's head down to the basement and see if you're every bit as good on my table as at the pool hall."

"All right." Dante eyed Beverly. "Will the ladies be joining us?"

"I don't think so," Beverly said. "Tenesia and I were just catching up—"

"Nonsense," Eric said brusquely. "I think you should both come down for a while. You can bring me some luck and maybe Tenesia can do the same for Dante."

"I don't know about that," Tenesia said coyly. "But I think it would be fun to watch you play a game, if it's all right with you, Beverly. I can't stay very long, though."

Beverly wrinkled her nose. "Guess I'm outnumbered. Fine."

Eric grinned. "Then that settles it." He patted Dante on the shoulder. "Let's go rack 'em up."

Dante peered at Beverly, sensing she wanted an explanation from him while knowing he couldn't tell her what she wanted to hear any more than she could explain to him why the hell she was staying with the likes of a dangerous man such as Eric Fox.

***

Eric was glad to have a home audience for what he hoped would be some competitive games of pool with him coming out on top more often than not. He stood on one side of the pool table while Dante lined up a shot. It allowed Eric to view Beverly and Tenesia as they sat on bar stools, observing the action. Tenesia was still as beautiful as he remembered in a sophisticated way, though not quite the measure of Beverly's beauty. He'd once gone after Tenesia, as any hot-blooded man with too much to drink would. Beverly had gotten bent out of shape about it, believing they had gone all the way, but he'd managed to smooth things over by convincing her that she was the only woman he was interested in.

Now Tenesia was back and looking as sexy as ever. Though tempted, he'd leave her alone this time. With Marilyn satisfying his sexual needs and Beverly his woman, Eric wasn't going to allow his libido to get him into trouble that he might not be able to get out of. Besides, something told him that Tenesia, barely over her broken relationship, had already moved on in her mind. He saw how Tenesia looked at Dante. She was attracted to the dude.

Maybe Beverly was, too, though Eric doubted he was her type. Most writers didn't make enough money to support high-maintenance women like Beverly, who loved being pampered and spoiled, which he was only too happy to do to keep her satisfied. Besides, he would never allow her to leave him for Dante or any other man. Beverly made him whole in the ways that counted most. He didn't want to lose that, knowing how hard it was to find.

On the other hand, if Tenesia needed some action, she could try to work her magic on Dante. Eric had no idea if the man was banging someone in Los Angeles, maybe even a wife, but that didn't mean Tenesia couldn't get off with him now. He had a feeling Dante wouldn't object, just as Eric wouldn't under other circumstances.

"You've got the table" Dante got his attention.

Eric gazed at him, then at what was left on the pool table. He grinned. "Looks like you fell a bit short of your goals."

"Yeah," groaned Dante.

"I'll see if I can take advantage of that." Eric met Beverly's eyes. He could see she was absorbed in thought. Perhaps she was still pissed about the vibes between him and Tenesia and feeling a bit insecure. Who knew where her mind was these days? He suspected she was bored, having never really gotten into him playing pool, which was the reason why he never took her to the pool hall. But he wanted her present tonight, mainly to show her off to Dante. Tenesia was bonus eye candy and someone who, if she played her cards right, could get Dante into bed.

Eric ran the table successfully and racked the balls for a second game.

SIXTEEN

Beverly could hardly keep her eyes off Dante. When he walked into the house, her jaw dropped. More than once she'd thought that her sexual liaison had been a setup by Eric to catch her in the act. Now she wasn't sure what to believe as she watched him playing pool with the same confidence and poise that he displayed in taking her to bed. But she had only gone to that hotel by chance and picked up Dante on a whim. Eric couldn't have forecast that and planted Dante as a trap. Yet, what were the chances that Dante would meet Eric at a pool hall and then come to the house? He appeared to be just as flabbergasted to see her, if she read his expression correctly.

I don't want my lover and my man becoming friends, if they aren't already in cahoots. It could only lead to disaster.

Just as troubling to Beverly was the way Tenesia was checking out Dante. It was obvious that she was attracted to him. Though Beverly had gotten no indication that it worked both ways, she feared that if she was able to seduce Dante, Tenesia might be able to as well if she wanted. The thought infuriated Beverly. Dante was hers—at least so long as he was in Detroit and was not a spy for Eric. She had no intention of letting Tenesia go after another man she was involved with, if, in fact, she had gone after Eric.

But how can I stop her without admitting my involvement with Dante? Beverly wasn't sure she could trust Tenesia, whose very timing in showing up tonight was suspect. She was afraid that Tenesia could then possibly reveal her secrets to Eric and get her in even hotter water. It was killing Beverly not to be able to talk to Dante one-on-one. As it was, Eric kept him busy playing pool, and Dante hardly looked her way twice. Was this some kind of damned game to him? Or was there something more to the story?

"You really know your stuff," Tenesia remarked over her glass of wine to Dante as he calmly sank another shot and claimed a third victory over Eric, compared to one loss.

He shrugged. "Just hit a few lucky shots at the right time."

"Yeah, right. That must be why Eric doesn't know when to quit."

Dante laughed. "Speaking of which, I'd better get going."

"Don't let us stop you," Beverly thought to say, trying not to sound as upset as she felt.

"One more game," Eric cut in. He put a couple of hundred-dollar bills on the table as enticement. "If you win, it's yours."

"Keep your money," Dante said, waving it off. "I like it when the games are just played for fun. I'm afraid I still have to leave."

Beverly felt warmth ripple through her when he gave her a long look before quickly turning away, lest Eric home in on the fact that they knew each other prior to tonight.

"Will you still be in town on Saturday?" Eric asked him.

Dante sipped his drink. "Yeah, I should be. Why?"

"I'm a member of the Detroit Yacht Club," Eric said. "I was thinking of taking the boat out in the afternoon on Saturday."

Dante looked at him with interest. "What type of boat do you have?"

"It's a fifty-five-foot Sea Ray Sundancer."

Dante flashed a half smile of recognition. "Nice."

"Why don't you join Beverly and me?" urged Eric.

Beverly peered at Dante. *Say no, say no.* If this wasn't some stupid game by Eric, she didn't want Dante to go along with it, pulling them both into a potentially dangerous situation.

Dante met her eyes. "I suppose I could use a few hours out on the water. Sure, why not?"

"Cool." Eric's mouth curved upward. "And you're welcome to come, too, Tenesia, if you're free."

"I am," she was quick to say. "I'd love to check out your boat." Tenesia eyed Beverly. "If that's fine with you?"

Beverly was steaming. Of course it wasn't fine with her. Not one damned bit. She didn't want Tenesia anywhere near Dante. Or even Eric, for that matter. But with the three conspiring against her and no plausible explanation she could use to voice her objections without arousing Eric's suspicions, Beverly knew she didn't have a leg to stand on.

"Of course," she answered evenly. "Why wouldn't it be?"

"Thanks," Tenesia said gratefully.

"Then it's settled," Eric declared. "We can meet here at two and head over to Belle Isle."

Dante grinned. "Sounds good to me."

Beverly sneered at him. She had never felt so edgy before, not knowing what the dynamics were of this unlikely friendship between her lover and the man she was living with. Then there was the very real possibility that her old friend, fresh off a broken romance and still as lovely as ever, might make a play for Dante, unaware that Beverly was having sex with him.

Over her dead body.

Even with that conviction, Beverly was at a complete disadvantage in dealing with the situation. First, she needed to talk to Dante alone, without Eric's intimidating presence, which might be a tall order tonight, as he seemed to be watching her every move as if he knew she had something to hide. Or someone hiding in plain view.

Tenesia had gotten a weird vibe from Beverly ever since Dante arrived. She couldn't quite put a finger on it. Was Beverly attracted to Dante? How could she not be? The man was drop-dead gorgeous. Tenesia could only imagine the rock-hard body beneath his clothing. She suspected he was a superlover who would have a woman crying out in sexual bliss all night long.

Maybe Beverly had been conjuring up the same images? She certainly seemed to be checking Dante out every time Eric wasn't looking. Could she have known Dante beforehand? From what Tenesia had gathered, Dante and Eric met at the pool hall and Dante was only in town for a few days, visiting from California. As far as she knew, Beverly had never set foot in the Golden State.

So why was Beverly giving her the cold shoulder and acting put off about her accompanying them on the yacht? She thought they had cleared the air prior to Dante's arrival, but now the tension was back.

Tenesia was done trying to figure out what went on in Beverly's head and why. She had staked her claim to Eric, and Tenesia got the message loud and clear: stay away from him. She had no problem doing that. But Dante was a different story altogether. As far as she was concerned, he was up for grabs as a stranger in town who looked like he could use a little loving from someone who could use a little loving as well from a hot male who was dripping with sex appeal.

Tenesia left at the same time as Dante. He graciously walked her to her mother's car, and they exchanged a few polite words before he got into his car. If she'd had her way, they would have driven away in the same vehicle and gone straight to his hotel and jumped into bed. But that wasn't to be. Besides, she had to show some restraint now, which wasn't easy for her. In the past, that had been her downfall with men. She didn't want to scare Dante off before he got a chance to know her. She would make her play on the boat while Beverly and Eric were otherwise occupied.

"Why on earth would you invite a man you hardly know to go out on the boat?" Beverly confronted Eric once they were alone. If this was some kind of trick to get her to confess to sleeping with Dante, she wanted to know now, whatever the consequences may be.

Eric had a drink in hand. "I don't know. It seemed like a good idea at the time. Besides, I thought you liked having more people around to socialize with."

"I do," she said evenly. "But not just anyone."

"I don't see what the big deal is," he said, eyeing her. "Dante seems like a nice guy. He also brought out my competitive juices. So maybe I want to show off my boat to him, knowing I can't lose there."

"So this is a masculinity thing?" She stared at him, trying to read any sign in his features that indicated he was on to her and Dante.

"Yeah, I suppose." Eric tasted the drink. "I also thought it might help Tenesia feel better if they were paired up."

Beverly's nostrils flared. "Oh, for heaven's sake, Eric," she whined, "Tenesia doesn't need anyone's help to get laid."

He chuckled. "You sure about that? Looks like her transcontinental adventure blew up in her face. Seemed to me like Dante is her type. And I got the feeling she agreed with me."

Damn you. The last thing I want to hear is that Tenesia's after Dante. "Any man is her type," argued Beverly. "Including you."

Eric's brows knitted into a frown. "I hope we're not going to rehash that crap again. I told you nothing happened between us."

"I believe you," she said, deciding it was best to tone down her indignation. "All I'm saying is that Tenesia is a big girl and can find her own men. She's also on the rebound and shouldn't be pushed toward someone." *Especially not Dante.*

"Okay, okay, I get it. You don't want me playing matchmaker with your friend and my pool buddy. But what's done is done. It's no big deal. The outing has already been set up, unless you want to call Tenesia and tell her not to come."

Beverly felt the intensity of Eric's gaze, as though daring her to bite the bait, which might then make him question her motives. Or did he already know about her and Dante and was just waiting for her to slip up or admit it?

"She can come," Beverly said, relenting. "Whatever happens between her and Dante, if anything, is none of my business." *It's totally my business, but I can't let him see that and possibly fall into a trap, if that's what this is.*

"I'm happy to hear you say that." Eric moved up to her as they stood in the living room and ran a hand down her cheek. "Otherwise, I might think you were attracted to the dude."

She swallowed thickly but kept her cool. "Dante's a nice-looking man," she admitted. "But I'm with you."

"Yeah, you are," he said firmly. "And I appreciate that, even if I don't always show it."

"You show it enough," Beverly offered, thinking of the fairly lush life she had with him, minus the sexual sparks. She also had to admit that she didn't love him, further weakening their relationship.

Eric grinned thinly. "Glad you feel that way. I like you too much to let someone else come along and steal you away from me."

"I'm not looking for anyone else," she said levelly, unnerved by his tone and forced expression. *Does he know about me and Dante, and this is his way of torturing me?*

"Good to know," he said stiffly. "Neither am I."

He kissed her on the mouth, and Beverly tasted the alcohol, which was a big turnoff. Yet, she allowed the kiss to continue, fearful that to do otherwise might be playing right into his hands admitting that something was going on between her and Dante. Beverly had to ask herself just how much of what she and Dante had was real and how much was little more than an illusion with some other objective in mind. She wasn't sure she wanted to know the answer.

SEVENTEEN

It had begun to rain when Dante got back to the hotel. He shook off the wetness, more consumed with the unexpected situation he walked into at Eric Fox's house. Never in a million years did he imagine that Beverly was involved with one of the men Dante intended to kill. How could he have not put two and two together that the older lover she snuck out on at every opportunity was none other than Eric the hitman? But how the hell could he have figured that out, given the scant information Beverly shared about her other life?

Did she know what Eric did for a living? If so, did she give a damn that people like his brother were dead now as a result of Eric's actions on behalf of Leon Quincy?

Dante went to his room and grabbed a beer before sitting on the chair. He thought about the wide-eyed, stunned look on Beverly's face when he showed up to play pool with Eric. What was she thinking? That he was somehow working for Eric and decided to take a dip in the honey before earning his pay by exposing her? He would have been happy to tell her that it couldn't have been further from the truth, even if he couldn't tell Beverly exactly what his real intentions were. Certainly not before he finished off Eric and his boss.

Dante downed a swig of beer. He saw the jealousy in Beverly's eyes every time Tenesia flirted openly with him through words, gestures, and body language. It was the same way he felt at the thought of Eric putting his hands on her. The same hands were stained with the blood of Russell and others. Only now was Dante beginning to understand just how much of a hold Beverly had on him, tapping into his libido like crazy, as well as messing with his head. He'd even imagined taking her on that pool table, with her long legs wrapped around his back and her warm breath tickling his face while he was on top of her, deep inside her body, lustfully making love.

But that was tempered by his beef with Eric and the fact that she was his woman. Meaning, she, too, became Dante's enemy as long as she was living with the man who pulled the trigger and snuffed out his brother's life. That didn't stop him from wanting her in the worst way, even with the sudden new twists that confronted them in their clandestine affair. Including Tenesia, who Beverly clearly saw as a competitor for his attention.

The knock on the door gave Dante a start. He took another gulp from the bottle and set it on the table; then he strolled to the door, his mind still occupied with conflicting thoughts. Opening it, he saw Beverly standing there, dripping wet and looking sexy as hell, in spite of the irritation clouding her face.

"Just *who* the hell are you?" Beverly demanded, storming her way past Dante into the room. She wiped wet hair from her face, not particularly caring that she wasn't at her best.

He closed the door, facing her. "You know who I am," he said calmly.

"I know nothing. You say your name is Dante from Los Angeles, in town to do a story. Is any of that true?"

"Yes, every word," Dante maintained.

She rolled her eyes. "And I'm supposed to believe that you just *happened* to show up at the pool hall where Eric was and wormed your way over to his house?"

"Yeah, that's pretty much how it happened. Only I didn't worm my way over there. He invited me, and I accepted."

"Are you in cahoots with Eric?" she asked.

"Cahoots?" His brow furrowed. "Not a chance. I don't have any type of secret alliance with him."

She sighed. "Have you known all along that the man I was living with was Eric Fox?"

"How could I have known?"

"You tell me," she insisted suspiciously.

"I would if I could," he said. "You came on to me, remember? I've been following your lead. I had no idea that the man who challenged me to a game of pool was the same man you were with. You weren't exactly forthcoming about that part of your life, and I didn't ask for anything more than you were willing to divulge."

Beverly was still taken aback and wondering if he was being straight with her. Or was he Eric's puppet who had caught her in a trap? It occurred to her that Dante could be a con artist who had followed her the first time they had sex and put two and two together, with some scheme to extract money from her to keep him from telling Eric about them. But he had never asked her for anything that she wasn't willing to give him.

So why did she still feel something wasn't right here? Or had being shaken up by everything that happened tonight, including Tenesia's sudden appearance, affected her judgment?

"Why did you take Eric up on his offer to go out on the boat Saturday?" Beverly wanted to know. "Or is this whole thing just some big joke to you to play around with other people's lives?"

"It's not a joke." Dante stepped up to Beverly and put his hands on her shoulders. "I accepted the offer to go on the boat because I wanted to spend more time with you. I couldn't bear the thought of him touching you, kissing you, being inside you. If being on the boat diverted his attention from you, it would be worth every minute."

Beverly felt heat creep between her legs. "What about Tenesia?"

He blinked. "What about her?"

"I could tell she was into you." As if he hadn't noticed, and he was probably turned on by it.

"I wasn't into her," he claimed. "Only you."

She wanted to believe that with all her heart. Not to mention her body, which was aching to be touched, teased, tasted, and stroked by him.

"Prove it," she challenged him.

Dante tilted his head and gave her a searing kiss that left Beverly light on her feet. He pulled back and stared ravenously into her eyes. "You need more proof?"

"I don't think so," she murmured. As far she was concerned, this was all the proof she needed to give herself to him this night, undaunted by the risky nature of coming to Dante when she did, not knowing if it would get back to Eric.

She grabbed Dante's shirt and this time took the initiative by smashing her mouth hard into his and slipping her tongue inside and practically down his throat, so badly did she want him.

"Take me to bed," she said lustfully into his mouth.

"No person on earth could stop me from doing just that," he told her fiercely.

Beverly took those words to heart, and Dante scooped her in his arms even as their mouths went back on the attack.

Dante helped Beverly remove her wet clothes before stripping naked himself and slipping on a condom, eager to get inside her. But he resisted this urge until doing some foreplay to get her ready for him. He began kissing and massaging her breasts and nipples, feeling her trembling at his touch. He brought kisses down her stomach, crossing the thin patch of hair between her legs, before arriving at her most sensitive place.

He inhaled her scent, driving him mad with desire, and licked her clitoris relentlessly until she came noisily, holding his head prisoner and quivering while experiencing the sexual high. Her body was still trembling when she let him up and he moved up the length of her body.

"I need you inside me to finish the job," she said longingly, spreading her legs wide to receive him.

"I need it even more," he declared, his nipples tingling with anticipation. Dante bent his knees slightly for leverage and guided himself quickly into the wetness of Beverly's vagina. She brought her legs up and clutched his buttocks. He sucked in a deep breath and began to make love to her slowly, knowing that the urge was too great to continue at this pace.

After a couple of minutes of withholding his needs, Dante lost that control and went at it with a greater sense of urgency. His thrusts became more fluid, powerful, enhanced by Beverly's cries while in the throes of satisfaction. She sucked on his mouth greedily, ran her hands across his head, and their bodies molded into one as Dante ejaculated deep inside Beverly. The bed shook while the moment seized them, and they relished the pleasure of the intensity of simultaneous orgasms.

Dante fought to catch his breath and control his heart rate once they climaxed, and he rolled off Beverly and onto his back. Their skin was touching and still hot from their passion. He gazed at Beverly and felt she never looked more beautiful than after sex. He wished that no one else was in the picture so they could do what they just finished whenever it suited their fancy. But that wasn't the case. She was involved with a man who didn't deserve to live. Even if it hurt her in the process.

"What are you thinking?" Beverly asked him in a murmur, kissing his arm.

"If you really want to know, I was wondering how you ever managed to get away from Eric tonight without arousing his suspicions." Dante had gotten a good sense from the man that he was the jealous type and had her on a short leash. If he only knew.

"He left the house on business," she explained.

He applauded her courage, considering the type of man she was living with. How much did she know about his dark life?

"What type of business does he do at night?" Dante was curious about her take on this.

"Didn't say. He doesn't talk to me much about what he does. I only know that he's a stock investor and financial planner."

And a cold-blooded killer. Dante imagined that the bastard used his blood money to invest in legitimate things. It didn't change the facts about the type of monster he really was.

"You still took a big risk coming here," Dante said.

"I decided I needed to see you," Beverly told him boldly.

"I'm glad you did," Dante admitted, stroking her hair.

"How could I not?"

"We would've talked things through sooner or later."

She moved her wet hair to one side. "Is that what you call what we just did—talking?"

He chuckled. "More than one way to talk."

"And I think we've probably discovered all of them," she said sexily.

"Perhaps," he suggested. "Or it could be there's a lot more to discover."

"Hope so."

Dante leaned over and kissed her hotly, feeling his penis harden again. More than that, this unlikely turn of events in discovering that the woman he'd been sleeping with belonged to Eric Fox gave Dante a new weapon to get back at his brother's killer. He'd take something precious from Eric the way Eric took away Russell. And after the bastard had gotten what he deserved, he would send him straight to hell.

Beverly wasn't sure what she would say if Eric was home when she returned. Would he somehow know she'd been with Dante? Maybe he would even smell their sex on her. How would he react to her betrayal? Did she even care at this point?

I can't help being turned on by Dante in ways I've never been turned on by a man before. If that means I lose Eric and the benefits of living with him, I'll just have to deal with it.

She didn't consider that to be the worst-case scenario. Not like how she would feel if it were Dante who walked out of her life forever.

When Beverly arrived at Eric's house, she noted that his car wasn't in the driveway. She breathed a sigh of relief, as she wasn't quite up to having to deal with the issues of their relationship that were becoming more thought provoking with each passing day. At the same time, Beverly wondered what type of business Eric was up to this night. Might he have followed Tenesia home and picked right up where Beverly had once believed they had left off? Or could he be seeing someone else, a relationship she wasn't privy to?

I'm being overly paranoid again. It wasn't all that unusual for Eric to meet with some clients at night, but it didn't mean there was something sexual going on. She should be grateful that he wasn't home yet. Otherwise it was she who would have some major explaining to do.

Beverly went inside, ignoring the rain, which was still coming down. She removed her wet clothes for a second time in the last two hours and threw them in the washer, adding some other clothes and washing them in case Eric decided to snoop. Then she took a quick shower and slipped into a nightgown for bed.

She had nearly fallen asleep when Eric got home. Feeling exhausted, she hoped he wasn't in a rare mood these days for sex. Dante had satisfied her more than she could have asked for this night, as he did every time they were together. She pretended to be asleep as Eric moved quietly around the bedroom. She could hear him undressing.

Finally, he slipped into bed beside her. Beverly felt his body move up to hers as she faced away from him. Eric draped an arm across her but said nothing.

Shortly, she heard him snoring. She lay awake a little longer, thinking about how much she wished it were Dante sharing her bed and keeping her up and in no mood to sleep as their passions erupted once again and had them all over each other with utter abandon.

EIGHTEEN

The following afternoon, Leon sat in the back of his limousine alongside Spencer while his driver took them to Seven Mile Road and the store now known as Kline's Shop. It was time to pay the piper, and he hoped Paul Kline was ready to do business. Aside from that, Leon had some other issues to deal with. Someone was stealing his drug shipments, costing him and his colleagues a bundle. He strongly suspected it was Clay Randolph, a punk who used to work for him and who had decided he was better off doing his own thing. Leon had warned him not to do it in his backyard. Apparently he hadn't gotten the message. *I'll see to it that he does, and it will also serve as notice to others who are thinking about messing with me.*

"You think he'll play ball?" Spencer asked, scratching his head.

Leon sneered. "He'd better. Or else he might end up with more in common with his predecessor at the store than he could ever dream of."

"Yeah." Spencer laughed.

In minutes, the driver pulled up outside the store. Leon considered the driver one of his most loyal employees. At forty, Henry Chamberlain had been part of his posse since day one. He'd grown up in the area, and he knew it backward and forward and was always ready to go on a moment's notice. He also knew how to keep his mouth shut and ignore any sensitive information he overheard.

"Keep the car running, Henry," Leon ordered. "We shouldn't be too long."

"No problem, Leon," he replied.

Leon got out on Spencer's side and looked around routinely, making sure nothing seemed out of order. Paul Kline had checked out as legit, so there should be no problems to deal with later.

There were a few customers inside the store. Leon had Spencer take a walk so as not to attract unwanted attention while he waited patiently for the place to clear. When it did, he walked up to the counter, where Paul stood, looking uncomfortable. Leon wondered if he still had a gun beneath that counter and knew how to use it.

Spencer joined Leon as he eyed the storekeeper. "Remember me?" Leon asked.

"Yeah, I remember you."

"Then you know why I'm here?"

Paul frowned. "Yeah, I know."

Leon maintained an even façade. "You have twenty-five hundred for this month?"

Paul paused. "I want to be clear. This protection money will buy me what?"

Leon held his hard gaze. Why was he asking? Maybe just to try to justify it to himself? Whatever worked.

"It buys you peace of mind," he responded. "You get to operate your business without anyone doing anything to harm it—or you."

"And you can really guarantee that?" Paul asked skeptically.

Leon grinned, glancing at Spencer, who remained steel faced. "Yeah, I can guarantee it. So long as you pay up every month on time—the fifteenth—everything's cool."

Paul wrinkled his nose thoughtfully. "All right, you win." He opened the cash register and took out several hundred dollars, sliding it across the counter.

Leon blinked. "Hope this ain't all you got."

"It's not." Paul gave him a dour look. "I don't keep that much here. Wait just a minute."

Leon sucked in an impatient breath, mindful of what would happen if the dude tried to screw him over. He watched Paul return from the back room, a thick wad of bills in his hand.

"There—that's the rest of it," he said.

Leon grabbed the money, confident it would add up as he stuffed it in his jacket. He had corralled another sucker into paying up and fattening his pockets and those of his associates. In a couple of months he would up the protection fee to double what it was now. The dude would have to take it out of his own profit margin. Such was the price of doing business in a neighborhood Leon saw as belonging to him.

"We're cool, Paul," he told the shopkeeper. "This way, I can keep the bad guys away and you can keep running your business smoothly."

"If you say so," Paul muttered.

Leon grinned. "See you later."

"Yeah, later," Spencer added.

Back inside the limo, after taking a moment to savor his latest triumph, Leon had Henry drive a few blocks until they came upon Officer Roger Menendez. He was walking the beat, doing his regular rounds as part of the city's efforts to keep businesses safe. Leon watched the dark-skinned, chunky Latino seemingly sleepwalking before he noticed the limo.

Leon opened the window as the officer approached.

Menendez stuck his face in the opening. "Leon, what's up?"

"Got a little something for you," Leon told him and slipped him an envelope with cash.

Menendez took it and looked in both directions. After seeing nothing out of the ordinary, he riffled through the bills and put the envelope in his pocket. "I take it Paul Kline is on board?"

"Yeah, he's down with it."

"Smart man," Menendez smirked.

"I can be pretty persuasive," Leon acknowledged. "Ain't that right, Spencer?"

Spencer grinned. "Yeah, most definitely."

Menendez chuckled. "I'd better get back to the grind. Be seeing you around."

Count on it. Leon nodded, closing the window. He liked having some corrupt cops on his payroll. They came in handy in more ways than one, while having every bit as much to lose as he. But they weren't half as clever, which kept him in the driver's seat, so to speak.

Leon had Henry take him home, where he had some other business to attend to.

"Did we get all that?" Ben Taylor asked through his earpiece after Leon Quincy and his muscle left the store.

"We recorded the whole transaction," his partner and lover, Lynn Fry, said proudly. "Quincy just made you the official victim of a shakedown. Little room for him to wiggle out of that."

"Good." Ben imagined her wiggling beneath him in bed while he was inside her body. "The dude's going down but not yet. We want to have him dig a deeper hole for himself, so that when, and if, he ever sees daylight again, he'll be too old to know when the sun is up."

"The hole just got a little deeper," Lynn said. "Quincy met with Officer Roger Menendez, paying him off."

Ben was glad to hear that to help build the case against Quincy. "The man doesn't waste any time making sure his cronies' hands are stained with corruption."

"Seems like Quincy senses that big brother may be watching and is looking for some leverage, just in case it all falls apart."

"He certainly won't find it with the feds," Ben made clear. He conceded that Quincy's testimony could be vital in getting the stiffest sentences they could for crooked cops. But they were even more interested in having the cops turn on Quincy to help bring down his entire operation.

"My sentiments exactly," Lynn voiced into his ear.

"We'll let Quincy tighten the noose around his neck a bit more before we move in for the kill."

"From the looks of it, it won't take him long to hang himself."

Ben agreed. "Got to go. Later." In this instance, he meant it literally as they had taken the undercover make-believe spouse idea to a whole new level. The department would likely frown upon it, but things like this happened when attractive people were paired together and began to develop sexual feelings for each other. He didn't know if there was any future for them, but was definitely willing to continue to enjoy the present.

As for being a temporary storekeeper, he had gained a whole new appreciation for what they had to go through. Especially when thugs like Leon Quincy tried to strong-arm them, often succeeding. Well, his time for bullying people was running short.

Ben heard someone come in the store. He recognized the tall, fit, bald man from before.

Dante felt a chill as he entered the store his brother had owned. He wasn't sure what had driven him back here. Perhaps it was the one place in Detroit where he felt connected to Russell. After all, this had been his pride and joy and what Russell believed would give him the means to have a comfortable retirement. How could he have ever imagined that it would be cut short?

"You find everything you need?" the male voice asked.

Dante looked up from the aisle where he had distractedly ended up. He recognized the man as the new owner. "Yes, thanks." He grabbed a box of crackers for effect.

"You were in the other day, weren't you?"

Dante wondered why he was asking. "I might have been."

"You said you knew the previous owner."

"Yeah, I did," Dante said.

"I'm Paul Kline." He stuck out his hand.

"Dante." Meeting his eyes, Dante shook the man's hand, finding he had a firm grip.

"So did the last owner of the store, Russell Sheldon, ever talk to you about people trying to force themselves into his business?"

Dante played dumb, unsure where this was going. "Not sure I follow you."

"You know, some local guys asking for protection money?"

Dante thought about nearly bumping into Quincy and his henchman the last time he was here. But why would Kline ask him about it?

"Maybe," he said tentatively. "Why? Is that what they're doing to you?"

Paul ran a hand across his chin. "Yeah, seems like that's part of the deal if you want to have any success operating a business around here."

Dante regarded him. "So you're paying up?"

"Don't really see where I have much choice."

"You could go to the police," Dante suggested, though he knew full well that they were not entirely dependable. Certainly not in Russell's case.

"I don't get along too well with cops," Paul said. "And I'm not sure I could count on their help."

"Probably not." Dante thought about Russell's stubborn nature and refusal to buckle under even when his life was on the line. He hoped Paul took a different course, because he hated to see Leon Quincy enforce his will on someone else. Even so, it wouldn't be for long, though.

"You think Russell Sheldon got caught up in a similar circumstance and ended up being killed for it?" Paul asked.

Dante felt the man was probably on the up and up, but he was a little concerned that he was asking too many questions to the wrong person. Was he an undercover cop or FBI? Or had he been watching too many TV crime dramas?

Does he know I'm Russell's brother, in town to avenge his death? Dante didn't see how that was possible, as he'd told no one of his plans, including the private investigator he'd hired to find Russell's killer. Still, he had to tread water carefully so as not to blow his cover or intentions.

"I wish I knew why Russell was killed," Dante replied. "Since the official cause was robbery, I guess I have to go with that, even if I have my doubts."

"To tell you the truth, I have my doubts too," Paul said. "But, as a businessman, I'll do what I have to do to stay alive and keep my store running."

"That's probably a good idea." Dante left it at that. He held up the box and added a pack of chewing gum. "Well, I think this is all I need right now."

Paul smiled. "Okay, let's go ring it up."

Dante followed him, while thinking about taking care of those who murdered Russell and were apparently extorting Paul Kline.

Ben got on his cell phone after Dante left, calling his partner and lover.

"Missed hearing my voice so soon?" Lynn asked teasingly.

"You could say that." He half smiled, wishing this was strictly a personal call. "I need you to get me what we have on Russell Sheldon."

"The guy who used to own that store?"

"Yeah," Ben said, having only taken a cursory glance at what seemed at the time to be unrelated to their investigation.

"We don't have much," Lynn said. "It's a local case. He was a victim of robbery, as I recall."

"Maybe." Ben thought about Russell's friend Dante, who seemed to believe otherwise, though he was reluctant to say much, as if afraid or overly cautious. Normally, Ben wouldn't give much credence to a layperson's views on crime. But there was something about the man that made him curious enough to reconsider the official line on Russell's death. "Could be Russell Sheldon was killed because he wouldn't cooperate with Leon Quincy."

"That's a bit of a stretch, isn't it?" questioned Lynn. "I mean, the area has seen its fair share of robberies in recent times."

"True," Ben conceded. "But it's also been targeted by Quincy for strong-arming business owners and threatening them with serious bodily harm if they don't capitulate. Could be the two are totally unconnected. But since we already suspect Quincy of being behind the murder of an informant, he may have more blood on his hands than we thought."

"Point taken," Lynn said. "I'll see what I can dig up."

"While you're at it, see if any other local store owners have run into harm's way in the last year or so," Ben directed, more than curious. "If there's a clear pattern, we'll have another angle to pursue Quincy and his associates."

NINETEEN

Beverly could barely contain herself when she met Marilyn for lunch at a seafood restaurant in the mall. Everything that happened last night was almost a blur, except for the intensity of her lovemaking with Dante, of which every moment was still fresh on her mind and stimulating.

"Don't say I told you so," Marilyn uttered in hearing about Tenesia's return as she bit into a piece of fried shrimp. "I knew it would never last between her and the player musician she ran off to be with."

"Looks like you were right," Beverly said thoughtfully. "Apparently Tenesia's back to stay."

Marilyn rolled her eyes. "She's got some nerve showing up at Eric's house after trying to sleep with your man."

"She says it was all in my head."

"And you believe her?" Marilyn jutted her chin. "That bitch would say anything to get back on your good side now that her ass has been dumped."

"Maybe I did overreact before," Beverly suggested while forking some rice. She wanted to give Tenesia the benefit of the doubt in the absence of any hard evidence to the contrary. She also wanted to believe that Eric had kept his penis in his pants instead of going after one of her girlfriends. This was perhaps one reason she felt so comfortable with Marilyn. She wasn't Eric's type. And likely not someone Dante would go after, either. Beverly only wished she could feel as confident about Tenesia, especially where it concerned Dante. She wouldn't put it past her to try to seduce him. Not if she could help it.

"Your first instincts about her were probably correct," Marilyn said, wiping her mouth with a napkin. "My advice is to never leave her alone with Eric. Unless, of course, you no longer care whether they do the nasty, now that she's back and looking."

"I do care," Beverly told her, setting aside her own outside sexual interest. She was still with Eric and didn't want one of her friends taking him to bed. "If Eric's having trouble getting it up for me, I sure as hell don't want to see him getting a hard-on for Tenesia or any other woman."

Marilyn sipped some water, gazing at Beverly. "So what was this other thing you couldn't wait to tell me?"

Beverly sighed. "You're not going to believe this. . . ."

"Hmm . . . must really be something. Go ahead, shoot, girl."

"Eric invited someone he met at the pool hall to come over last night."

"That's nice. And . . . ?"

Beverly paused. "It was Dante."

Marilyn's mouth became a perfect O. "Wait a minute," she said. "Let me get this straight. You're telling me that the *man* you've been sleeping with on the side *knows* Eric?"

"Yes," Beverly said, still finding it hard to believe herself. Even Dante's explanation was a tough pill to swallow, except for the fact that he hadn't done anything to cast doubt on his story.

Marilyn's head fell back with laughter. "That is just *too* funny."

"Not really." It was anything but.

"I wish I had been there to see the reaction on your face when Dante showed up."

"I nearly passed out with worry, fear, embarrassment, you name it," Beverly admitted.

"And Eric was clueless about you and your pool-playing lover?"

"Apparently. He never gave any indication that he suspected anything," Beverly said. "Knock on wood."

"What about Dante?" Marilyn asked, spearing another piece of shrimp. "Could he have known about you and Eric beforehand and was playing you for some reason?"

"I don't know what reason that would be." Beverly put her fork down. "Dante seemed just as shocked to find out that I was Eric's girlfriend."

"You think?"

"Dante couldn't have known I was with Eric before I walked into that hotel bar. It was all just a coincidence that he met Eric at the pool hall and Eric decided to invite him over."

Marilyn tasted her iced tea. "Maybe so, but it's still weird."

"That's putting it mildly," Beverly said. "Even weirder was that Tenesia was still there and made it clear that she wanted Dante."

"That bitch!" Marilyn fixed her eyes on Beverly's face. "Doesn't she *ever* give it a rest?"

"She had no idea that Dante and I were involved," Beverly said, defending Tenesia. "And I wasn't exactly in a position to spring it on her. Not when Eric wouldn't let either of us out of his sight."

"So how did you handle the obviously awkward situation?"

Beverly took a breath. "I just prayed that neither one of us slipped up and said something that would give us away."

"I take it you didn't?" Marilyn asked.

"I don't think so." Beverly tasted her soup, but it was cold. "But Eric invited Dante and Tenesia to go out on the boat with us Saturday."

"What?" Marilyn's lower lip twitched. "Why them instead of me and Spencer?"

"It had nothing to do with you."

Marilyn frowned. "That doesn't answer my question."

Beverly could see that she was hurt. The reality was, Eric and Spencer weren't that close, though Eric did some consulting work for Spencer's employer, Leon Quincy. And Marilyn and Eric were not as friendly as Eric and Tenesia were. Beverly personally would have preferred that Marilyn and Spencer accompany them on the yacht. At least she wasn't sleeping with Spencer.

"Eric wants to show off his boat to Dante," Beverly said. "He's also trying to play matchmaker with Tenesia and Dante."

Marilyn's eyes grew. "Bet that really pissed you off."

"You're damned right it did." Beverly did not pull any punches. "Particularly when Tenesia was only too happy to agree."

"And Dante?"

"He's coming as well, but not for the reasons you might think."

"So tell me the reasons I'm not thinking," Marilyn pressed.

Beverly mused about their night of passion, reliving the most intense moments, of which there were many. She gazed at her friend. "Dante wanted to be there because he couldn't stand the thought of my being alone with Eric."

"You mean he's jealous of Eric?"

"Yeah, a little, I'm sure," Beverly said, lifting her glass of water. "Just as I'm sure Eric would raise hell if he knew about Dante."

"You're right about that," Marilyn concurred.

"Especially if he knew I went to be with Dante last night."

Marilyn's eyebrows lifted simultaneously. "You didn't?"

"I did." Beverly could scarcely believe it herself. "I had to see him. I needed to confront him about his friendship with Eric and to reassure myself that we were still involved. When I left, I had no doubt about that much."

"And you did this right under Eric's nose?"

Beverly nodded. "He was out himself—he said it was for business. I got back just before him, so he never knew I was gone."

"You've definitely got guts, girlfriend." Marilyn chuckled. "I really hope you know what you're doing— and *who* you're doing it with."

"I hope so too," Beverly told her. "It just feels right with Dante, you know."

"It used to feel right with Eric."

"That was before Dante entered the picture. He brings me to life sexually. Eric doesn't anymore."

Marilyn sat back. "Why don't you leave him, then, so you can have Dante full-time?"

"I want that," conceded Beverly truthfully. "I'm just not sure Dante does."

"So end things with Eric. If Dante doesn't want to be involved in a relationship, find someone else who does and offers great sex in the bargain."

"I'm thinking about that," Beverly said, pausing. "But I'd rather wait and see how things go before I abandon ship and give up Eric."

"You mean all the stuff he gives you, including a place to live?"

Beverly looked at her. "Yes, and the security of being with him." She knew it sounded like all she cared about was his money and material possessions. Maybe that was true to some extent. It was also true that she still enjoyed being with Eric, if only in a more platonic way.

"I wouldn't wait too long to make up your mind about which way you want to go," Marilyn advised. "The longer you dangle the two men like puppets, the more likely it's going to blow up in your face."

Beverly heard her words and was unnerved by them. All she wanted was to be happy, just like everyone wanted. Being in a great relationship with one guy who would take care of her had been what she thought was most important. Now she wondered if being with someone who made her heart race and caused her body to tingle all over whenever he touched her wasn't the way to go, whether he had deep pockets or not.

Dante fit the bill over and beyond money. She just needed to know how he felt about them in a relationship beyond the physical part. Or had he even thought that far ahead?

Marilyn was livid that Eric didn't invite her and Spencer to go on his boat. In fact, she had never been on his damned boat, though she'd heard about it and his belonging to the yacht club. Now he'd asked Tenesia and Beverly's lover to join them for a cruise on the Detroit River.

Take a deep breath and calm down, girl. Things won't stay the way they are right now forever.

Marilyn reminded herself that she was the one who knew how to get Eric up and keep him going, not Beverly. It was only a matter of time now before he learned of her betrayal and kicked her to the curb. *That's when I'll step in and show him the type of woman he truly wants.*

She thought about Beverly's laughable predicament. Dante and Eric as pool buddies, with Tenesia ready and willing to open her legs for Dante. It was something that Marilyn imagined Tenesia would have been willing to do for Eric, too, had she not beaten her to the punch. While Beverly was so hung up on Tenesia going after her man, she'd never considered that Marilyn would be the one to seduce him and keep him coming back for more. It pleased her knowing that Beverly had been so shortsighted, which worked wholly to her advantage, rather than Tenesia's.

Now that Tenesia was back in town and still on Beverly's radar, it was a perfect scenario for Marilyn. She would use Tenesia to further drive a wedge between Eric and Beverly, causing Beverly to act even more reckless in sleeping with her lover man, Dante. That way, Eric would see her for what she truly was: a tramp who couldn't satisfy him or be faithful to the man who put her up in a grand style Beverly didn't deserve.

Marilyn was in her car when she phoned Eric. He answered right away. "I need to see you," she said stiffly.

"I've been thinking about you too," he said seductively.

"Can you get a room at the motel?" Her voice softened. She wanted to make him feel like a man before laying into him.

"When?"

"I can be there in an hour."

"I'll see what I can do," Eric said.

Marilyn assumed that meant he would be there. She hung up and turned her thoughts to Tenesia, ready to pay her a little visit. While they were cool, there had always been some distance between them in vying for Beverly's friendship. Now that she had won the battle, thanks to some misinformation and Tenesia's own weaknesses and inability to regain Beverly's trust, Marilyn hoped to take full advantage of that for her own purposes. Namely, to have Eric all to herself.

She pulled into the driveway of the small brick house where Tenesia's mother lived. Marilyn imagined that Tenesia must have really been hard up to have to come crawling back to her momma. *Better her than me.* She put on lip gloss, then got out of the car and headed up a pebbled walkway. She rang the doorbell and collected her thoughts while waiting to see Tenesia again.

The door opened and Tenesia stood there, better looking than Marilyn remembered. For an instant, she froze. She didn't want to say the wrong thing. Or tip her hand as to her true motivation for being there.

Marilyn showed her teeth. "Hey, there, girl."

"Marilyn." Tenesia smiled. "Nice to see you."

"You too." She gave Tenesia a hug. "Beverly told me you were back in town."

"Yeah, I'm back," Tenesia said. "Come in."

Marilyn went inside and smelled food. It admittedly made her hungry again, but she refused to lose her focus. "How's your mother?" she thought to ask, hearing that she hadn't been well.

"She's sleeping right now. Her doctor tells me that her prognosis for the future is good, as long as she continues to take her meds."

"That's nice to hear."

"I was just about to make myself a waffle," Tenesia said. "Can I make you one?"

"Sure, sounds tasty." Marilyn hated that Tenesia was being so kind to her, but she wouldn't let that distract her from her mission.

They went into the kitchen, and Tenesia poured Marilyn a glass of orange juice. "What's Spencer up to?"

"Not much," Marilyn said, sitting in the breakfast nook. "Mostly working and trying to keep out of trouble." She tossed that last part in just because.

Tenesia laughed. "Yes, men and trouble often seem to go hand in hand."

Marilyn seized the moment. "Yeah, I heard things didn't work out with you and—"

"Manute," Tenesia finished. "Guess it just wasn't meant to be."

"It's better that you found out before things went any further." Marilyn tasted the orange juice.

"You're right," Tenesia agreed. "I just wish I had seen his true colors before I dragged my butt across the ocean."

"Live and learn," Marilyn said coolly, deciding this was a good time to work on her. "Look, I want you to know that I never believed any of that stuff about you and Eric."

"Oh, really?" Tenesia lifted a brow. "I was under the impression that—"

"It was the wrong impression," Marilyn interrupted. "I just didn't want to get caught in the middle between you and Beverly."

"I understand." Tenesia put a waffle on Marilyn's plate, then set down the tub of margarine and some maple syrup. "It's cool and all water under the bridge now."

Marilyn decided not to wait until Tenesia sat down before digging into her waffle. "So I hear you've set your sights on a new man. . . ."

"I have?" Tenesia batted her eyes innocently.

"Dante, Eric's pool friend."

"Oh . . . him." Tenesia chuckled. "Is that what Beverly told you?"

Who else? "Well, she did tell me there were some strong vibes between you and Dante."

"Hmm . . . I got the impression that she was put off by my attraction to Dante, though I'm not sure why." Tenesia sat down. "Are things okay between Beverly and Eric?"

Marilyn considered the question. "As far as I know, they're really happy together," she lied. "Just like me and Spencer. I'm sure you misread Beverly. I know she thinks Dante's a hottie, but she has her man, Eric. That leaves Dante up for grabs while he's in town. I say go for it, if you feel strongly enough about him, and see what happens."

"That's exactly what I plan to do," Tenesia said enthusiastically. "Eric invited us both out on his boat Saturday. And I hope to make the most out of it."

Marilyn resisted displaying her annoyance at being shut out of the party. But it just might work out in her favor at the end of the day. While Tenesia swooped in and went after Dante, Beverly would sulk and maybe do something stupid in her desperation, leaving Marilyn to pick up the pieces in Eric's life and his bed.

"I wish you luck," she told Tenesia with a persuasive smile on her face.

Eric checked into the motel and waited for Marilyn to arrive. He'd made up an excuse for not being able to go with Beverly to pick out a nice outfit for their day on the boat. She seemed to take it in stride, but he could tell she was royally pissed. Just like she'd been pissed when he'd invited Tenesia and Dante along for the ride. Beverly had gotten spoiled, monopolizing his time and spending his money. He tolerated it for the most part because she was so damned good looking and everyone knew it whenever she was on his arm.

There was still a sore spot between her and Tenesia, though. Eric hoped to rectify that by pushing Tenesia off on Dante so Beverly could feel confident that nothing was going on between him and Tenesia. The fact that Beverly saw Dante as practically some drifter stud who had no business in their lives didn't faze Eric. He understood that she was trying to look out for his best interests. But he didn't need protecting. He liked that Dante had more than held his own on the pool table and even seemed to know a little about boating. If Eric could give him Tenesia as a going-away present, why not? He assumed Dante had as much an appreciation for fine women as he did.

This brought Eric's thoughts to Marilyn. She was definitely not Beverly. Or even Tenesia, for that matter. But she had her own way of doing business. Sexual business. It made him keep coming back for more, not knowing what the next trick was up her sleeve, but accepting the challenge. Eric wondered what Spencer would think if he knew he was bedding his wife. Was he man enough to come after him, as Eric would were the shoe on the other foot?

Eric laughed to himself. Better for Spencer that he wasn't the wiser to Marilyn's infidelity. Otherwise, he might have to take Spencer out and that wouldn't set too well with Leon Quincy. But Eric couldn't worry about that. He did work for Leon, but he wasn't his servant. He looked out for number one first and foremost.

At the moment, that meant getting some action from Marilyn, who clearly needed him just as much this afternoon, and he intended to deliver.

TWENTY

Beverly sometimes wondered why she even bothered to ask Eric to accompany her anywhere but the bedroom. And that wasn't happening too much now since she'd turned her attention to Dante in that department. Maybe it was because she was still trying to see if there was anything left for them. Or if it had turned into a lost cause.

Things had seemed so simple before Dante had turned her life upside down. Now she could rarely get him out of her head. The great sex had awakened her to new possibilities with a man even beyond multiple orgasms and moaning. But she still needed Dante to be on board before she made some major changes in her life. Were they on the same page there? Would Eric cause trouble for both of them if she bolted?

Beverly pushed those thoughts aside as she looked at the women's apparel in the fashionable boutique. If Eric insisted that she had to go boating with her lover and a woman who Beverly believed might have her eye on him, she at least wanted to dress the part, believing Tenesia surely would. She picked out several nice outfits, intending to narrow it down to one. But she wasn't sure she could. Eric had given her carte blanche to buy what she wanted, so Beverly justified her spending spree on that basis since they were still living together—even if it was Dante's eyes that she wished to captivate.

She showed some restraint and settled on two out-fits, though she still couldn't decide which one she would wear on Saturday.

Beverly took out her cell phone and called Dante, hoping he was available. "Hey," she said when she heard his suave voice.

"Hey, back."

"What are you doing?" she asked, picturing him with Tenesia.

"Thinking about what we were doing last night," he said seductively.

"Hmm . . ." Beverly allowed her mind to wander to that steamy hour or so. "Good thing to think about."

"Are you ready for more phone sex?"

She smiled dreamily. "Not exactly. I called so you could help me pick out something to wear on the boat that will keep your eyes glued to me." *And not on Tenesia.*

"My eyes will be on you no matter what you wear," Dante told her.

"Oh, really?" She was happy he felt that way.

"I'm sure you'll look great in anything you wear, just as you do when you aren't wearing anything."

"That's nice of you to say—and naughty too," she added, feeling a slight tingling sensation between her legs.

"I'll try to keep my naughtiness in check," he said with a laugh. "Tell me about your outfits."

Beverly described a rose-colored three-quarter sleeve, boatneck top and straight-leg, ankle-zip jeans, and then a purple puffed-sleeve, twist-neck knit top, and ebony, wide-leg Capris. With both outfits she planned to wear her new slingback flats.

"I'd go with the twist-neck top and ankle-zip jeans," Dante told her. "Why not mix it up a bit?"

"Consider it done." Beverly liked that he was willing to show some initiative and creativity. Something that was nonexistent in Eric when it came to what she wore.

"I can't wait to see you again."

"Same here," she sighed and thought about wanting to keep things hot and heavy between them well beyond his return to L.A. But now was not the time to talk about it. Especially when this relationship currently seemed to be in the here and now category, though she hoped to change that. "So, if a strong gust of wind sent me overboard, would you be able to jump in the water to save me?"

A chuckle came out of Dante's throat. "Are you asking me if I can swim?"

"Can you . . . ?"

"That's pretty much a prerequisite if you live in California," he answered. "I was on the swim team way back in high school. So, yes, if you find yourself taking an unexpected dip and need my assistance, I won't let you drown."

"Good to know." Beverly smiled, taking solace in those words, picturing him in some Speedo swim briefs. As it were, she could swim but would much rather have Dante come to her rescue. She hung up and purchased her outfits.

Dante walked through the hotel lobby toward a restaurant for a bite to eat. He felt upbeat after talking to Beverly, in spite of the negative part of her association with Eric Fox. Dante wished she hadn't been caught up in his beef with the man who murdered his brother. It was much better when he knew she was staying with a faceless, nameless man whom he could detach himself from and from what was going on between them. Now he had to deal with the fact that his deception as to his true motives for being in town had become personal on a romantic level. Beverly was bound to be affected one way or another before this was through, but he saw no other way around it short of abandoning his mission. And he didn't see that happening, not while Eric Fox and Leon Quincy were still able to walk free after what they did.

At a table, Dante studied the menu, though his mind remained on Beverly. He looked forward to seeing her on the boat Saturday with the new outfit, having no doubt that it would go well with her sexy body. The fact that Eric would likely be hanging all over her was irritating as hell, to say the least. He wondered what had prompted Beverly to be attracted to such a man. Surely she must have gotten some indication of the asshole he truly was.

Not that Eric would necessarily go out of his way to show that side of his true nature if he didn't have to. The man was clearly a smooth operator and had used this to his advantage to entice Beverly into being with him. But that façade could only last so long before his true colors started to show.

Dante wasn't sure he could wait that long before enlightening her. He had not come to town looking for romance or the likes of one smoking-hot sexy lady like Beverly. But it was what it was, and he had to deal with it and any ramifications that came with the territory.

He ordered his meal.

Marilyn swallowed the length of Eric's stiff penis, resisting the urge to gag when it went to the base of her throat. She was willing to put up with that to get him off. She moved up and down him, watching his eyes shut tightly as he enjoyed the oral copulation. When she felt he had reached the point of no return, she focused her stimulation on his shaft, licking and kissing until he came mightily. His body trembled during the orgasm, and Eric held on to her head, guiding her while he achieved the ultimate gratification.

Satisfied that she had given him just what he wanted, Marilyn got off her knees and wiped her face. "Did you enjoy that?" she asked as if having the slightest doubt.

Eric grinned while taking a deep breath. "You *know* I did."

"There's always more where that came from."

"Is that a promise?" He put his flaccid penis back inside his pants.

"Yeah, it's a promise." As long as she got what she wanted. "I'm sure you like it better being inside me." It was certainly much better for her.

"Whichever way we can get it going, I'm down with it," he declared.

"I'll bet." She looked him in the eye. "So how come *I* wasn't invited out on your boat?" *Better be a damn good explanation.*

Eric kept a straight face. "Been talking to Beverly, have you?"

"Did you think I wouldn't?" Her lashes fluttered. "I talked to Tenesia too."

He pursed his lips. "I invited Tenesia and this dude named Dante I met as a spur-of-the-moment type thing."

She narrowed her eyes. "So I'm good enough to suck your penis, but not to go for a boat ride?"

"It's not that," he claimed. "I thought you didn't like the water?"

Marilyn wished he hadn't remembered she'd said that, under the circumstances. "I don't," she admitted.

"But being on the boat isn't the same thing as being in the water."

"So you can go the next time," he offered.

"Yeah, so you say," she pouted.

"It's no big deal."

"It is to me," Marilyn persisted. "How do you think it makes me feel to hear that Tenesia shows up in town and you're giving her the damned royal treatment, even though Beverly hates her guts because she thinks Tenesia was fooling around with you?"

Eric held her cheeks. "Who cares what she thinks. We both know the truth."

Marilyn looked at him knowingly. "Which is?"

"That it's *you* who keeps me happy."

"You sure about that?" Marilyn asked doubtfully.

He gave her a hard kiss on the mouth. "Yeah, I'm sure."

"So why are you still with Beverly? She doesn't know the first thing about pleasing you sexually." Marilyn hoped being so direct didn't backfire, but she needed to knock Beverly off her high horse.

Eric sighed. "Come on, let's not go there."

"Let's," she persisted.

He gazed at her. "You know how I feel about you, but Beverly and I belong together. I thought you understood that."

Marilyn bit into her lower lip. It took everything in her to keep her cool. He was so blind when it came to Beverly. *Bet you wouldn't think she was Miss Goody Two-shoes and your soul mate if you knew she was have steamy sex with your new bud Dante. Would you kill her as payback for being nothing more than a cheap whore?*

In spite of wanting to spill her guts, Marilyn stopped short of that, fearing it could backfire on her. It was better he learned the truth on his own, which seemed a given as Beverly got deeper and deeper in her involvement with Dante. She forced a smile. "Yes, I do understand, baby," she cooed. "I was only trying to say that Beverly is so lucky to be with you. I hope she doesn't throw it all away someday."

"I don't think she will," Eric said. "I won't let her."

"In that case, you can have us both and everyone's happy," Marilyn told him with a forced smile, even as she planned to ultimately have him all to herself. And Beverly could go to hell if she didn't end up with Dante, or worse. Tenesia would do just enough to keep things interesting.

Eric smiled. "Now, *that's* what I like to hear."

She puckered her lips and kissed him to reaffirm her position and give the guise that she was more than willing to take what he gave her until it was time to collect much more.

Eric left the motel feeling satisfied that Marilyn had taken care of his physical needs. There was little doubt in his mind that she enjoyed getting him off in her mouth, vagina, or with her hands, knowing that her best friend was unable to stimulate his libido these days. He wondered if Marilyn might be starting to want more than he could give her. She had to know she could never take Beverly's place in his life. Didn't she?

He could never quite figure out the jealousy women had toward one another. The lines between friendship and rivalry were often blurred. Men like him played on this, getting the most out of women like Marilyn. Eric only hoped she didn't overstep her bounds and mess things up for them, good as they were. Pressing for what she couldn't have was a surefire way to make him cut ties and go in a new direction.

But he wouldn't jump the gun yet. Things between him and Beverly were still not where he wanted them to be. Certainly not in bed. That was where Marilyn came in. So long as she did her part without making waves, everything was good. As for Beverly, he had her covered too. She liked all the beautiful things in life, and he gave them to her. Going out on the boat was just another example of the perks of being his woman.

He wasn't too concerned about the still somewhat frosty relationship between Beverly and Tenesia. Time healed all wounds between friends. If Tenesia and Dante hit it off, that would be even better. For all Eric knew, they would fall head over heels with each other, and Dante would take Tenesia back with him to Los Angeles. Or at least pave the way for that to happen down the line. Meaning Beverly could focus only on him, a relationship that Eric had no intention of seeing fall by the wayside.

Spencer sat in the living room, watching the baseball game and drinking malt liquor. He wondered where Marilyn had gone. She was always doing one thing or another when not hung up on her favorite soap operas and romance novels. He was cool with it for the most part. She was entitled to go out without him getting jealous like a schoolboy. He trusted her to be true to him and their marriage. After all, she went along with him working for Leon and didn't ask too many questions for which she might not like the answers. So why shouldn't he respect her as the woman he'd chosen to be his wife?

Still, Spencer found himself suddenly wanting more reassurance from Marilyn that they were in this for the long haul. Having a child would do that. He'd never really wanted one before now, feeling that the kid would only be subjected to the hardships that life brought. Marilyn seemed to agree, more or less, having never indicated a strong desire to be a mother. But things changed. A boy or girl might be a good thing for him and Marilyn. They could even ask Beverly to be the godmother. Since she didn't have any kids, either, he imagined this would be a good way for her to have one to dote over without all the responsibilities that went along with it. That would fall on him and Marilyn. Assuming he got her to go along with the idea.

Hearing the car drive up, Spencer peeked through the wooden blinds. It was Marilyn. He waited for her to come in, sipping his drink thoughtfully.

"Hey, baby," she said with a smile. She had a bag in her hand.

"Hey." He looked up at her. "What've you been up to?"

"Just came from the store. Before that, I was with Beverly, and then I went to see Tenesia."

"When did she get back?"

"Couple of days ago."

"She here to stay?" he asked.

"Looks like it."

Spencer recalled that Tenesia had run off with some dude to England. He knew that she and Beverly were tight and Marilyn felt a little like the third wheel. Now that Tenesia was home, he hoped that didn't interfere with things between Marilyn and Beverly, which seemed to be going well.

"I want to talk to you about something," he told Marilyn.

She regarded him tentatively. "Okay."

"Sit." He patted the cushion beside him. She plopped onto it, and he kissed her. "You taste nice."

Marilyn beamed. "Only for you, baby."

Spencer liked hearing that. It also made for a good setup for what he had to say. "I've been thinking . . ." he began.

"That's good," she said lightly.

"I want us to have a baby."

Her eyes grew wide. "*Where* did that come from?"

He put a hand on his heart. "I just think it's time for us to start a family."

Marilyn licked her lips. "We can talk about it."

"We're talking about it now," he said, sensing she was stalling. "I know this wasn't a direction we wanted to go, but now I feel different."

"But will you feel the same way tomorrow? Or next week, after the seed has been planted?"

Spencer mused, tasting his beer. Those were good questions.

"This is too serious to be wishy-washy about," warned Marilyn.

He agreed. But it was something he wanted, mainly to keep her too busy to be out and about too much instead of home taking care of her kid. He also liked the thought of having a boy he could groom to take after him. Only, his boy would do better with his life and associations.

"I really want us to have a kid," he reiterated, putting his large arm around her. "You'd be a great mom."

"You really think so?"

"Don't you?" he questioned.

She paused. "I guess. If not, I could learn to be."

He grinned. "You'd do this for me?"

"Of course," she said. "If that's what you want, we can try to get pregnant."

"I love you, babe."

"Same here," she told him, showing her teeth.

Spencer smiled broadly. He was feeling more secure about things between them and hoped it didn't take too long before Marilyn sprang the news that she was pregnant.

Marilyn was taken aback by Spencer's sudden desire to have a child. Who the hell had he been talking to? Did he have any idea what it took to raise a child in this day and age? Would he be around to do his part? Or expect her to carry the full load?

Could they even afford to have another mouth to feed when his income was barely enough to make their lives comfortable?

More importantly, Marilyn could only wonder how that might impact her relationship with Eric. If she were saddled with a child, any chance they had to be together as a couple would pretty much disappear. She couldn't allow that. Not when it was Eric she wanted and not Spencer.

But if she rejected Spencer outright, he may get suspicious that something was going on with her outside their marriage. So she would pretend to not take her birth control pills when they had sex. What he didn't know wouldn't hurt him. And by the time Spencer found out the truth, it would be too late. She would have gotten Beverly out of the way and claimed Eric as her man, leaving Spencer to lick his wounds alone.

Pretending they might as well get started now, Marilyn unbuckled Spencer's pants, pulled out his penis, and got him hard. Then she climbed atop him and slid onto his erection. She would have preferred Eric to be inside her, but since they never got to that point this afternoon, she needed to get her fix somewhere. Spencer would have to do for the time being.

TWENTY-ONE

Beverly sat beside Eric up front, while Dante sat next to Tenesia in the back of Eric's car, as they drove toward Belle Isle. It was hardly the arrangement she preferred, as Tenesia was clearly seeking to sink her claws into Dante and Beverly was helpless at this point to do anything other than listen to Tenesia openly flirt with him. Beverly tried to ignore this while fantasizing about Dante and the sexual things he did so incredibly well that elevated her libido and made her heart skip a beat.

These delicious thoughts were broken when Eric started talking about his boat and the time they spent on it, reminding Beverly that she was still his woman, whether he was the man she wanted to be with or not. She had to walk the line between keeping her lover a secret from both Eric and Tenesia and letting Dante know in no uncertain terms that she was willing to fight to hold on to what they had with each other. That included fending off Tenesia and going around Eric and his misguided attempt to pair Dante with Tenesia.

"You do any boating in L.A., Dante?" Eric asked, looking into the rearview mirror.

"I've gone out on the ocean a time or two on a friend's boat," he responded.

"Cool. Maybe Beverly and I can get out your way sometime, and you can show us a good time in Hollywood."

"Yeah, I can do that if you come out."

Beverly felt ire in her stomach at the invitation, even if she was sure Dante only meant to appease Eric. How could she stand being in Los Angeles with Eric there trying to show her off as his when her body would belong only to Dante?

"I'd love to go back to Los Angeles someday too," Tenesia chimed in. "I was there a couple of years ago, visiting a friend, and had a wonderful time."

Beverly bristled. *I'm sure you did. And you think you'd have an even better time if you were on Dante's arm. It's not going to happen.*

She sucked in a deep breath, not wanting to let jealousy get the better of her. Dante knew what she offered him in bed and doubted Tenesia could ever measure up, though she would no doubt try. Beverly would make the best of an uncomfortable situation and get it over with. Then she could turn her attention and see if things between her and Dante could move to a new level.

Tenesia was aware of Dante brushing against her more than once as they rode to the dock. It felt good to be touched by a man again, even if unintentionally, after things had turned frosty between her and Manute for some time before she'd had enough. Dante seemed to be a good catch. From what she'd gathered, he was single, as was she. Not to mention the man exuded sexuality to go with his bald good looks.

She still sensed that Beverly didn't approve of her attraction to Dante, though Marilyn had suggested otherwise. Tenesia wanted to believe that Beverly would be happy for her to move on from Manute without going after Eric. Unless, of course, Beverly had already turned her attention elsewhere. If so, obviously Eric wasn't the wiser. Tenesia wouldn't jump to conclusions about Beverly. Not the same way Beverly had about her in erroneously pointing the finger at her in sleeping with Eric.

Tenesia would focus her attention on the hot hunk beside her and see what happened. If he gave her even an inch of interest, she would take it from there and make sure he never regretted it. Especially if he turned out to be a one-woman man, which didn't seem to be the case for most men, as Manute had illustrated by breaking her heart and trust.

Tenesia softly brushed her bare knee against Dante's trousers to see what type of reaction she would get. He regarded her with a half smile that seemed genuine enough and nearly made her melt. She smiled back, only imagining how much he could set her body on fire in bed.

"It's a real beaut, ain't it?" Eric asked Dante after they stepped aboard the yacht.

Dante took a sweeping glance, admittedly impressed with what he saw. It must have cost him a pretty penny. The boat was undoubtedly financed by Eric's earnings as a murderer. The thought irked Dante. He would have preferred to be going for a boat ride with Russell . . . and Beverly as his lovely date. Instead, he had to suck it up and put on a good front for now, in spite of a strong desire to throw Eric's ass overboard when they got far enough out.

"Yeah, it's something," Dante told him.

"Let me show you around. It gets even better once you check out the control station, galley, and state-rooms," Eric bragged.

"Sounds good." Dante cast his eyes on Beverly. Wearing her sexy new outfit, she looked good enough to eat, causing a stirring in his loins. She met his gaze, and he could read the hunger to be with him in her beautiful face. It worked both ways. He only wished she had not taken up with Eric, who suddenly grabbed hold of her hand as if she were his damned property, like the boat, as they started to walk around.

Dante turned to Tenesia. She was wearing a body-hugging, blue print, split-neck tunic and white cropped cargo pants. She'd been checking him out since he got to Eric's house. It wasn't lost on him that Beverly resented this attention and might be pissed at him for seeming receptive to it. While he understood her position, considering the affair they were having, she was still involved with Eric at the same time. In Dante's mind, this meant they weren't exclusive to each other, all things considered.

Not that he was averse to having Beverly all to himself. In fact, it was pretty much all Dante thought about these days apart from avenging Russell's death. Eric and Leon still had to pay for what they had done. He couldn't take his eye off the ball in that regard, as killing them would bring instant satisfaction. But he had to play the hand he was dealt and not just go off firing shots no matter who got caught in the cross fire. Dante just wasn't certain that what he and Beverly had found in each other could withstand what would go down inevitably.

Whereas that wasn't an issue with Tenesia, who seemed more than ready and willing to have something happen between them. Dante thought about exploiting this in trying to wean himself from the powerful hold Beverly had on him, which he feared would only end up badly for both of them.

***

Eric guided the boat down the Detroit River on a gorgeous sunny day. He was glad he'd decided to take it out impromptu. It gave him and Beverly a chance to spend some romantic time together and Tenesia her opportunity to put the moves on Dante, which seemed to be going according to plan.

He gazed at Dante, who was standing beside him, looking as though he had something on his mind. Eric was curious. He liked getting to know a man from the inside out. What made Dante tick, other than writing and playing pool?

"What's going on with you, man?" Eric asked in a friendly voice.

Dante grinned, holding a bottle of beer. "Just chilling and enjoying the ride."

"Yeah, it's nice out here. Perfect day to be on a boat."

"I agree."

"So what do you think of Tenesia?" Eric asked point-blank, aware that she and Beverly were below deck.

"I think she's hot," Dante said without preface.

"Yeah, definitely hot. I think she has her eye on you."

"I'm getting that feeling too." Dante scratched his chin. "I also know she just got out of a bad relationship."

"Doesn't mean she's not ready to move on with you."

"I suppose," Dante said, sipping the beer.

"Can you handle someone stacked like that?" Eric decided he may as well be direct and see if the sparks he sensed between them were real or imaginary.

Dante chuckled. "Yeah, I think I could."

"Thought so." Eric gave a little laugh. He realized that Dante wasn't a local and it might take more than just sex appeal for him to want more from Tenesia than a quick lay. "You seeing anyone in L.A.?"

"No, not really."

"What does that mean?" Eric angled his face to look him in the eye. Either he was or he wasn't.

Dante met his eyes, unblinking. "It means I go out with women, but there's no one special in my life."

Eric grinned. "Sounds like me before I hooked up with Beverly. Was married once, but it wasn't until I met Beverly that I felt I'd found my true soul mate." The fact that he was bedding Marilyn, and others who had come before her and after his involvement began with Beverly was, inconsequential. She was the one he was with and the one who was living in his house.

"Soul mates, huh?" Dante tasted more beer. "Sounds serious."

"Yeah, very serious," Eric admitted.

"You plan to make an honest woman out of her or what?"

Eric looked out over the water thoughtfully. "If you mean marriage, I don't know about that. Putting a piece of paper in front of you can pretty much ruin whatever you had going for you." That was certainly the case when he made the mistake of marrying Gloria.

"I wouldn't know about that, since I've never been down the aisle," Dante said. "But I do know that when I find that very special woman in my life, I'll do whatever it takes to make her happy, as long as I'm happy too."

"I like the way you think." Eric chuckled. "Maybe Tenesia can be that special lady?"

"Who knows," Dante said, seemingly leaving the door wide open to such a possibility. "I'll take each day as it comes."

Eric stared at him curiously. "So what do you think of Beverly?" He'd caught the dude checking her out from time to time. It didn't really bother Eric, as most men found Beverly as captivating as he did. In fact, this was part of her allure, knowing others wanted what he had. Did that include Dante?

"I think she's gorgeous," Dante responded bluntly. "And I also think you're one lucky son of a bitch to have her to come home to every night."

A grin played on Eric's lips. "Yeah, damned lucky I am at that. She's a keeper, and I'm not about to let her go. I can tell you there would be hell to pay for the bastard who tried to take her away from me."

Dante gave him a knowing look. "I'd feel the same way if I were in your shoes." He sipped the beer. "Taking away someone who means so much to you is definitely reason for fighting back hard."

Eric nodded in agreement. He imagined that if Tenesia played her cards right, she just might become that lady Dante would fight to have and hold.

"So are we cool, then?" Tenesia asked Beverly as they sat in the master stateroom. She had wanted to talk to her alone ever since they boarded. Tenesia needed to know what Beverly's true feelings were toward her since Beverly seemed to vacillate between warm and downright frosty.

Beverly blinked. "Yes, why wouldn't we be?"

"I don't know. I thought we'd gotten past the issues with Eric, but I'm getting vibes that you still have a problem."

"You're wrong," Beverly said calmly. "I don't have any problem with you."

"Then you're okay if I go after Dante?" Tenesia surveyed her face with a steady gaze. "I've seen the way you look at him."

Beverly laughed. "You've seen only what you want to see. I'm not interested in Dante. I have Eric, remember? If I have any issue with you and Dante, it's only concern for you as my friend. I know you've barely been out of a relationship with someone you packed your bags and went off to England with. Now you're back, and the first man you meet, you're ready to hop in the sack with."

"I never said that," Tenesia voiced defensively.

"You didn't have to," Beverly countered. "I've seen how you look at the man. Besides, I know you're hurting after what Manute put you through. I just don't want to see you get hurt again by falling for another good-looking guy you barely know who will be leaving the city when his work is done."

Tenesia felt relieved to hear Beverly's thoughts and know that she was only looking out for her best interests, just like the old days, rather than looking to have her cake and eat it, too, with two gorgeous men.

"I appreciate your concern for me," she told her, "but I'm a big girl and can take care of myself."

"Like you did when you hooked up with Manute?" questioned Beverly. "Forget I said that. You're right. What you do is none of my business. If things work out with Dante, more power to you both."

"Thanks for having my back." Tenesia smiled at Beverly. In spite of the distance between them of late, she really did appreciate having Beverly as a friend again.

Beverly shrugged. "No problem. After all, I'm sure you have mine too."

"I do," she promised, even though Tenesia wasn't sure if Beverly believed her.

Dante gave Beverly a long, tongue-tingling kiss as her back pressed up against the paneled wall in the forward stateroom. "I've been wanting to do this all afternoon," he said hungrily into her mouth.

"Me too," she murmured, a mixture of adrenaline and fear that they could be caught coursing through her veins. And what would that do to her fragile friendship with Tenesia, who was hoping to make a play for Dante? Not to mention what Eric's reaction would be. She feared that he and Dante could easily come to blows on the boat, well away from shore.

Beverly unlocked their mouths. "We'd better bring up those snacks before they get suspicious."

Dante sighed. "Yeah, you're probably right. Eric's been watching you like a hawk. He's also warned me that anyone who messes around with you will have to answer to him."

She shivered at the notion but kept a brave face while staring into Dante's eyes. "You're not afraid of him, are you?"

"No," he said confidently. "The better question is, are you?"

Beverly wasn't sure how to answer that. Eric had been gentle to her for the most part, but had shown more aggressive behavior at times toward others. Given his desire to keep their relationship going, she could only imagine how he might react if she were to leave him for Dante. The thought was definitely unsettling.

"Maybe a little," she admitted.

"Do you want to leave the boat with me?" Dante asked her firmly, surprising Beverly. "I won't let him hurt you."

Beverly took solace in his words. But did he mean what he said? Was he prepared to take on a much greater role in her life? Or did he think that a short-term solution would keep her safe from Eric and somehow protect her broken heart as she longed for Dante?

"I'd like to talk to you about us, but not now." She gazed into his eyes. "I'll be fine. We'd better get back."

"All right." Dante held her gaze. "Just keep your guard up."

Beverly intended to do just that. Still, she couldn't help but wonder if Dante knew something more than he was telling her to give her reason to be concerned for her safety.

TWENTY-TWO

Tenesia purposely had a neighbor drop her off at Eric's house so that Dante could give her a lift home after the boat ride. She was happy that he was more than willing to, even if Beverly regarded her crossly for a long moment before appearing to reconcile with the fact that as a grown woman Tenesia had to do what was best for her. Or at least take a step in the right direction. She hoped that step began with Dante.

"How long have you been a writer?" Tenesia asked him as they rode to her place.

"Oh, about half my life in one form or another." Dante changed lanes. "I've been writing professionally for about a decade now."

"I've always wanted to write a novel," she confessed, "but I can't seem to get started. Maybe you could give me some tips."

"I write nonfiction, which is totally different," he pointed out. "Still, I'd be happy to give you some ideas to motivate yourself so you can plunge headfirst into your novel."

Tenesia smiled. She loved watching him talk so smoothly to go with his attractive features. "I'd like that."

"So where are we headed?" Dante asked.

This was where Tenesia felt it was time to make her move and see where it led. "How about to your hotel room?" she boldly suggested.

He turned to her. "You sure about that?"

"Yes, if you're game." *Say yes, say yes.*

Dante looked at the road and back at her. "I'm game."

She beamed. "Good. Then so am I." *Maybe I can get my love life back on track with him. If things go right, I could be packing my bags for L.A.*

At the hotel, Tenesia almost felt like Dante's lady as they walked through the lobby and everyone seemed to stare at them. Or more like admire them.

Once they were in Dante's room, any nerves she had seemed to subside for what might happen next.

"Can I get you something to drink?" Dante asked, casting his eyes toward Tenesia.

"I'll have whatever you're having."

He thought about pouring them both a glass of wine or beer, but decided neither of them was there to drink. Besides, they'd had enough alcohol on the boat to loosen any inhibitions they might have had.

Against his better judgment, Dante pulled Tenesia over to him. She was definitely nice looking, with kissable lips. She just wasn't Beverly. But where was she right now? With that asshole Eric, probably in bed with his dick in her, getting off. That thought infuriated Dante since he'd rather be the one inside Beverly. Yet when he offered her the chance to leave Eric right then and there on the boat, she declined. That told Dante that at least on some level she wasn't prepared to walk away as Eric's live-in lover. Perhaps because she knew the type of man he was and was fine with it. Except when she wanted some action on the side.

Why should I long for her when it's not convenient for her to be around, especially when another woman wants me?

Dante gave Tenesia a hard kiss. Her full mouth contoured nicely with his, and she sucked his lips as if they were candy. He broke their lip-lock and met her eyes. They were hungry and unapologetic. He kissed her again. Then he cupped her breasts through her clothing. They were high and fit well in his hands. He felt her leg pressing against his erection, as if trying to will it to burst through his twill pants.

As Dante imagined them naked and making steamy love, Beverly's face kept slipping into his mind, along with her body and scent. No matter how much he wanted that not to be the case, he realized that there was no escaping the sexual hold she had on him. Even while kissing another woman passionately.

He broke away from Tenesia's arms, which had slipped around his neck, gazing at her.

"What's wrong?" she asked. Her voice was full of desperation.

"I'm sorry, I can't do this," he told her.

"Is it me?" Her eyes widened.

"No." Dante ran a hand across his mouth.

"Are you involved with Beverly?" Tenesia asked candidly.

The question caught him off guard, though it was clear to Dante that the two ladies had some issues when it came to sexual interests. While he would like nothing better than to appease her curiosity with the truth, the chance that it might get back to Eric prematurely was a risk Dante wasn't ready to take.

"No, I'm not sleeping with Beverly," he said, keeping his tone level. "I've been seeing a woman off and on in L.A. It's been more off than on lately. Guess I wanted to put her out of my mind for at least a little while, but that wouldn't be fair to her or you."

Tenesia looked at him with a grim stare. "I guess I won't take up any more of your time, then."

Dante wished the situation had been different, but it was what it was. "I'll take you home."

"Thanks, but I'd rather take a cab."

"All right." He knew she was pissed, as was he, albeit for different reasons. In his case, Dante was pissed that he wanted Beverly all to himself, while she was apparently content to be shared by two men. The fact that one was a killer who Dante was after only complicated matters regarding how it would affect Beverly and whether he should even give a damn.

He saw Tenesia out, telling her what she probably didn't want to hear, but what Dante believed to be true. "You're an attractive lady, and you deserve to be with someone who can be devoted only to you."

Tenesia eyed him. "You know what? You're right. I do. I was hoping that someone might be you. But I've been wrong before." She touched his face. "Thanks for being straight with me."

Dante nodded. *I only wish I had been, but that wouldn't have helped either of us.* He closed the door and thought about Beverly. How far could he go with her while she was sleeping with the enemy when she wasn't with him?

Beverly was in the lobby when she spotted Tenesia moving toward the exit. Ducking behind a marble column to avoid being seen, Beverly felt anger boiling inside her. She knew Dante had offered to take Tenesia home, but hadn't expected him to bring her to his room. She was sure it was Tenesia's idea, as she had made her intentions perfectly clear and Beverly had hardly been in a position to voice her complaints too loudly.

Had Dante slept with Tenesia? If so, why was she leaving now? It seemed to Beverly that she was pissed. There was only one way to find out.

Beverly took the elevator. She had used the time Eric afforded her when he insisted he had to meet a client. Though she complained, Beverly had secretly hoped he might leave her alone so she could be with Dante. She hadn't expected to have nearly run into Tenesia and then have to explain the unexplainable.

At Dante's door, Beverly sighed and then knocked. She hoped he would be as happy to see her as he seemed to be when he'd given her a soulful kiss on the boat a couple of hours ago.

The door opened, and Dante's eyes grew at the sight of her. "Beverly."

"Yes, it's me," she said. "Were you expecting someone else—perhaps Tenesia?"

His face showed no expression. "You saw her?"

"Were you hoping I wouldn't?"

Dante half grinned, allowing her in. "It's not what you think."

Beverly rolled her eyes. "That's what they all say."

"Nothing happened between us," he said with a straight face.

"So why was she here? And why did she leave?"

Dante was silent.

"Let me guess," Beverly said. "Tenesia came on to you, and, like most men, you just couldn't resist her charms?"

"I did resist when all was said and done," he told her stiffly. "I was too busy wanting you, even though I knew you were with *him*."

"I'm not with him now," she declared. She was aroused, knowing that Tenesia had failed to seduce Dante because she wasn't her.

"I can see that." Dante studied her. "So what? You stepped away from Eric out of jealousy?"

Beverly met his eyes. "I stepped away because I couldn't bear the thought of another moment without you being inside me."

"Neither could I." He grabbed her shoulders and leaned into a deep kiss. "Guess we were both on the same wavelength."

"Yes, very much," she uttered in a breathy voice, and dove back into his mouth for more solid kissing.

Dante backed her into the bedroom as their mouths were locked, maintaining the kiss at the foot of the bed, before Beverly broke away, her need for him too strong. She unbuttoned his shirt and ran her hands across his chest and flat stomach. He began removing her clothes. She couldn't get naked fast enough, and she was overcome with desire to see him totally naked and craving his touch.

In bed, they resumed kissing, and Dante's sure hands made their way between her legs, where he began to gently stroke her. Beverly gasped from the sensations that his fingers produced. She could feel her wetness, which he brought about so masterfully. She bit his lip, trying hard not to come at that exact moment, preferring to wait until he was inside her.

"Make love to me now," she pleaded.

"We'll make love to each other," he responded huskily and put on a condom before sandwiching himself between her legs, splayed wide and ready for him.

Beverly grunted from the primeval force from when Dante entered her, filling her insides with his sex tool. She arched her back and felt her buttocks clutch while he drove into her, making her cry out with unbridled joy. She brought him deeper and deeper inside her with each thrust, locking their groins in sexual harmony as his chest flattened her breasts and her nipples grew taut.

Dante propped Beverly's legs over his shoulders while he quickened the pace of their sex. His low moan and sporadic breathing matched hers as each went after the other without pause. Their slick bodies moved lustfully this way and that in the midst of their passion and pleasure.

Beverly sucked on Dante's lips and shamelessly rubbed her clitoris against his hard body as her climax exploded, ripping through her like a lightning bolt. Even as she absorbed the nearly overwhelming sense of fulfillment, Beverly held on to Dante and braced herself for the onslaught of his potent orgasm, which shook the bed and left her feeling totally weak and satisfied.

"Whew," she said afterward with a little chuckle. "Sex with you is, well, out of this world."

Dante laughed. "So it's like alien sex, huh?"

"Not quite. We're definitely human in what we do to each other."

"Yeah, man and woman, and our all-consuming passion."

Beverly sucked in a deep breath, inhaling the redolence from their steamy sex. Her feet were tangled with Dante's and one breast was squished against his chest. She was happy to be the one in his arms instead of Tenesia. At this point, it didn't even matter if Tenesia hooked up with Eric if he was who she wanted and vice versa. Beverly only wished it could be that simple. It was obvious that Eric didn't want to see their relationship end and might not step aside without causing trouble if she asked him to.

But it was a chance she was willing to take. His money and being an older man to look after her were no longer enough to make Beverly feel whole. She needed the type of sizzle that Dante had brought into her life. Could he say the same about her?

She gazed up at this face. "Take me back to Los Angeles with you," she said straightforwardly.

His eyes fell on hers. "Seriously?"

"I think we're really good together, and I'd like to build on that, see where it goes." In her mind, Beverly was sure it could go far, but she didn't want to overstep her bounds without knowing if he felt the same way.

Dante smoothed an eyebrow. "I think I'd like that too. . . ."

She frowned. "Do I hear a *but* in there?"

He touched her knee. "What about Eric?"

"What about him?"

"Do you think you can live without the things he brings to the table?" Dante met her eyes.

"If you're talking about his house and stuff like that, the answer is yes," Beverly responded positively. "I won't lie. I've enjoyed the things he's given me, but I like even more what you've given me. It won't be a problem for me to leave this behind and start a new chapter of my life with you."

Dante took her hand and kissed it. "In that case, I say let's do it."

"Really?" Her voice was ecstatic.

"Yeah. For now, though, I think you should stay where you are until I wrap up my assignment. That way, Eric won't have time to do something stupid that I may not be able to prevent."

Beverly wanted to object, not wanting to spend another day meeting secretly. But the sensible side of her knew he was right. As long as she was still in the city, Eric could make her life hell, and even be a downright danger to her health and well-being. Besides, she didn't want to crowd Dante while he was here for work and make him have second thoughts about being together.

"How long should I keep up the charade with Eric?" she asked, trying hard to be patient, not normally her strong suit.

"Not too much longer," Dante answered evenly. "Just give me a little time to tie up some loose ends."

"I'll hold you to that." Beverly was excited at the prospect of starting a new relationship with someone who made her feel so alive. They had certainly gotten off to a blazing start.

"I'm counting on it."

Dante gave Beverly a brilliant smile and kissed her, pushing his tongue into her mouth. She received it eagerly while nibbling on his mouth and thinking about a future that could potentially give her everything that was truly important.

Dante made love to Beverly again, exhausting them both after pushing themselves to the limit while they explored every part of each other. Neither of them wanted her to leave, but they understood it was in their best interests. Dante stood by the window with a view of the city, sipping alcohol pensively. He could never have anticipated that coming to Detroit would bring him face-to-face, body to body with a beautiful woman whose seduction he'd succumbed to time and time again. Like her, he wanted to extend what they'd developed over and beyond the great sex and interesting communication. But that had to be balanced with his need to finish what he'd started. What he'd come to Detroit for.

Perhaps once Beverly knew the real reason why he'd come, she might want to run the other way and not look back. Of course, he still wasn't sure she was as innocent as he'd hoped she was where it concerned her involvement with Eric Fox. Maybe she even knew that the bastard had murdered his brother and ignored it all for the mighty dollar that he'd thrown at her to keep her tethered.

Dante wouldn't judge her prematurely, as he had definitely fallen for the lady and hoped Beverly's character was as strong as her appetite for hot sex. In the meantime, he thought it best that they keep a low profile on their affair so they wouldn't tip their hand. It would be time soon enough to let Eric know that Dante had snatched Beverly away from him and there wasn't a damned thing he could do about it.

Dante expected the man to try, though, knowing that Eric had a bigger ego than he did. That was when he would be waiting for him and see to it that Eric drew his last breath as he watched his woman having sex with someone who would turn out to be his worst enemy.

TWENTY-THREE

Eric climbed inside the limousine and sat next to Leon. Across from them was Spencer. For an instant, Eric thought about the fact that he was banging the dude's wife and Spencer didn't have a clue. Better to keep it that way for both their sakes. Eric didn't want that to come between him and Beverly, especially now that Tenesia had turned her attention toward Dante, keeping Beverly from being jealous over something unfounded.

"Glad you could make it," Leon told him.

"You called, so I came." Eric rubbed his nose. "What's up?"

Leon grinned. "That's what I like about the man, Spencer. He likes getting right down to business just like me."

Spencer cracked a half smile. "Yeah, Eric is all business."

Maybe not all business, big man. Eric suddenly got turned on as he imagined Marilyn going down on him, as she did so well. "That's why things work so smoothly with us," he told Leon. "We understand each other." At least he understood the man insofar as his penchant for doing whatever was necessary to keep his operation running smoothly, including killing people.

"So let's get right to it, then," Leon said and nodded at Spencer. He opened the briefcase beside him, removing an eight-by-ten photograph and passing it to Eric.

The man in the photograph looked familiar to Eric. He was in his early thirties and had black micro braids and a patch of hair under his lower lip.

"Name's Clay Randolph." Leon pointed a finger at the picture. "He used to work for me."

"Yeah, I remember," Eric said thoughtfully.

"Unfortunately, the dude stabbed me in the back by going after drugs that belonged to me. He showed me absolutely no respect, and now he's got to pay for it."

Eric met Leon's eyes. "You want me to take care of him?"

"Yeah," Leon said tersely. "Make sure it's a clean hit that can't come back to my doorstep and give me even more problems to deal with."

"You won't have to worry about that," Eric assured him, taking pride in his professionalism. "I'll take him out, and you'll never see Randolph again—alive."

"Good." Leon nodded at Spencer, who took an envelope from the briefcase and gave it to Eric. "As usual, it's half your payment and Randolph's address. Once the job is complete, you'll get the rest."

"Not a problem." Eric slipped the envelope in his jacket pocket. No need to count the money. He and Leon were cool. Their professional relationship necessitated a certain amount of trust both ways and had worked out well for him thus far.

"Stop the car," Leon ordered his driver after he had driven around the block and was now back where they started.

"I'll be in touch," Eric said to the one who had just hired him to kill a man. He gave Spencer a cursory nod, and Spencer nodded back.

Out of the limo, Eric walked to his car, already plotting his strategy as to how best to get his target alone. Clay Randolph would soon wish he'd never crossed

Leon, just as Russell Sheldon and others had made the mistake of doing.

Dante had followed Leon from the time he left his house with another man in the limousine to his meeting with Eric for what Dante suspected might have been plans for another targeted hit. Or could it be that Eric was bowing out of the business of murder to focus on saving his relationship with Beverly? Dante very much doubted this. Eric was too arrogant to walk away from a good thing for him in working for Leon Quincy. And since the authorities hadn't done a damned thing to break up this relationship based on killing anyone who got in Leon's way, there was no real reason for either man to discontinue what they were doing.

The only way it would happen was if someone else put a stop to it. Dante intended to be that man. Having missed the chance to off him at his house, he'd been following Leon for days now, trying to figure out his routines and shortcomings that might present another opportunity to strike. A driver took him everywhere, and Leon was often accompanied by a large man, who, Dante assumed, was his bodyguard. Leon tended to surround himself with a parade of attractive young women, who were probably sent out on the streets when not servicing him. Dante recalled that his private eye, Floyd Artest, had described Leon as a pimp, among other things.

To Dante, Leon Quincy was first and foremost a cold-blooded killer who had orchestrated the hit on Russell. And for what? A little money, which, from the looks of Leon's lavish house and extravagant lifestyle, he probably didn't really even need. It was all about power and intimidation.

Well, soon, he would see what it was like to be on the other end of the stick. Dante would find a way to get to the asshole if it was the last thing he did, while limiting the risks to his own health and well-being. But first, he wanted to deal with Eric, the triggerman, who had taken Leon's dirty money to dispose of Russell like yesterday's garbage.

Only after the two bastards had received their comeuppance could Dante seriously think about trying to work on his relationship with Beverly, one that seemed ripe with potential that could carry them a long ways.

"My source at the Detroit Police Department said that they're still standing by the robbery angle as the reason behind Russell Sheldon's death," Lynn told Ben after she hung up the phone that had interrupted their intimacy.

Ben studied her taut alabaster skin and ran a hand along her smooth arm while trying to stay focused on Lynn's news. "I was afraid they'd say that," he groaned.

"You think there's a cover-up?" Her blue eyes widened.

"Not necessarily. I think at the very least it was a less-than-thorough investigation. Or it might have been made to look like a robbery."

"Other than the fact that you're the target of a shake-down as the new owner of the store, what are you basing your theory on?" she asked pointedly.

Ben looked at her. "Isn't that enough?" He saw no reason to bring up Russell's friend Dante, who had confided in him his ideas but was probably too concerned about his safety to want to come forward with anything other than innuendos. "Call it a hunch. If we could tie Sheldon's death to Leon Quincy, it would be another nail in his coffin."

"I think we're pretty close to burying him, so to speak."

"So do I, but nothing says we can't add another feather to our collective caps if there's more to hang on him."

Lynn laughed. "You know you're cute when you use clichés to bolster your argument."

Ben grinned, admiring her shapely breasts. "You're cute even if you fail to utter a single word."

"You'd say that when you have me stark naked for your eyes to feast upon."

"Probably," Ben admitted, though he still stood by his words. "Did you come up with any other store owners in the area who were recently murdered?"

"Yes, there was one we already knew about," Lynn responded, stretching out her long legs. "An informant by the name of Kurt Braddock was shot to death just over a week ago. Turns out he owned a salon a block away from the store where you're working undercover. But since he was apparently killed for what he knew rather than what he wouldn't do, there may not be a connection, per se, to his business interests and Sheldon's death."

"Or maybe there is and no one wants to delve into it."

"Maybe we should just stick to what we've got going on now," she suggested.

He peered at her sexy body and began to get an erection again. "I think you're right."

Lynn colored. "I wasn't talking about that."

"I was," Ben said lasciviously. He kissed her lips lingeringly. "We can get back to the other stuff later."

"Yes . . . later," she murmured, pushing him down on the bed and climbing atop his hard body.

TWENTY-FOUR

"I miss you too," Beverly was telling her thirteen-year-old brother, Cody, over the phone on Sunday afternoon.

"Promise?" he asked.

"Double promise." She smiled. "So put Mom on the phone."

"Okay, I'll get her."

Beverly sat firmly on her stool in the kitchen, sipping coffee. Eric was out doing his thing, which was fine by her. The less time they spent together, the easier it would be when it was time to say good-bye. At least as far as she was concerned. But she was not convinced that Eric would simply allow them to go their separate ways without raising hell. Or worse.

Guess I'll just have to wait and see. Beverly was emboldened by the fact that Dante wanted her as much as she did him, making any short-term aggravation worthwhile.

"How are you doing, Beverly?" her mother asked routinely.

"Well . . ." Beverly took a breath. "I'm leaving Eric." She knew that would please her.

"Hallelujah," Etta voiced jubilantly. "Better late than never."

Beverly was inclined to agree, though she felt it was right on time. "You don't have to be so excited," she tossed out.

"I'm not. Relieved is more like it. He was never right for you."

He was for a time. "Not everything is meant to be forever." Beverly tried to rationalize it.

"So have you told him yet?" Etta asked.

"No." Beverly thought about Dante's desire that she wait for now for her own safety. "I plan to tell him soon, though."

"What are you waiting for, child? For Eric to convince you that you should stay with a man practically twice your age?"

"It's not that," Beverly said, sipping her coffee.

"Then what?" persisted Etta. "The longer you wait, the more difficult it will be. And I'm worried about how Eric will react to the news."

Beverly shared that feeling but couldn't allow it to keep her where she no longer wanted to be. "I'm moving to Los Angeles."

"Los Angeles? Since when?"

"Since I began seeing Dante," Beverly told her. "He wants me to move out there and build on our relationship."

"Maybe you ought to give relationships a break and see how you do on your own," her mother suggested.

"I don't do well on my own."

"That's because you haven't tried being apart from men for very long," Etta countered.

"I had a very good teacher," Beverly shot back.

"This isn't about me."

"I know." Beverly regretted bringing that up, not begrudging her mother for trying to make the best situation for herself and her kids, especially after Beverly's father left them to fend for themselves. "I just want to be happy. Right now, Dante makes me happy."

"What did you say he does for a living?" Etta asked.

"I didn't say," Beverly responded. "He's a journalist."

"Journalist, huh? And he's not secretly married with five children?"

"Not that I know of." Beverly chuckled. "Anyway, I doubt he'd want me to come to L.A. if that were the case."

"I hope this one works out," Etta surprised her by saying.

"So do I."

"I don't suppose you can come to Atlanta for a few days before you go all the way across the country?" Etta asked. "Cody misses his big sister. I miss you too."

Here we go with the guilt trip. "I'll see what I can do about that," Beverly said without making any promises.

After she'd hung up the phone, she took her cup of coffee and wandered around the house. She'd once thought it was the perfect place to live. Now she saw it as a prison that she wanted out of. Dante would make that possible, even if Eric had a problem with it. He would just have to get over it and find someone new for himself, as he had when she entered his life. She doubted they could continue to be friends, but hoped they could at least break up on good terms. That would be up to him.

Dante sat at a picnic table in the backyard of his brother's friend, Wesley Carson. Wesley had invited him over for barbecued ribs. It was a good time to chill after all the drama of dealing with Russell's death and trying to get past it. Dante wished he could have brought Beverly along as his date, but that wasn't possible while she was still living with his brother's killer. Dante had a major score to settle with Eric and intended to follow through with it in due course. But this afternoon was a happy time to spend with Wesley, his wife, Doris, and their daughter, April.

"You'll have to e-mail me some of your articles," Doris was saying to him while holding corn on the cob. "I'm very interested in the topics you've covered."

"I'd be happy to do that," promised Dante as he sipped punch from a paper cup.

"Thank you."

Dante smiled, looking at Wesley, who was standing over the pit and another slab of ribs. "Thank you both for making Russell feel right at home, just as I do."

"Believe me, it was, and is, our pleasure," Wesley told him. "Russell was a good man. So are you. He would have been happy to know that his big brother was looking in on us."

"Wish I had a big brother," April whined with barbecue sauce on her nose, mouth, and fingers.

"You may have to settle for a little brother," Doris said. "Or sister."

Dante's brow rose. "Does that mean . . . ?"

"We're working on it," she responded with enthusiasm. "These things can take time and you never know what the good Lord has in store."

"That's the truth," Dante said thoughtfully. He could only hope that Russell was at peace up there, even if his death remained unsettled down here.

Wesley sat down next to his wife. "Anything new in the investigation?"

Dante noted that April seemed to be off in her own little world. He met Wesley's gaze. "Not really," he said bleakly. "It's pretty much stalled at this point."

"That's too bad."

"Yeah." Dante picked up a rib, frowning. "It seems like too many cases get swept under the rug. I've given up trying to figure it out or seek answers, only to be stonewalled."

"I know what you mean," Wesley said.

Dante looked at him, then Doris, and realized he was turning a nice picnic into a downer. He put a wide smile on his lips. "Hey, we're supposed to be enjoying ribs and not dwelling on the negative. I'll be fine."

As if to hammer home that point, he sucked the meat off a bone and helped himself to another rib.

Leon thrust his penis inside Katrina, a twenty-one-year-old he'd turned out a month ago, after she ended up in his territory in search of crack cocaine. He was more than happy to feed her habit so long as she gave him something in return. When she wasn't putting out for him, she was making him money on street corners like his other hoes. She moaned as he moved in and out of her while playing with her obviously enhanced large breasts. He squeezed her nipples while she squeezed his erection deep inside her as she started to come.

That spurred him on to finish the job at the same time so she wouldn't be too tight for his pleasure. After sucking in a deep breath, Leon picked up the pace, spreading her legs even wider and bringing his groin closer. He shut his eyes as his orgasm took control, causing his body to shudder, along with hers. He was perspiring heavily but ignored it, while making damn sure he basked in the moment of sexual ecstasy. At the end, he leaned his face down and allowed her to suck heartily on his lips as he continued having sex with her even as his penis was losing size in a hurry.

"Was it good, baby?" Leon asked, rolling off her.

"Always, Leo," Katrina murmured, as he expected, still on her crack high. "You do it better than anyone else."

Leon grinned, inclined to agree with her, even if he suspected she would say that to any man who was on top of her and had spoon-fed her what she really needed to get off.

"Get up now and go take care of business," he ordered, never forgetting that no matter how much he enjoyed bedding his hoes, business always came first. That included having them turn tricks and sometimes sell drugs for him.

Leon smacked Katrina playfully on the ass and watched her giggle. He understood that making them think he really cared made it easier to get what he wanted from his hoes without having to resort to violence like some other dudes who pimped out women. Pity he couldn't always apply the same logic when operating other facets of his empire.

TWENTY-FIVE

Eric tracked Clay Randolph to a local park where he was conducting a drug deal under the cover of darkness. Clay, about six feet and slender, brimmed with confidence as he did his business before separating from the two men he was interacting with. Eric wanted to take him out right then and there, but thought better. Though the park was not exactly jumping with activity this night, he still chose to err on the side of caution and wait until they were alone and away from potential witnesses before completing his mission.

He thought about postponing the hit until tomorrow and going home to be with Beverly or maybe even getting some quick action with Marilyn. But then Eric saw Clay duck behind the bathrooms. He suspected the dude wanted to give himself a fix in semi-privacy before hitting the road for home or wherever junkie traitors hung out.

Eric pretended to go into the bathroom, but instead slid into the shadows and crept behind the building. He spied Clay leaning against the wall, about to inject himself, probably with heroin. Eric waited for him to put the poison in his veins and enjoy his last high before approaching him rapidly just as Clay was poised to leave.

Taking out his gun and getting an adrenaline rush, Eric had it pressed against Clay's head before he knew what was happening.

"What the—" voiced Clay, the needle falling to the ground.

"Get down on your knees!" Eric ordered.

"If this is a robbery, man," Clay told him, "take what I've got."

"I doubt you have anything I need." Eric pushed the gun's silencer into his temple. "Get down now!"

Clay complied, falling hard onto his knees. "Then what's going on?"

Eric supposed he owed him that much as a condemned man. "A former acquaintance of yours sent me your way. You remember Leon Quincy, don't you?"

Clay raised his chin. "That son of a bitch."

"I'm sure he's been called worse," Eric said wryly.

"Look, it doesn't have to be this way," Clay pleaded. "Whatever he's paying you, I'll double or triple it."

"You got that kind of cash lying around?" Eric was only mildly curious.

"Yeah, I got it," he said in a shaky voice.

Eric took a quick second to think about it. He wasn't going to double-cross Leon for some pathetic, disloyal asshole who was peeing his pants right now. "Sorry, nothing doing. You shouldn't have gotten on Leon's bad side. As a result, you got on mine. Now you've got to pay for it."

"Don't," Clay sputtered pleadingly. "Give me a chance to make it up to Leon."

"Wish I could, but in this business, there are no second chances."

Without wasting more time listening to his weak attempts to save his life, Eric pulled the trigger, silently sending a bullet into Clay Randolph's head. He slumped over onto his brain matter splattered on the dirt. Eric fired one more bullet into what was left of his face and, satisfied that Clay had breathed his last breath, put the gun away and left the scene. He made his way back into the park and blended in with others as if merely there to hang out.

After returning to his car, Eric called the one who hired him to do the job, feeling a sense of achievement and little remorse over the fate of his victim.

"It's done," he told Leon, understanding that nothing more needed to be said between them. Not until the next time his services were needed to eliminate someone who stepped out of line.

"I have to go out for a little while," Eric said unapologetically to Beverly, after making a call on his cell phone.

"But you just got home." Beverly looked at him with annoyance. Not that she couldn't get by alone. It was just that she had been by herself most of the day and was bored. If she had to pretend to be content with Eric for the time being, it might be easier if he were around a bit more.

"I know, and I'm sorry, but I have to take care of some business."

"What kind of business?" She hadn't necessarily wanted to call him out on this, but it was after eight and she thought most business deals were over by then. "If you'd rather not tell me—"

Eric's mouth curved up on one corner uneasily. "It's not what you think."

She batted her eyes at him. "And just what am I thinking?"

"That I'm slipping out to see another woman."

"Are you?" Beverly wouldn't put it past him. They hadn't exactly been burning up the sheets lately, mainly due to his inability to maintain an erection. Perhaps he had been getting his from someone else, just as she had turned to another man.

"I'm not sleeping around," Eric told her with such a straight face that Beverly was inclined to believe him. "You're the only woman I want."

"You're sure about that?" Beverly was hoping he would say just the opposite. She might be a tad pissed off about it, but overall, that would make things easier for both of them to part ways.

"Absolutely." He stroked her shoulder as she sat on a living-room chair. "I was just talking to Spencer. He wants to deliver consulting fees for work I did for Leon. I told him I'd meet him halfway. Call him if you don't believe me."

"I believe you," Beverly said, figuring he must be telling the truth. Otherwise she could easily have taken his challenge. But then if Marilyn answered and started talking to her about her affair with Dante, the onus for having something to hide would shift to Beverly.

Eric bent over and kissed her on the mouth. "I promise I won't be long."

Don't hurry back on my account. "It's fine," she said, wishing he hadn't kissed her. The only man's lips she wanted on her these days were Dante's. "I can find ways to keep busy."

He grinned lasciviously. "I'm sure you can."

Once he had left, Beverly thought about hopping into the Jacuzzi bath and stimulating herself while fantasizing about Dante. Then she had a better idea. Why not call him and see if she could drop by for a quick but powerful romp in his bed? If he was around, she couldn't imagine him objecting to the idea.

***

Spencer sat at the bar, tasting a beer. Now that he had personally verified that Clay Randolph was good and dead, Leon was satisfied and had dispensed him to pay Eric what was still owed him. Spencer wondered how Eric could kill so easily and seem to be unaffected by it. Or maybe he was but chose not to show it, figuring it was important for his reputation to keep up the façade.

Either way, Spencer supposed he could do the same thing if called upon. He knew how to use a gun and, in fact, had done target practice over the years and had become pretty accurate. If he were to progress to being an enforcer in Leon's organization, he wouldn't turn his back on it. Instead, he would take advantage of the opportunity given him. He'd never let it get personal, determined to keep that part of his life separate from working for Leon.

Spencer just wanted to do right by his wife, first and foremost. Marilyn was everything to him, and he wanted to keep her happy. Now that they were working on having their first child, he was excited at the thought of building their family and looking toward the future. He hoped that in a few years he would be able to take his family and relocate to Alabama or Mississippi, where he had relatives. He believed it would be a safer environment for Marilyn and their daughter or son, and possibly even a second or third child.

"Hey." The deep voice broke Spencer's reverie.

He looked up into Eric's face. "Hey," Spencer said, straightening his shoulders.

Eric sat beside him. "Looks like you were off in dreamland somewhere."

"Yeah, you could say that." Spencer thought again about Marilyn and her friendship with Beverly. He wondered if Eric appreciated his woman the way Spencer appreciated his. "Buy you a drink?"

"Sure, why not?"

"What'll you have?"

"I'll take a beer," Eric said.

Spencer gulped down the rest of his beer, flagged down the bartender, and ordered two more. The bartender quickly filled their mugs. Spencer paid, though he imagined Eric was bringing in more than him and was financially comfortable at this stage of his life, judging by his house and car, though neither measured up to what Leon had.

Spencer looked at Eric, who seemed pretty cool, calm, and collected, as always. He was admittedly a little intimidated by the older man, who was in better shape and kept his distance.

"You have something for me?" Eric asked with a catch to his voice.

"Oh, yeah." Spencer took the envelope of cold hard cash out of his pocket, sliding it across the bar toward Eric. "Leon wanted me to tell you he was pleased you took care of business so quickly."

Eric put the envelope away without looking inside. "I always do," he said characteristically. "Comes with the territory."

"Did Clay give you any trouble?" Spencer asked in a low voice.

"Nah." Eric put his mouth to the foam. "All he did was wet his pants and whine like a little baby. I've seen it all before."

"Yeah, guess so." Spencer sipped his drink. "You ever think about walking away?"

Eric grinned. "Sometimes," he admitted.

"So why don't you?" Spencer was curious.

"And do what? At my age, high-paying jobs don't come along every day. As long as I'm still good at what I do, I'll keep doing it."

"Makes sense."

"I could ask you the same thing," said Eric. "You're still young. Why not take your wife and start over elsewhere?"

Spencer mused about Clay Randolph leaving Leon's employ. Now he was dead. "Then maybe you'd have to come after me too," he half joked.

Eric cracked a grin. "Yeah, there's always that possibility." His mouth became a flat line. "On the other hand, Leon seems to respect you. I'm sure he wouldn't stand in the way if you wanted to try something else."

"Maybe not," allowed Spencer, though with some uncertainty. "Right now, I'm happy doing what I do. Like you."

Eric nodded. "I'll drink to that." His raised his glass, and Spencer did the same in agreement. "How's Marilyn?"

"She's good," Spencer answered thoughtfully. "We're working on having a baby."

Eric cocked a brow. "That so?"

"Yeah, it's the right time."

"Good for you." Eric drank beer. "Beverly never mentioned that to me. Not that she would."

"We're just starting to come to terms with it ourselves," Spencer said. "It was my idea, to tell you the truth. Seemed like a nice way to make our marriage stronger."

"Hope it works out for you." Eric rubbed his chin. "Well, I've got to get out of here. Beverly was already pissed that I stepped out."

"I understand." Spencer pictured Beverly being pissed. She was the needy type and likely milking Eric for all she could get as long as possible. He finished his beer and stood. "Better get home too."

Outside, Eric gave him a friendly pat on the shoulder. "See you around."

"Yeah, see you."

Spencer walked to his car. He would stop by the store and pick up some butter pecan ice cream, knowing it was Marilyn's favorite.

"I'm not sure how much longer I can keep pretending I want to be with Eric," Beverly said coarsely as she lowered herself onto Dante's erection. "Especially when I just want to be with you."

Dante groaned as she ran her fingers across his chest. "It won't be much longer," he promised. "Soon we'll be together, and he won't be able to do a damned thing about it."

"I want to believe you." Her body tingled as he played with her nipples. "I do."

"Then believe it. We're just getting started."

"I was hoping you'd say that." Beverly lowered her body and kissed his lips ravenously. "I want to taste you." She stuck her tongue in his mouth.

"Taste all you want," Dante told her, flipping their bodies over effortlessly and taking the lead in making love to Beverly.

Her buttocks clutched and her breasts heaved as Dante plunged in and out of her, going deeper with each thrust, driving Beverly crazy with desire. She brought her body up to meet Dante's firm torso while spreading her legs wide and curling her toes as the fever hit her. Beverly cried out loud when she came in waves, causing her body to shake almost uncontrollably.

She started to catch her breath and hung on for the ride when Dante unleashed his own powerful orgasm, moaning in her ear and quivering wildly as his powerful thrusts levitated Beverly. They kissed madly during the moment of impact, sucking each other's lips heartily with their heartbeats in sync.

"Now you see why I don't know if I can stand another day apart from you," Beverly told Dante with a deep sigh, still beneath him.

He held one of her buttocks and groaned. "Yeah, I know what you mean. But since I still have a little more work to do in town, and you'd be vulnerable just staying here, I think it's best to stick with the plan."

She pouted while breathing in the incredible scent of their sex. "If you say so."

"Don't take that the wrong way," he told her. "I want us to be together, but we have to be smart about this. You know as well as I do that Eric's not the type of man to just roll over and let someone else steal his woman from him. We can't risk having him try something stupid before we're in a position to leave the city quickly."

"You're right," Beverly said begrudgingly. "We'll do it your way."

"No, we're doing this *our* way."

Dante gave Beverly a deep kiss that left her lightheaded. It killed her to have to go back to Eric, but she didn't argue about it further, knowing that only made things harder and went against logic. She was glad that Dante was the sensible one about this, which was another reason why she liked him so much and was feeling more comfortable with him as her new man with each passing day.

When Beverly arrived home, she saw that Eric had beaten her back. A sliver of fear raced through her. What would she tell him when he asked where she had been? Would he be able to tell she was lying? Would her affair with Dante be exposed?

"You're back," Beverly said evenly as she entered the living room.

"Yeah, I finished my business quickly." Eric was sitting on a chair, gazing up at her. "Where were you?"

"I went over to Marilyn's for a few minutes."

Did she really see Marilyn? He needed to know if she was being straight with him or if something else was going on. Not that she'd given him any reason to believe she was fooling around. Still . . .

"I see." Eric watched her for any sign of wavering. "What's she up to these days?"

Beverly batted her eyes. "I thought Spencer might have told you."

"Told me what?"

"He wants her to get pregnant," Beverly said.

Eric relaxed his jaw. Maybe she did go to see Marilyn, after all. He'd check with her just to be sure. "Yeah, Spencer mentioned that. I take it she agrees?" He wondered what that would do to their sexual trysts. He had no problem having sex with a pregnant woman, so long as it wasn't his kid she was carrying. And it certainly wouldn't stop Marilyn from giving good head, which she did so well.

"I'm not so sure Marilyn's on board with having a baby," Beverly told him. "I think she'd rather wait awhile before going down that road."

"That wasn't the impression I got from Spencer," Eric said. "But then, it may have been more wishful thinking on his part."

"Maybe."

Eric took her hand. He liked how soft Beverly's hands were. "Are you still cool about not having children?" Or was it just him and she had merely gone along with it to please him?

She paused. "Of course. Not everyone has to have kids to be fulfilled in life."

"And are you fulfilled?" He looked her in the eye.

"Yes," Beverly said succinctly. "Why wouldn't I be?"

"Just checking to make sure," Eric told her. "As my woman, I want to give you whatever you want or need."

"Right now, I need to take a shower." She slipped her hand from his. "Then I want to get some sleep."

Eric remembered there was a time when neither of them wanted to get much sleep. He had only himself to blame for the change. He hadn't exactly been taking her to bed with lust in mind. On the other hand, he couldn't be blamed if she wasn't turning him on the way she used to. The way Marilyn did these days. He would try to change that. Eric didn't want their relationship to become sexless, but he could live with it as long as he still had beautiful, young Beverly by his side. She made him feel younger and the envy of many a man.

"Maybe I'll join you in the shower," he suggested, gauging her reaction.

"You're welcome to," she said sensually. "I have no problem rubbing soap all over your body."

A lascivious grin spread across Eric's face. "Likewise."

He was starting to remember what had attracted him to Beverly in the first place other than her incredible looks. It was the reason he could never give her up, at least where it concerned Beverly ever leaving him for another man.

TWENTY-SIX

FBI Agents Ben Taylor and Lynn Fry entered the police precinct at 10:00 A.M. Ben sensed that nearly every
cop they came upon recognized them as feds, which
was precisely what he wanted. Now that he had completed his undercover work at the store and had built a
solid case of racketeering charges against Leon Quincy,
it was time to step up the heat in trying to link him to at
least two murders connected to his criminal enterprise.
At the very least, Ben was counting on the two cops on
Quincy's payroll to get spooked into doing something
further incriminating that could be used as leverage to
secure their cooperation.

Ben led Lynn into the office of Detective Scott Mc-
Coy, who had been the lead investigator in the murders
of Russell Sheldon and Kurt Braddock.

"Thanks for meeting with us," Ben told the detective
after offering a perfunctory handshake, with Lynn doing the same.

"I always have time to meet with the FBI," McCoy
said.

Ben was not sure if he was being flippant. "That
makes our job easier."

"Have a seat and tell me what's on your mind."

Ben met Lynn's eyes, and they both sat on the other
side of his desk. They agreed not to play their entire
hand, unsure if McCoy was also in Quincy's hip pocket.
Even if he wasn't, the case against Leon Quincy was

too important to allow McCoy to spill the beans, inadvertently tipping off those who were on the take in the department.

"We're in the middle of a racketeering investigation," Ben said deliberately, "and I think you might be able to help us."

McCoy leaned back in his desk chair. "Not sure what I can lend to a racketeering investigation, but I'll try."

"We're looking into a couple of homicides that we think may be linked to our case," Lynn told him.

"I'm listening . . ." the detective said.

"Russell Sheldon and Kurt Braddock." Lynn gazed across the desk. "These are your cases, right?"

McCoy nodded. "Yeah, both Sheldon's and Braddock's cases are ongoing investigations, though neither is on the front burners. From what I understand, there's no indication that either murder is connected to your racketeering investigation."

"You may need to rethink that," Ben said, bluffing his way into what could be a dead end. "We believe that Russell Sheldon and Kurt Braddock may have been the victims of an attempted shakedown made to look like something else."

"Do you have any proof to back that up?" McCoy asked.

Ben was afraid he'd ask that. He had to be careful with his response. "It's mainly circumstantial right now," he conceded. "But if we could take a closer look at your files on these murders, it would be helpful."

"Knock yourself out. I don't want to stand in the way of your investigation. Personally, I think you're wasting your time. As I told Russell Sheldon's brother, the man's death fits the pattern of a typical store armed robbery. Even though he also seemed to have reservations about it, some crimes are merely as simple as they seem."

Ben wondered about the brother. Did he know something that might be germane to their investigation? "You have an address for the brother?"

"Afraid not," McCoy said. "I know he lives in L.A. Got his phone number somewhere." He pulled out a notepad and riffled through the pages. "Here it is. Dante Sheldon."

"Dante?" Ben's eyes grew.

"Yeah. You know him?"

"I might." Ben thought about the visitor who'd been in the store a couple of times. His name was Dante, and he claimed to be a friend of Russell's. Why lie about it? Or, for that matter, what did he know about Russell Sheldon's death? Ben wrote down Dante's number.

"Is there anything else I can help you with besides the file on Sheldon and Braddock?" McCoy asked.

Ben looked at Lynn and nodded. They worked well together, professionally and personally, understanding each other's cues.

"That should be all for now," Lynn said, standing, as did Ben. "If we need more information, we'll visit you again."

"Good luck with your investigation," McCoy said, getting to his feet.

"It's never about luck, Detective," Ben told him earnestly. "It's about doing a thorough investigation and achieving maximum results."

Once they were outside, Lynn raised her eyes up at Ben. "A bit tough on the detective, weren't you?"

"Not as tough as his superiors will be if he screwed up on two murder investigations that led to other crimes," he responded.

"Like shakedowns, drug dealing, and prostitution?" Lynn asked.

"Exactly. Even if Quincy's hands aren't dirty with these murders, chances are he was still involved in strong-arming Sheldon and Braddock for so-called protection money."

They reached their official vehicle and climbed inside.

"So what is it about Dante Sheldon that you aren't telling me?" Lynn asked from behind the wheel.

"I met him in the store," Ben responded thoughtfully. "I didn't realize he was Russell Sheldon's brother, that's all."

"Does that make a difference?"

"Not sure." Ben's instincts told him there might be more to the man than met the eye. He wondered if Dante had returned to Los Angeles or if he was still in town. If so, for what purpose? "I'd like to find out everything we can about Dante Sheldon."

"I hear you're going to have a baby," Eric said with interest, sitting up in bed as he wiped perspiration from his brow after some intense sex with Marilyn.

She blinked. "Who told you that?" As if she had to ask. Spencer with his big damn mouth. She wouldn't be at all surprised if he shouted it from the rooftops for the entire world to hear. Well, he was wasting his breath. It was never going to happen. Not with him as the father of her child, anyway.

It occurred to Marilyn that Beverly might have told Eric about Spencer's cockamamie plan to get her pregnant. Needing someone to confide in about this, she'd let it slip when Beverly phoned last night after another night of passion with Dante. Of course, Marilyn had agreed to cover her ass, knowing it was yet another thing she had on Beverly that she would use to her advantage sooner or later.

"Spencer passed along the news yesterday," Eric said, affirming Marilyn's suspicions. "We got together to take care of some business, and he told me all about it."

Marilyn didn't have to ask what type of business. She knew what Eric did for a living and how Spencer did just about everything else that Leon Quincy needed. Rather than frighten her, she was actually turned on by Eric's masculinity, penchant for violence, and cool-headedness under fire. If it were up to her, though, she'd prefer that he and Spencer didn't talk to each other about their personal lives. Just as Spencer knew nothing about her personal life with Eric, and Eric didn't have a clue about Beverly's intimate life with Dante. She suspected all the secrets were bound to come out one way or another. When that time came, everyone would simply have to face the music. Marilyn could only hope it gave her the great triumph over Beverly that she so craved.

"Don't believe everything you hear," Marilyn said, tasting him in her mouth from when she'd gone down on. She draped her leg across Eric's legs, keeping him pinned to the bed.

"So it's not true?" he asked.

"Would you care if it were?"

He paused. "Only if it were mine."

The idea of having his child appealed to her, though Marilyn knew Eric showed no interest in being a father with any of the women in his life. Could she change that in him down the line?

"I'm *not* pregnant," she told him flatly. "That's Spencer's dream, not mine. I just went along with it to get him to shut up."

Eric tossed his head back with relieved laughter. "You're rotten, you know that?"

"We both are, honey. Guess that's why we make such a good team."

"I think you're right." He kissed her nipple.

"Can we get rotten again for a little while . . . ?" Marilyn asked, feeling an urge to have him inside her, figuring they had just enough time to go another round before she had to go home and make dinner while pretending that was where she wanted to be.

Eric licked her other nipple. "Whatever makes you happy."

"You make me happy," Marilyn said honestly.

"Works both ways," he replied and began putting his hands all over and inside her.

Marilyn started to suck those tasty lips of his, while tingling between her legs. She felt like telling Eric she loved him and wanted this to become a permanent arrangement. But she didn't want to push it just yet. Especially when she sensed he was close to making the first move in recognizing that they belonged together in body, spirit, and soul.

TWENTY-SEVEN

Dante awoke and rubbed his eyes to the afternoon sunlight streaming in between the blinds. He'd slept in after last night's hot sex with Beverly and the conflicting thoughts going on in his head. He was beginning to believe he had finally found the woman of his dreams. Beverly was beautiful, passionate, great in bed, and unafraid of going after what she wanted. That was part of the problem. She had once wanted Eric Fox and got him. Never mind the fact the man was a cold-blooded murderer. Dante had to believe that Beverly knew nothing of his dark side. Either that or she deserved an Academy Award for her performance. From what he had gathered, Eric was pulling the wool over her eyes, just as he apparently had done to the authorities as Leon Quincy's enforcer.

Dante wanted Beverly all to himself. And it was no longer about taking something away from Eric, but rather being with a woman who Dante felt might be his soul mate. He wouldn't know for sure until they could spend time in a normal environment instead of a hotel bed. But before they could go there, he needed to finish the business that had brought him to Detroit. He had no illusions that it would be easy to take two lives, even despicable lives like Eric's and Leon's. Maybe that explained why he'd taken his own sweet time to go after them, apart from waiting for the appropriate moment. He wasn't a killer like Eric.

Yeah, I am. Eric and Leon turned me into a killer the moment they decided my brother wasn't worthy of living.

Now the time had come to pull the trigger as often as it took until they were both dead. Only then could he have some peace of mind and could Russell rest in peace.

Dante opened a drawer and took out the gun he'd purchased. He studied the weapon, took aim, and imagined shooting Eric, then Leon, right between the eyes.

The tap on the door gave Dante a start. He hadn't expected Beverly to come back so soon. Especially when he'd wanted her to play her part with Eric until he could make his move. Clearly Beverly couldn't get enough of him. Dante felt the same way. But now wasn't the time to get careless in their passion and romance. In spite of Eric's callousness, Dante didn't believe the man was a fool. Should Eric suspect Beverly was cheating on him, there was no telling what he was capable of doing to her.

We have to put aside our desires for each other and keep our distance for now; otherwise, this whole thing could blow up in our faces.

He couldn't let that happen. Not when he was so close to finishing his mission.

There was another, stronger rap on the door. "Just a minute," Dante called out. He put the gun back under some clothes in the drawer and threw on some slacks.

He opened the door and was surprised to see that it wasn't Beverly standing there. It was the new owner of Russell's store. What the hell was he doing there?

"Paul . . ."

"Actually, that's not my real name," he said. "It's FBI Special Agent Ben Taylor—"

Ben could see that Dante was taken aback by his admission. He supposed the same would be true were the shoe on the other foot. But since he saw Dante as a potential ally and not as an enemy, Ben hoped he would be cooperative, assuming he knew anything at all.

"Mind if I come in?" It occurred to him that Dante could be entertaining someone in the room, given that he was wearing only pants. However, because this was important and concerned his brother, Ben was sure Dante could spare a few minutes.

"Do I have a choice?" Dante rolled his eyes.

"People always have choices," Ben said calmly. "It's how they use them that often determines whether they're good or bad."

Dante gazed at him in thought before stepping aside.

Ben looked around the suite. He was impressed that Dante was staying there, as it must be costing him a pretty penny on a journalist's salary. "Sorry to just barge in on you like this," he told him.

Dante regarded him curiously. "How did you find me?"

"I have my ways," Ben said cryptically.

"So what's this all about, anyway?" asked Dante. "Why is an FBI agent pretending to be operating a small store in Detroit?"

"Good question," Ben said, anticipating such. He wouldn't get too much into specifics but did want Dante to feel he could trust him. "We're conducting an undercover sting involving a racketeering operation. The storekeeper role allowed me to do my job going after the suspects."

"Interesting, but what does any of it have to do with me?" Dante peered at him, still wondering what the connection was.

"We believe Russell Sheldon might have been the victim of an attempted shakedown that could be tied to our investigation." Ben met his eyes. "Russell was your brother, correct?"

Dante wanted to deny it but changed his mind. "Yeah, he was."

"Mind telling me why you said you were his friend?" Ben didn't want to treat him as a suspect or criminal, especially when he didn't know he was lying to a federal agent at the time. But there must have been some reason for the deception. Perhaps he was afraid, though Dante didn't strike him as a man consumed by fear.

Dante scratched his chin. "I just didn't see any reason to get into my personal business with a total stranger," he claimed.

"I don't recall asking you to," Ben said.

"You were running my brother's store. It seemed less painful if I was more detached when talking about him."

Ben wasn't sure he bought that, but had no real reason to contradict him. "I'll give you that." He paused. "Now that the truth is out, I got the distinct impression you knew something about Russell's death that you weren't telling me."

Dante swallowed. "I only know what the police told me."

"I spoke to Detective McCoy," Ben said. "He confirmed that he told you they believe robbery was the motive for your brother's murder. Are you buying that?"

Dante turned his eyes to the floor before lifting them again. "What do you want me to say?"

"Whatever you know that might be helpful to our case," Ben said. "For example, did your brother say anything about being pressured to pay protection money? Or name any names? Anything you can think of will help."

"Russell never told me anything," Dante said stiffly. "I wish to hell he had before it was too late."

"Then you do think he was being victimized by a shakedown?" Ben challenged him.

"I believe something was going down other than an armed robbery. If the police were serious about the investigation, they might have drawn the same conclusion."

"The FBI is on your side," Ben assured him. "We think your brother's death and at least one other store owner's death are part of this broad racketeering case. But proving it may be more difficult without any hard evidence."

"I wish I could help you," Dante said sincerely.

"So why are you in Detroit?" Ben asked.

Dante lifted a brow. "Excuse me?"

"I've checked you out. I know you're from L.A. I just wondered what your purpose is for being here—staying in this luxury hotel for what, going on two weeks now?"

Dante pursed his lips. "I didn't know I was breaking any laws."

"You're not—yet," Ben said.

Dante sighed. "I'm here on assignment," he told him. "I'm doing a piece on sex trafficking, if you must know. The hotel is being covered by my expense account."

Ben locked eyes with him. "I spoke to your editor. She said you had taken a leave of absence."

"I do some freelance work too," Dante said, unblinking.

Ben couldn't dispute this but remained suspicious. "In Detroit, on sex trafficking?"

"It goes on around the country," Dante pointed out. "Detroit is no exception. Maybe the FBI should be looking into it."

"Who says we aren't?" Indeed, they were cooperating with ICE agents in a separate investigation that was going after sex traffickers in Detroit and Chicago. As far as Ben knew, this was one of the few illegal things that Leon Quincy did not have his hands in, though he made up for it with a profitable homegrown prostitution business.

"So I needed a break from L.A.," Dante defended himself. "I also missed my brother and felt that coming to Detroit for a while would help me deal with his loss."

"Like hanging around the store he once owned?" Ben replied.

"Yeah."

Ben gazed at him. "So why do I believe there's more to the story?"

Dante shrugged. "Maybe because it's your nature as an FBI agent to be suspicious of everyone. And that includes an innocent man just trying to mourn his late brother."

"You have a point there," Ben agreed. Still, his intuition rarely failed him. He wanted to protect Dante from getting in over his head, especially if his purpose for being in Detroit was deeper and more dangerous than he was letting on. "I probably shouldn't be telling you this, but I will, anyway. We're close to wrapping up our racketeering investigation and plan to bring down the ones behind it. I'm trusting that you won't do anything stupid to get caught in the cross fire."

"I have no intention of getting in the way of your investigation, Special Agent Taylor," Dante said flatly. "As I said, I'm only here for—"

"I know what you said, and it's cool with me—as long as you don't break any laws." Ben narrowed his eyes in a way meant to intimidate. "If I thought you were out for blood and it in any way infringed on my investigation, I'd have to charge you with obstruction of justice, or worse, if you got blood on your hands. I know your brother wouldn't want to see that happen."

"No, he wouldn't," Dante agreed. "I get it. I have no plans to take the law into my own hands, especially when the local police are so capable."

Ben caught the sarcasm there. He agreed with him that the police investigation was lacking in tying Russell Sheldon's death to Leon Quincy's operation. Maybe it was because the connection really wasn't there. Or, more likely, they weren't privy to the information that the FBI had at its disposal regarding Quincy, some of which had since been shared with the locals. Either way, Ben wanted this case over badly and hoped that it might result in a few souls resting peacefully when all was said and done.

"Fortunately, the FBI is very capable of doing a thorough investigation where it concerns crimes within its jurisdiction, including murder." Ben tilted his face but kept his eyes on Dante. "I'm sure we understand each other. Hope you enjoy the rest of your stay in the city."

Even in saying this, Ben saw little joy in reliving the death of a sibling, something he knew all too well, having lost his sister twenty years ago, when she was hit by a drunk driver. The hurt never went away, no matter how distant the memory. He imagined it was the same with Dante. The only question was whether the man planned to deal with his grief constructively or destructively.

Dante saw Special Agent Ben Taylor out while doing his best to keep up appearances as a disgruntled but innocent brother of a murdered man. He suspected that Ben could see right through him as if he had a window into his thoughts.

Damn, the feds are onto me. How?

Had he done something to tip them off that he was in Detroit for the sole purpose of killing the two men responsible for Russell's death? Maybe his body language gave him away when he visited Russell's store and talked too much to an undercover FBI agent.

Either way, this changed the equation. For all he knew, Taylor or one of his colleagues would be tailing him now, waiting for him to commit attempted murder so they could arrest him and toss him in the slammer, maybe alongside Leon Quincy and Eric Fox. The thought of being associated with such scum sickened Dante. Not to mention what it would do to Russell's memory if Dante were to circumvent the law in seeking justice and get caught in the process, meaning his efforts would have wound up doing more harm than good at the end of the day. He doubted Russell would ever want that, no matter how much he felt he owed it to his brother to make his killers pay.

Dante made himself a drink. *It's over. I can't go after those bastards now.* It wasn't worth it now that the FBI had apparently homed in on Quincy's enterprise. Even if Taylor couldn't make the case that Leon Quincy was behind Russell's murder, with Eric pulling the trigger, Dante figured that as long as they both went down for subsequent federal crimes that put them away for the rest of their lives, he could live with that. The alternative was to simply ignore Taylor's not so thinly veiled warning to not interfere in an FBI investigation . . . or else, and take his chances by seeking revenge.

I'm better off quitting while I'm ahead and letting the feds do what the local cops couldn't, or wouldn't, do—get the bastards who robbed Russell of a bright future.

Dante's thoughts drifted to Beverly, the one good thing that had come out of his time in Detroit. She was terrific and kept his libido high whenever they were together. It was time he was straight with her. She deserved to know the kind of monster she was living with. Then they could both pack up and get out of the city and take a chance on each other and a life together full of possibilities. Hopefully, Eric would be too busy dealing with the feds to be bothered by Beverly's exit from his life. But if Eric did choose to come after them, Dante would have every right to defend himself and Beverly, if it came down to it, and he wouldn't hesitate to do so.

TWENTY-EIGHT

"Stop here, Henry," Leon instructed his driver. They were in the empty parking lot of an abandoned building, save for one other vehicle. He recognized the official car of Detective Stanley Dillard, who had summoned him for a meeting, saying it was safer than speaking over the phone. Admittedly, this had unnerved Leon. He didn't like it when someone else was calling the shots. But, given that he and the detective were in business together and both stood to lose if something went wrong, Leon had to respect him if he felt it was urgent that they speak.

After Henry opened his door, Leon slid out alongside Spencer. Leon saw Dillard with his back to them, standing at the end of the lot overlooking the city.

"Wait here," Leon told Spencer, stopping him in his tracks.

"You're sure?" he asked, his face filled with concern.

"Yeah, I'll be fine." Leon doubted the detective was leading him into a trap. It would only come back to haunt him. "I'll call out if I need you."

Leon walked across the lot, maintaining a cool and calm façade, until he reached the detective, who turned and faced him.

"What took you so long?" Dillard asked, unsmiling.

Leon's brows knitted. "I didn't know I was on your time clock."

"We both are." Dillard wrinkled his nose. "We may have a problem. The FBI has an ongoing investigation into racketeering in Northwest Detroit. You could be targeted."

Leon's heart skipped a beat. The last thing he needed was the feds on his ass, especially when Dillard was on his payroll specifically to run interference for any such investigations. He met the detective's eyes. "So get the target off my back."

"Wish it were that simple. I can't control what the FBI does and doesn't do."

Neither could he, which pissed Leon off. "What do they have?"

"They're probably looking into all your operations, loan-sharking, bribery, prostitution, drug dealing, and shakedowns."

That definitely concerned Leon. He wanted it to concern the detective as well. "You'd better find some way to help me out here. You can't afford this type of heat any more than I can."

"I'm helping you right now," stressed Dillard. "There's only so much I can do. Oh, and there's one other thing. . . ."

Leon wasn't sure he wanted to know. "What?"

"The agents are trying to link the deaths of Kurt Braddock and Russell Sheldon to their investigation. I hope your hitman covered his ass."

So do I. He assumed that Eric Fox had taken care of business without any loose ends. "I'm sure he did."

Dillard rubbed his long nose. "In that case, you may not have much to worry about there. But it doesn't change the fact that we both have to look over our shoulders. I suggest you rein in your people and keep a low profile for the time being."

Leon wasn't too keen on suspending operations, costing him money and emboldening his adversaries to try to swoop in like vultures. But he also had no desire to spend the rest of his life in a federal penitentiary, rotting away and cursing how he'd ended up there.

"I'll do what I have to," he told the detective. "I suggest you do the same."

Dillard nodded. "I believe you have something for me."

Leon had almost forgotten that he owed him another payment for being a set of eyes and ears on the police force. He had a mind not to give him a dime after being told news he didn't want to hear. But every time he paid off Dillard, it was one more reminder that he owned the detective and would make damned sure they were cell mates if he went down, right along with Officer Roger Menendez.

Leon took the envelope out of his pocket and passed it to Dillard. "There will be a lot more if you can get the feds to poke their noses elsewhere."

"That won't be easy."

"Never said it would be," Leon stated.

"Can't promise anything, but I'll try."

Leon took that as a possibility the detective could throw the FBI off stride or, at the very least, minimize his exposure in their investigation.

"Keep me informed," Leon ordered.

"Yeah." Dillard scratched his pate. "In the meantime, I think it's best if we don't meet again until this thing blows over, if it does."

"I think you're right," Leon said as self-preservation kicked in. He considered that he might have to take the detective out if it seemed in his best interest to do away with him, rather than risk the dirty detective testifying against him.

Dillard sniffled. "See you later."

Leon watched him walk away, seemingly as fast as he could without running. He was tempted to do the same but refused to panic prematurely. Or show weakness in front of Spencer and Henry.

He would play it by ear and stay ahead of the game, while laying low for a while, if this was what it took to keep the government from coming after him.

"Looks like Leon Quincy has just added more fuel to the fire to burn him," Lynn said after Ben joined her in a car.

He'd gotten word that things were starting to fall into place with their investigation. Ben could hardly wait until they could slap the cuffs on Quincy and those he employed to do his dirty work.

Lynn passed photographs to Ben. "We caught him having a private chat with Detective Stanley Dillard in a parking lot at Broadhurst and Sixteenth Street. They never had a clue that our man had a front-row seat in the building, getting plenty of still shots and video."

"I had a feeling going to see Detective McCoy just might shake things up a bit in the department," Ben said. There was no proof McCoy was actually dirty. But Ben had passed along information that, as anticipated, got McCoy's attention and made its way straight to Quincy.

"Definitely scared Dillard enough that he wanted a face-to-face with Quincy," Lynn said.

Ben studied the pictures, focusing on one where Quincy was clearly passing an envelope to Detective Dillard. "Got you both," he said with satisfaction.

Lynn smiled. "Sure looks that way."

"Hope it was worth it to Dillard to throw his career away to be in bed with an asshole like Leon Quincy."

"I'm sure Quincy made it worth his while as a means to supplement his cop salary," Lynn said.

"Can't put a price on freedom," Ben said. "Dillard and his buddy, Officer Roger Menendez, are about to find that out the hard way. Once we put the squeeze on them, they'll be trying to outdo each other to hand us Quincy on a silver platter, along with his other cronies."

"There's something else you should know," Lynn said. "A couple of days ago, a petty drug dealer named Clay Randolph was found shot to death at Edge Creek Park." She handed Ben a photo of the victim. "Word is he used to work for Quincy and may have become competition that he could easily do without."

"Hmm . . ." Ben mumbled thoughtfully. "That seems to be the pattern with Quincy and anyone who gets on his bad side. It's not enough to rough them up or threaten to kill. Only their actual murders will do."

Lynn brushed hair from her face. "You're thinking of Russell Sheldon and Kurt Braddock?"

"Yeah, I suppose, given the circumstances that left their deaths questionable in relation to Quincy's operation." Ben mused about Dante Sheldon. The man definitely appeared to have more on his mind in hanging out in Detroit than doing a piece on sex trafficking. Not that he had anything against more exposure about this dirty aspect of prostitution in the city. Ben hoped that Dante had gotten the message and wouldn't try to be a one-man vigilante against those he deemed responsible for his brother's death, with Leon Quincy likely at the top of the list. Otherwise, Dante would only end up suffering, too, either by going to prison or getting himself killed. Neither of which would bring his brother back.

"Maybe Dillard and Menendez can shed some light on these murders in connection with Quincy," Lynn said.

"Yeah, I was thinking the same thing," Ben told her. "The same is true for some of the other people in Quincy's inner circle, like Spencer Ramsey. Amazing what the prospect of doing hard time can do to shake up memories and fill in the blanks."

"You're right about that." Lynn chuckled. "Are we ready to bring Menendez and Dillard in? Or even Leon Quincy himself?"

Ben was tempted to say yes and see how it all unfolded. But he was experienced enough to know that people like Quincy became most unpredictable and prone to errors when running scared. "Let's give them another day or two to rattle their nerves and see what else they do to build the case for us."

"If that's what you want."

Ben looked at her and realized she was what he wanted beyond this case. He thought the feeling was mutual. Once they had Quincy and company put away, they could talk about where they would go from here as a man and woman who seemed to mesh quite nicely behind closed doors. He hoped that would be the case in public as well.

TWENTY-NINE

Beverly invited Marilyn for lunch at a bistro not far from the hotel where Dante was staying. It was time to let her best friend in on the news that she had only shared thus far with her mother. She wondered if Marilyn would think she'd taken leave of her senses in giving up a good life with Eric for an unpredictable one with Dante. Or would she believe it was about time that she followed her heart, rather than what had been the most comfortable situation for her—being with someone for whom money never seemed to be an object?

"So what's this big news you couldn't wait to tell me?" Marilyn asked over her chicken sandwich.

Beverly wiped mustard from the corner of her lips after she took a bite of her corned beef sandwich. "I've decided to move to Los Angeles to be with Dante." *There, I said it, and I'm only asking for her support.*

Marilyn's eyes fluttered. "You're actually walking out on Eric?"

"I wouldn't quite put it that way," Beverly said. "But, yes, our relationship is over. It's time."

Marilyn smiled. "I agree. It's been obvious for a while now that things weren't clicking anymore with you and Eric."

"I know. I really did want it to work for us. Then Dante came into the picture and made me reevaluate everything I thought I wanted in a relationship."

Marilyn took another bite of her sandwich. "The big question is, have you told Eric you want out . . . ?"

Beverly sighed. If it were up to her, she would have done so by now. But she acquiesced to Dante's desire that she wait just a while longer. She could only hope it proved to be a smart move.

"I plan to tell him shortly," Beverly replied calmly.

"Why delay?" Marilyn frowned. "Are you having second thoughts already?"

"Not at all," she insisted and then explained why she hadn't packed her bags and moved out yet. "Dante and I really want to be together. He just doesn't want me left alone with Eric pissed while he's doing his assignment."

"Maybe you should be concerned. Eric's not the type of man you mess around with," Marilyn warned.

Beverly cocked a brow. "And how do *you* know what kind of man he is?" she asked. Not that she disagreed with her assessment. "You and Eric haven't exactly spent much time together."

Marilyn took a moment while drinking pink lemonade. "He and Spencer work for the same man," she pointed out casually. "Spencer told me that Eric has a temper and isn't afraid to act on it."

"He's never hit me," Beverly pointed out. But did that mean Eric was incapable of this if he felt he was being disrespected? Or wronged by an unfaithful girlfriend?

"And that's supposed to make you feel you have nothing to worry about by stringing him along?"

"I never said that." Beverly didn't consider what she was doing as stringing him along. It wasn't like there had been much romance between them in recent memory.

"Besides, you and I have talked about him enough times to know that the man treats you like a queen," Marilyn said. "How do you think he will feel when his queen decides she wants to move to another man's castle?"

Beverly hated being put on the defensive when she was doing what was best for her, even if not for Eric. "He'll just have to deal with it," she responded tonelessly. "It's not like we're the first couple to ever break up. It happens all the time."

"Not to Eric Fox."

Beverly stared at her. "Whose side are you on, anyway?"

"Yours, of course," Marilyn said quickly.

"I was starting to wonder, based on the way you're chastising me for just trying to get on with my life like any normal woman who's found a man she wants to make a life with."

"I'm sorry if you took it the wrong way." Marilyn sighed and put her sandwich down. "I want you to be happy, and I'm glad you seem to click with Dante. All I'm saying is, I think you should grab your things and get the hell out of Eric's house as soon as possible."

Beverly's mouth opened. "You mean without telling him I'm leaving?"

"Not necessarily," Marilyn said levelly. "But there will probably never be a totally right time to give him the news and have him be cool with it. If Dante's that concerned about when you should tell Eric you no longer want to be his woman, and you feel the same, maybe you're better off just leaving him a note. Then maybe after he's had time to adjust to the news, you can talk to Eric about it once you're in L.A. with your new man."

Beverly hadn't considered leaving Eric without even saying good-bye. Not after all he'd done for her. But maybe that would be a way out without having to deal with the drama likely to come from his displeasure and his attempts to get her to stay. Would Dante be okay with her moving into his hotel room before he finished his article? Or was he not open to compromise when all she wanted was to be with him right now?

"I'll think about that," she told her. "I don't want to hurt Eric or drag this out any more than I have to. But the bottom line is we're both adults and should understand that these things happen sometimes and we both just need to move on with our lives."

"I agree, and I'm totally in your corner," Marilyn said. She reached across the table and took her hand. "You need to do what you need to do. I'm sure that even if Eric's initially pissed about it, he'll eventually realize that it was for the best and that there's someone else out there for him too."

"I hope so." Beverly smiled, squeezing her hand. She was glad to have Marilyn there to talk to and get this off her chest. But there was still the hard part of talking to Eric face-to-face—unless she left him a good-bye note. Maybe once she was out of the picture, he would realize they were no longer right for each other and find someone else to share his life with.

The ringing of her cell phone jarred Beverly from her thoughts. She took out the phone and saw that Dante was the caller. A happy feeling caused her stomach to churn. She met Marilyn's eyes before answering.

"Hey," she said, always eager to hear his voice.

"I need to see you," Dante told her firmly.

It sounded serious. "I'm just having lunch with a friend."

The Hitman's Woman   293

"It's important."

"All right." Beverly felt a little nervous, wondering if he was calling off their plans to start a relationship. "Are you at the hotel?"

"Yeah."

"I can be there in five minutes," she told him.

"I'll be waiting," Dante said and disconnected.

"What was that all about?" Marilyn asked curiously.

"Dante wants to see me."

"Oh . . ." Marilyn looked at her wide-eyed. "Is everything all right?"

"Not sure." Beverly's heart was racing. "Guess I'll find out soon."

"Go," Marilyn told her. "I'll pay the bill."

"Are you sure?" After all, Beverly had invited her to lunch and knew that Marilyn often pinched pennies.

"Positive. It can be on you the next time."

"All right." Beverly stood. She gave Marilyn a hug. "Call you later."

"Good luck," Marilyn said with a smile. "With everything."

Marilyn could barely hide her glee. That bitch was finally leaving Eric alone so she could shack up with another man she hoped would be her equal. This meant that at last Marilyn could have Eric all to herself and kick Spencer to the curb and any fantasies he had about her having his child. Now Eric would finally see Beverly as nothing more than the gold-digging tramp she really was.

I know he'll be mad as hell and probably want to strangle her. Marilyn considered that very thing while driving and listening to some rap music. It was up to her to make Eric forget all about Beverly. He didn't need her when there was someone much better to share his bed, house, and heart with. Surely he would see that and feel the same way, especially after Beverly left him, maybe without even having the guts to tell Eric to his face.

I have a mind to call Eric right now and share the good news. Marilyn put that urge on hold, realizing the worst thing she could do was come across as the bad girl in this triangle of infidelity and deceit. She would wait it out for Beverly to hang herself and be there to comfort Eric, which he would surely need as he licked his wounds and dealt with a damaged ego.

In the meantime, Marilyn would continue to play along as the devoted wife of going-nowhere Spencer, while knowing that wouldn't be the case much longer. She started singing the rap song, suddenly feeling as if things were finally beginning to fall into place in her life thanks to Beverly's reckless behavior and risky decisions.

Dante opened the door. "Hi."

Beverly smiled softly. "Hey."

He kissed her ruby lips, enjoying how they felt on his. "Thanks for coming."

"You made it sound important," she said.

"It is."

Dante shut the door and gazed at Beverly's face. It was beautiful as always with a complexion that brought out her best features. He'd love to strip off her clothes and make love to her while exploring every part of her body. But this time there was more on his mind. He wished to hell they had met under circumstances that didn't lead to Eric Fox. But neither of them could help that. They had to take things as they were and go from there.

He walked to the wet bar. "Fix you a drink?"

"Okay." She met his eyes uneasily.

Dante made them both a cocktail, handing her one. "Let's sit down."

"You're scaring me," Beverly said. "Please don't tell me you're reconsidering my coming out to California with you."

"No, it's nothing like that." Dante took her hand and led them both to the couch. He wasn't sure how she would take this, but it needed to be said. "I want you in L.A."

She sighed. "And I definitely want to make this transition in my life."

"I know." He tasted his drink, realizing this was harder than he'd thought it would be, not quite sure where to start. Or if she would listen. "I haven't been entirely honest with you."

"About what?" Her eyes expanded. "You're married? You have a girlfriend? What?"

"Nothing like that." Dante paused. "It's about Eric...."

"He knows about us?" Fear registered in her voice.

"Not from me."

"What about Eric?"

Dante could only hope he wasn't telling her what she already knew or suspected on some level. "He's not who you think he is."

Beverly's brows creased. "What are you talking about?"

"Eric is a hired killer," Dante said bluntly.

"*What?*" She shot him a look of disbelief.

"The man you're living with kills people for a living."

"And how do you know this?" she asked with suspicion.

Dante tasted his drink and paused. "He murdered my brother."

Beverly put her glass on the table. "None of what you're saying makes sense to me."

"I know, and I'll try to put it to you straight," he told her, taking a breath. "The man Eric works for, Leon Quincy, is not your average businessman. His business is illegal—loan-sharking, drug trafficking, and prostitution. Eric is an enforcer for him. When Quincy needs someone silenced, he calls Eric to take care of it. He murdered my brother, Russell, after he refused to pay Quincy protection money for his store."

Beverly shook her head. "No. Wherever you got your information, you're wrong," she insisted. "Eric is a consultant and investor—"

"He's a damned killer!" Dante raised his voice, finding solace in the fact that she was clearly oblivious to his alter ego. "Forget whatever Eric told you. He's got blood on his hands."

She glared at Dante. "Why are you telling me this?"

"Because I thought you needed to know the truth before we go any further," he said lowly. "You deserve that much."

"I don't know what to say." Beverly sighed. "This doesn't make any sense. Eric is a hired killer?"

"I can assure you that I didn't make it up," Dante insisted, though understanding how this news could take her aback. Who would want to believe this about someone who presented a different picture for the world to see? Or, in this case, the woman who lived with him. "I have it on good authority."

"Whose authority?" she demanded. "Who would tell you such a thing?"

"A private investigator who's nothing if not thorough," he told her, feeling she had a right to know how he'd come to point the finger at Eric.

Beverly rolled her eyes broodingly. "So this whole thing—me and you—has been about your brother and Eric all along?"

"What you and I have going on has nothing to do with what Eric did to my brother," Dante explained. "I had no idea that you and Eric were involved when you came on to me downstairs that night. You never told me his name. It wasn't until I saw you at his house that I put two and two together."

She gazed at him sharply. "So it wasn't an accident that you were at the pool hall when Eric was there, was it?"

"No," Dante admitted. "I followed him there."

"For what?"

"To get more information about him and then . . ."

"Then what?" Beverly demanded.

He sucked in a deep breath and locked his eyes on hers. *I might as well come clean about it if I want us to get past this.* "I wanted to kill him."

She put a hand up to her mouth. "Oh no, you were *using* me this whole time to get to Eric," she reiterated.

"No, I wasn't," Dante said firmly and reached out to touch her. "Not from the start."

Beverly recoiled. "Don't touch me."

He complied, wishing he could comfort her in some way, short of taking back what she needed to hear. "I didn't plan to get involved with you. It just happened, and is totally separate from my beef with Eric."

"If that's true, why weren't you just straight with me from the time you realized I was living with Eric?" she challenged.

Dante ran a hand across his mouth. He had hoped to use her as a pawn to get into Eric's head. But he'd abandoned that plan when he realized he cared too much about her to want to put her at risk. He doubted she would believe this, given the skepticism in her tone. But there was an even more important reason why he hadn't put everything on the table from the start.

"I wasn't totally sure where you stood insofar as what he was doing," Dante admitted.

Her eyes narrowed angrily. "So it was okay to keep having sex with me, even if you thought I condoned killing people?"

He resisted the urge to touch her again. "I thought it was pretty likely that you didn't know anything about it."

"Yeah, *right,*" she muttered.

"But another side of me wasn't convinced you'd believe what I had to say about Eric," he told her.

She curled her lip. "And why should I believe you now when you've been misleading me from day one?"

"Because I felt it was time that you knew what was going on." Dante swallowed thickly. "Things might be going down soon, and I don't want to see you get hurt."

"Like I'm not already hurt?" Beverly hissed. "By more than one person."

Dante felt her pain. "I'm sorry you have to be caught in the middle of this."

"I don't think you are. Otherwise, you wouldn't have been leading me on when all you really wanted to do was kill Eric for what you claim he did to your brother."

"I was never leading you on," Dante stressed. "We both got what we wanted from each other. As far as my 'claim' about Eric, it's a fact. My brother's dead because Leon Quincy ordered a hit on him when he wouldn't pay up."

"If this really happened, why haven't you gone to the police?" Beverly questioned.

"I did and got nowhere with them."

"So you're taking it upon yourself to be an avenging angel?" Beverly asked acerbically.

Seemed like a good idea until the FBI got in the way. Dante sighed. "I'm not going after Eric anymore, even though I'd like to, if only to stop him from taking out anyone else." He leaned forward and placed his hand on her shoulder. This time, she didn't push it away. "The man's a menace to society. You're not safe as long as you stay in his house."

Her eyes blinked twice with cynicism. "But you're the one who told me I needed to stay there while you were—"

"I know what I said," he replied, cutting her off. "Now I believe you're better off getting the hell out of there."

Now she pushed his hand off her shoulder. "And do what? Move in with you here?"

"If that's what it takes. At least he won't know how to find you. Not easily, anyway." Dante had no doubt Eric, with his ego, would try to find her, which made him all the more dangerous.

"And what about your plan for me to move to L.A. with you?" Beverly tossed out. "Or was the whole journalist bit just a lie?"

"It wasn't a lie," Dante told her. At least not the profession part. "That's what I am, and I do live in Los Angeles. I'd still like you to come out there with me and we'll see how things go."

"And if they don't go according to plan, then what?" Beverly pouted. "I'm out on the street, forced to make a life on my own?"

"Wouldn't that be better than living with a bona fide murderer?" Dante said in a more abrasive tone than he'd intended to. "Or are you incapable of taking care of yourself?"

"Go to hell!" she blared.

"I'm not judging you."

"Sure sounds like you are. I thought you were different. Now it seems that you're just like other men I've fallen for who turned out to be phony."

"I'm not phony where it concerns us," Dante assured her. "That's why I asked you over here, because I genuinely care for your health and well-being."

"I think you care more about yourself," Beverly accused him. "Well, don't expect me to just go along with whatever you tell me, because it's not happening."

Beverly rose so quickly that she nearly lost her balance. Dante got up, prepared to catch her if necessary. "Let's talk about this some more," he implored her.

"You know what? I'm not sure what to believe right now," she said, clearly flustered.

"I understand your confusion, but I'm not your enemy."

"How do I know who or what you are, Dante, if that's really even your name?" Beverly took a breath. "I have to get out of here."

"Don't go back to Eric's house," he said earnestly.

She gazed at him wide-eyed. "Why shouldn't I? Am I really in any more danger with him than you? If you were, or are, willing to kill him, are you any better than you claim he is?"

Dante was speechless as Beverly stormed out of the room. Every fiber in him wanted to run after her and talk some sense into her. But it was clear she was in no mood to listen. Were he to burst into Eric's home and confront him, it could lead to violence and Beverly could become a victim. Besides, if the FBI was truly about to put the clamps on Leon Quincy's operation, surely the trail would lead to Eric, meaning his days of killing were likely numbered.

I'll just have to lay low for now and see what happens. Hopefully, Beverly will come to her senses after she cools down and not put herself in danger by making Eric aware of what she knows about him.

If the man felt she had become more of a liability than an asset, Dante had no doubt Eric would rather kill Beverly than have her potentially testify against him in court. Or he might sweet-talk her into believing that he was just a law-abiding businessman who was being unfairly targeted by the feds.

Dante wouldn't put anything past that bastard. All he knew was that Beverly had become too important to him to let her slip through his fingers. He would not let her become another victim of Eric, like Russell. Or had the whole thing started to spin out of control now, with him powerless to affect the outcome?

THIRTY

Beverly hoped she didn't get a ticket for speeding. She couldn't help herself, as it was a means to blow off steam. Just when she'd thought she found her knight in shining armor with Dante, it turned out he'd had his own agenda in bedding her. Now what was she supposed to think? Could his accusations about Eric be true? Was the man she'd been living with truly capable of being a killer?

She'd always sensed there was something secretive about Eric. But a cold-blooded murderer for hire? He had chosen not to fully discuss his business with her, and she accepted this as simply who he was, balanced against the man who seemed to worship the ground she walked on. Was that all just an act to cover his dark side? Or were Dante's accusations against Eric unfounded? He had given her no proof that Eric was responsible for his brother's death or that Leon Quincy was behind it.

What was she supposed to believe?

I'm so confused right now. Am I really in danger if I stay with Eric for another day or even an hour? Or was everything Dante said baloney?

Beverly slowed down, realizing that killing herself would not help matters. All she'd wanted was to start a new life with Dante and put the past behind her. But he had to mess things up by throwing this crap at her and leaving their future in doubt. She really didn't know what to think at this point other than she wasn't prepared to just walk out on Eric without confronting him about these scary charges. Killing people for a living was too monstrous to envisage for the man she had been living with. Yet, she was left with no choice other than to accept the very real possibility that everything Dante told her about Eric was true.

Beverly willed herself to gather the courage to face Eric, while praying it didn't come at a cost she would never want to pay: her own life. Only then could she sort things out and see where she wanted to go from there. When all was said and done, she might discover that she didn't belong with Eric or Dante. Maybe being on her own for the first time wouldn't be such a bad thing. Especially if the alternative was to be with someone she couldn't trust to be real.

Beverly saw Eric's car in the driveway as she drove up to the house. Her heart skipped a beat as she parked behind him, knowing that whatever happened in the next few minutes, things would likely never go back to the way they were. She wasn't sure how he would take this, but she wouldn't turn back now. Not with so much at stake. She desperately needed to sort out the hearts and motives of the two men in her life.

Eric had finally done it. He'd bought tickets to the Bahamas for him and Beverly. She had two weeks to pack, and then they were away from Detroit for a couple of weeks of fun in the sun. He was sure she would be pleased by this, as she had wanted to go somewhere, just the two of them. He certainly looked forward to spending some romantic time with her and trying to get back what they had been missing in their relationship. Hooking up with Marilyn from time to time certainly had its benefits, but Beverly was the woman he wanted as his lady.

He heard the familiar sound of her car driving up and peeked out the bedroom window in time to see her get out. *I suppose she was hanging out with Marilyn again.* Part of Eric liked this, for he wanted his lover to be his eyes and ears when he wasn't around. The other part felt uneasy with the two women in his life spending too much time together, potentially complicating things for him. On the whole, he was sure Marilyn would keep her mouth shut as she had just as much to lose as he should their affair ever come out. Spencer would probably leave her ass, and Marilyn might not get as lucky again to find someone who would marry her until death do them part, as seemed to be the case with Spencer. Good thing she walked on water in his eyes. Just as Beverly did as far as Eric was concerned.

Now she would get to swim in it, too, on Paradise Island. Eric grabbed the itinerary, tucked it in his blazer pocket, and headed downstairs to greet his woman. Beverly walked in the door, looking very hot in a sleeveless, V-neck blue dress, her legs bare and sexy down to her flat sandals.

"Hey, baby," he said, hands behind his back. "I've got something special for you."

When Eric tried to kiss her, Beverly turned her face so he ended up with his lips on her cheek. He looked into her eyes and could tell that something was wrong.

"What's the matter?" he asked, figuring she and Marilyn had it out or something.

Beverly gulped and stepped into the living room before turning on him. "Is it true?"

"Is what true?"

She paused. "What is it you say you do for Leon Quincy?"

Where did that come from? Eric maintained his poise. "I do some consulting work for him."

"Consulting on what?"

"Investments," he maintained. "Why are you asking?"

She stared at him through frightened eyes. "Do you kill people for Leon?"

The words gave Eric a start. Who the hell told her? Marilyn? Why would she? Maybe Gloria, as some form of payback? Should he continue to deny it?

"Who's been pumping this garbage into your head?" he demanded, hoping his tough tone would be enough to get her to dismiss it.

"It doesn't matter," she uttered tentatively. "I just want to know the truth."

Eric took a breath. He wasn't ready to let her in on that part of his life, if only to protect her. If she knew the full story, then Leon could one day target her if he saw her as a potential threat to his crime organization. Eric had made the mistake of confiding in his ex, and she tried to use it as leverage in controlling him. It had backfired. Not only did he leave her, but he also made her swear to never breathe a word of what she knew to anyone or she'd face the consequences.

Had Gloria done the unthinkable and blabbed to Beverly out of vengeance? If so, she would regret it more than she could possibly imagine.

"The truth is I have no idea what you're talking about," he lied without a muscle in his face twitching. "Leon is a businessman like I am. He doesn't go around killing people or asking someone else to do it for him. Certainly not me."

Beverly cast her eyes up at his thoughtfully. "I want to believe you."

"You can," Eric insisted. "I'm not a monster. Obviously someone wants you to believe that. Who told you this?"

She stood mute for a moment. "It's not important."

"It is to me," he insisted. "When someone tells my lady I'm a killer, I shouldn't have to defend myself."

Beverly regarded him tentatively. "And I shouldn't have to wonder if the man I've been living with is a hitman for the mob, or whatever."

"Then don't," Eric pleaded in a serious tone.

"When I've asked you more specifics about your work, you've always sidestepped it, making me feel foolish in the process." Her brow creased. "Why is that?"

Eric kept his cool, though hating that he'd been put in this position. "If I made you feel that way, it was never my intention," he said with a straight gaze. "Had nothing to do with trying to hide anything from you. I just thought you'd be bored listening to me droll on about consulting, investments, and such."

Beverly locked eyes with him. "So those late-night business meetings and quick trips out of town . . ."

"Were all perfectly legit," he finished equably. "I don't work for some damned thug, any more than your friend Marilyn's husband, Spencer, does." He let that settle in, not above using his lover if the situation called for. "Now I'd like to know who's behind this ridiculous allegation."

Beverly averted his stare. "Never mind."

Eric bristled. Why was she stonewalling? Who had she been talking to? Could the cops have told this to her? Eric wondered if they were targeting him in relation to Leon Quincy. He was aware that there had been numerous investigations into Leon's activities, most of which failed to gain traction. Maybe they had someone on the inside. Eric had done his best to cover his tracks and didn't think they could build a solid case against him, unless it was Leon who was willing to stab him in the back to save his own neck. That seemed very unlikely, as the authorities would certainly consider Leon a bigger fish to fry than him.

Still, it bothered Eric that Beverly was throwing this in his face while dodging his desire to know the source. Could be the cops asked her not to reveal it. Or maybe she was protecting someone else.

He glared at her. "Did this mystery person offer any actual evidence of this outrageous charge?" he asked, hoping she didn't provide anything he might find difficulty refuting.

Beverly sighed. "I was never given any proof, only accusations."

Eric felt relieved, but was determined to get to the bottom of it. "Accusations are a dime a dozen," he told her. "They are also slanderous. If I ever find out who's behind this, I'll—"

"You'll *what?*" she regarded him nervously.

He hated that she was calling him out on what someone had spoon-fed to her. *I'm not about to bite the bait.* "Sue, of course," he answered easily. "What did you think I was going to say?"

"Nothing." Beverly looked away pensively. "Can we just forget this?"

Not a chance in hell. "Yes, consider it forgotten." Eric had gotten so flustered that he'd almost forgotten his surprise for her. He couldn't allow this to spoil the mood he'd wanted to create. In fact, maybe this was the perfect time to show her his softer side. Unlike the portrait someone was trying to paint of him, even if it was true. She'd never have to know that.

Eric ran his hand across her cheek and felt Beverly react, unsure if it was in appreciation or fear. He chose to believe the former. "I was going to present this to you after we'd had a glass of wine," he told her. "But I think under the circumstances, I should give it to you now." He removed the trip itinerary and handed it to her. "I purchased first-class tickets to Nassau and Paradise Island in the Bahamas."

Beverly expressed surprise as she studied the itinerary. "This is nice," she said unevenly. "But I'm not sure—"

"Don't let others mess things up for us." Eric frowned. "Let me show you who I *really* am and how much I care for you. Please . . ."

He didn't allow her to say another word, instead kissing Beverly on the lips while counting on his charm and her love for the good life to win out over anything else.

Inside, Eric was still seething that someone was trying to let his secret out of the bag and destroy their relationship in the process. He intended to find out who and do something about it.

Half an hour later, Beverly was left alone while Eric went out. She might have feared he was going after Dante, except she hadn't revealed him as the source of her accusation. Had it been a mistake to mention it to Eric? He had appeared unflustered, by and large, by the notion he was a hired killer, as his anger seemed more aimed at who was behind it. Could she blame him? Had such a charge been leveled against her by someone, she, too, would be royally pissed, knowing it was totally untrue.

But was it? She couldn't shake the feeling that there was more to this than Eric let on, in spite of his staunch denials.

She sat at the kitchen table drinking, coffee. Her head was spinning as she wrapped her mind around the notion that she might know far less about the man she had been living with than she had realized. Yes, Eric had professed his innocence in any part of killing people. But Dante seemed pretty certain that his information was solid, even if he gave her nothing to support it, other than his own apparent obsession with Eric and Leon Quincy.

Do I believe the man I've fallen in love with, who may have just been using me with no serious intention of having a relationship? Or do I believe the man I'm living with, who I don't love?

If she stayed with Eric and he truly was a hired killer, Beverly doubted she could ever forgive herself. And what would happen to her if he decided she knew too much? Would she, too, be murdered and end up being another forgotten soul? What if she were tossed in the river afterward and her mother wasn't able to give her a proper burial?

I'm just thinking crazy now. Can I really side with someone I've known for less than a month over a man I've been with for over a year? Doesn't Eric deserve the benefit of the doubt, even if Dante comes across as credible, if not totally convincing?

Beverly wasn't sure what to think or do. She'd received a text message from Dante, asking if she was all right and to call him. She did not respond, feeling it might merely be playing into his game of vengeance and possibly a case of mistaken identity. It would certainly take work for him to convince her he was sincere in their mutual seduction and plans to build a relationship.

She looked at the hotel brochures Eric had given her. Beverly's hands were actually shaking as she read the info on the five-star hotel and amenities it offered, including direct access to the beach. She could really use a vacation right now. But could she really enjoy it if it was with someone who didn't do it for her romantically or sexually these days? Or would it really just be delaying the inevitable, which she'd have to deal with later?

I need to talk to someone about this. Beverly grabbed her cell phone and called Marilyn. She welcomed the sound of her best friend to be the voice of reason to help her decide how to handle these new developments that threatened to throw a wrench in her plans for a new life with Dante.

THIRTY-ONE

"Beverly just phoned and asked me to come over," Marilyn told Eric. "She sounded kind of funny."

Eric listened to her on the speakerphone as he drove. He was hoping Beverly would call Marilyn when he left. "Someone's been bad-mouthing me, and she won't tell me who the hell it is. I have some ideas, but I want to know for sure."

"Why would someone want to talk about you to her?"

"That's what I need you to find out," he said.

"I can't promise she'll tell me anything," Marilyn uttered.

Eric dismissed that, even if he realized she was only trying to cover her ass in case she fell short of what he needed. "You're Beverly's best friend," he reminded her. "Make her tell you everything about where she heard that I was working as a hitman for Leon."

"Wow, she told you that?"

"Yeah." He stopped at a light. "I need to know what I'm dealing with here."

"I understand," Marilyn said. "I'll see what I can get out of her."

"You do that." Eric was determined to get to the bottom of this. If the authorities were trying to use Beverly to get to him, he needed to know. If the source was someone else, then that person would have to deal with him.

"I assume you denied working for Leon in that capacity?" Marilyn probed.

"Yeah, I acted as if I had no idea what the hell she was talking about." Eric made a left turn. At the time, it seemed like denial and outrage were his best moves. He liked the fact that Beverly was the one person in his life who knew nothing about his illegal activities. He preferred to keep it that way. At least for now. Maybe at some point Eric would come clean with her when he felt she was ready to handle it. Such knowledge would bind them together even more, for it would be another reason he could never let her go.

"And Beverly bought it?" Marilyn asked.

"I don't know," he admitted. "For her sake, I hope so. At the very least, it buys me time to try to get to the bottom of this."

"I'm sure you will—or we will."

He stiffened. *There is no we, other than for sex.* But he had no problem having her believe otherwise while he dealt with this new wrinkle in his relationship with Beverly. "I'd better let you go," he told Marilyn.

"I'll let you know what I find out," she said.

"I'm counting on it."

Eric hung up, eager to know who was behind Beverly's shocking accusation. And, more importantly, why they'd told her. He thought about the trip to the Bahamas. He hadn't been sure how Beverly would react when he told her about it. For all he knew, she would toss the itinerary in his face, wanting nothing more to do with him. But she seemed receptive to the romantic trip, which he was happy to see. It was even more important now that they get away from Detroit for a while. He needed her more now than ever.

What he didn't need was someone he'd once been married to trying to sabotage their relationship. Which was why Eric had decided to pay his ex a little visit, as she had been the first person to come to mind as the one who would be foolish and bitter enough to let Beverly in on knowledge she had no damned business knowing.

Gloria Fox had just returned from the spa where she gave herself a well-deserved day of pampering. She also wanted to look and feel her best for a date tonight with her ex-boyfriend, Hal Ketchum, whom she'd started seeing again. Yes, she had once upon a time actually thought she might get back together with her ex-husband, Eric. But he'd made it perfectly clear there was no chance of that. He preferred to continue bedding that bimbo Barbie doll Beverly instead of being with a real woman who could put up with all his idiosyncrasies. Not to mention share his deep, dark secrets that not every woman could handle.

Indeed, Gloria once felt she couldn't handle it. What woman wanted a husband who made a living being an enforcer for the likes of such men as Leon Quincy and, before him, Vincent Miller? But she'd tried to make it work, hoping that having a baby might be enough to get Eric to be a real man and not a killer. Eric had rejected the idea of becoming a father and real husband, making Gloria believe he really didn't love her at all. So she ended things. Or he had. She'd given up trying to figure out who left whom. All that mattered was that it had stopped working between them, and it was time to cut their losses.

Then she'd gotten drunk recently, run into Beverly, and made the mistake of thinking she wanted Eric back. Gloria had sobered up pretty quickly and come back down to earth. Especially after Eric threatened her if she didn't back off and stay away from his girl toy Beverly. Then Marilyn put in her two cents, warning Gloria to leave Eric and Beverly alone. It didn't take much for Gloria to read between the lines. Though she knew Marilyn was supposed to be Beverly's best friend, it was quite obvious that Marilyn had her eye on Eric. Only, Beverly was too self-absorbed to notice where the real threat to her relationship was coming from. But that was her problem. Gloria washed her hands of them all. She was moving on with her life now and hoped Hal would continue to be a part of it.

When the doorbell rang, Gloria thought Hal might have come early for an afternoon in bed before more of the same tonight. She didn't even bother to look out the window for his car. Nor did she need to primp, since she'd just had that done for her.

Opening the door, Gloria was unpleasantly surprised to see Eric standing there. He had a scowl on his face, and she could only wonder what reason he had to be upset with her.

Beverly closed the door after Marilyn came inside. She was thankful her friend had dropped what she was doing to come over. As it was, Beverly had no one else she could talk to about this. Certainly not her mother, who would no doubt say, "I told you so," about Eric, even when there was no proof that he was the cold-blooded killer Dante made him out to be. And not Dante, either, since he was hardly impartial where it concerned Eric and was unwilling to consider that his so-called facts might be wrong. That left Marilyn, who Beverly trusted perhaps more than anyone else. She knew Marilyn had her back and was at least willing to listen before forming an opinion.

"So what's going on?" Marilyn asked as she sat in the living room on the couch.

Beverly sat on the loveseat, tucking her legs beneath her. "Where do I start . . . ?"

"How about by telling me what happened when Dante asked you to come over?" Marilyn suggested.

"All right." Beverly rubbed her hands as she thought about Dante's chilling words. "Seems like there's more going on with Dante than he led me to believe."

"Like what?"

Beverly sighed. "Like he isn't in Detroit to do a story," she said, having never considered his believable tale might not be true.

"You're saying he's *not* a journalist?" Marilyn looked at her curiously.

"I really don't know whether he is or not." Beverly didn't care right now about that part of who he still claimed to be. "What I do know is he had an agenda that has nothing to do with journalism."

"Tell me what he's up to!" Marilyn said insistently.

Beverly sat back, meeting her gaze. "Dante says that Eric works as a hired killer for Leon Quincy."

Marilyn's eyes bulged disbelievingly. "*What?*"

"He thinks Eric murdered his brother on orders from Leon." The accusation shook her to the core, as much for its shock value as the idea it could be true.

"That's crazy," Marilyn said, rejecting the information.

"That was my reaction," Beverly said waveringly. But as far-fetched as it seemed, she couldn't help but wonder if there was any merit to it.

"Who the hell is his brother?"

"He had a store," Beverly said. "I think Dante said his name was Russell."

"So wait a minute. You're saying that your lover secretly has a vendetta against Eric because he blames him for his brother's death?"

"Yes, that's pretty much it. And he feels the same way about Leon."

"So Dante was *using* you as a pawn to get to Eric?" Marilyn asked suspiciously.

Beverly shrugged. "He says he never realized I was with Eric until he saw us together."

Marilyn's brows rose. "And you *believe* that?"

"There's no way Dante could have known who I was when I first walked in that bar." Beverly shifted and put her feet on the floor. "We didn't do much talking that night." She warmed at the thought of their incredible lovemaking, remembering how thorough Dante was in appeasing her every sexual need.

"Whatever," Marilyn said, waving her hand cynically. "The bottom line is he's given you a load of crap in his misguided targeting of Eric."

"How can you be so sure?" Beverly regarded her thoughtfully.

Marilyn paused, then snapped her head back. "Do you *really* think Eric could be killing people without you having any knowledge of it?" she challenged.

"No, but, how well do I *really* know Eric?" Beverly had to ask. "Yes, we've been together for a year, but I don't know any more about his work than what he's told me. What if the whole thing is a lie and he really *is* a killer?"

"Well, what did Eric say about it?" Marilyn leaned forward. "I assume you confronted him?"

Beverly sucked in a deep breath. "I had to."

"And . . . ?"

"He said it wasn't true," she replied. "Eric insisted that his work for Leon was legitimate and had nothing to do with killing people."

Marilyn scowled. "Well, of course it doesn't. Don't forget that Spencer also works for Leon. And I can promise you he's definitely *not* involved in any criminal activity. If he were, I'd know it. That means Eric's hands are clean too."

"I guess you're right," Beverly said, noting that Eric had indicated the same thing. Or was Marilyn just as clueless as she was when it came to exactly what their men did in Leon's employ?

"I know I'm right," Marilyn maintained. "Eric is a decent man. I don't know why Dante pointed the finger at Eric for his brother's death, but I'm sure he has the wrong man. Otherwise, the police would've been all over him and Leon too."

"Good point." Beverly could not argue with her logic, no matter how convinced Dante seemed to be with his allegations that Eric was a very dangerous man to her and others. She was still very troubled by the whole thing. It certainly did nothing to help move her relationship with Dante along. Or had that been his plan all along: to rattle her so much that she pulled away from him, rather than the other way around?

"Did you tell Eric anything about your relationship with Dante?" Marilyn asked with interest.

Beverly shook her head. "It wasn't the right time to get into that." She wasn't sure if there ever would be a right time, all things considered.

Marilyn swallowed. "So where do things stand with you and Dante?"

"I really don't know," she said candidly. "The chemistry is still there. But he's been operating under false pretenses, and I don't know if we're on the same page anymore."

"And what about Eric?" asked Marilyn. "Do you plan to stay with him now that things have turned frosty with Dante? Or do you still want out, since you've made it pretty clear you don't really want to be with him anymore?"

Beverly considered the question, with the answer staring her right in the face. With everything that had happened between her and Dante and the serious questions she had about Eric, there was no way she could continue being with him.

"I want out," she told her sincerely.

Marilyn smiled. "Makes perfect sense. It's obvious that it's time for you to move on with your life, whether Dante's in the picture or not. I'm telling you this as your best friend."

"Eric bought tickets for us to go to the Bahamas in two weeks," Beverly said tonelessly, certain this would get a reaction from Marilyn. Knowing this was something she and Eric had talked about, Beverly had hoped their relationship status would be resolved before then. Evidently Eric had his own game plan for their future.

"He *what?*" Marilyn looked at her in disbelief.

Beverly swallowed. "Eric showed me the itinerary and brochures after I asked him about Dante's accusations."

"Wow." Marilyn sucked in a deep breath. "I assume you told him you didn't want to go?"

Beverly pressed her lips together. "I didn't say one way or the other," she admitted. She had certainly wanted to reject it, but with Eric staring at her for approval, she didn't want to bruise his ego at a time when she'd already called his integrity into question.

"You can't go on a romantic trip to the Bahamas with Eric!" Marilyn insisted. "Why string him along when you'd rather be there with Dante?"

"I'm not sure that's the case anymore." Beverly was confused where it concerned Dante. Yes, she would love to be on an idyllic, romantic island where they could enjoy each other's company and have steamy, all-consuming sex. But, given Dante's underhandedness and questionable motives for romancing her, she would definitely have to think about whether she wanted to continue her relationship with him. And that was assuming he still wanted to be with her now that his true mission had been revealed.

"So what are you going to do?" pressed Marilyn. "Pretend to be content as Eric's woman *just* to get a free trip to the Bahamas?"

Beverly glared at her. Sometimes she honestly wondered if Marilyn's tough love was a bit over the top. Why wasn't she supporting whatever choice she made instead of criticizing her? Beverly decided it was just Marilyn's tough personality. She'd made her point, though. Beverly had already begun to come to terms with the fact that it wasn't working with her and Eric and a trip to the Bahamas or anywhere else wouldn't change that. Even if things fizzled between her and Dante, she could no longer stay with Eric as if they were the all-American couple, when both knew they were anything but that. Eric would just have to accept it and let her go.

"I'm *not* going to the Bahamas with Eric," she told Marilyn steadfastly.

Marilyn's lips twitched into something resembling a contented grin. "I think that's a smart choice all the way around. Eric might be mad at first, but he'll get over it."

"I don't know about that," Beverly said, "especially after I accused him of being a killer. How could he not believe the two are intertwined?"

"Even if he does, that's his problem," Marilyn said harshly. "It doesn't change the fact that you've turned your attention to another man, whether that works out or not." She took Beverly's hand, meeting her eyes. "Trust me when I tell you that you're better off parting ways with Eric. And the sooner, the better, no matter what else might be in store for you."

Beverly took those words to heart, finding it hard to deny her feelings for Dante and no longer feeling anything for Eric. She would have to do the right thing and move on with her life, wherever it took her.

THIRTY-TWO

Eric's annoyance with Gloria over what he believed might be her betrayal was tempered by her appearance. He could see that she'd gotten her hair, nails, and makeup done, and it looked like she was wearing a brand-new outfit. Even her perfume agreed with him. Her entire package turned him on more than he'd expected, especially given the circumstances for him showing up at her house. He wondered if she'd given herself the spa treatment to celebrate ruining his life. If that were the case, it would be the biggest mistake she'd ever made.

"I need to talk to you," Eric said in a coarse voice, not giving her a chance to say no as he forced his way inside the house.

Gloria looked uncomfortable as she rounded on him. "I'm expecting company, so whatever you have to say, say it quickly and leave."

Company, huh? Eric was only mildly curious, but much more interested in whether she was the one who told Beverly something he didn't want her to hear.

"Have you been talking to Beverly?" he asked with narrowed eyes.

Gloria frowned. "What would I talk to her about?"

"Someone has been blabbing to her about what I do for Leon," Eric said.

She smirked. "I see. And you think it was me?"

He stepped up to her. "Give me a good reason to believe it wasn't you, and it better be a damned convincing one."

She took a step backward. "I'll give you three good reasons. One, I got the message the last time to stay out of your life. Two, I also got the message when Marilyn showed up and put her big face in mine to warn me to stay away from you and Beverly. And three, I'm dating Hal Ketchum again and am happy to be with someone who actually enjoys my company. I have no interest in screwing up your life the way you screwed up mine. If someone is out there whispering bad stuff about you in your girl toy's ear, you better look elsewhere."

Eric softened his hard stare. He believed she was telling the truth, though he imagined she wouldn't lose much sleep if his world fell apart. Maybe things would have turned out differently for them had they tried a little harder and given in more. In spite of everything, he supposed he still wanted her to be happy. As long as it didn't infringe upon the life he was trying to build with Beverly.

"All right," Eric said. "Maybe you weren't the one."

"Why didn't you just tell Beverly what was going on from the start?"

"That worked out pretty well with you, didn't it?" His voice was wry.

"I never held that against you," she claimed.

Eric's features softened. "Maybe we should've had that kid."

"We can't go back," Gloria said. "You made that very clear."

"It's for the best," he told her, realizing that neither of them was quite right for the other. Beverly was a much better fit for him at this time in his life.

"I think so." Gloria looked at her watch. "If that's all, Hal will be here any minute. I'd rather you weren't here when he comes."

Eric grinned. "No problem. See you around."

He drove away from the house, almost wishing Gloria had been the one to give Beverly the information. She would have been easier to deal with. Instead, Eric was left fearing that it might have been the cops who approached Beverly. Did that mean they were onto him? Or was someone else trying to poison Beverly's mind against him? He needed to get to the bottom of it for professional and personal peace of mind.

Eric thought about Marilyn. What the hell was she doing threatening Gloria? No one asked her to interfere. He'd have to have a little talk with her. On the whole, Eric supposed he couldn't find too much fault with Marilyn having his back as she seemed to, even while stabbing her best friend in the back.

He wondered if she had gotten anything from Beverly about who fed her the information about him.

Marilyn drove home, her mind preoccupied with what she'd learned from Beverly. That bitch had gotten herself involved with a man who had it in for Eric and was using her to accomplish his objective, no matter what the circumstances were when Beverly began spreading her legs for him. There was little doubt in Marilyn's mind that Eric was guilty as charged of killing Dante's brother. She recalled Spencer telling her about an uncooperative store owner by the name of Russell whom Leon had ordered taken out, which, of course, was Eric's specialty.

And Eric had bragged about it to her himself one afternoon after they had sex, telling her he'd made it look like a robbery and no one would be the wiser. Since the case had gone cold with the police, Marilyn assumed Eric had gotten away with it, like his other murders. But now, Dante had come along and was trying to stir up trouble.

He'd also opened Beverly's eyes to the true nature of the man she was staying with. Marilyn doubted that Dante had convinced her, especially when she had done a good job to dissuade Beverly from believing it was true. Marilyn had her own agenda. Since she wanted Eric for herself, the last thing she needed was for him to go after Dante, with Beverly being the grand prize for whoever was left standing when the dust settled.

Marilyn felt that would be less likely if Beverly simply left Eric, wherever she ended up, without the drama of Dante's accusations hanging over Eric to go along with the fact that Beverly had been sleeping with him. Once Marilyn had gotten her claws into Eric as her man, she had no problem with him getting rid of Dante before he came after Eric.

But, for now, she wanted to keep this interesting turn of events to herself. Her thoughts turned to the trip to the Bahamas that Eric had planned for him and Beverly. It really irked Marilyn that he continued to treat that bitch like a queen while being clueless that Beverly would have been fantasizing only about her lover while Eric was inside her. Assuming he could even get it up, as Beverly clearly had no idea how to get his libido in gear.

If things went according to her plans, Marilyn would be the one Eric took to the Bahamas, with Beverly out of his life for good. In fact, she wouldn't even mind if they relocated to Nassau. Particularly if the police began closing in on Eric and they needed to get away to somewhere the cops would never find them.

Soon Eric will come to realize that I'm the only woman he needs and can truly count on through thick and thin.

When Marilyn's cell phone rang, she took it from her purse and saw that it was Eric. She smiled, knowing he was eager to hear how things had gone with Beverly. She let it ring a few more times before answering.

"Did you talk to her?" Eric asked eagerly.

"Yes, I just left."

"Did she say who told her about me?"

Marilyn paused deliberately. "She said it was some private eye, but didn't say who he was working for. I got the feeling that the man was just fishing, hoping to rattle her into maybe helping him get more information about you."

"At least it wasn't the cops," Eric muttered. "But still—"

"I don't think you have anything to worry about," Marilyn told him optimistically. "I think that between us, Beverly's pretty much convinced that it's all a lie or a big mistake."

"I hope so. I don't want her mixed up in that side of my life."

"Of course not. Wouldn't want to burst her bubble, would we?"

"What's that supposed to mean?" he asked, his voice lowered an octave.

"Nothing," she quickly said. *I hate that he keeps putting her on a pedestal. Pretty soon she'll be knocked off her high horse, and I'll take her place.*

"Why did you pay Gloria a visit?" Eric asked sharply.

That bitch went and blabbed it to him. "I was just trying to get her off Beverly's back," Marilyn lied. "Believe it or not, she's still my best friend."

"Yeah, well, do me a favor and leave my ex-wife up to me from now on."

"No problem."

Actually it was a problem. She didn't want him to start pining for Gloria again. *I won't allow him to dump Beverly and go back to his ex. Where would that leave me?*

"Thanks for helping me out with Beverly," Eric said in a nicer tone.

"You know I'd do anything for you, baby." Marilyn made her tone soft and sexy.

"Yeah, I know." He paused. "Talk to you later."

"All right," she told him sweetly. *I'll make sure we do much more than just talk.*

Marilyn had already begun making plans to move into Eric's house when Beverly moved out. That, of course, would mean leaving Spencer. A small part of her didn't want to hurt him. But she couldn't help it if her heart and body belonged to another man. Spencer would just have to find someone else. Maybe he could go after Gloria. Or even Beverly, if Dante no longer wanted what she had to offer.

Marilyn could care less, as long as Eric was her man—and hers only—full-time. And, with everything she knew about him, she figured he owed her that much and a whole lot more.

THIRTY-THREE

Dante drove around that evening feeling helpless as he had not heard from Beverly in spite of sending her a couple of text messages. Had she told Eric about them and what he accused Eric of doing to his brother? Would Eric come after him now? Would the bastard hurt Beverly now that she knew his dark secret?

If he harms one hair on her head, he'll have to deal with me. Dante touched the handgun in his pocket. Using it against Eric and Leon would solve all his problems. Or would that merely create bigger problems, such as having to deal with the aftermath right in the middle of an FBI investigation?

The truth was Dante felt he needed the gun now more for self-defense than taking matters into his own hands to avenge Russell's murder. He had chosen to leave it up to Special Agent Ben Taylor and his colleagues to go after Leon Quincy and his posse, including Eric. But that didn't mean he would sit back and make himself a target. Or have Beverly in danger because of something he'd told her.

I can't just go barging into Eric's house and rescue Beverly like some hero in a comic book. For one, she might not need rescuing if she'd kept what he'd revealed about Eric to herself. Then he would only be placing her in more danger by exposing his relationship with her. It also occurred to Dante that by putting most of his cards on the table, it had changed the nature of his relationship with Beverly by revealing his hidden agenda. She had taken it with expected skepticism, questioning his true motives and feelings for her.

Eric had grown to care for Beverly well beyond their ravenous sexual appetite for each another. He still wanted her to come back to Los Angeles with him and further tap into the forces that made him feel so good in being with her. As far as he was concerned, he was able to easily differentiate between having her as a lover and Eric as his mortal enemy. Maybe in time Beverly would come to see things the same way. Until then, all he could do was wait and wonder.

Dante found himself in front of the pool hall he'd once followed Eric to. Having nothing better to do, he decided to go in, shoot some pool, and have a drink before calling it a night and dreaming about Beverly.

Inside, he ordered a beer and found an empty pool table. Shooting a little pool would take his mind off other things, most of which were beyond his control.

"You're still in town?" Dante heard the familiar voice.

He turned and saw Eric standing there. A trickle of concern struck Dante, as if the man were about to accost him. He nearly went for the gun tucked inside his sport coat, but held up as it didn't appear as though Eric meant him harm at the moment. Apparently Beverly had not spoken to him about working for Leon as a killer, with Russell being one of his victims. *Or maybe she had and left my name out of it.*

"Yeah, still here," Dante said blandly, then decided to add, "Not for long, though."

"Figured as much. Want to keep shooting alone or a little competition?"

I prefer to shoot alone if you're the competition. "A little competition sounds good," Dante said in a friendly tone. "Rack them up."

A few moments later, Eric broke the balls. Dante wished he could blow his brains out right now and be done with it. But since there were plenty of witnesses and he could actually hinder the case against Leon Quincy, to say nothing of being arrested himself for murder, the desire quickly subsided.

"So how did things work out between you and Tenesia?" Eric asked over his shoulder.

"We didn't really click," Dante told him candidly, holding his mug of beer. He suspected Eric had tried to set him up with her to deflect his own interest in Tenesia, perhaps for Beverly's sake.

"Too bad," Eric said. "Thought you'd want a piece of that in a hurry."

Dante gave him a fake chuckle. "She's a nice lady, just not for me."

"That's cool." Eric regarded him curiously. "Have you found interest in anyone else while you're here? Or do you have someone waiting for you back in L.A.?"

Was he testing him regarding Beverly? Did he suspect something was going on between them?

"No to both questions," Dante answered coolly. "Right now the work has been enough to keep me going."

"Yeah, I guess I can understand that." Eric calmly called his shot, draining it into a side pocket. "Me, I prefer to have some balance between work and play."

Dante sipped his beer musingly. "Then I guess I should ask you how your playmate Beverly is doing?"

"She's good."

"You mean good in bed?"

Eric grinned. "Yeah, definitely, along with just about everything else."

"Glad to hear you've got a nice thing going there," Dante lied. It was killing him inside.

"Yeah, we do. In fact, we're headed to the Bahamas in two weeks." Eric's voice rang with excitement.

Dante nearly lost his cool hearing that. He wondered if Beverly was okay going on a romantic trip with a man who she had at least considered might kill people for a living. It burned Dante up to think of Eric making love to Beverly on the beach or anywhere else. He doubted the man could hold a candle to him in satisfying her. Otherwise Beverly would never have found the need to stray in the first place.

"That's nice," he made himself say.

"I think it's just what we both need to put a little more spark into the romance," Eric told him and missed the shot.

"Whatever works for you, man." Dante could only hope Beverly came to her senses before it was too late. He lined up a ball and drilled it into a corner pocket.

After Dante won the game, he let Eric win the next before taking the tiebreaker himself. He rejected Eric's offer to stop by his house to shoot some more pool in private. Besides, not believing Beverly wanted to see him right now, the last thing Dante wanted was for his presence to make Eric suspicious, putting him and Beverly in danger.

He left as Eric found another challenger and turned his attention to him, as if not having a care in the world. Dante expected that to change soon one way or another.

Eric went home after being out all day. He'd wanted to give Beverly a chance to chill after she'd leveled the accusations at him. He seemed to have won her over before he left, punctuating it with the trip to Paradise Island and Nassau. Getting Marilyn to throw doubts into her head was a smart move on his part. Now he could only hope that whoever it was who was feeding Beverly information had moved on to someone else.

It bothered Eric that someone was on his case. And maybe Leon's too. He planned to talk to him about it first thing tomorrow and see if they could put their heads together to figure out if there was a need to be concerned or not.

As expected, Beverly had already gone to bed. He watched her for a moment, wondering if she'd gotten what she heard out of her system. He sincerely hoped they would get past that and move on with their lives. The fact that their relationship was outside what he did for a living grounded him. Eric hated to have to bring Beverly into his other world and have her lose some respect for him in the process. But he preferred that to losing her at all. She was his woman, and he would not let her leave him, so long as he was still walking among the free.

After taking a shower, Eric slipped into bed. Beverly stirred but did not wake up. With her back to him, he put his nose into Beverly's shoulder, inhaling her scent. It turned him on. He slid a hand between her legs and began to stroke her softly.

She reacted, awakening, and pushed him away. "Stop it!"

He kissed her shoulder. "I need you," he said softly.

"I just want to sleep tonight," she pleaded. "I hope you'll respect that."

Eric kissed her body again and then backed away. He suppressed his desire and left her alone. Having his way with her against her wishes would only hurt his cause in maintaining her trust. There would be time later to have sex, especially once they were in the Bahamas and away from the current climate. He would rediscover what it took to satisfy his woman and try to be patient with her. In the meantime, he had Marilyn to take care of his immediate needs, and more.

Beverly breathed a sigh of relief that Eric didn't press the issue of wanting to be intimate. She tolerated him holding her while snoring, but knew she didn't want any more sex between them. Not when it was Dante who still aroused her wildly whenever he entered her mind or body. What she didn't know was if what they had could be sustained, given his personal vendetta against Eric, regardless of if it was justified or not.

Either way, Beverly had made up her mind to leave Eric. This would be her last night staying in that house. She couldn't bear to have him touch her any longer and expect more. She certainly couldn't accompany him to the Bahamas and pretend they belonged there together as a romantic, loving couple. Since he was still a good-looking, smart, and successful man, Beverly was sure he would have no problem finding someone to take her place in his life. Eric was used to being the one to decide when a relationship was over, as with his ex-wife. But this time, she intended to make the decision and hoped he would take it like a man and not make it harder than it needed to be.

Beverly was up early the following morning. She left Eric in bed asleep and made herself a cup of coffee. She hoped to tell him it was over this evening, once she had her bags packed and he couldn't try to talk her out of it.

"Good morning," Eric said, entering the kitchen, fully dressed in one of his power suits.

"Morning." Beverly sipped her coffee and tried to make things seem as normal as possible.

"Sleep well?"

Not really. "Yes," she told him.

"So did I." Eric poured himself a cup of coffee. "Look, regarding what you were told about me—"

"Let's not talk about it," Beverly said hastily.

"You're sure?" He gazed at her. "I don't want this to come between us."

"It won't." She tried to keep her voice steady, knowing that the allegations had affected the way she saw him, even if she was still on the fence about whether there were any merits to Dante's charges. How could she possibly see Eric the same way at the mere possibility that she could be living with a stone-cold killer?

Moreover, even before this came up, she had begun to see him as someone who was too old for her and on a different wavelength in many ways, in spite of his willingness to take care of her.

"I'm happy to hear that," Eric said, sitting at the table. "By the way, I saw Dante last night at the pool hall."

Beverly reacted but shut it off just as quickly, realizing he was eyeing her unwaveringly. Did he know about them? Had Dante said anything? Was Eric reading the truth in her face?

"Oh, your friend," she uttered nonchalantly. "How's he doing?"

"Good," Eric responded over his coffee. "Guess he's leaving town shortly."

Beverly bit her tongue at the thought of Dante leaving without her. Or had that been his plan all along? Maybe his desire to get revenge for his brother's death overrode anything they had done and talked about in terms of a life together.

"I'm sure he'll be happy to get home," she suggested and then realized that the statement suggested she'd known him longer than Eric believed. "I mean, who wouldn't want to get back to sunny Southern California?"

Eric grinned. "Yeah, you got that right." He paused. "I thought he might have hit it off with Tenesia after we went out on the boat. But I guess any sparks between them fizzled."

"I'm sure Tenesia will do just fine on her own." Beverly tasted her coffee. She was thankful that Dante didn't fall under Tenesia's spell and sleep with her. Even if it was obviously what Eric was hoping, as if to keep Dante from going after her. Or perhaps it was so he could keep his own lust for Tenesia in check.

"I'm sure you're right." Eric put his mouth to the mug and stood up. "I've got to go take care of some business."

The first thought in Beverly's mind was that his business was to kill Dante. It scared her. "What business?" she had to ask.

"Same as always," he said calmly. "Consulting work. I've got an appointment with Leon, then others."

It sounded straight enough to Beverly, even with the dark thoughts Dante had planted in her head with no proof whatsoever. She had to accept that Eric was truly an honest businessman until she found out otherwise.

"See you when you get back," she told him with a faint smile.

"Okay." Eric bent down and gave her a brief kiss on the mouth.

Beverly chose not to get up for any prolonged show of affection. She was past that now with him. She just wanted them to go their separate ways, doubting they could remain friends. She had never been able to maintain a friendship with any of her ex-boyfriends, most of whom were bitter with the breakup. Eric would probably feel that way too. If so, it couldn't be helped. It was just the way it had to be.

She waited for him to drive off before rising. Though there was much to do, there was only one thing on Beverly's mind at the moment.

And one man.

Dante.

THIRTY-FOUR

The moment Dante opened the door with his sexy bare chest staring her in the face, Beverly felt her libido go into overdrive. When she looked up and locked eyes with him, reading the lust in his eyes, which matched her own, it was all she could do not to jump his bones on the spot. Instead, she pushed him inside and kicked the door shut.

"Kiss me," she demanded, too desirous of him to want to think about the future or anything else other than to have him deep inside her.

Dante grabbed the back of Beverly's head and brought his lips down to hers for a searing kiss that took her breath away. "I was worried about you," he said into her mouth.

"How worried were you?" she asked breathlessly, her body longing for his.

"Enough to go over there and get you."

Hearing him talk about rescuing her turned Beverly on even more. "I'm here now, and I need you to make love to me."

"I need it too," Dante said huskily.

He lifted her up in his arms and carried Beverly to the bedroom. After laying her on the bed, he spread her legs. "I want to taste and smell your sweetness first."

"Go right ahead," Beverly uttered daringly, though she knew that as hot as she felt right now, it wouldn't take long for her to come with his mouth working wonders down there.

She watched as he put his head beneath her dress. Since she wasn't wearing any underwear, she was more than ready for him to bring her joy.

"Hmm . . ." Beverly's moan deepened as Dante licked her clitoris over and over, then began kissing and sucking. The sensual sounds of his oral gratification were music to Beverly's ears and sheer pleasure for her body.

She ran her hands back and forth across Dante's smooth head while trembling as her orgasm approached. She thrust her groin into his face uncontrollably, and her back arched with the sensations rapidly spreading throughout her.

When Dante lifted his head, he licked his lips. "You're so wet and delicious," he murmured.

"Whose fault is that?" she asked unabashedly.

He sighed. "You drive me crazy, and I think you know it."

"It works both ways," Beverly admitted, feeling the urge to have him inside her.

"I'm going to take you now," Dante voiced urgently and slipped on a condom.

"I want you inside me," she uttered longingly, needing his fullness to complete her satisfaction.

Beverly opened her arms and legs, welcoming Dante as he came down to her and drove his erection deep inside. She gasped from the sheer power and pleasure of his penetration and repeated thrusts, bending her knees while she pressed against his rock-hard body. He licked her nipples generously, sending waves of sensations across Beverly's breasts. She desperately sought out his lips and sucked voraciously.

Their bodies, slick and lustful, pressed against each other closely as they made love with zest and intensity. Beverly reached a second and third orgasm, rocking her body and soul, before Dante succumbed to his own potent climax. Crying out, he drove deep into her, and she absorbed his erection as far as it could go, holding on to him while he released his seed. They finished the shared seduction by kissing each other with open mouths, their tongues caressing, while their bodies remained locked in coitus.

Beverly sucked in a deep breath, continuing to cling to Dante as she lay atop his moist, hot frame. She kissed him one more time before rolling to the side and coming back down to earth. She had been so caught up in the moment and man that everything else had been pushed to the back of her mind. Until now.

"This doesn't mean I buy anything you said about Eric," she said, inhaling the scent of their lovemaking.

Dante faced her. "I take it you didn't tell him what I said?"

Beverly turned his way. "I told him everything you said, but I left out who gave me the information."

"How did he react?"

"Eric denied he was a killer for Leon," she said flatly.

"Did you honestly expect him to say anything else?" Dante asked. "The man's not going to come out and admit he's a hired gun. Certainly not to someone he wants to put him on a damned pedestal."

"I don't put him on a pedestal," Beverly retorted. "Far from it."

"Maybe I should have said it was the other way around."

She narrowed her gaze. "He told me he saw you last night."

Dante's expression registered his surprise. "I went to the pool hall to try to take my mind off things, and he showed up."

"Yeah, *right*," she scoffed.

"I didn't go there looking for him," he insisted. "Hell, he was the last person I wanted to see last night, not knowing what was going on with you or if you were in harm's way."

"As you see, nothing happened." Beverly sighed. "I just needed time to think."

"So did I." Dante looked at her, and his tone grew serious. "Eric may have been on his best behavior for his own reasons, but I can assure you that he's a very dangerous man. It's only a matter of time before his criminal activities blow up in his face, and I don't want to see you caught in the middle."

"You haven't given me any proof that Eric's done what you say," she reminded him. "How can I be sure it's not a case of mistaken identity or some other game you're playing?"

"This is not a game," he told her. "And it's no case of mistaken identity. I hired a very capable private investigator to find out who killed my brother after the police seemed to turn a blind eye. He led me right to Eric and Leon Quincy. I have no doubt they are the ones responsible."

Beverly eyed him dubiously. "If true, why not pass along what you know to the police and let them handle it instead of trying to do it yourself?"

Dante paused while thoughtfully moving his hand across her smooth thigh. "From what I understand, the FBI is already focused on Leon Quincy's operation," he said. "And I'm letting them handle it. I only want to handle you. . . ."

His hand slid up her thigh, and Beverly closed her eyes for a moment to savor it before pushing his hand away. "It will take more than sex for us to move our relationship forward."

"I know." He gazed at her. "I want it to happen. I assume you do too. Otherwise you wouldn't be here right now, basking in the afterglow of some really hot sex."

Beverly blushed. "So I'm still into you. It doesn't mean I'm not mad at you for keeping important things from me."

"I'm sorry I didn't tell you sooner," Dante said. "The important thing is that you believe me now and get the hell away from Eric."

"I'm leaving him today," she said, though still reserving judgment about Eric as a killer. If he really was working for Leon in that capacity, Beverly wondered if Spencer was also involved in criminal behavior that Marilyn wasn't aware of.

"Does that mean the trip to the Bahamas is off?" Dante surprised her by asking.

She gave him a surprised look. "He told you about that?"

"Yeah, he couldn't say enough about his plans for you and him over there."

Beverly could only imagine their conversation, while wondering how Dante was able to refrain from bursting Eric's bubble by telling him about them.

"There won't be any trip to the Bahamas," she told him resolutely. "At least not with Eric."

Dante's eyes lit with satisfaction. "Good. Maybe you should move out when he's not home. It might be better if there's no confrontation."

Beverly didn't necessarily disagree, especially if Eric was the killer Dante believed him to be. But if he wasn't, didn't she at least owe him enough to woman up and tell Eric she was ending their relationship? She didn't want to hurt him, just be honest and hope they could part amicably. Or was that even possible at this stage?

"I think you're right," she remarked, feeling it was better to be safe than sorry.

"Glad we agree on this." Dante kissed her cheek. "Do you want me to go there with you?"

I would love that under other circumstances. Beverly sighed. "Probably not such a good idea. If Eric were to come home before I left and saw you there, it would only make things more difficult all the way around."

"I understand." Dante's eyes crinkled. "Just remember, I'm here if you need any help."

Her eyes batted. "And how long will you be here?" She hoped she didn't sound desperate to accompany him to Los Angeles. Or maybe she was, as the thought of being apart from him was one Beverly didn't care to contemplate.

"As long as it takes," he answered succinctly.

She showed her teeth. "Good answer."

Dante raised his mouth to hers, and Beverly devoured his lips with a long kiss and plenty of tongue as the room began to get warm again, with little chance it would cool off until they had satiated each other's sexual needs again.

Dante walked into the local FBI office. He was a little uncomfortable with the surroundings, given the fact that he had very nearly killed two men out of anger and revenge. These actions would have made him a wanted man, and his visit there could have had a whole different twist. As it was, he had come there voluntarily to try to help the FBI with their investigation. An investigation that Dante hoped would result in Eric and Leon being arrested and tried for their crimes.

Barely an hour had passed since Dante's passionate lovemaking with Beverly had ended. His feelings for her continued to grow every day. Obviously, she shared his sentiments, in spite of the burden Eric Fox had placed on their relationship. Now that they had reached this point, Dante really wanted to see things with Beverly move on to a new and exciting level. One that was away from Detroit and the negative vibes he got there as the place where Russell had lost his life.

It was hard for Dante to let Beverly go back to Eric's house, even temporarily. It was obvious to him that Eric was domineering and unlikely to allow Beverly to simply walk away. *I have to respect her decision to get in and out on her own, knowing how my presence would only complicate matters at this point.* He only hoped she wouldn't underestimate Eric and what the man was truly capable of, or hesitate for one minute to call him if she needed his help to get away from Eric's grasp and move on with her life.

This was the very reason Dante had decided to turn to the FBI. If they were on to Eric, he wanted them to step things up for Beverly's sake. If Eric had managed to slip under their radar, Dante wanted to make sure he was front and center, alongside Leon Quincy.

Dante was greeted at the door of an office by Special Agent Ben Taylor, who shook his hand firmly. Ben introduced him to a nice-looking FBI agent named Lynn Fry.

"I was surprised you wanted to meet with me," Ben told him.

"Guess we've both been full of surprises," Dante said dryly, remembering how he'd once believed Ben was a mild-mannered store owner named Paul Kline.

Ben grinned. "Yeah, I suppose." He pointed toward a chair near his desk. "Have a seat and tell us what's on your mind."

Dante sat down and Lynn sat beside him, while Ben remained standing.

Feeling all eyes on him, a moment of hesitation swept over Dante and he wondered if maybe this wasn't such a good idea. The last thing he wanted, or needed, was to be looked at as a suspect rather than a person hoping to help them. Dante was holding a folder, which he put on his lap. It contained info that would either work for him or against him. He was banking on the former.

He opened the folder and pulled out a photograph of Eric. "This is the man I believe murdered my brother. . . ." Dante passed it to Ben and watched him study it with the trained eye of a law enforcement professional. "His name is—"

"Eric Fox," Ben finished, handing the photograph to Lynn.

"You know about him?" Dante asked, though the answer was obvious.

"Yeah, we know our fair share. The better question is, how do *you* know about him and what makes you think Fox had anything to do with your brother's death?"

Dante had been prepared to be grilled. He wouldn't let it get to him. Or stop trying to do right by Russell without getting himself into a mess of trouble.

"I hired a solid private investigator to look into my brother's murder," Dante said. "After months, he came up with Eric Fox as the shooter."

Ben and Lynn gave each other a conspiratorial look.

"Is that so?" Ben asked.

Dante gazed at him. "Yeah, and I'm confident Eric is the right person."

"And what else did this private eye tell you?" Lynn asked curiously.

"He told me that Eric was acting on the orders of another man." Dante pulled out another photograph, handing it to her. "Leon Quincy, local crime boss. Ring any bells?"

Again he watched the two FBI agents exchange knowing glances. Dante could tell that he was onto something. Maybe this had been the right move to make.

Ben took a look at the second picture and then eyed Dante. "Got anything else for us?"

"What else do you need?" he challenged him.

Ben wrinkled his brow. "So how long have you been sitting on this information?"

"Long enough to know it's the real deal," Dante told him. "I want to know if you plan to use this info to get the ones who murdered my brother, Russell."

Ben paused. "We're very familiar with Eric Fox and Leon Quincy," he said calmly. "Both are bad news."

"That didn't exactly answer my question," Dante said, wondering if they were merely stringing him along.

Lynn faced him. "All we're at liberty to tell you is they are part of our broader investigation."

Dante's brows knitted. "Hey, I came to you, hoping you would help me since the police don't seem to give a damn that my brother was murdered. Maybe it was a mistake to—"

"You did the right thing," Ben said firmly. "Your information has been helpful, and it will be added to our own. I can't promise you'll get everything you're after, but you can rest assured that the days of freedom for these men are numbered."

Dante swallowed. He would settle for that at the moment, realizing taking the law into his own hands was no longer an option.

"I hope so," he told them.

"Do you mind giving us the name of your private investigator?" Lynn asked, leaning toward him. "Maybe he or she can provide more information that could be helpful in building a case against these men."

"It's a he." Dante no longer had a need to protect his source, given that his own agenda had changed in the scheme of things. "His name is Floyd Artest."

She jotted it down, and Ben got his attention. "So I imagine you'll be leaving town soon?"

"Yeah, I will," Dante replied. Not soon enough to suit him. But there was still some unfinished business.

He couldn't very well ask the FBI to protect his lover from the man she was planning to distance herself from. It might make them wonder if he had something else to hide. Or if she did. Dante was banking on the fact that Ben and his partner would put Eric out of commission before he had the opportunity to make Dante regret that he hadn't taken the man out himself.

"Thanks for coming in," Ben said as they stood toe to toe.

"Just doing my civic duty," Dante said wryly. "Whenever you slap the cuffs on Eric Fox and Leon Quincy, I'd love to be a witness."

Ben grinned crookedly. "I'm afraid it doesn't work that way. When an arrest goes down, we prefer that the public is out of the loop as much as possible to avoid collateral damage. I'm sure you understand our position."

"Whatever you say." Dante glanced at Lynn, who smiled faintly. He got the drift. *Stay the hell out of the way so you don't get hurt.* He would heed the advice—as long as they did their job in a timely manner and Beverly didn't find herself in trouble and needing to be rescued.

Dante stepped outside the FBI office, feeling as though he had dodged a bullet. After all, he had come to Detroit on a deadly mission and came that close to carrying it out. Fortunately for him, it was not a crime to want to do something that you never did. Still, he couldn't help but think that his visit to see Ben could have had a totally different outcome had the circumstances been slightly different. As it turned out, he and the FBI agents were on the same side, which was more than he could say for the police, who had done little to go after those responsible for Russell's death. Maybe now justice was not so far off.

Driving to a park near the river, Dante found a secluded spot with large evergreens as his cover. He took a bag containing the gun, which he'd wiped clean of any fingerprints, and threw it out into the water as far as he could. He had no further use of the firearm and wanted to make sure that the piece never fell into the hands of anyone else, either.

"So what do you think?" Lynn asked Ben after Dante left.

Ben sat back in his desk chair. "I think the journalist in Dante has done a damned good job to zero in on Leon Quincy and his top enforcer, Eric Fox."

"It's not like he didn't have a vested interest," Lynn pointed out. "The man seems pretty convinced that they're responsible for his brother's death."

"He may be onto something. The pieces fit, along with some circumstantial evidence that ties Quincy to strong-arming local proprietors who fail to pay up. It's not a stretch at all to think he would resort to taking out those like Russell Sheldon and Kurt Braddock to make a point, if nothing else."

Lynn glanced at her notepad. "I'll give this Floyd Art-est a call and see what he has to offer."

"Meanwhile, I think it's time we picked up Detective Stanley Dillard and Officer Roger Menendez," Ben said. "My guess is they'll have plenty to say about this to save their own asses. Then we can bring in Quincy, Fox, and their other associates." Ben felt a sense of excitement at the prospect of closing down Leon Quincy's operation once and for all.

"That will certainly make the agency happy."

"And a lot of other people too," Ben voiced. Perhaps beginning with Dante Sheldon, who clearly took what happened to his brother personally and apparently had gone to great lengths to even the score. Ben hoped to help him in that regard.

"I can't wait for this investigation to be over," Lynn said, touching his hand in a way that was not bound to draw suspicion but let Ben know she cared for him. "That way we can focus on something else."

Ben smiled at her. "I'd like that." He didn't know if they had a future or not, but he was certainly up for exploring the possibility of an extended romance while they enjoyed each other's company right now.

THIRTY-FIVE

Eric sat next to Leon in the lowly lit, out-of-the-way restaurant. Spencer and another member of Leon's posse, Moses Wright, were also at the table. With his concerns about the authorities being onto him, Eric had called the meeting, hoping to get some answers about what might be going down.

"What's on your mind?" Leon asked, peering at Eric. "It better be good."

Eric steeled his nerves, glancing at Spencer. "Someone's been snooping around, passing along information about me."

"What kind of information?" Leon's lips pursed.

Eric took a breath. "What I do for a living . . . working for you."

Leon's eyes grew with unease. "I thought you were a pro."

"I am." Eric resented the insinuation that this was his fault. He'd been damned careful doing Leon's dirty work. But one could never be too careful in the business of murdering people, especially if the authorities were after bigger fish and able to put two and two together.

"You have any idea who's behind it?" Leon asked.

"I was hoping you did," Eric responded tautly.

Leon paused. "You been talking to anyone about my business and yours, including your woman?"

Eric met the hard gazes of Spencer and Moses. He suspected they would like nothing more than to lay this on his shoulders. But he wasn't about to be intimidated by them.

"I think you know me better than that," Eric replied, keeping his composure. "That's not the way I work."

"You sure about that?" Spencer asked. "Maybe something slipped out while you were in bed with Beverly—"

Eric was barely able to refrain from laughing at the suggestion. Had he known better, he might have thought Spencer was onto him and Marilyn, whom Eric had inadvertently slipped info to from time to time during pillow talk. But he couldn't detect any signs that Spencer knew he was bopping his wife, who seemed to know plenty about what her husband did for a living. Eric was confident that Marilyn knew how to keep her mouth shut regarding Leon's operation for all their sakes. Not to mention their sexual trysts.

"Nothing slipped out," Eric insisted, looking Spencer squarely in the eye, and then turning to Leon. "Look, I came to you not to have the finger pointed at me, but because I wanted to see if you were aware of anything going down as far as a law enforcement probe." He knew that Leon had crooked cops on his payroll, who would likely know if something was happening that could cause Quincy's entire organization to crumble.

Leon lifted his coffee cup and sipped. "I'm sure the cops are always hoping to get lucky. But there's nothing specific that makes me believe I'm being targeted." His eyes shifted to the other men at the table and back to Eric. "I suggest you find out who's behind this, as you put it, 'snooping,' and get rid of the problem. That way, we can all rest a little easier and keep business running smoothly."

"That sound like something you can handle?" Moses asked brusquely.

Eric regarded the husky, forty-something man with thin, slicked-back graying hair. "Yeah, I can handle it." As if he would say differently, knowing Moses had been vying for his job and wouldn't mind one bit if he took a fall or suddenly became expendable in Leon's eyes.

"Then we're good," Leon said, dabbing the corners of his mouth with a napkin. "Keep me posted."

"I will." Eric took this as his cue to leave, and he was happy to do so, fearful that in spite of Leon's indication to the contrary, he was up to his neck in something that involved a criminal investigation. This, of course, remained to be seen. For now, Eric would keep his eyes and ears open for anything that raised a red flag. If he was headed for a fall, it wouldn't be without a fight.

Still, he would feel much better if he knew exactly who he was fighting, to give him the edge he needed to come out on top.

Eric left the restaurant alone and gave Marilyn a call. He was in the mood for some no-strings-attached, tension-relieving sex. Marilyn had never rejected him yet. He saw no reason for that to start now.

Leon waited until Eric had gone out the door before taking a breath and looking at Spencer and Moses. Both men had shown surprise when he told Eric that he was unaware of any investigation into his activities. Now Leon felt he owed them an explanation, since he needed their continued loyalty and silence, should there be any arrests.

"I think it's best if Eric believes this is all about him and not about us," Leon said calmly. "If the feds are out to get us, we need to start distancing ourselves from Eric. Right now, he's a potential liability who may have gotten a bit sloppy. We don't need the type of trouble

Eric could bring to the organization if he is tied to any of the hits I ordered."

"You want me to take him out?" Moses asked eagerly, his thick brows bridged.

Leon considered that this might solve one of his problems. He feared that Eric might talk if push came to shove and make his life miserable in the process. On the other hand, if he were killed, it might cause an even deeper investigation that could lead right to Leon's door, putting everything he had going on in jeopardy.

"Not yet," he responded. "Let's wait and see if Eric will do himself in and save us the trouble."

"He's not a fool," warned Spencer. "The dude will be looking over his shoulder and be ready to defend himself, whoever goes after him."

"He ain't Superman," Moses argued.

"True, but he is one of the best in the business at what he does," Leon pointed out. That was exactly why he had hired Eric in the first place, to get rid of certain people who became expendable. Now it appeared as if Eric himself was being targeted. Leon wasn't sure if it was more personal in nature or part of a broader campaign to go after him. He didn't really care at this point.

I have to look out for number one, first and foremost. If that means selling out Eric to whoever wants him in custody, or dead, then so be it.

Leon straightened his shoulders and smoothed his silk tie. Feeling the heat, he was already planning to skip town and take his operation with him. That didn't necessarily include Spencer or Moses, both of whom could prove to be more liabilities than assets when all was said and done. He wasn't about to tell them that, though. Not as long as he needed them to be on guard for possible infiltration into the organization by the feds—or others who were out to get him.

"Let's keep an eye on Eric for now," Leon ordered his men. "If things get out of control, and he becomes more of a problem than a solution, we'll deal with him. . . ."

THIRTY-SIX

Beverly had packed her bags and was hoping Eric didn't show up till she was gone. She was more than a little concerned about how he might react to her ending their relationship so abruptly, especially if he was half as dangerous as Dante had suggested. In spite of the fact that Eric had mainly shown her his good side, Beverly strongly suspected it was only what he wanted her to see, and not who he truly was.

Maybe I should have allowed Dante to come along as insurance, in case Eric returns and goes ballistic. But wouldn't Dante's presence as the other man with whom she was set to start a new relationship only have exacerbated the situation, complicating matters and all but ensuring a confrontation?

Feeling antsy, Beverly brought her bags downstairs and put them in the living room. She had taken everything Eric had given her, but would give it back if that was what he wanted. She wouldn't make a fuss over the items, even if many were expensive or rare. In spite of her reputation among some as a high-maintenance gold digger, she rejected the label. There was nothing wrong with taking what the men she was involved with had chosen to give her. There was also nothing wrong with turning her back on it for a relationship of substance with a man who had stolen her heart to go along with her sexuality and romance.

When her cell phone buzzed, Beverly saw that it was her mother. She let it go to voice mail, then listened to the message. As expected, her mother was checking on her progress, or lack of, in ending things with Eric. *I'll call her later, when I have something new to say about the subject matter. Otherwise, she'll just get on my case about procrastinating or making bad choices, which she wouldn't have made in the first place.*

There was a knock on the door, which startled Beverly, who had been so absorbed in her own thoughts. She hadn't heard anyone drive up, but didn't rule it out given her preoccupation. Obviously Eric had a key, so she was confident it wasn't him, thank goodness.

Looking through the peephole, Beverly was surprised to see Tenesia White. They hadn't spoken since the day they went out on the boat with Eric and Dante and Tenesia had tried to seduce Dante.

Beverly sucked in breath and opened the door. "Hi, there." She pasted a smile on her face.

"Hey, girl," Tenesia said. "I was in the neighborhood, so thought I'd stop by."

"You're always welcome." *Though not for long, unless it's Eric you came to see.*

It was only after Tenesia had walked through the door that Beverly remembered she'd put her bags in the living room.

"Are we going somewhere?" Tenesia asked, her tone full of curiosity.

Beverly had considered giving her an evasive response, not wanting to let the cat out of the bag before speaking to Eric. But she decided it made little difference at this stage if Tenesia knew the truth.

"I'm leaving Eric," she said, trying to keep her voice from shaking.

Tenesia cocked a brow. "Really?"

"Yes. He doesn't know that yet, but . . ."

"So what happened?" Tenesia asked, flipping her hair to one side. "I thought things were good between you two."

Beverly wasn't going to tell her about Dante. That would only lead to too many questions and possible conflict, which she didn't need right now.

"I just need to move on," Beverly said succinctly. "We had our time, but it's over now."

"Sorry to hear that."

Are you? Or did Tenesia see this as good news, considering she was available to go after Eric? "Anyway, if you want Eric, you can have him."

Tenesia frowned. "I don't want him," she stated. "I never have, Beverly. It was all in your head."

"Maybe it was," Beverly conceded. "Nevertheless, it's over and done with. I'm looking forward to getting on with my life and wish Eric only the best."

"And I wish you only the best." Tenesia gave her a hug. "I hope you believe that."

Beverly was beginning to. She'd never wanted a man to come between her and Tenesia. She could only hope that Dante never would when all was said and done.

"I do," she told Tenesia, fighting back tears. "So what's been happening with you these days?"

"Not too much. Taking care of my mother and trying to find a job." Tenesia's face lit up. "Oh, I've started dating again."

"Really?" Thoughts rolled through Beverly's head as she recalled seeing her leaving Dante's hotel. Was she still pining for him? "Anyone I know?"

Tenesia smiled. "I don't think so. He just got a job transfer here from New Jersey. We're taking it slow for now. I'll have to see if he turns out to be the man of my dreams. Haven't had much luck in that department."

"So maybe after a few frogs, it's time for you to find your prince," Beverly suggested, happy that she seemed to have gotten Dante out of her system.

"Could be," Tenesia said sincerely. "I hope everything works out for you too. If not with Eric, then someone else."

"Thanks." Beverly felt as though she had found her prince, lover, friend, and so much more in Dante. She only wanted the opportunity to make this work, and he had given it to her. The hard part was not so much in breaking up with Eric but having him accept it graciously so they could both have a clean slate to get on with their lives. But if he chose to make things difficult, there was nothing she could do about it as her decision had been made and there was definitely no going back.

Eric held Marilyn's head while she orally gratified him. He listened to her sucking noises while she took in his entire erection, turning him on. At the last moment, he decided he'd rather climax inside her vagina than her mouth this time. He brought her up and pushed her against the wall. Moving in between her legs, he lifted Marilyn's skirt and was happy to see she wasn't wearing any underwear.

His hard penis bore deep into her as she propped her thighs on his hips. The thick, wet feel inside her stimulated Eric's penis as he thrust in and out. He ignored Marilyn's loud moans and fantasized instead about Beverly, as though she were the one he was making love to. He grabbed one cheek of Marilyn's big ass and squeezed while continuing to go at it hot and heavy, working up a sweat.

"I'm coming I'm com—" she uttered, clutching his shoulders and shaking uncontrollably.

Eric didn't let go of her as he felt his surge about to release. Picking up the pace, he drove hard into her while breathing heavily and feeling his heartbeat quicken. When the moment of impact came, Eric grunted unevenly and gave it one more mighty thrust while his orgasm subsided.

He pulled out of her and watched his erection disappear and with it, his interest in being with Marilyn any longer this day. She'd given him what he needed and now it was time to go back to Beverly.

"You do it for me every time, baby," Marilyn cooed, licking his cheek.

"Same here." Eric zipped his pants. "Unfortunately, I've gotta go."

Marilyn's forehead furrowed. "Where?" she demanded. "To be with *her?*"

"Yeah, Beverly." He saw no reason to say otherwise. "You know she's my woman."

"*I'm* your woman!" Marilyn glared at him. "*I'm* all you need."

Where was this coming from? "Not quite," Eric said, trying to be nice about it. "I need you part-time. I need Beverly *all* the time."

"But she doesn't need you," Marilyn said nastily. "Not like I do. Make me your number-one woman and you'll never regret it."

Eric was beginning to regret it right now. She was being unreasonable and clingy. Things he hated in women. Especially those who had little to offer him other than their mouth, breasts, and vagina, not necessarily in that order.

"I thought you were happy being with Spencer?" He didn't really believe that, but it sounded good. In truth, it was obvious that the man couldn't keep her interested in him in the bedroom. But he still wanted her the rest of the time. That had to count for something, didn't it?

Marilyn rolled her eyes. "Right, just like you're happy being with Beverly. We both know she can't keep up with you in the ways that count most."

"I'm talking about you and Spencer." Eric hoped to dodge any more discussion about his relationship with Beverly before things turned ugly.

"There's nothing to talk about," she spat. "I don't love Spencer. I love you!"

"*What?*" Eric's eyes bulged. He hoped she wasn't serious.

"You heard me. You're the love of my life, and it's time everyone knew about it, including Beverly."

"Are you out of your mind?"

"My mind is perfectly fine, thank you," Marilyn retorted. "I stand by my feelings for you."

Eric sighed. The last thing he wanted was to see their little arrangement come to an end. But she was obviously making it hard, if not impossible, to keep it going. Not when she was talking such nonsense. Maybe he should have seen this coming. Or maybe she was simply going through a situation with Spencer and projecting her true feelings in the wrong direction. Either way, it was time to move on.

Before he even realized what was happening, Marilyn had wrapped her arms around his neck and was kissing him while murmuring, "You're mine, baby, not hers."

He yanked her away, wiping his mouth with the back of his hand. "Whatever has gotten into you today, I can't deal with it," he said. "I thought we both understood what this was about." Eric was happy to spell it out. "We're here for uncomplicated sex. That's it. Anything else you've conjured up is strictly in your head.

I'm with Beverly and always will be, if I have any say in the matter."

"You don't have a say," Marilyn tossed back at him with a catch in her voice. "Your Little Miss Perfect Beverly isn't the loyal, loving woman you think she is."

"What the hell are you talking about?" Eric suspected she was grasping at straws, somehow hoping to drive a wedge between him and Beverly for her own misguided purposes.

"I'm talking about Beverly and her plans for a life that don't include *you!*"

He narrowed his eyes, not liking the sound of that, though refusing to believe a word of it. "I don't have time for this crap. I'm out of here."

Marilyn grabbed his arm. "You'd better make time. You need to hear what I have to say. . . ."

Though it was clear to Eric that she was desperate to hold on to him and whatever fantasies she had conjured up, something about her gloating expression got his attention. "You've got one minute to get it off your chest," he snorted, ripping her hand off his arm.

She sighed, locking eyes with him. "Beverly's leaving you. . . ."

"*What?*" Now Eric knew she was delusional. He and Beverly were an item, and she wasn't going anywhere, except to the Bahamas with him.

"She's been having an affair with another man right under your nose," Marilyn stated wickedly. "When you and I have been getting it on, she's been doing her thing, too, and loving *every* minute of it."

Eric felt the bile rise in his throat. He grabbed Marilyn roughly by the shoulders and shook her. "You're lying through your crooked teeth."

"I'm telling you the truth," she maintained. "I should've told you long before now, but Beverly told me in confidence and—"

The more he thought about it, the more Eric considered that maybe there was something to this. The fact was Beverly had been acting strange lately, as if something was going on. And she hadn't been interested in sex, giving him one excuse or another. Could it be that she was getting some elsewhere? The mere notion infuriated him, never mind that he had been spending time with Marilyn, which had clearly been a mistake.

He tightened his grip on Marilyn's shoulders. "Who is he?"

She looked him in the eye. "Dante," she said gleefully.

Eric's heart skipped a beat at the name. "Dante, my . . ."

"Yeah, that's right. Your pool buddy's been doing your woman."

Eric couldn't believe what he was hearing. "Dante's cool. He wouldn't go after Beverly."

"Oh, yes, he would, and he *did*," Marilyn insisted. "They've been having sex even before you met him at the pool hall. Both of them made a fool out of you and have been laughing about it behind your back ever since."

Eric's nostrils flared. He wanted to dismiss this cockamamie tale out of hand, but looking at her gloating face, he was sure that Marilyn got the whole story directly from Beverly, who had no idea just what a bitch her so-called friend was. Eric could care less about that, though. His only interest was in the fact that Beverly was cheating on him with a man he had invited into his home, not knowing Dante had his eye on Beverly the whole time.

"How long have you known about this?" Eric demanded, shaking Marilyn.

"From the very beginning, when Beverly seduced Dante at his hotel," she practically bragged.

Eric did the math. It infuriated him to think of how many times that asshole had actually slept with Beverly. "And you *never* bothered to tell me?"

"Hey, I'm loyal to Beverly too," Marilyn said contemptuously. "At least I was before I began to see the type of woman she really was. I wanted to spare you all her sex drama, knowing you wanted to believe she was a damned saint when it came to keeping her legs closed except for you."

"That two-timing bitch!" Eric felt sick to his stomach at the stark betrayal by Beverly and Dante. He also hated that Marilyn knew all about it, hanging on to her secret until the right time to throw it in his face.

Marilyn smiled crookedly. "So you see . . . she's not Miss Goody Two-shoes, after all. I know I'm bad, too, but I never pretended to be anything else—not with you, anyway. This is why we belong together. I understand you and respect you as a man and lover. But Beverly was only using you as a sugar daddy until a younger guy who could satisfy her sexual urges came along. She doesn't give a damn about you. The sooner you realize that, the sooner you can put that bitch out of your mind."

I'm putting you out of my mind and life before anyone else. "What hotel is he staying at?" Eric demanded.

She told him. "I'll bet he's with her right now." She poured it on. "Get used to it, 'cause Beverly's dumping you to be with him."

"Like hell, she is." Eric was already plotting his next move beyond getting Marilyn out of his life for good.

"Oh, there's one other thing you need to know." Marilyn raised her chin triumphantly. "It was Dante who told Beverly about you."

"How did he know?" Eric's mouth became an O. He wondered if Dante was an undercover cop or FBI agent.

"Dante's brother owned a store and was shot to death. He blames you and Leon for it." Marilyn twisted her lips. "I tried to convince Beverly that Dante was way off base, but evidently he's made a believer out of her. They plan to skip town together."

"Over my dead body!" Eric blared, releasing her from his grip. His indignation was now directed elsewhere.

So it was no accident that I happened to run into Dante at the pool hall. The bastard has been trailing me from the start. He wormed his way into my life, stole my woman, and probably hoped to kill me as part of the bargain in his plan for revenge.

"Forget about him and that bitch, Beverly!" Marilyn pleaded, grabbing his shirt. "We don't need them. We have each other."

"We have nothing," Eric shouted, ripping her hands off him. "You and your deceit and manipulation disgust me."

Her face contorted into a pout. "You don't mean that."

"I mean every last damned word." His gaze narrowed. "You could never come close to Beverly in any respect, you hear that?"

"This isn't you talking." Marilyn desperately wrapped her arms around his waist. "I know you're pissed about what Beverly and her lover Dante have done to you, so you're taking it out on the one person who would do anything for you."

Eric pushed Marilyn away and back-smacked her. "You didn't do the one thing I needed from you most— tell me what was going on with my woman," he yelled.

"I didn't want that to mess up things between us," she stressed, touching her stinging cheek.

"No, you didn't want to mess up any stupid fantasy you had about some dream life for us." His lip curled. "Well, it's not going to happen now—or ever! Beverly is still my lady, and nobody will stand in the way of that."

"She's not worth your love," Marilyn hissed. "Or is this what you call love, putting your penis in my mouth instead of hers?"

Eric felt like hitting her again, but suspected that was exactly what she wanted, to play the victim and hope maybe he'd come crawling back to her. He checked his temper while wishing he had never hooked up with her.

"What we did was all about sex—nothing more," he made clear. "Now even that's over with. Get the hell out of my face and go back to your husband. Maybe you can worm your way back into his good graces, though if I were him, I'd toss your ass out on the street. That's just what you deserve."

"I deserve you," she cried, reaching out to him. "Let's forget everything that's happened and go to the Bahamas. Beverly may not be interested in that, but I am. You can trust me to do right by you always. Can she say the same?"

Eric didn't want to hear another word about it from her. Yes, Beverly had betrayed him, and he would deal with her and her lover Dante. But he'd be damned if he would ever want to take up with the likes of Marilyn, who wasn't his type physically or mentally.

"It's over, Marilyn," he said tonelessly. "Get that through your head and don't ever contact me again. And stay the hell away from Beverly. I think you've done enough as her backstabbing friend."

"Please, don't go," Marilyn uttered frantically, trying to block his way. "I love you."

"You don't know the meaning of the word!" Eric tossed her to the floor and glared at her with hatred before leaving the room.

He sucked in a deep breath, trying to wrap his mind around what he'd just learned about Beverly and Dante. They would pay for humiliating him. First, he would make it clear to Beverly that she was not walking out on him for that bastard. Not if she wanted to keep breathing. Then he would see to it that Dante got the same thing his brother got—only worse.

Eric went to his car, intent on carrying out his plans and regaining control of a situation that was threatening to get away from him.

THIRTY-SEVEN

Marilyn was mad as hell at the way Eric had treated her. She didn't deserve it the way she worshipped him and kept all his secrets as though they were her own. She'd known it was a risk telling him about Beverly and her tawdry affair with the man named Dante, but the time seemed right to put her cards on the table and hope that Eric was man enough to know who he truly should have as his woman. But, no, he'd rejected her like other men in the past, before Spencer came along.

She had thrown herself at Eric, done things she had never done sexually with Spencer, all because she wanted what belonged to Beverly. Now just like that—it was over. And for what? So he could try to win Beverly back while taking out Dante and anyone else who stood in the way? Wasn't it obvious that Beverly wanted nothing more to do with him, having made her choice to be with another man?

Marilyn wiped the tears from her cheeks as she sat on the motel bed, feeling miserable, betrayed, and, most of all, vengeful. She would be damned if she stood back and allowed Beverly and Eric to somehow end up staying together, leaving her sitting on the sideline, pretending to be happy for Beverly while knowing full well she was anything but.

She dug her cell phone out of her purse and called Beverly. *You'd better pick up, bitch! I want you to hear it from me before Eric gets the chance to do whatever he thinks he needs to in order to win you back.*

Marilyn doubted he had a snowball's chance in hell to do that. Not the way Beverly had talked about Dante, what a fantastic lover he was, great looking, and more. But she couldn't take the chance that somehow Eric might overcome the odds and convince or coerce Beverly into staying with him. Marilyn felt she couldn't live with that.

"Hello." She heard Beverly's voice, sounding a bit edgy.

"Hey." Marilyn thought carefully about what she should say. "I need to see you."

"What's wrong?"

"I'd rather not say over the phone," Marilyn told her. "It's important."

"Why so secretive?" questioned Beverly.

You'll find out soon enough. "It's, uh, a rather sensitive subject," was all Marilyn would tell her. "I promise it won't take long."

Beverly hesitated. "All right."

Marilyn asked her to come to the motel, which was still hers for the day. It was a good out-of-the-way place that Eric likely wouldn't think to come back to. Not until it was too late.

"I'll be waiting," Marilyn said simply before disconnecting. She would use the time it took for Beverly to get there to ponder everything she had to say, knowing that it would very likely end their friendship forever. At this point, she didn't really care. She wanted Beverly to hurt as much as she did.

Beverly tossed her bags in the trunk of her car, her eyes darting around for any sign of Eric's car approaching. Thankfully, he didn't show up at the last moment, making a tense situation even worse.

On the road, Beverly mused about this meeting with Marilyn. She sounded pretty strange on the phone and more cryptic than usual. And what was with the motel? She could only speculate about why Marilyn wanted to meet there instead of at her house or a restaurant. Maybe she and Spencer had a big fight and she moved out. As far as Beverly knew, things were cool between them. But what did she really know about the state of their relationship?

As it was, she had her own relationship problems. Starting with ending one and beginning another. In both instances, there was a cloud in the air that did not appear as if it was ready to dissipate overnight. Only time would tell if Eric was really Dr. Jekyll and Mr. Hyde. Or an innocent man, albeit no longer her guy.

She drove into the motel parking lot and parked in front of the room number Marilyn had given her. A moment later, Beverly was at the door, more than a little curious about why she wanted to meet her there. Had Marilyn not sounded so distraught, she might not have come. But because Marilyn had been there for her time and time again, Beverly felt obliged to see what was going on with her.

She knocked on the door. It opened right away, and Marilyn stood there, looking disheveled. There was a welt on her left cheek, and she had clearly been crying.

"What on earth happened?" Beverly asked, eyes expanded.

Marilyn did not speak, and her mouth was tight as she stepped back inside the room.

Beverly went inside. Immediately she picked up the musky scent of a man's cologne and assumed it was Spencer's. Or could it have been someone else's?

"Who did this to you?" She regarded Marilyn. "Did you have a fight with Spencer?"

"He knows," Marilyn said simply.

"Who knows what?" Beverly was confused.

"Eric knows about you *and* Dante."

"How?" Beverly's left eyebrow shot up. "*You* told him?"

Marilyn paused. "Yeah, I told him everything you wouldn't."

Beverly was shocked and bewildered. "But why? How could you? It wasn't your place to tell him."

"And it was yours?" Marilyn's lashes descended over her glare. "You had your chance and kept putting it off, so I did it for you."

Beverly's head snapped back as if she'd been slapped. It still hadn't registered about what was going on here. She couldn't imagine why her best friend would do such a thing behind her back.

She looked around the room, noting the bed wasn't made, and back at her. "Wait a minute. Are you saying Eric was here—in this room?"

"Yeah, he sure was." Marilyn touched the side of her face, wincing. "And he made sure I didn't forget."

"Eric hit you?" Beverly didn't want to believe he would be violent toward Marilyn, even if she blindsided him with news he didn't want to hear. Equally troubling was why they would be meeting in a cheap motel room in the first place.

"Isn't it obvious?" Marilyn batted her eyes. "He didn't like what I had to say and reacted like an asshole."

"I'm sorry to hear that." Sorrier than she knew. "I still don't understand why you made my business your own. I confided in you as a friend and counted on you not to go back and blab it to Eric. Or am I missing something here?"

Marilyn laughed cynically. "Yeah, I think so. Do I really have to spell out every detail for you, girlfriend?"

Beverly glanced around again, focusing on the bed, which had clearly been used by maybe more than one person. She locked eyes with Marilyn, hoping what she was thinking was wrong.

"Maybe you *should* spell it out," she directed her.

Marilyn got up in her face, her mouth twisted into a sneer. "Okay. I've been sleeping with your man—actually, there wasn't much sleep going on. Or should I say, the man you used to call your own until you found someone else to spread your legs for."

Beverly took an involuntary step backward. Apart from trying to wrap her mind around the stunning betrayal, she was shocked by the cruel way in which she had said it. She was like a totally different person to Beverly.

"How long?" That was all she could think to ask her.

"Long enough to keep him coming back for more of this." Marilyn gloated and ran her hands up and down her body. "I gave Eric what you couldn't, or wouldn't, and made him feel like a man."

"You bitch!" Beverly impaled her with an angry stare, feeling like she had been violated in the worst way by someone she had trusted. Instead of Tenesia, it had apparently been Marilyn all along who Eric had been bedding on the side, even while pretending to be a one-woman man. "How could you do this to me? I thought you were my friend."

"You only thought what I wanted you to believe," Marilyn stated venomously. "You were always the attractive, slender one all the men craved, while I was always your overweight friend that men never noticed. Do you have *any* idea how that made me feel? Of course not. You were too busy having your way with any man of means who looked your way twice. When you set your sights on Eric, I decided that I deserved him more. So I took him from you in the ways that

counted most—in bed. And he loved *every* second of
what I gave him. So did I."

Beverly noted that she was speaking in past tense.
Judging by the way Eric had worked her over and was
no longer there, it was clear that their dirty affair had
come to an end. Beverly didn't know whether to laugh
or cry. Eric had given her the perfect out for a relationship that was going nowhere, as he had proven himself
to be a first-class asshole like so many men in going
after her so-called best friend. More troubling was
that Marilyn had such a low self-esteem and a jealous
streak. Beverly had never seen anyone cheat on her
husband out of spite and desperation, just to take Beverly's place in a sexual relationship.

"I hope to hell he was worth it to you," she told
Marilyn in a decidedly unfriendly voice. "From where I
stand, we've both been screwed by Eric. And for what?
To put one over on me and make yourself feel better as
a woman?"

"Look who's talking," Marilyn retorted. "Eric gave
you everything, and you tossed it all away the first
chance you got for a man who was only using you to get
to Eric. You don't deserve him."

"And *you* do?" Beverly's nostrils expanded. She put
aside the notion Dante had used her, choosing to believe that he truly cared about her, no matter what his
beef was with Eric. Obviously the same could not be
said for Eric, who proved to be a self-centered bastard
who saw her only as eye candy he was free to disre-
spect in the worst way. Just as unsettling to Beverly
was Marilyn's attitude about the entire scenario, which
she never saw coming. "You think Eric smacking you
around and leaving you here high and dry is the way
you deserve to be treated? Does Spencer deserve to be
with a backstabbing bitch who thinks so little of herself
and what it means to be a true friend?"

Marilyn tried to hit her in the face, swinging both hands wildly, but Beverly deflected them with her forearms and pushed her away. She stepped back, putting more distance between them, resisting the urge to strike back physically herself. "The truth hurts, doesn't it?"

"Go to hell!" Marilyn said sharply.

"I think you've already been there, *girlfriend!*" Beverly responded sarcastically. "Eric is all yours, if you can get him back. I'm finished with him . . . *and* you."

"This isn't over," Marilyn said, wiping tears from her eyes.

"Keep telling yourself that." Beverly moved toward the door. "It was over the moment you showed your true colors. I hope it hurts like hell, because it definitely hurts me to know what a fool I've been where it concerns you much more than Eric. Good-bye, Marilyn."

Beverly got out of there as quickly as she could, with the air stagnant from betrayal and disgust. At this point, she had absolutely no interest in confronting Eric and hearing his lame excuses for choosing Marilyn, of all people, to cheat on her with. As far as Beverly was concerned, she wished she had never hooked up with Eric and hadn't chosen Marilyn to be her friend and someone she could put her trust and loyalty in. Obviously both had proven to be big mistakes that she would forever regret!

Eric arrived home and saw that Beverly's car was not in the driveway. Damn. Where the hell was she? As if he had to guess. She'd gone to be with that asshole Dante. The mere thought grated on Eric's nerves. No one cheated on him and got away with it. Especially someone he put on a damned pedestal, where she might have stayed had Dante not come to town on some revenge mission, stealing his woman as a bonus.

He headed inside, wanting to see if Beverly had actually flown the coop for good or had merely gone to see Dante for sex before returning, pretending everything was good between them. Since Beverly didn't know he was onto her affair with Dante, Eric wouldn't have been surprised if she'd continued to play games with him. Would she actually have gone to the Bahamas as planned, pretending she was still his lady while bedding another man?

Eric cocked a brow with indignation when he saw the note on the kitchen table. Damn. That bitch had left him and didn't have the guts to tell him face-to-face. Did she really think for one moment he would allow her to shack up with a dude he had tried to befriend, unaware at the time Dante was his enemy in more ways than one? Eric suspected Marilyn had tipped her off that he knew what was going on. He could only imagine her glee in sticking it to Beverly.

He would deal with that bitch later. Right now, Eric only wanted to go after Beverly, whom he still considered his woman, while doing what he needed to do to get Dante out of their lives permanently.

I'll make that bastard wish he'd never come to Detroit hell-bent on revenge before setting his sights on Beverly.

Eric stormed out of the house and into his car, where he headed for the hotel where Dante was staying.

THIRTY-EIGHT

Dante answered the phone on one ring when he saw that Beverly was the caller.

"Eric knows about us," she said in a shaky voice.

Dante swallowed as he stood in his room. "How?"

"My girlfriend Marilyn told him." Beverly paused. "She's been sleeping with Eric and used whatever I told her in confidence to further her own devious objectives."

"I see." Dante could tell that she was taken aback by the betrayal, perhaps even more than knowing Eric was aware of their relationship. Obviously Marilyn was a real piece of work. And so was Eric, not too surprisingly. "Where are you?"

"In my car. I just left a motel where Marilyn was only too happy to tell me about her and Eric, along with spilling the beans about our affair."

"Maybe she did us a favor," Dante reasoned. "That includes opening your eyes to just what type of man you've been living with, over and beyond what's already come to light."

"How can you be so cool about this?" Beverly asked, sounding irritated. "This was the worst thing that could have happened."

"Actually, it isn't." Dante disagreed. "The *worst* thing would've been if you'd let him off the hook for being the murdering thug he is."

She paused. "Obviously the man I thought I knew never existed."

Dante was happy to know she was finally coming to terms with that. The one thing he never wanted was to pull Beverly away from Eric while she still somehow believed he was being miscast as the bad guy.

"Don't beat yourself up about it," he told her. "Eric has been a master of deceit and manipulation. Well, that's about to come to an end."

"Please don't tell me you're going after him," she said nervously.

"I'm not," Dante assured her. Not that he wouldn't love to get a piece of Eric, maybe two or three pieces. Instead, he was leaving that up to the authorities. "But the FBI is in hot pursuit of him and his boss, Leon Quincy."

"And you know this how?"

"I visited their local office earlier today and got the word straight from the agents working the case. They know all about Eric and what he's been up to. They might even be able to tie my brother's murder to their racketeering investigation."

"Though Marilyn didn't say, I think she might have told Eric that you came here looking for him on account of your brother," Beverly said, her voice tinged with regret. "I never imagined that she and Eric were—"

"It's okay," Dante said. He couldn't blame her for confiding in a friend who then used that friendship against her. "How could you have suspected? I knew Eric would figure out who I was in due course, assuming I didn't tell him first. It's just as well that everything's out in the open now. No more secrets and lies, starting with Eric and his very dark side."

Beverly sighed. "I can't believe what a fool I've been."

"You weren't a fool for wanting to see the good in someone you cared for," Dante told her. "Eric is a fool for, well, every despicable thing he's done, including hurting you."

She sniffled, and Dante suspected Beverly was crying. Not that he could blame her. Eric had proven to be a real bastard across the board, not to mention a very dangerous man. She had a right to be emotional when trying to process all this and get on with her life. Dante intended to be right there by her side to help her make the transition from a hitman's woman to his own lady.

"Do you have your bags?" he asked.

"Yes."

"Good. I'll be waiting for you. And be careful."

"I will," Beverly promised as her voice shook.

As he hung up, Dante was certain he was now a marked man. At the very least, Eric now knew he was having an affair with Beverly. And might well know he was onto him as a hired killer for Leon Quincy, with his brother being one of the casualties.

Though Dante doubted Eric would be able to get his room number from the staff, assuming he'd found out where he was staying, Dante phoned the front desk anyhow as a safety precaution to that effect.

After hanging up, Dante called Special Agent Ben Taylor. It seemed like a smart idea to give him a heads-up on these recent developments. He figured that since it wasn't a crime to have an affair with a suspected hitman's girlfriend, they ought to know that he and Beverly were in danger because Eric suddenly had a whole new reason to kill. Dante could only hope the FBI stepped up to the plate and nabbed Eric before things got out of hand and he had to defend himself by any means necessary.

***

For a moment, Beverly feared Eric was following her. She imagined him accosting her in the hotel parking lot and shooting her in broad daylight, similar to a woman she had read about recently who was murdered by her ex-boyfriend. The thought unnerved Beverly. She didn't want to die with too much to live for. But she would rather be dead than have to live with someone who not only cheated on her with her best friend, but also was a hired killer who clearly had no conscience.

Looking again in the rearview mirror, Beverly watched as the Cadillac she thought was Eric's veered off in a different direction. She breathed a sigh of relief. *So that wasn't him. It doesn't mean he's not out there looking for me—and Dante.* As calculating and cunning as her ex-friend had proven to be, she wouldn't put anything past Marilyn, including her telling Eric which hotel Dante was staying in. Or maybe he had forced it out of her. Either way, Beverly was sure Eric would come after Dante, intent on killing him. After all, that was how he made his living, sad as it was for Beverly to believe. Only now it had become personal for Eric.

Beverly parked and left her car. She raced across the lot, expecting to spot Eric or his car at any moment, seeking to prevent her from going to Dante. But such was not the case. Stepping inside the hotel and its warm ambiance, she felt a little more secure. With people moving about, Beverly doubted that Eric would try anything in plain view. Still, she worried. Did the hotel give out room numbers to strangers? She feared Eric could be waiting around any corner to pounce on her so she could lead him straight to Dante's door.

Even though she got into the empty elevator alone, Beverly felt it couldn't close fast enough, imagining Eric slipping in at the last second and forcing her to take him to Dante's room before killing them both.

Wasn't that how professional killers operated? They took advantage of every opportunity to get the job done effectively without fingering themselves in the process.

But no one got on the elevator before Beverly reached Dante's floor. She hurried to his room, and the door opened before she could even knock.

Dante embraced her. "Thank goodness you made it safely," he said gratefully.

"Yes." She felt protected in his muscular arms. That didn't mean she believed either of them could afford to take Eric for granted. Not when Beverly knew that even though he had crossed the line in more ways than one, he would not sit back and allow her and Dante to go off into the sunset. Especially since Dante knew that Eric was a hired assassin, giving Eric another reason to want to kill him.

"Everything's going to be all right," Dante said comfortingly, still holding her.

"I want to believe that," she uttered into his shoulder. "I wouldn't put anything past Eric at this point."

"Neither would I." Dante stepped back. "That's why I just brought the FBI up to speed on Eric and the latest details. From what I understand, they think they have more than enough now to arrest him. They've put out an APB on the bastard."

Beverly took some solace in that even as she was still trying to digest that the man she had been living with could be capable of committing murders for pay. Between that and having an affair with Marilyn, she could only imagine what other skeletons might have been in Eric's closet.

"I'd just like to put him behind me and get on with my life," she said.

"You and me both," Dante told her.

She met his eyes. "Are you sure this isn't more than you bargained for to be with me?"

He grinned. "I think we've both gotten more than we bargained for out of this. As far as I'm concerned, that's proven to be a good thing. After all, I have you to look forward to building something special with."

His words touched Beverly's heart, and she acted on emotion when she put her hands on his cheeks and kissed Dante on the mouth. He kissed her back, and their mouths opened, their tongues drawing each other into the kiss even more. In that moment, Beverly managed to put everything else on hold while enjoying the intimate expression that made her feel she wouldn't want to be with anyone else on earth right now.

She broke away from his mouth, touching her tingling lips. "I've fallen in love with you," she told him, though the timing might have been off. Beverly wasn't sure how he would respond, but she needed to say it. This was the only thing that made sense to her these days.

Dante gazed deeply into her eyes. "I'm feeling it too," he said, holding her waist.

"Really?" Beverly couldn't have hoped for more.

"Yes, really. We're definitely on the same wavelength. You're beautiful, wonderful, sexy, and fun to be with."

Her cheeks rose when she smiled. "I could say the same things about you."

He pulled her a little closer. "As soon as we get past this current situation, we can explore our feelings more deeply."

Beverly looked forward to that. She wouldn't push it, knowing that as long as Eric was a thorn in their side, they likely wouldn't have much of a future. She kissed Dante again. "I can wait until then."

"So you've got all your stuff," Dante reaffirmed.

"Yes. Wait . . ." A thought occurred to Beverly.

"What is it?"

"I left the diamond brooch my grandmother gave me in the dresser," she told him.

He met her eyes. "Maybe you should just leave it."

"The brooch means a lot to me." Beverly got maudlin. "It was the one thing I promised my grandmother I'd always hang on to. I was so flustered in stuffing everything I owned into my bags so I could leave that I somehow forgot the brooch."

"'Nuff said." Dante touched her chin. "We'll go get it."

"Are you sure?" Beverly didn't relish the thought of confronting Eric. Or putting them both in his crosshairs.

"Yes, it's cool. We can be in and out of there in no time flat. Besides, with any luck, the feds have already nabbed Eric."

"One could only hope," she said thoughtfully, resting her head on Dante's chest for a moment of comfort.

Eric took a deep breath to try to calm his ire at the idea that Beverly had been sleeping with Dante, a man who was out to get him. In the ideal world, he would love to simply whisk her away to the Bahamas and forget this stunning betrayal ever happened. But how could he when Dante was out for blood and had stolen his woman's body and maybe her heart too?

I can't let it go, and I won't give up Beverly to that bastard. Once he's out of the picture for good, I'll forgive her for cheating on me and things can go back to the way they were.

But that wouldn't include his fooling around with Marilyn, who turned out to be an unstable, scheming little bitch who could have ruined his life if he'd let her. Eric wondered if she would tell Spencer and if he would kick her out as she deserved. Either way, Eric had to focus on getting back what was his and no other man's. Beverly. He should never have taken his eye off the ball. It was a mistake that wouldn't happen again, or at least not until things were right between him and her.

Eric drove into the hotel parking lot and found a place to park. He checked the pistol in his pocket, making sure the silencer was intact. After putting the gun away, he left the car and headed for the hotel.

He walked through the lobby, pondering how to get someone to give him Dante's room number. It shouldn't be too much of a problem to bribe some greedy bellhop or housekeeper to get what he wanted.

Eric was just about to put his plan into action when, before his very eyes, he spotted Dante and Beverly across the lobby, moving briskly toward the door. Dante was holding Beverly's upper arm while playing the black knight in shining armor to protect her from him.

Think again, bastard. You're the one who's going to need protection when this is over.

Eric resisted the desire to take out his gun and start shooting. He hadn't gotten where he was by operating recklessly in front of witnesses.

Instead, he waited for Beverly and Dante to exit the hotel before going in hot pursuit.

THIRTY-NINE

Marilyn wasn't sure how she made it home, as her head was in a fog. How could everything go so wrong? She'd thought Eric would prefer her over that cheating bitch Beverly, especially when he combined that with the fact that her lover Dante also wanted revenge against him for killing his brother. But no, he still wanted Beverly and was willing to forgive and forget just to have her in his life to give the appearance that they were a loving couple. As always, Marilyn came in second to the woman she had grown to hate with a passion.

She wouldn't let it end there. If Eric thought he could just cast her aside now that he no longer wanted her to suck his dick, he had another thing coming. He would pay for treating her like a common whore. Eric wouldn't end up back with his tramp, assuming Beverly would want to stay with him after learning that he had been screwing her best friend. Marilyn doubted Eric would be able to sweet-talk his way out of that one.

She knew that he was still a very dangerous man and wasn't used to a woman not giving him what he wanted. In this case, it was hanging on to Beverly, even if Eric had to take out Dante and keep her locked away as his prisoner. Maybe that would serve her right. Then Beverly could see the real Eric, whom he'd somehow managed to hide from her until now.

I hope they both rot in hell.

Marilyn dabbed at her eyes and got out of the car. She looked at Spencer's car parked in front of hers. He was home early. In this case, she considered it right on time. There were things he needed to hear.

Inside, she found him in the den, half dozing with a baseball game on. She grabbed the remote and cut the television off, gaining his attention.

Spencer sat up. "Hey, just getting back?"

She wrinkled her nose. "What do you think?"

His brows rose. "What's wrong?"

Marilyn moved closer, touching her sore cheek. "Something happened."

"Your face." Spencer studied her. "Were you in an accident?"

"No." She made her eyes water.

"Then what? Talk to me, baby."

"Someone hit me," she said tonelessly.

"*What?*" Spencer stood, towering over her with concern. "Who did this to you?"

Marilyn sighed. This was harder than she expected, but it needed to be said. Especially now that there seemed to be no chance that she and Eric would ever get back together.

"I've been cheating on you." Her voice cracked. "I'm sorry."

His brows creased. "Who is he?"

She licked her lips and looked up at him. "Eric Fox."

Spencer studied her with fury. "You're joking, right?"

"I wish I were." Marilyn wiped her eyes.

"That sonofabitch," he cursed. "For how long?"

She considered telling him just how many times they had slept together or otherwise engaged in sexual acts, but had actually lost count. Besides, she had no desire to hurt him any more than necessary.

"Long enough that I couldn't take it—or him—anymore," she lied. "I knew it was wrong, and I wanted to end it today." She took a deep breath and wiped her runny nose with the back of her hand. "But he rejected that, insisting that he was fine with the way things were, having Beverly and me at his beck and call. When I told him again that I was done, he hit me and said he'd kill me if I tried to end the affair before he was ready to. I was afraid he might carry out that threat, since that's what he does for a living." She touched her tender cheek again and started to cry theatrically. "He forced me to have sex with him today, just to show who was calling the shots and make sure I didn't forget it."

Spencer's eyes bulged as if they were about to pop out. Seeing the fury in his eyes, Marilyn feared that he might become physical with her. It was a chance she'd been willing to take if it meant Eric would get his too.

When Spencer reached out to her, Marilyn actually flinched. But then he put his arms around her and pulled her to his chest. "It'll be all right," he said soothingly.

"I never stopped loving you," she told him, hoping he believed it. "It was never about that. I messed up with him and don't ever want to see his face again."

"You won't have to." Spencer tightened his hold on her, and Marilyn could feel him trembling. "I'll kill him for what he did to you."

Marilyn gulped from the finality of his words, but they were pleasing music to her ears. For this was exactly what she'd hoped he would say as her means to get back at Eric for taking away the one chance at happiness Marilyn thought she had. She would settle for sweet revenge against the man she now hated with a passion, right alongside Beverly.

***

Spencer was beside himself with rage that Eric had defiled his wife. He had never considered that Marilyn would cheat on him, especially with the likes of Eric Fox. But Eric had a way with the ladies, just as Leon did. Once Eric set his sights on Marilyn, Spencer wasn't surprised that she fell under his spell as an older, suave, more established man who happened to be the boyfriend of Beverly, who, Spencer knew, Marilyn had always felt inferior to. Like a hound dog sensing easy prey, Eric had taken advantage of this vulnerability when he went after Marilyn.

As if it wasn't bad enough that the bastard was having sex with his wife behind Spencer's back while not even giving a hint of it in their conversations, Eric had laid his filthy hands on Marilyn and sexually assaulted her. This had crossed the line in a way that was totally unforgivable. He could not let Eric get away with this and live with himself as a man who still loved his woman, no matter what she'd done to destroy their marriage and everything he'd worked for to make what he thought was a pretty good life for them.

Spencer took the box down from a shelf in the bedroom closet. He removed his .357 Magnum revolver and checked the loaded cartridge. Stuffing the gun in his pants, he half zipped his jacket, knowing what must be done. Eric would never again hurt Marilyn or any other woman, including Beverly, who must have also had the wool pulled over her eyes regarding this tryst between Marilyn and Eric.

Downstairs, Spencer found his wife sitting in the breakfast room, stuffing her face. He had become used to this as her way of dealing with adversity. He didn't necessarily like it, but right now he had other things on his mind, such as doing right by her after what Eric had put Marilyn through. When the dust settled, Spencer hoped they might still have a marriage worth working on.

"I'll be back," he told her, knowing that might not be the case for a long time.

"I'll be here," Marilyn responded, barely able to look at him, as though she understood what was going to happen and it was with her blessing.

"Love you," Spencer said glumly and then walked away without hearing her response. At this point, there was only one thing on his mind: killing Eric Fox for seducing and violating his wife.

FORTY

Beverly had feared they would see Eric's silver Cadillac in the driveway and would have to face him. But, to her relief, his car was not there. She wondered if he was out looking for her or Dante, or both of them. She was nervous no matter what, not knowing what to expect from Eric with the information Marilyn had fed him. Not to mention Beverly's new knowledge that the man she'd been living with was a murderer for hire. All she wanted was to get in and out of the house as soon as possible. Maybe then, Dante could take her away from Detroit so she would never have to deal with Eric again or Marilyn and all she'd done to betray Beverly's trust and friendship.

"You ready?" Dante asked from behind the wheel.

He put his hand on hers, and Beverly couldn't help but shake from nerves. She met his eyes and felt some comfort. "I think so."

"Then let's do this. If Eric happens to be inside, I won't let him hurt you," he promised.

"And what about you?" She looked at him. "If Eric's the killer you think he is, then you're in every bit as much danger as I am, if not more."

Dante jutted his chin. "Don't worry about me. I can take care of myself. That doesn't mean I'm taking Eric lightly. Anything but. Yes, the man's a stone-cold killer and wouldn't hesitate to take us both out if he has the chance, which is why we won't stay here a moment longer than necessary." He leaned over and gave her a light kiss on the lips. "We'll get through this, I promise."

She flashed him a soft smile, playing on his optimism while longing for the life they could have together when this was all over.

Dante led the way as they went inside. Beverly looked around the foyer and into the living room, wondering if Eric might be lying in wait. She saw no sign of him.

"The brooch is upstairs," she told Dante.

"Figured as much," he said. "Go get it. I'll be right behind you. I don't plan to let you out of my sight until we're out of here."

Beverly smiled gratefully at him. "Thank you for being so understanding."

Dante grinned. "You'll have plenty of time to thank me later."

They mounted the curving stairway, and Beverly led the way to the master suite. The fact that she'd shared it with Eric in good times made her a little uneasy in Dante's presence. On the whole, though, there was nothing left inside her for Eric, and she had no problem with Dante being there to see her put that chapter of her life behind her for good.

Beverly found the diamond floral brooch made of eighteen-karat yellow gold in a small pouch in the back of the bottom drawer of the dresser. She grabbed the piece of jewelry. "Got it," she told Dante happily.

"Great," he said. "Let's get the hell out of here."

"Well, well, well, look who's here," the deep and recognizable voice said.

Beverly and Dante turned to find Eric standing in the doorway. He was holding a gun pointed directly at them.

"This must be my lucky day," Eric said wryly. "I get to see my woman keeping company with my pool buddy."

Dante glared at him but was determined to keep his cool under fire given the stakes of one wrong move. "I wondered if you would show your sorry ass before we left."

"How could I not?" Eric bristled. "And you're not going anywhere." He aimed the gun at Dante, then Beverly, ushering them back into the room.

"You don't have to do this, Eric," Beverly uttered.

Eric fixed her with narrowed eyes. "Why him?" he wanted to know.

She batted her lashes. "I could ask you the same thing about Marilyn."

Eric reacted, clearly caught off guard that she knew. "Oh, you know about that?"

"She was only too happy to tell me," Beverly said sharply. "Marilyn was my best friend. What does that make you?"

"A man," he responded matter-of-factly. "Just like this asshole. Only I did it just for the sex. Whereas we both know Dante boy here was only using you to get to me."

"Not true," Dante voiced edgily. "We met by chance. I didn't need Beverly to get to you. I knew exactly where to find the bastard who murdered my brother."

Eric smirked. "Russell, I believe his name was. I should have seen the resemblance the first time I saw you at the pool hall."

"If you had, I would've killed you then," Dante admitted, the reality of it sinking in, along with the ramifications if he had carried out an act of murder and had to live with himself afterward.

"Too bad you didn't when you had the chance," Eric said, aiming the gun at him. "Now it's you who's about to die. Only then will my revenge be complete, and Beverly and I can get back to the life we had."

"Do you honestly think that would *ever* be possible?" She looked at him with incredulity. "I could *never* be with you after—"

"No, you don't get it," Eric said, cutting her off. "This isn't up for debate. You're my woman for as long as I say. Unless you'd rather die right here and now with your boyfriend. The choice is yours. . . ."

Dante didn't want to give her even a moment to contemplate it and make it easier for him to shoot them both. "No, the choice is yours," he declared. "The FBI has the bead on you and Leon Quincy. There's an APB out on your ass even as we speak."

"You're lying," Eric gritted his teeth.

"No reason to at this point. They've been investigating Quincy for some time now. The feds know all about his crime operations, including employing you as a hired killer. The whole thing is about to come crumbling down around him. My advice to you is to quit while you're ahead, Eric. Maybe with what you know, you can cut yourself a deal."

Eric regarded him thoughtfully. "Not interested. If I go down, it won't be until you're dead." He looked at Beverly. "What's it going to be? Do we go away somewhere and start our lives over after I get rid of this punk? Or do you want to see what it feels like to die for someone unworthy of your affections?"

Beverly met Dante's eyes out of what he thought was uncertainty before glowering at Eric. "If I have to die to get away from you, then so be it. You totally disgust me for everything you've done as a human being. I hope you rot in hell!"

Eric's nostrils expanded. "If that's the way you want it," he hissed.

Dante watched him direct the gun at him unevenly from about five feet away. He figured he had maybe one chance to lunge forward and deflect Eric's shooting arm. Or die trying. Just as Dante was about to make his move, he saw another man come up behind Eric. He was holding a pistol and calmly placed it to the back of Eric's head. Without preface, he pulled the trigger.

As brain matter flew out from Eric's shattered face, he went down in a heap, clearly no longer among the living. Beverly screamed, and Dante held her, studying the overweight man who stood over Eric, peering down at the corpse before firing another bullet into what was left of Eric's head. Dante recognized the triggerman as one of Leon Quincy's henchmen.

"You picked the *wrong* woman to violate and take advantage of, you stupid bastard," the man said roughly. "I couldn't let you get away with it."

He looked up and aimed the gun at Dante and Beverly.

"Spencer—" The name sputtered from Beverly's mouth fearfully. "Don't . . ."

Spencer gazed at her and lowered the weapon. "My beef ain't with either of you." He turned and walked out of the room.

Before Dante could assess what had just happened with a trembling Beverly still in his arms, he heard a booming voice that sounded like Special Agent Ben Taylor ordering Spencer to drop his weapon. He apparently complied, as Dante heard footsteps in the hallway and then a friendly face entered the room.

"What took you so long?" Dante asked Agent Taylor. He was wearing a bulletproof vest and holding a firearm.

Ben gave him a direct look. "Sorry. These things take time." He looked down at Eric, lying in a pool of his own blood. "Looks like Fox was put out of his misery."

"Someone had to do the honors," Dante said un-apologetically.

"I suppose that's one way to look at it." Ben shouted out to other agents that their target was dead and the coast was clear. He looked at Beverly. "Are you all right?"

"Yes," she replied, still clinging to Dante.

"Good." Ben put the gun in his shoulder holster as Agent Lynn Fry came up behind him. "We'll need statements from both of you on exactly what went down in here. I'm sure you'll be happy to cooperate."

"Of course." Dante spoke for both of them. Eric was just one piece of the puzzle that needed to be solved. What about the kingpin himself, Leon Quincy?

As though reading his mind, Ben said, "By the way, you'll be happy to know we picked up Leon Quincy on a small airstrip where he and two of his ladies were attempting to flee the country and responsibility for all the havoc he caused. His days of terrorizing Detroit business owners and others who got in his way are over."

Dante's face lit up with the news, knowing his brother could now rest in peace, for his death had been avenged.

"Thank you," Dante told the FBI agent and his partner.

"Just doing our job," Ben said, offering a smile.

Dante kissed the top of Beverly's head. "This nightmare is over—for both of us."

She winced, looking at Eric's shattered remains. "Yes, I think it is," she uttered as Dante looped his arm around her waist.

He liked the feel of their bodies side by side. This was a terrifying ordeal Dante fully intended to put behind them for good. He looked forward to the two of them being able to share their dreams and a life together away from Detroit and all the bad memories it conjured up.

FORTY-ONE

On a sunny afternoon, Beverly took a small bite out of Dante's chili dog as they walked along the Santa Monica Pier. She'd elected not to get one herself, as she wanted to maintain her slender physique. Beverly had barely swallowed the food and was thinking about sexual nourishment with Dante when he leaned down and gave her a mouth watering kiss.

"That's so much tastier," she told him, touching her tingling lips.

"For you and me both," he said in a sexy voice. He put his arm around her possessively.

This was one time when Beverly was happy that her man was territorial, as she felt the same way about him. It had been three months since she'd moved to California and taken up residence at Dante's home in Los Angeles. With Dante's encouragement, she had enrolled in art school to pursue a hidden passion. Both had left behind the dark drama associated with Eric Fox and Leon Quincy. In Beverly's mind, it represented a chapter in her life that she'd just as soon forget. She doubted that would be possible, especially where it concerned her ex-best friend. Marilyn had proven to be a vindictive and callous bitch who had used her own husband to do her dirty work, leaving them both paying the price.

Beverly sucked in a calming breath of ocean air. She spotted the amusement park and grabbed Dante's hand. "Come on. Let's go for a ride on the Ferris wheel."

He grinned. "Sounds good to me."

An hour later, they were taking a stroll on the beach, arms around each other like lovebirds. Beverly found herself totally at home with the laid-back California lifestyle. More importantly, she was ensconced in the serious relationship she had begun with Dante. They had taken things beyond their sexual attraction to a new state of awareness and appreciation of each other's strengths and interests.

She tugged on his waist. "Maybe we should cut this short and do something else that's on my mind."

"And what would that be?" Dante asked with a smile.

"Do I need to spell it out?" she teased him.

"How about if I do that for you?"

"Go for it."

He gave her a very passionate kiss that Beverly felt right down to her toes. "Am I on the right track?"

She tasted her lips. "I'd say you have a one-track mind."

Dante laughed. "Puts me in pretty good company, don't you think?"

"Oh, yes, always," she agreed wholeheartedly.

They made love and explored each other thoroughly while discovering new ways to pleasure each other, along with employing tried-and-true ways. Dante waited atop Beverly until she was in the throes of her orgasm and begged him to complete the process before releasing his own pent-up needs and climaxing deep inside her. He held her quavering body and put his tongue in Beverly's waiting mouth while they came together in a moment of ecstasy.

Afterward, she laid her head on his chest and fell asleep. Dante ran his hand through her hair, reflecting on the forces that had brought them together as a loving couple who had their whole lives ahead of them. He'd gone to Detroit for all the wrong reasons and left for all the right ones. With Eric dead and Leon Quincy on the verge of being put away for a very long time, Dante felt satisfied on behalf of his brother. He was even more content that he'd come away from what could have blown up in his face with the first woman who had ever reached the depths of his soul. Beverly had given Dante what he had been missing in his life: someone who could keep up with him in and out of bed. They were not rushing anything, letting their love grow at its own pace. He fully expected that she would always be an important part of his life and that marriage and children were something the future held for them.

The thought brought a wide smile to Dante's face, and he kissed the top of Beverly's head and then her lips, sensing that she wouldn't mind one bit if he woke her for more mutual pleasuring and intimate romance.

Notes

Notes

Notes

ORDER FORM
URBAN BOOKS, LLC
78 E. Industry Ct
Deer Park, NY 11729

Name: (please print): _____

Address: _____

City/State: _____

Zip: _____

QTY	TITLES	PRICE
	16 On The Block	$14.95
	A Girl From Flint	$14.95
	A Pimp's Life	$14.95
	Baltimore Chronicles	$14.95
	Baltimore Chronicles 2	$14.95
	Betrayal	$14.95
	Black Diamond	$14.95
	Black Diamond 2	$14.95
	Black Friday	$14.95
	Both Sides Of The Fence	$14.95
	Both Sides Of The Fence 2	$14.95
	California Connection	$14.95

Shipping and handling-add $3.50 for 1st book, then $1.75 for each additional book.

Please send a check payable to:

Urban Books, LLC

Please allow 4-6 weeks for delivery

ORDER FORM
URBAN BOOKS, LLC
78 E. Industry Ct
Deer Park, NY 11729

Name: (please print): _____

Address: _____

City/State: _____

Zip: _____

QTY	TITLES	PRICE
	California Connection 2	$14.95
	Cheesecake And Teardrops	$14.95
	Congratulations	$14.95
	Crazy In Love	$14.95
	Cyber Case	$14.95
	Denim Diaries	$14.95
	Diary Of A Mad First Lady	$14.95
	Diary Of A Stalker	$14.95
	Diary Of A Street Diva	$14.95
	Diary Of A Young Girl	$14.95
	Dirty Money	$14.95
	Dirty To The Grave	$14.95

Shipping and handling-add $3.50 for 1st book, then $1.75 for each additional book.

Please send a check payable to:

Urban Books, LLC

Please allow 4-6 weeks for delivery

ORDER FORM
URBAN BOOKS, LLC
78 E. Industry Ct
Deer Park, NY 11729

Name: (please print):_____

Address: _____

City/State: _____

Zip: _____

QTY	TITLES	PRICE
	Gunz And Roses	$14.95
	Happily Ever Now	$14.95
	Hell Has No Fury	$14.95
	Hush	$14.95
	If It Isn't love	$14.95
	Kiss Kiss Bang Bang	$14.95
	Last Breath	$14.95
	Little Black Girl Lost	$14.95
	Little Black Girl Lost 2	$14.95
	Little Black Girl Lost 3	$14.95
	Little Black Girl Lost 4	$14.95
	Little Black Girl Lost 5	$14.95

Shipping and handling-add $3.50 for 1st book, then $1.75 for each additional book.
Please send a check payable to:
Urban Books, LLC
Please allow 4-6 weeks for delivery

ORDER FORM
URBAN BOOKS, LLC
78 E. Industry Ct
Deer Park, NY 11729

Name:(please print):_____

Address: _____

City/State: _____

Zip: _____

QTY	TITLES	PRICE
	Loving Dasia	$14.95
	Material Girl	$14.95
	Moth To A Flame	$14.95
	Mr. High Maintenance	$14.95
	My Little Secret	$14.95
	Naughty	$14.95
	Naughty 2	$14.95
	Naughty 3	$14.95
	Queen Bee	$14.95
	Say It Ain't So	$14.95
	Snapped	$14.95
	Snow White	$14.95

Shipping and handling-add $3.50 for 1st book, then $1.75 for each additional book.

Please send a check payable to:

Urban Books, LLC

Please allow 4-6 weeks for delivery

ORDER FORM
URBAN BOOKS, LLC
78 E. Industry Ct
Deer Park, NY 11729

Name:(please print):_____

Address: _____

City/State: _____

Zip: _____

QTY	TITLES	PRICE
	Spoil Rotten	$14.95
	Supreme Clientele	$14.95
	The Cartel	$14.95
	The Cartel 2	$14.95
	The Cartel 3	$14.95
	The Dopefiend	$14.95
	The Dopeman Wife	$14.95
	The Prada Plan	$14.95
	The Prada Plan 2	$14.95
	Where There Is Smoke	$14.95
	Where There Is Smoke 2	$14.95

Shipping and handling-add $3.50 for 1st book, then $1.75 for each additional book.

Please send a check payable to:

Urban Books, LLC

Please allow 4-6 weeks for delivery

ORDER FORM
URBAN BOOKS, LLC
78 E. Industry Ct
Deer Park, NY 11729

Name: (please print):_____

Address: _____

City/State: _____

Zip: _____

QTY	TITLES	PRICE

Shipping and handling-add $3.50 for 1st book, then $1.75 for each additional book.

Please send a check payable to:

Urban Books, LLC

Please allow 4-6 weeks for delivery